1982

a whole loaf: stories from Israel

a whole loaf

stories from Israel

EDITED BY

SHOLOM J. KAHN

THE VANGUARD PRESS, INC., NEW YORK

Library of Congress Catalogue Card Number: 61-17541

Manufactured in the United States of America

To Chava and Tamar

CONTENTS

EDITOR'S ACKNOWLEDGEMENTS

THANKS ARE due to the many individuals who have contributed to the making of this book:

To the person behind the scenes, Mr. Samuel Katz, manager of Karni Publishers, who has contributed so much (besides one of the translations) at every stage of the editorial process that his name should appear on the title-page as a collaborator.

To all the translators for their labors, promptness, cooperation, and patience in the face of necessary tamperings with manuscripts.

To the friends who, accepting me as a comparative student in the field of the modern Hebrew short story, were so generous with their counsel in guiding me along unknown paths. Dr. Haim Toren set my feet right at the beginning; and Messrs. Aryeh Lifshitz, Meshullem Tochner, I. M. Lask, and Haim Hefer were of help at various stages. Naturally, though all these have earned my gratitude, they must share none of the blame for any errors of judgment or fact which may still remain.

To the late Mr. Yitzchak Shenhar and to Dr. Zalman Shazar, who, engaged upon a similar project recently published with the support of the Jewish Agency (*Tehilla and Other Israeli Tales*), cooperated so pleasantly to assure that our labors did not overlap.

To Mr. Haim Hazaz, for his friendly advice in clearing up some obscurities, and for his liberal attitude towards my unconventional tactics in translating his Yemenite story.

The contents of this book are published with the kind permission of:

Mr. S. Yizhar for *The Dead and the Living*

Mr. M. Shamir for *Doctor Schmidt*

Mr. H. Hazaz for *The Lord Have Mercy*

Mr. Y. Yaari for *The Judgment of Solomon*

Mr. N. Shaham for *The Seven*

Mr. A. Meged for *The Party*

Mr. B. Tammuz for *The Roll of Canvas*

Mr. Y. Hurgin for *Reb Shmelke of Safed*

Mr. Y. Mossinsohn for *Polka*

Mr. Y. Bar-Yosef for *The Lateborn*

Mr. Y. Shenhar for *Country Town*

Messrs. Shocken Books for *Metamorphosis* and *A Whole Loaf* by S. Y. Agnon

Messrs. Tarshish Books for *Shaitana* by M. Smilansky

Messrs. Rubin Mass for *Enigma* by Y. Zarchi

INTRODUCTION

I.

WHEN WE read a Greek tragedy,' wrote Taine, 'our first care should be to realise to ourselves the Greeks. . . . I would give fifty volumes of characters and a hundred volumes of state-papers for the memoirs of Cellini, the epistles of St. Paul, the Table-talk of Luther, or the comedies of Aristophanes.'

So too the reader of this collection will be tempted on its strength to ask: 'What are those Israelis *really* like?' But he should beware: part of the answer to that question may be found here, but only a fragment. What he will actually find are translations of fifteen stories from the modern Hebrew which have moved, amused, and in general pleased the Editor. Here are fifteen *good* stories, but not necessarily the best or the most representative. For one thing, the classic writers of the Hebrew Renaissance, whose works belong chiefly to the 19th century and almost exclusively to Europe (Mapu, Mendele, Peretz, Frishman, Feierberg, Bialik), have been deliberately excluded; also, many an excellent story-teller of our own day has had to be omitted for lack of space. Thus, to generalize on the basis of these stories alone would be like approaching America's life and literature through a single collection of contemporary short stories, and without a knowledge of Irving, Hawthorne, Poe, Melville, Twain, or Henry James.

What distinguishes this volume from most previous similar collections* is the fact that these are all stories of the 20th century,

* With the exception of *Palestine Stories, Selected and Translated From Hebrew*, by I. M. Lask, Jerusalem, 1942. Five of Mr. Lask's authors are

and, with one exception, they reflect life in Palestine, or the State of Israel. All these writers, with two exceptions (Smilansky and Zarchi), are still alive and creative. Three literary generations are represented—as usual: the old-timers, the middle-aged, and the youngsters—but with the accent on the contemporary.

Within these limits of time and place, the basis of selection was literary value and universal human interest— in brief, a good story. Yet, after the selection had been completed, it was found that somehow, in their variety if not in their number, these fifteen tales manage to mirror many of the typical experiences and rich traditions which have gone to make up modern Israel. To give really adequate expression to those experiences and traditions would be an enormous task, since all six continents are represented today in the tiny Holy Land, and its recent history has been extraordinarily dynamic, passing within half a century from Turkish to British rule and thence to Independence; and, in cultural terms, from the Middle Ages to the Atomic Age. This is a modest sampling from a very large storehouse; and the emphasis is on action, character, significance, style, technique—rather than on history or sociology.

II.

Still it will help the reader, who may be entering upon almost unknown territory, to see these tales in some sort of historical perspective. For that reason, they have been arranged, not by the ages of their authors or their dates of publication, but by a logic inherent in their subject-matter and themes.

The seven stories in Part I pivot, in one way or another, around the struggle for national independence. The first group of four begins in the period of Arab attacks (1936-1938); introduces the

also represented here, but six younger writers whose work began to appear only during the last decade appear in our Table of Contents—out of a total of fourteen authors.

Yemenite as a type, against the background of World War II; and includes a treatment of one result of Hitler's persecutions. A second group of three, by younger writers who emerged during the last decade, are all stories of the War of Independence and its results: a battle episode—an excellent war yarn, a crippled veteran's plight, and a complex confrontation of the attitudes of a representative of the older generation with those of the sabra youth.

The eight pre-war stories of Part II go back in time, supplying background for Part I. First, a European story by S. Y. Agnon, the great master who dominates this half-century of Hebrew fiction—a brief bow to that Old World which itself sprang, in ancient times, from a fusion of East and West similar to the one being attempted again in Israel today. The remaining seven stories are divided into three groups. First, two Eastern tales, one Arab and one Jewish. Then two stories of immigration and pioneering settlement on the land. Then, passing to the spiritual center, Jerusalem, three very human tales of the New City, depicting some of its infinite variety, Orthodox and modern, which custom cannot stale; and culminating in Agnon's important second contribution: a symbolic fantasy of man's hunger for 'the whole loaf' of existence.*

III.

From Yizhar's embattled farmers, to Tammuz the questioning young sabra; and from Agnon the European, through pioneering and growth, to Agnon in Jerusalem. There is a great deal of modern Israel typified in these pages, and it is presented in a suitable variety of styles. Here are the comedy and satire of Churgin's Reb Shmelke, Bar-Yosef's spoiled child, and Hazaz's tragi-comic Yemenite; and the tragedy or pathos of Zarchi's unhappy divorcée, Yaari's torn

* Further discussion of the historical backgrounds, and of individual authors and stories, may be found in the 'Biographical and Critical Notes'.

mother, and Meged's tortured cripple. The styles range from the sensitive social realism of Shenhar, through the more psychological and introspective realism of writers like Yizhar and Meged, to the romantic exoticism of Smilansky and the Kafkaesque symbolism and allegory of Agnon.

With apologies for betraying our own caution concerning the danger of large generalizations on so slender a basis of evidence, we may still venture to suggest that there are at least three traits strongly in evidence here which we, at least, associate (not exclusively, of course) with Jewish character: humor, emotional sensitivity, and conscience. Above all, perhaps, the probings of conscience—in relation to God and one's own self and one's fellow-man and the ideals of society—are strongly felt in such varied contexts as Agnon's hungry man and divorced couple, the soldiers of Yizhar and Shaham, Shamir's conscientious doctor, and Tammuz's troubled sabra. Indeed, one of the heartening outcomes of reading these selections is the picture one gets of Israel's younger generation, in particular, as maintaining the age-old Jewish traditions of self-criticism and spiritual search. There may not always be a sure mastery of style or technical resources, but there is a readiness to experiment, to try new ideas and explore fresh areas of experience, which is reasonably well represented in the six stories from the younger writers.

IV.

A brief word about some problems of translation. The mainstay of this volume is, of course, Mr. I. M. Lask, the veteran dean of translators from the modern Hebrew, whose work is already familiar to the English reader. His five renditions have been supplemented, however, by those of nine other translators, a veritable new generation of craftsmen, with a wide variety of backgrounds and degrees of experience. For one thing, their English has been learned in many corners of the world: England, South Africa, the United

States, Europe—and one is from far-off New Zealand! Inevitably, under such circumstances, differences of idiom and usage will be felt. The Editor has done what he could to reduce such elements of linguistic idosyncracy, but some departures from this norm undoubtedly remain.

Two rather special linguistic problems presented themselves: first, the presence of Arabic words and phrases in the Hebrew, as well as of Hebrew usages which are an intimate part of the Israeli scene (a word like 'kibbutz', for example); and second, the very special Hebrew of the Yemenites. The first problem has been solved by keeping a certain number of Hebrew and Arabic words in the translation, with the expectation that they will prove to be familiar to many readers, who know by now that 'Shalom' means 'peace'. However, a brief Glossary is appended for the uninitiated.

The second problem was more subtle and difficult. The Yemenites, we are told, speak dialects which have been largely influenced by Arabic idioms. In Shamir's story, the Yemenite farmer is given a somewhat broken and ungrammatical Hebrew, the general effect of which has been approximated in the translation. But Hazaz's Yemenites are as much more complex than this as his knowledge of the Yemenite is deeper—he has written a number of novels treating exclusively of Yemenites—and his mastery of Hebrew style is greater. The Editor, searching for some equivalent in English for the language of Hazaz's Yemenites, was struck by the many affinities *in this particular story* with certain qualities of Negro character and dialect: racy humor; carelessness with respect to grammar; familiarity with the Holy Scriptures; sincere religiosity which sometimes descends to superstition; folk idiom and readiness with epithets; frankness concerning sexual matters; and, in general, a certain likeable 'primitive' quality. He therefore makes so bold as to present here Hazaz's very Jewish Yemenites speaking a sort of Negro dialect, with the belief that this is as close as he, or anyone, could get in the English language to the total effect of Hazaz's

Hebrew. It should be unnecessary to add the cautions that Yemenites are, of course, not Negroes; and that the two stories by Hazaz and Shamir are far from doing justice to the variety and richness of Yemenite society and culture.

This last is another form of the warning with which we began. No aspect of Israel's rich and ever-changing scene is more than glimpsed at here: not the Eastern Jew, not the German Jew, not the kibbutz, not the Israeli farmer, not Tel-Aviv, not even Jerusalem. But what can one do? Sufficient unto each volume are the translations thereof.

THE HEBREW UNIVERSITY

JERUSALEM, 1957

a whole loaf: stories from Israel

THE DEAD AND THE LIVING

by S. Yizhar

I.

SHRAGA HAD been watching through the entry, and welcoming each arrival with a bright look, pointing to the ladder and then suffering afresh until the next arrived. Now he saw Abrashka emerging and running, barely managing to cover a few paces, then suddenly clutching at his left side with his hands and running an additional three paces before he collapsed. Only after that did he realise that there had been a shot, indeed several, one after the other. Abrashka raised himself again, shot once with his rifle, and apparently found the bolt hard to handle; for he produced his pistol and shot once with that as well, then tried to stand up only to fall back once more. Then Shraga dashed out, caught him under the armpits and pulled him backwards through the gunfire, dragging him to the entry where somebody else helped get him into the room.

He was still breathing, rested his hand on his belly, murmured 'It's here . . . I'm done for' while blood welled under his hand; and beneath the heads bowed helplessly over him his soul departed. Abrashka was no longer there. Shraga straightened himself slowly, responding to the looks fixed on him by shrugging his shoulders and then snorting through his nose, turning round and withdrawing into the darkness. For a few minutes, which seemed to grow increasingly menacing, there was a dark confusion pressing down heavily until Shraga returned with the oil lamp in his hands which he shone this way and that until he placed it at the head of the corpse, and said: 'That's how it is . . . Abrashka . . .'

Who cried? No, there was no crying. We won't cry. (Oh dear distant mother, you may burst into bitter weeping, mother burst into bitter weeping, Abrashka will not stand erect any more, he will never rise again, no and only no.)

'What's going on here?' said Aaron, climbing down the ladder, then approaching and staring. 'What? Abrashka!' Now it suddenly became understandable, and the tears gathered. But we won't cry. There was a frozen awe. Abrashka's shirt was stained along the sides, round by the belt, with blood; and the shirt was so lively, so everyday, and the creases in it were all living creases, the shirt wasn't at all dead. Only the body that was in it had crusted, grown hard and was so dead . . . And so far away, so much not with us, so far beyond . . . And all of a sudden! What do you know about sudden! And there was nothing to say, nothing at all, so they kept quiet.

At first consciousness was stupefied and the startled heart cried out. When it became hoarse, the awakening consciousness began cutting, and that was far, far more dreadful: To comprehend the ungraspable! Whose were these approaching feet outside that were so familiar . . . No, he would not come back any more . . . Not he . . . Aaron kneeled down beside Abrashka, felt his pulse, put an ear to his heart (such an empty breast!) and it seemed for a moment as though something moved there, the slopes of the abdomen, or an eyelid; but the head hung back, downwards—that cruel reverse slackness. And Aaron stood up. 'Nothing to be done,' said he pressing his lips together, then added very quietly, 'Back to your stations, everyone.' The four or five fellows in the little room stepped backwards, and when they reached the gloom in the corner each one slipped off in his own direction. Aaron and Shraga were left alone, with the light of the lamp above the body that was gradually losing its warmth.

'So suddenly . . .,' said Shraga. 'Rushing over . . . and suddenly . . .' 'Yes,' answered Aaron. 'It's always sudden.' 'He was such a lad . . .' Shraga began, but Aaron interrupted: 'You stay down here and I'll go up. And you don't need to talk . . . It's just beginning here now.'

What was this everything here, how unsuitable any word is, how much it isn't that, and all so not good, God in heaven, this thing that was spoken about, which had been foreseen—how absolutely it isn't like this, and there is no restoring, no correcting, nothing at all, and forever . . . Shraga bowed his head, shifted slightly, then turned back and once again it seemed for a moment as though what was lying there had taken a deep breath . . . Fear possessed him, a strange fear, a sense of the abysmal nothingness of your being, with a double will: to forget and to remember, such a kind of shadow of death, while wherever you try you see ahead a falling into nothingness and a desperate confusion hurtling down. And what was more, the shooting had begun again, and you had time only to dash to the windows. And shoot once more? All just as it had been, over again? If only there were somebody yelling instead of keeping quiet, yelling, yelling and weeping, shrieking, saying what a pity it all was, how bad it was, not to have such an Abrashka any longer, that it was wrong—just to yell, there's no point in this silence! To be sure, once again you don't know what has point and what hasn't. And in the few paces to the window the desire swelled and grew heavy, for something entirely different with nothing in it of all that is now and here, something distant and different and good and beautiful; meaning Estherka. Her tone of voice when she would take the paper in the morning from where it was stuck into the shutter and run her eyes over it and report what she found, while the room would be half dark and half early morning light, and you could grin at her over the glass of tea, already packed with the day's meal into your basket, and you had to go out to work. But how would Estherka be when she opened the morning paper and saw — — — Dead! That's that? Dreadful! And it was quite dreadful enough to come to the fellows who did not know yet, and to go on without the first word being: Boys—Abrashka! But their shining foreheads and the way they stood declared that they already knew it all, and there was nothing to hide.

'Well, then,—shooting?' said Shraga, clearing his throat; and they were serious, they were grave and helped Shraga to keep to the point, saying: 'They're shooting all the time.'

'But they won't get into the courtyard. They'll die but they won't get in!' And there was no need to answer him that they all knew, and did not know, all that he knew and did not know.

'The branches hide things up above, but you can see everything from here,' Shraga went on about the business that was not the real business at all. 'We can sling a grenade or two when they come close.' 'Fallen.' Such a famous word and so meaningless. And that is not all kinds of things, but just exactly as this is now. 'I'm going upstairs for a minute,' said Shraga, bursting with the need to see people, or to say something to Aaron, or pass by somebody who didn't believe in him yet, or something—to go out, to move round for a moment.

II.

You could not reach the ladder in the entry room without passing by him once again. And like a light breeze trying to throw back and raise the curtain as it grows stronger, so from time to time one's awareness approached an understanding of something not understood, now understanding and thinking back, blowing and ceasing, and then trying to grasp what was not there.

And, for a moment, there shrieked a voice from within which he knew spoke only part of the truth, shrieking and saying that . . . it was all nothing, empty phrases. Then, for a moment, yet another voice shrieking, and apparently with more truth, saying that it was necessary to dig a hole as soon as possible and hide this remnant in it, the slightly opened lips and the fallen head with the stretched neck and upraised chin; until there started up once more that speech which can be delivered so easily out of the whole traditional thesaurus: He was this and that and he was, and he was . . . The only truth in it all being the word 'was'—in the past.

Shraga climbed up the ladder. To pass as the only one with knowledge among the many who did not know was ticklish and burdensome enough. But the way they stood above, and their dropped voices, showed that here as well they already knew everything and were gravely silent, so that if you yourself had not been serious as well, you would have been liable to burst out laughing maliciously. Shraga approached Jacob and met his gaze, which passed swiftly over his face and then dropped down:

'Is it true, Shraga?' Jacob mastered his voice. 'Yes, true.' 'And... all over?' 'All over.' And they continued starting out of the black window. Then Shraga said: 'And that seems to be a new stage.' 'Mmm. That's how it is.' 'And it's not over yet—and there are still more stages.' 'Yes, it's going to drag on and on.' 'And what do you think?' 'I don't think at all.' 'And it suddenly seems to me that all the same there's some way out here.' 'The fact that we're standing here is better than a hundred thoughts.' 'That so?' 'That or something like it.' 'So it's necessary to gird yourself, as they say, to gird yourself, that's what, I tell you!'

And it seemed as though they all had to take hold of one another's hands, all those who were here, and start singing Hallelujah and go out to the world with joined hands and go on like this with this strange feeling, with this astonishing brotherhood, with this sort of incomprehensible 'almost-understood.' 'I'm looking for Aaron,' Shraga suddenly excused himself and went off to look for him. If only Abrashka were here now to give him some advice about this mad business . . .

'Food has to be prepared, the men are hungry,' said Aaron without the slightest shadow accompanying his words, except the shadow in your heart. 'There are several chickens they brought from the courtyard, there's bread and there's tomatoes. Go and prepare the food, Shraga.' So Shraga went off to the western veranda where he found Nathan; and by the small southern balcony was Yitzhakale, and they're the best two for preparing grub. Were it not for some vacuum in the heart which even this friendly task could not bridge properly—maybe things would not appear so desperate.

Nathan groped about and found a primus and a big pot in one of the corners. He put the pot on the fire and thought: Let them eat something and drink a little tea, and everything will be different! Yitzhakale, still busy with the tomatoes, seemed to answer: 'Just what I said all the time—if only they'd listened to me a little earlier!' 'What did you say all the time?' Nathan wanted to get to the root of the matter. 'Everthing. All of this. I warned them, but they wouldn't listen to me. We could have been out of the courtyard an hour or two ago. Then it would have been dead easy to get by, one-two.' Nathan gave a long yawn: 'I'm dying to sleep, like a dog!' Shraga, who was still there, confused and washed out, bestirred himself then and said: 'Look: how carefully you crawl and crawl before you catch the bullet, so many preparations . . .' And Nathan retorted on the spot: 'If anyone's afraid of the bullet—the bullet will catch him.'

But Shraga could not feel at ease anywhere, and absentmindedly folded his hands behind his back and walked up and down the room. Words hung heavy on the tip of his tongue, but it did not help him that the shooting was growing heavier; and he bowed his head and got onto the ladder and left, just murmuring: 'Now they think the courtyard is theirs.' It seems that you can never say what seems to be going on now, to say for instance, that it's so near: it's already far away. And even if you should finally know how to say everything—to whom are you going to say it? And what will come of all this palaver? And there are still ever so many fine distinctions and things that gradually become clear, and you can't be satisfied with the mist of weariness and the confusion outside. There's also a kind of emotion, a fury of abomination, a lust to smash and destroy and avenge, you don't know on whom to take it out and you don't know how; and maybe all you want is to go off to some special tiny corner of your own and lie down on the ground and shrink together and feel how the muscles are melting with fainting pain, and give way to your own exclusive and private and personal mood, absolutely private; and devote yourself to that very little, that very little, which once again may be simply called, in brief, Estherka.

Somebody dashed running across the room with two rifles in his hand. That's it, to overcome, to gird yourself and to drive to the devil everything complicated, and to know and remember that one of ours has fallen while several of theirs have already gone down, and death is still here and his hands are prowling round to snatch what he can, and there is a struggle for survival here, a war to take hold, and if you hold on or let go here—it isn't merely your own fate that is being decided but also that of many others here and there at isolated settlements all over the country, who have to hang on like you or let go. Now there is something in that, when you remember that there are others like you and they haven't forgotten you, and the job you're doing and your own life are part and parcel of the big undertaking, and so on and so forth; and yet for some reason all these are only fine phrases that are far from the truth. For the heart feels sour, so sour, far beyond any supposed deeds of daring, beyond sacrifice or all kinds of things; and you have to hide this well, because you're among people who believe in and look up to you, and because apart from that 'they' aren't going to get into the courtyard, they aren't, you can perish and all, but they won't get in, devil take it.

And Shraga went down the ladder, and everything that a man's brain could think vanished in all directions, and in the place which had grown empty was the same quiet as surrounded Abrashka lying there with the lamp at his head, and the feeling that the current was running fast and the shores were steep, and you would not pass but would be swept along until you got stuck wherever you were going to get stuck.

And in this way Shraga approached the window and looked out in the deceptive light and once again picked up the vanished thread and knew what the other three here also knew; one solid piece of knowledge which it is is hard to define or name, but which heals and puts heart into one, together with the wish to be obstinate. 'They're preparing food already,' said he to them and felt that he had expressed the essential thing. For what did 'bad' mean? Except that you want to be obstinate and can't. 'And prepare the grenades,' said he, carefully taking the detonator, slipping it into place and slowly and cautiously screwing it tight, feeling the rough outer nipple with his thumb nail.

Naturally, that was how it had once been, so-and-so had a wife and son and so-and-so a bosom friend, and now there was nothing more than your body and those bodies with it; and there was no yesterday and no once upon a time; and there was only a now, a now that could be felt; and they were still standing and still shooting, and there were bullets, and there would also be food right away, and nobody was going to enter this courtyard, and that's how life was. No, no more apprehensions, no more reckonings, and you might do anything you liked, you men, anything goes, your soul was in your own hands and your life was free for all, and you could waste what you liked, and nobody thought about what was going to happen, and who gave a damn what would happen afterwards? Even if the one lying in the next room was waiting for you, and maybe you would be joining him right away. It didn't count at all, there was no calamity or wrong in it if you fell and died now, there was nothing to it, in all faith; now you were beyond caution and 'worthwhile' and 'has-to-be,' now you were prepared for anything. For instance, they would approach and you would lob a grenade at them. 'You can see much better down here than upstairs,' said Shraga easily, and the others answered: 'We see real fine.'

That whisper was healthy, genuine, the heart of the matter. Shadows moved in the empty space, there was nothing beyond that. Every-everything was here. In a little while there would be such ease that it would make no difference whether it would go on and on like this for another day or another week or ever so long: it wasn't frightening. Spit, pal, spit at every kind of nervousness and melancholy and all such things, and do the simple tasks, because that's what it is to live. Human life! Pah, how good to be alive! Here all of a sudden was a wave of cool air blowing between the stinking rags of smoke, and how fine to breathe cool air and to feel all the limbs of the body as well as the hunger that was there, and properly (they're preparing food already!). And it's good and fine to eat, devil take it, and it isn't at all nice to remember that on one side of the wall somebody is lying, while on the other side of the wall lie a few of theirs; devil knows if it's nice or not, but that's how it is, to tell the truth, that's the way it is. And what else? If only this smoke weren't there, the smoke is so unnecessary, making the head ache, making the soul feel stuffy, not giving you a chance even to come to yourself levelheadedly! That's just how it always is, when you're already prepared to accept things and put up with them—it turns out at once that you have to do it quick and sweating, and that there's dust and it stinks, and all in all it's no good—and as for all those fine and lofty things, to hell and the devil with them.

They were clearly out for the corner of the courtyard. And in through the tumbled-down fence. Then they would open the two gates, then fire would encircle the house and prepare to finish it off. But one grenade flung precisely at that corner by the fence would work wonders. So he held the grenade in the palm of his hand, gripping the embossed squares, the fate of the men engraved on the palm of the hand, holding the fate of the men inscribed in the embossed squares and diamonds which would burst apart and tear apart; such a big hand, that can hold the hoe, or lead a mule down the slippery slopes of the wadi, or hold screws cleverly and fit the screwdriver to them, and knows so gently and excitedly where the shadowy and pleasant places are with such-and-such an Estherka, and it's a fist and it's a stroker, and it grips the criss-crossed grenade opposite the box of matches, and rubs one against the other with a brief, sharp movement, and holds tight when a cascade of sparkling fire bursts out, and it lifts and aims beyond the window, this iron egg which whispers and counts two, three, four, and a tremor thunders with a white flare, and in spite of the fact that tens of thousands of years have passed since then, the hunter's cry resounds in the heart and hands and legs of a man. Run with cruel shouts and skin and cut and scalp, or be where the killing is done, and eat the heart of the one who fell, or dabble in his blood or something—and an ancient fire lights up in the eyes.

Somebody said 'swell!' at one side—and in the corner of the fence, in the mingled light and shade, there was a diminishing flurry and a harsh silence. Then someone groaned out there and said, 'Ahhhh' very long and annoyingly. And again somebody said, 'Let him choke!' And the inner tension linking the throat with the stomach was very attentive and also responded with a hidden echo.

III.

And it is a good thing if somebody in this house, one at least, naturally not you, knows what all this is about. No, only not to be killed! Let the bullet hit the hand or the leg or any place, as long as it isn't a place you die of. It's such a pity to die, if only you knew! 'Ah, they didn't expect such a fat chunk as that!' somebody beside the window said with pleasure. 'It's tremendous!' 'And still,' said another, 'they don't clear off, they're hanging on like ticks.' And the first one added, 'We've already moved and moved and there's nowhere else to move to, so now it's their turn, they've

fellow, 'let the one who sent him, water him; let him fill up with the mouthful he came here for!' 'Belly wounds,' Shraga found a decent way out, 'mustn't be given water!' 'And are you sure,' the lively fellow went on, 'he's not the one who shot Abrashka?! And what would he give you if you were lying wounded by his house? A bullet, that's what he'd give you!'

'Ach, *ya Allah*, ach!' wailed the voice outside, 'water!'

'We'll fetch him in to the steps, let him lie there!' The fellow from the cowshed went on tackling the problem, 'or we'll call one of them to drag him to them.' 'No use talking,' decided Shraga. 'You can't go out. It's all hard, and that's hard as well.'

'Hey!' came a voice from upstairs, 'one of you come up and fetch the food.' 'You go,' said Shraga to the pitying fellow who could find no rest, and he answered: 'All right, but I'll do without my share. Abrashka on the one side, and this fellow on the other, and then sit down to eat!'

IV.

He came back with the smell of scorched chicken making a widening circle round him, tomatoes and cucumbers in his pocket, a loaf of bread under his armpits, and promptly forgot his vow. They all stood chewing and peering out of the window, gnawing and not thinking about anything, chewing voraciously, chewing their fill, and you had to be tough and sure enough we are tough, and you get used to anything, and if you don't get used, you have to get used. Maybe you imagined a different meal and another landscape and other ways—but no: eat like this and live like this and rip off a chunk of meat and then round it down with a tomato and nibble at a cucumber, and everything grinds under the teeth, mixed with spittle and splinters, and you block off every twitch of doubt with bread, and the hands give you no rest, no opportunity—'Without any thoughts, comrades,' the stuffing hands say, 'and without monkey-business, comrades!' The grinders and the fangs and the chewers agree, and the important thing is to stuff yourself! Finally comes a faint belch.

Since the pause lasted for a long time, the ears were listening restlessly. In the strange silence outside they could already catch the sound of one cricket and then another, those crickets who are concerned with nothing but their own songs, blinded by their melody they see and hear nothing and merely disembarrass their hearts of more and more and more of all that has been stored there. And this goes to show how, while you are still dashing about and messing up the roads, the world goes on following its precise, indifferent, just, and absolutely perfect ways.

And Shraga, in whom the two furrows which life ploughs in every man's face from the wings of his nose to the corner of his mouth were exceedingly deep, running from the corners of the eyes till they divided the chin into a separate block, accompanied by a few channels and cross-branches round the mouth, the temples and the forehead—Shraga found the room too small for walking up and down in. Apart from which this pacing in a cage upset the others, and it was already so very necessary to have something else, something else already, that some kind of a doorway should be opened . . . Yet at the same time you are so afraid that the suffering voice will start asking for water again, and you promptly abominate your appetite, that filthy need to be full, and you turn and go to the window facing the grove. When had all this business of the grove taken place? Ages ago! And beyond the grove were the fields. It seems that the whole world is not wood, courtyard and house. There are also fields, there are valleys. There is a sky above all this. Interesting. The sky has all but been forgotten. And beyond our three thousand dunams there are other thousands of dunams, ploughed, harvested, forsaken, split up with wadis, and growing trees; and year after year people go out and plough them, go out and spend all the day in the fields and shrivel up in the sun, and hope for the coming year. And the nights are spacious, so spacious and empty, silence streams under them, it is hard to find anyone to talk to. And you don't know how to talk either. You open your mouth, but any real true word, anything of what you really want, is more than you can express.

Sometimes in the field, when you straighten up for a moment in the middle of your work and want to bend down again, it seems, for some reason, that there is something above, and you pause to gaze for a moment and see there is nothing, not even a cloud; yet you were so sure there was something there, and even more than sure, and that it really must have been something important; and you start looking all round, shading your eyes with your hand and searching, and there's nothing, and so how could you have been so sure? And only a little surprise or not surprise but something else, just so . . . So near the thing, so hard by it, just a step between you and the true knowledge, and in all truth what? In all truth nothing, you just imagined, and it was only so much confusion. And that's how it is . . . Words, words . . . Lots of words for strengthening the weak hands of others, the failing knees of somebody else, while you yourself just have a feeling of oppression. There's Abrashka who's already gone. There's a courtyard which has been burned. There's a little wood from which everybody ran away, and it's smoking. And there are three thousand desperate dunams. There are thirty men trapped in the house. There's dwindling ammunition. There's a tiny boat and a mounting tempest. And there's an overwhelming desire not to be here, and there's a clear, small core of knowledge that you can't dodge being here. There are two feelings: one of absolute wonder, and one of vanity of vanities. One has neither doubt nor question, while the other is entirely weariness and distaste and a wish for something else. One is of the regular guys who takes things as they come, easily, a feeling of 'let it come'; and the other, grave and childlike and hopeless.

And it's all liable to go on and on. Nobody will sleep tomorrow either. And for that matter we were prepared for much worse than this after all. Still, if only for just the bare fraction of a moment, if only Abrashka were alive. He never managed, he never at all managed so much together at once.

It must certainly be two o'clock in the morning already. The fire in the grove was dying down. What were they up to now? Such a long night as this is. Beyond the smell of smoke there is also another smell, a hard smell, a smell of horror, and maybe it was the smell of blood. What was the whole business like? A tree. As long as it grows in its proper place, we forget that it grows and may not grow some time, so mightily does it grow. Now that it has been cut down you are startled to see how empty the place is, how disconsolate, how lacking . . . Or maybe it is the scent of the gradually approaching Autumn . . . Autumn, winter, rain . . . God in Heaven, where does all this point?

Then, like a malicious hand shaking somebody awake out of deep sleep, there now rose again the groaning entreaty from outside: '*Hawaja*—water!' And it started a shudder of hatred, of pity and of helplessness. 'Shraga!' began the fellow from the cowshed, 'he's beginning all over again.' 'Well, he won't continue very long,' Shraga comforted him, and the fellow turned a shocked eye back. 'No, I can't bear it, I'm bursting!'

'You'd better be happy it's him howling out there and not you,' the lively lad answered excitedly. But Shraga spread out his fingers near his ear and moved them gently: 'Well, well, it will pass, everything will pass.' A frightened cow chose that moment to low briefly and ear-splittingly, and destroyed all his good intentions, so that Shraga could only finish: 'This will pass, I tell you, everything will pass.'

DOCTOR SCHMIDT

by Moshe Shamir

I.

A SMALL LEMON-COLORED Morris car crossed the Yarkon bridge between Ramatayim and Petach Tikvah. The criss-cross shadows of the high, steel girders were woven into the asphalt bridge. The river ran slow and green under it, and aged eucalyptus trees cast their shadows from both banks.

As soon as the car had crossed the bridge, it moved to the right side of the road and picked up speed. The driver, his unlit pipe between his teeth, was Dr. Schmidt, whose eyes, like the pipe, showed not a flicker of light. They were half-closed, partly from the glare of the sun setting on the horizon, but mainly because of the sense of weariness which never left him.

In the rich complex of his personality—compounded of deft fingers, an active brain, a wealth of knowledge, stubbornness, amiability, and physical vigor—his eyes were always the first to tire. You would never succeed in revealing the Doctor's fatigue judging only by his movements, by the humor in his conversation, by the strength of his will or his mental alertness. All these had a tremendous staying power and could never be overcome by weariness. Only his eyes would close, and because of this he would often baffle people with whom he was talking by a sad, tranquil look which was difficult to interpret—even while he would be participating fully in some activity.

Now, after a day of hard work and travel, he held the steering wheel lightly, his eyes half-closed. In a few minutes he would pull up at the office in Petach Tikvah and would ring home once more. 'This will be the fifth time,' he said to himself. The first had been when he had set out from Tiberias in the morning. Miriam had answered the telephone and said that No, there had been no word although one couldn't tell, but nevertheless it would be best if he would hurry home. From the Jordan Valley he rang twice. He sat in the bustling, stifling offices, swallowed grapefruit juice and waited for his call—while giving final instructions to the local cowhands for coping with the epidemic.

Once again Miriam had answered. Her voice was overcome with dejection, and he imagined her standing there in her blue house-coat, her orderly hair tied in a bun on top of her head, her large eyes full of suffering. 'No dearest, not yet. There has been no message, no phonecall, no telegram. Perhaps he will contact us before three. You know . . . how stubborn he is. He may leave without coming home at all . . .'

He could see the tears silently filling her eyes, her mouth straining, forcibly controlling her throat to speak calmly so that he should not be aware of her grief, lest he hear the cry welling up within her, lest the aching shame be conveyed to him.

From Haifa he had phoned a fourth time. He sat in the Department's district office, which was buzzing with clerks, typewriters and telephones—and waited for the call to come through. There was a steaming cup of black coffee in front of him. An Arab youth kept going out, returning, and thumbing noisily through his papers. Doors were opened and closed by busy clerks—and the eternal smell of lysol and shaving soap and khaki clothes dominated everything. When the call came, he trembled. It wasn't Miriam who answered the phone, but one of the neighbors, who had to shout over the bad connection. 'Your wife received a telegram from your son. It looks as though he is coming home for a short while—before he leaves. I don't know. But Dr. Schmidt—I don't know . . . He may arrive any moment, you can't tell. I will tell her, of course.

Mrs. Schmidt left the key with us. Yes, Yes. Shalom, Dr. Schmidt. Goodbye . . .'

II.

They were waiting for him now at Petach Tikvah. He would have to check the reports of the local clerks and of course they would add their usual complaints and all sorts of suggestions. He would have to stop there, investigate and work, since the epidemic had also struck in this district, no doubt about that. Perhaps this would require serious attention, his full attention. This cursed plague had spread over the country like a storm, penetrated every nook and cranny and deposited its poison in every crevice. In reality it was not one epidemic, but two or three.

The fatal chicken pest had begun in the Arab villages and struck down their thin, neglected chickens. It had then penetrated to the Jewish settlements and destroyed even the strongest birds in their coops—those strong white Leghorns which cackled during the day and scratched at night. Then there was the dread foot and mouth disease, which had attacked nearly all the farms in the Jordan Valley and was still spreading. You would look at the heavy Friesian cows and the tall Damascus breed, and to see them suffering in their animal dumbness was heartbreaking. And, last but not least, there was that cursed horse plague. They didn't know exactly what it was yet, but it had already managed to strike fatally in many stables at various places throughout the country, and this had happened just at the time of the autumn plowing.

Two weeks ago the little Morris had begun to bump along the roads and narrow paths, raising clouds of dust and sounding its horn, passing through farms and Arab villages, panic-stricken district offices and gas stations. First and foremost, the epidemic had to be isolated. Those places already affected were segregated, and a strict quarantine was imposed on all farms throughout the country, as well as on the roads. British and Arab police stationed on the main highway received strange orders which they did not understand. Drivers of the huge red trucks coming from Damascus and Beirut loudly cursed the thorough examination, but the foreign cigarettes they offered were of no avail. The gates of the Jewish farms were locked, their soil covered with lime; drums of lysol were placed on both sides of them bearing large signs: 'Disinfectant.'

All this activity was due to the efforts of that little Morris which had rushed everywhere, conscripting people, explaining, threatening, placing some on guard and spurring others to activity. The Arab fellaheen were overcome by fear of the accompanying policeman, of the official documents, of the syringes and veterinary instruments. Only one policy was effective in their villages: to frighten and isolate them, burn the stricken animals and dead birds, forbid all communication with neighboring villages, and promise reward and punishment. But in the Jewish settlements, the cowhands and poultrymen were quiet, understanding people who penetrated to the heart of the problem. They would listen attentively, accept advice with thanks, and carry out the instructions fully. They would accompany the car to the road, gravely shake hands with the vet and, at his departure, immediately lock the gates.

Those had been dark days for the cowhands of the Jordan Valley. One by one the big cows fell. First they would begin to drool yellow saliva between their teeth, in black, sore-scarred mouths; then they would sway on their legs, hooves covered with festering sores. The sight of those tottering animals was heart-rending. Although whole cowsheds lost their milk, their health, their very sustenance, the cowhands were restrained and comprehending, and through the car window Dr. Schmidt would jokingly declare: 'I'm not worrying about you. Whatever you've lost is lost, but if you bring the epidemic down to the Emek there'll be the devil to pay! Don't you dare to go anywhere near there. Don't even stick your noses out. Do you hear? Well, don't despair.'

Don't despair—God! They had received a telegram from his wife Miriam saying:—'The troops are going overseas. No word from Shlomo. Return home immediately . . .'

III.

That had been yesterday. The telegram had awaited him in the Department's office in Tiberias. The troops were leaving—perhaps for the firing line. Shlomo had not been home since the winter, December—nearly a whole year. The roads were teeming with soldiers going home to snatch a farewell leave of a few hours. One short order could transport thousands to infinite distances. Perhaps—to the firing line . . .

But today there had been six, eight, ten farms waiting for him along the road taking him south. Were they supposed to know that there was a certain Shlomo, that he had not been home an entire year—and that now he was being taken away? Were they supposed to visualize his high, pale brow, his sad eyes, his incredible stubbornness? Unwillingly, Dr. Schmidt had made his visits to the farms—farm after farm, hour after hour. But at some station a railway engine is already getting up steam, darkened carriages are waiting; on some distant horizon guns are reaping their grim harvest of death. There is a lot of mud in the world, epidemics, horse carcasses lying along the roads and soldiers climbing over their warm bodies.

Yes, this horse plague. What would they say at Petach Tikvah? What if this epidemic had not yet struck there, and he wasn't required? What if Shlomo is sitting in his uniform on the sofa opposite his mother, finding it difficult to make conversation, fiddling with the radio and then turning it down, glancing idly at the daily newspapers? Mother is silent—from time to time making some prosaic comment: 'I think Father will be here soon, they told him you were coming.' He is answering with a growl, or with a smile, or looking into her eyes . . . standing by the window, hands in his pockets . . . smoking and staring into the ashtray with narrowed eyes: 'You know Dad. He's probably operating at this very moment on some cow, or drawing blood from a donkey, or talking to the man in charge of the sheep-pen . . .' His laugh sounds unnatural and awkward, and Miriam is gazing at him with a prayer in her eyes.

Here is Petach Tikvah. The Morris pulls up in front of the office with a jerk, Dr. Schmidt jumps out and, coat-tails flying, sweeps into the outer room.

'Shalom. Good evening. How are things? Bring the papers into the other room. Get me Tel Aviv on the phone. My home. Thanks.'

In his office, he sits down at the desk, takes off his coat and hat, tosses them aside, and pulling the telephone towards him, leans back in his chair.

Shlomo's high, pale forehead . . . well, a father's soft spot! Only yesterday he was still an infant in swaddling clothes . . . they had to raise him in cotton wool—he was so weak and soft. And then, then one day he swaggered into the study smoking. 'Dad,' came from behind a cloud of smoke, 'Dad, I have a driving licence.' He had literally jumped out of his baby clothes. Then he'd come home in the early hours of the morning, sprawl on the bed in his smart suit and sleep with his shoes on until dawn, when he'd get up and walk about the house like a shadow. He was constantly complaining about the food, the furniture, the books, and his clothes. Evenings he'd sit, lighting his cigarettes one after the other. Then: 'Dad, give me the keys to the car. Don't wait up for me. As usual.'

Mother and father would wait wordlessly in their easy-chairs. Even when he had closed the door behind him, and stolen out like a burglar, silence would reign between them. Each lost in his own thoughts, they would seek refuge in books, letting the lowered radio continue to disturb the stillness. But they could still see him: pale, elegant, hair slicked back, the white silk scarf round his neck emphasizing the deep-blue weave of his suit. They'd hear the car as it noisily left the yard—and even then, for a long while, they wouldn't dare to look at one another . . .

The telephone buzzed. Dr. Schmidt seized it nervously. 'Hallo. Who's calling? From the farm? Which farm? No, tell them that I'm not in. I won't go, and that's all there is to it!' He hung up. To hell with them. Someone else can do it. We'll send someone tomorrow.

Gutterman entered unexpectedly, uncalled. He had never looked so stupid, superfluous, and dilapidated. Files in hand, he stood in front of the desk. The two gazed at each other silently a while, until suddenly the phone sprang to life again. Seizing the receiver nervously, the doctor shouted into it: 'Hallo. Dr. Schmidt. Petach Tikvah.'

As he waited for the line to stop crackling, he went back to that evening when Shlomo, dressed in grey flannels, white shirt neatly pressed, had stood by the door, the moment when he could stand it no longer.

'Shlomo, don't go out tonight. Mother is ill. We'll need you.'

'Me? Since when am I needed here?'

'But Mother is ill.'

'She'll get well without me.'

'Shlomo, a minute . . . (but Shlomo had grabbed the doorhandle and leaned on it slightly)—You know how long I've kept quiet. I've wanted to talk to you, *to talk* to you! But it seems that I can't. If you go . . .'

'I'm going.'

He had run forward and thrown open the door for his son, and as he did so their hands touched. Then he bowed deeply: 'Get—out!' Shlomo smiled, went out—and was swallowed up by the night . . .

Suddenly, Miriam's voice came through the receiver. He couldn't catch the first few words. Her voice was trembling, her strength and courage drained from her. 'He hasn't come yet. Some of his friends I met said he may still come. They have to be back at Lydda by seven-thirty . . .'

The doctor glanced at the watch on his wrist—fourteen minutes past six. He shouted into the telephone: 'What do you mean "he may"? Didn't he get leave like all the others? Has something happened?'

'I've been sitting here waiting for him. I switched on all the lights in the house, prepared supper, packed a parcel . . .' Her voice choked with the tears she couldn't control. But she continued: 'Sorry . . . don't worry. But come immediately. For my sake. If Shlomo won't come—then you come. Right away. They'll understand, they'll manage without you for once. Will you come?'

'Of course I will. And dry those tears—because Shlomo is standing outside and looking through the window.'

'How I wish he were! Come—right away.'

'Don't worry, I'll manage. *L'hitraoth* . . .'

'Shalom.'

He replaced the receiver . . . A week after that evening which had left its bitter taste of folly, Shlomo had knocked at the door and come in dressed in the uniform of the British Army, the Jewish Brigade. Miriam was still ill, and night after night she would wake him as she sobbed into her pillow. He would get up, light his pipe and sit by the dark windows until morning. Shlomo had come in uniform, his pale forehead hidden under a silly pointed cap, his slender body clothed in greenish khaki, and dragging his heavy black shoes as he walked. Schmidt didn't talk much, as if he were being faithful to what he had said then: It seems I don't know how to talk to you. Shlomo would keep vigil at the foot of his mother's bed whenever he came home, and would reply quietly to all her questions, shutting him out. But even with her he was apathetic. Then they had been transferred from place to place and Miriam had risen from her sick-bed. And then winter had come, December weather, and he had not been home since. But now in Lydda, at seven-thirty exactly, the engine would whistle and set out on its journey, and a steel helmet would cover the pale forehead . . .

Doctor Schmidt looked up at Gutterman, who had not moved all this while: 'Take those papers back. I'm going.' He stood up, gathering his brief-case and coat, and added: 'You sign the monthly report yourself. I'm not going to do any more today. If anyone rings, tell them I've been in and left. Don't ring me at home. Well, it doesn't matter—you can ring me if you need me. Open the door, please.'

IV.

Coat, hat and brief-case in hand, he went into the outer room, nodded to the telephone operator, and opened the door. Coming up towards him on the steps outside were a Yemenite couple. In her arms the woman carried a baby wrapped in swaddling clothes. There could be no doubt as to their origin or class, from their clothes. On his thin body the man wore ragged, borrowed khaki trousers, obviously not made for him, and a badly worn coat. The woman's bones were covered with black trousers, above which hung some rags, and she wore a filthy shawl on her head.

Doctor Schmidt took in the whole of their plight at a glance. He saw them without pity, but he was unable to escape without saying anything. Unwillingly, he asked: 'Where are you going? Whom do you want?'

The Yemenite was startled, and his wife also stopped at his side.—'Doctor Schmider. They tell me here . . .'

'What's wrong? What do you want him for?'

The Yemenite paused two steps below and looked up at him. His wife lowered her head and hugged the baby tighter. As though aware of the identity of the man standing before him, the haggard, balding farmer began talking rapidly, swallowing as he blurted out his story: 'The horses, Doctor. Two horses— they sick all of a sudden. The Lord knows—both not moving. Sweating something terrible. One more than the other, and he swollen too. They tell me, wait, the Doctor he come. They not die yet, they only sick. They say they not die from that there sickness. They not die—but I got to work. They say, Schmider he come and see what to do . . .'

The doctor let him talk on, but it was absolutely clear to him that he would have to go and look at the animals. Within three days the plague could spread and destroy the entire district. It was essential that he investigate this case, even though—what was the time? In one hour the train leaves Lydda—damn those horses! He turned round, shouting 'Wait here!'—and flung open the door. Inside, Gutterman was leisurely drinking the tea in front of him. His elongated head, narrow eyes, big hands, and enlarged jawbones were all completely engrossed in this task. The doctor thundered at him: 'Gutterman, get the instrument case . . . and bring the certificates, and the pistol . . . and please give me an overall, any one will do. Immediately, Gutterman, and hurry!'

Going outside again, he found the man and woman exactly where he had left them. 'I'm going to your place,' he shouted to the terrified pair, who followed him with their eyes, and threw his coat and hat into the Morris. In the meantime Gutterman had appeared at the head of the stairs, and stood waiting in confusion.

'What are you standing there for? Come on, you're coming with us.' And opening the back door for the couple he commanded: 'Get in!' The frightened Yemenite, suspicious of this offer, timidly suggested: 'Never mind, Doctor. I show the way. No need. We go like this.'

'Do as I say, and don't be a fool. I'm in a hurry—get in!'

Gutterman bent his huge body and, groaning loudly, forced himself into the seat next to the driver, holding the instrument case in his lap. Painstakingly, the Yemenite climbed in and sat in the back. His wife stood silent and motionless, the child in her arms. Dr. Schmidt felt his blood coursing to his head, but, clenching his teeth, he regained control of himself with a tremendous effort. 'Get in, damn it!—Are you a human being or not?'

She was finally persuaded by her husband's entreaties and increasing shouts: 'Get in, Miriam—come on, *yallah*, we go in the car, so what . . .?'

The doctor set the car in motion, immediately the woman had got in and crouched on the back seat. They moved off before the door was closed, and for a short while it swung on its hinges until Gutterman turned around and slammed it shut. As they glided through the streets of the town, a smile broke out on the doctor's face at the sudden realization: Fancy that—there was a Miriam in both places. They soon turned into a dirt road bordered on both sides by trees and houses at irregular intervals. In winter these empty fields would become lakes of stagnant water, and in spring they would be covered by carpets of anemones, groundsel and poppies. Now, only dust rose from the desolate, grey fields. The car swayed slowly between wheel-tracks and puddles. 'There, Doctor, behind huts, in Yemenite quarter. Turn right here, this here side . . .'

The Morris turned right between two rows of closely crowded wooden huts and came to a quick stop. Puddles of sewage water, stacks of bricks, and scattered piles of rubble and garbage blocked the road completely. 'We'll get out here.' The doctor announced his decision with a finality which left no room for objection. 'We'll walk from here. The car can't pass. Come on, *yallah*, no time to waste!'

Gutterman got out last, straightened his weary body, gathered his heavy overcoat about him, and tucked the instrument-case away under his arm. The mother and child trailed along behind, but the Yemenite's spindly legs carried him quickly over the familiar ground. 'Here sir. Behind that there hut. Then another one . . . Then my house. You see the horses. It not so bad. A son I have, and he go in the army. He run away from home. I say to him, You dog, you do this your father, what'll we eat. Then he spit on me, not give a damn, and go in the army, and I not hear from him nothing. I not know where he be now, where they sent him. Now I alone myself with horses. I work for Koblosky, but he's a swine, he not give enough even for bread. I think we get work building, I harness horses—they start—they not going. They sweat something terrible, one swollen. My heart jump. If they die . . . I die. Now the Doctor see . . .'

V.

It seemed as though he had seen this selfsame yard many a time before: the small, one-roomed hut, the filthy area, the wagon thrown together from rickety boards. The Yemenite ran ahead leading the way, but his wife had entered the hut immediately, leaving the door wide open. Inside could be seen a bare table standing by the windows, and the clay floor. A boy, skinny and with close-cropped hair, stood in the doorway staring at the newcomers.

The Yemenite led the way to the horses standing in a corner of the yard. A number of twisted boards over their heads formed a kind of shelter, and a makeshift manger—two crates propped up on poles—was absolutely empty. 'They not eat nothing. Not this much. Nothing,' explained the owner of the two miserable animals, lifting a finger. Doctor Schmidt approached the two drab, emaciated male nags. One was shaking all over, sweating, his bloodshot eyes protruding from their sockets. A thread of yellow saliva drooled from his drooping lower lip. The other horse was also covered with sweat, shaking, nodding its head sadly, and its swollen veins looked like black cables.

The doctor stood before them in silence. There was no need to examine them. 'Peste Angina,' he mumbled to himself, not intending that his voice reach the mystified Gutterman who was standing close by. Peste Angina, African Horse Plague. Shaking off the weary distress which had overcome him momentarily, he turned round and spoke to the two waiting men. 'Nothing can be done. You will receive ten pounds for each of them. Did you bring the pistol, Gutterman? Give me the certificates. And you, mister, dig a big hole immediately and bury the two carcasses as deep as you can. Tomorrow someone will come to see whether you have done it . . .'

The Yemenite stood silent staring in bewilderment. 'No understand, Doctor. They no good? Not get well? Why they die? Not get well? Not so bad. Look, they standing.'

He hadn't the strength to argue. The doctor continued as though he had not heard: 'Come inside with me, please. I'll sign the certificate. You can take this to the district office tomorrow and you will receive twenty pounds . . .'

'Why twenty pounds? What they do to the horses?' he mumbled as he went over to them. Gutterman had not yet done a thing.

'Gutterman!' Dr. Schmidt startled his assistant out of his reverie. 'Do as I told you. And you, mister, if you don't want the money— I won't sign the certificate. I have no more time to waste . . .'

From his inside coat pocket, Gutterman brought out a long-barreled pistol and strode towards the horses. The Yemenite backed towards them and joined the unfortunate beasts.

'No!' he burst out suddenly, screaming wildly, 'you not kill them . . . kill me first . . . you not got to kill, they still good. They work. Come, kill me! . . .' Finding his path blocked by the raving Yemenite, Gutterman stopped short and turned helplessly to the doctor. The Yemenite also was gazing at him with madly pleading eyes. Hearing the cries, the wife rushed out to join them with the baby in her arms. 'Take him,' she sobbed. 'Take him and kill him. Kill me. Kill the woman.' Helplessly she raged at Dr. Schmidt: 'I swear, by your father's life . . . Where we get food, where? These here horses, they all we got. They go, work a bit, not work. Eat a bit, then not eat. So what. Look at the house. Look at the baby. Look at me.'

Dr. Schmidt looked at his watch. Seven o'clock. Well—good luck, Shlomo. And that whole quarrel . . . see how your eyes are laughing again. They leave Lydda at seven thirty. But there is no need at all to shoot healthy men through the head. Such a fate is only for sick horses, no one else but sick horses.

VI.

He went quietly up to the thin, excited man, and with a slight gesture prevented his unconscious retreat. Of itself, his hand came to rest on the farmer's shoulder, and only a ragged sleeve was between them. He said: 'Your horses are suffering from a terrible sickness. It is a plague which comes from Africa. It will infect other horses, donkeys, and mules. Even if your horses get well—and I don't think there's a chance of their recovery, just look at them—in any case, they are now threatening the lives of hundreds of horses in the district. Do you understand? All the horses of all the carters, the cooperative settlements, and the private farmers would be affected. The same thing would happen to all their horses. They will shake all over, they won't eat, won't work—they will die. Understand?'

Greeted by a dense, stubborn silence, the doctor turned to Gutterman and said drily: 'Take him inside and give him a certificate for two horses. Afterwards see to it that he buries them. Give me the pistol.' The owner of the horses stood between his two beasts, not uttering a word, as though he had neither heard nor understood what had been said. Gutterman approached and motioned him to move, but when he did not stir—he put his long arm around his shoulder and began to lead him in the direction of the house. The Yemenite now began to resist. He screamed, lashed out with his fists—but he was dragged on. 'You rats, you cut my throat . . . kill me . . . come, burn the house. You go way, you. Let go me. I not thief, you dog. You not shut my mouth. Leegggoooooo!!!'

An excited group of neighbours stood in the street by the broken fence. Many of them seemed like brothers of the screaming man, in stature, dress, and features. They looked at the horses, listened to the shouts, and shook their heads. They shook their heads in pity, but not one of them climbed over the fence.

Although Gutterman did not succeed in closing the door, he kept his prisoners inside the hut. Dr. Schmidt went up to the horses. One of them drooled saliva and would have died in two or three hours' time. We will have to send policemen to dig a grave, this man is out of his mind and won't do anything. The horse's head sagged loosely, its scraggy mane full of straw. The doctor placed the pistol barrel to its ear, a quiver passed over the half-paralysed beast, and he pressed the trigger. The shot was not frightening, and yet the horse staggered immediately and fell on its side. At that moment the shouts from the house became louder, the woman wailed, the children cried, and Gutterman's solid form blocked the doorway.

The other horse shook its head nervously. Dr. Schmidt stroked it and patted its wet swollen muzzle. While doing this he grabbed its nostrils and squeezed them. At first the horse was surprised and resisted a little, but soon it yielded and was quiet. Its large head remained steady, turned upwards and back. With his free hand Dr. Schmidt put the pistol to its ear. At that very moment the Yemenite managed to force his way through the door, but the shot re-echoed and the horse sank immediately without a tremor, and with no loss of blood.

The bereaved carter clutched the doorpost of his hut at the sight before him. He groaned, and his sobs choked within him as his shoulders shook convulsively.

'Did you make out a certificate? You had better send policemen over to bury the horses immediately. If only one mosquito lights on the carcasses it will spread the plague like wild-fire.' He glanced at his watch again. Seven-fifteen. The group of spectators stood quietly by the fence, and the thin Yemenite, sobbing silently in the doorway and leaning his head on the post, did not move. 'Come on, let's go.'

When they reached the road, the heavy puffing of someone running suddenly reached their ears. 'Schmider, Schmider!' The doctor stopped, and turning saw the Yemenite lean on the fence with both hands, and gasp: 'I swear, now I take everything. My wife and children. Lock the door. Spill kerosene. Let fire take us to Hell. You destroy my house. May that eat you till you die. You destroy my house . . . Your house be destroyed too. I hope the Lord destroy your house. Your sons die like my horses you kill. Die, die . . .'

They walked on, crossed the road, avoided the scrap-heaps and puddles. Black wondering eyes stared at them from the doorways, and at the end of the street the car stood like something from another world.

'You come over here yourself tonight to supervise the burying of the horses. And see if you can help him with something . . .'

'Yes, sir.'

They entered the car. Dr. Schmidt started the motor, and his glance fell on the hands of his watch. Seven-thirty. The engine is blowing its whistle and letting off steam, the carriages are beginning to roll—and the boys are off to the firing line. The Morris began to move forward, and suddenly splinters were flying: a window-pane was shattered and the stone landed on the back seat. The doctor accelerated the car as it jolted along the furrowed road. A shout pursued him, once, twice, thrice:

'Your house be destroyed, murderer—your house be destroyed!'

THE LORD HAVE MERCY!

A Yemenite Story, by Hayim Hazaz

I.

SA'ADYA ARAKI didn't on no account consent to volunteer for the Army, like was being expected of every man's son in the prime of his life and all there and without no children. So the members of the Draft Board in Jerusalem, they come and kick him out of his job with the carpenter, where he made his living. Sa'adya, he just stood there and folded up his tool-kit and left the shop with a mighty peculiar expression. It was hard to tell, if you know what I mean, whether he was welcoming the Sabbath or taking leave of it: he looked glad on the right, and awful sorry on the left.

His missus, Badra, she saw things the way he did, and she wanted what he wanted.

'Why, man,' says she, 'y'is d'on'y husban' ah'se got. Is ah gonna give mah honeybunch, mah sweetiepie, mah big buck, to study war? Not on yo' life! Not on yo' lives, damn yo' souls! An' ah don't mean yo' pappies'! Ah'll see 'em dead first! No, suh!'

Now Sa'adya, he made the rounds of all the carpenter shops in town and kept asticking his nose into every corner where he scented a job, but he couldn't smell out a thing, seeing as how he didn't have no work card.—'Has y'got yo' exemption?' they all asks him, like they is singing hymns or a love song.

So he give up trying to make a living, and he goes to work on the missus, to get him a little exemption at home by making her pregnant. Man! he kept at her night and day, astrutting and acourting and atussling her like he was a rooster.

'Ah'se gotta get me a son!' He was sot on that. 'Come hell or high water, ah'se gotta have one.'

But nothing seems to do him no good, not the day tussling nor the night tussling, and things is looking pretty dark.

So he takes hold of the missus and he totes her to the Yemenite Rabbi, and from the Rabbi to the wise men of the Kurds, and from the Kurds to the Mugrabis, and all the rest of the tribes found in Israel. Says he, if they all can't bring him no help from Heaven, why let it come from the other place, so long as they helps him!

But! just as he was no damn good to her hisself, so he couldn't get no use for her from all the spelling and charming of them witch doctors. When the Lord He shuts a door, no mere human man ain't going to open it.

From all the worries that was eating him, and from the wolf aprowling at his door, and from it all—he began to pine away, and the meat on his bones it got shrivelled and dried up like a carob, and he kept astorming and afretting all day, and his heart was bitter and his mind was cross. The way the world was looking to him, he had no peace, nohow.

'Oh Lawd!' he pours out his troubles, complaining to his Maker. 'How come Y'All make dis here trouble on'y fo' me? Why is ah worse'n de udders? Y'All got Kurds, an' Urfals, an' Chalabs, an' all sorts o' queer critters Y'done made fo' Yo' Cre-a-shun, an' dey all gets 'em litters as fast as jackrabbits, an' ah'se d'on'y man cain't git nary a one. Is Y'All doin' hit, God fo'bid, on pu'pose? Why? For what cause? What sin ah done? So dey all kin cotch me an' draf' me an' beat de stuffin' out o' me in dis here war? Lawd, Lawd!'

The biggest gripe Sa'adya had in his heart was against his poor wife, and, not once and not twice, he'd jump on her and use hard words, and he'd tell her off:

'What d'hell use ah got fo' ya, if y'is dry an' y'don't do me no good?' he'd yell at her as if he was aiming to swallow her up.

'Y'kin bu'n in hell a t'ousan' times, damn yo' soul, y'bitch!'

'Ah ain't dry, an' dere ain't nuthin' wrong wid me.' Badra bows herself down, as meek as a lamb, and answers him. 'Dis here ain't mah fault. Hit's de Lawd's doin'. If'n He-All wanted hit, we'd done had us a son a'ready . . .'

'Can't fool me none wid dat high talk! Talk ain't 'nuf! When a hen don't lay no eggs, she goes t'de butcher!'

Right off, when she heard him talking thataway, the tears began to flow.

'Why y'blamin' me?' she clucked through her tears. 'Am dis here sometin' ah kin do? Do hit res' on me? Wasn't Sarah, mudder o' Israel, a dry one? An' wasn't Rachel, mudder o' Israel, a dry one too? Till de good Lawd, He blessed 'em, an' sho' 'nuf Abra'm got'm a son when he was ninety-year-old . . . Jes you wait, ole man. De Lawd has plenty. We-all is still mighty young, we still got time.'

'Y'go 'n give dat line o' talk t'de Draf' Board,' says Sa'adya, aboiling and apuffing at her. 'Dis here chitchat o' yourn ain't doin' me no good. Ah'se gotta git me a son! One way or 'nudder—t'git shet o' dis here draf'! . . .'

Pretty soon the town got wind of what was going on, and the news was spread around, from neighbor to neighbor, from stonecutter to chipper, from chipper to muler, from muler to porter. So some, they picked themselves up and came to give Sa'adya a load of heavy advice and tell him about all sorts of sure-as-hell-fire remedies; and some, they just came to give him the giggles and sound off to him the kind of stuff that ain't fit to print. The womenfolk too got a kick out of getting fenced into this here chickencoop, and they were kept pretty busy with Badra, telling her sometimes things that helped, and sometimes things that didn't.

'Looky here, Badra gal,' they give her a sharp look and say deliberate like. 'Mebbe yo' ole man he's weak, he ain't atryin' an' aworkin' 'nuf; mebbe he jes ain't doin' no ridin' an', po' t'ing t'ain't yo' fault nohow.'

'What y'all blowin' 'bout? . . .' says Badra, and her face gets red as a live coal in a breeze. 'He's as healt'y and as hot as dey come! Like a rooster!'

'Well, now, sometime bein' healt'y don' help an' bein' like a rooster don' help,' says they, trying to draw her out by talking. 'Mebbe his ball-stuff ain't sharp . . .'

'No, no, no, no!' Badra rocked her body like a water wagtail and put their doubts to rest by her tone and her look. 'Sharp 'nuf, sharp 'nuf . . . Bless de Lawd, de man is healt'y as a stud-hoss. He's all dere an' got what hit takes.'

'Den y'try an' git'm t'take ya t'a doctor. De doc kin tell if'n de trouble is his'n or yourn.'

'Ai, ai! De Lawd protec' me. How'll ah strip me nekked an' show mah innards 'fore de doctor! Ain't dat a shame?'

'So, who care? Y'be sure o' one t'ing: y'ain't agoin' out from dat dere doctor widout you'se acarryin' twins . . .'

'So *dat's* hit? *Dat's* hit, y'bitch? A jinx on yo' pappies, y'good-fo'-nuthins! Dat's how y'talkin'? . . .'

Sa'adya, he had no rest or peace of mind. He ate lots and lots of ginger and coconuts, and eggs that Badra mixed with butter, and all kinds of that there grub as is good for the man-stuff. Everywhere he went he kept apestering people and asking their advice, ahustling and abustling, afretting and afuming, this way and that, looking for a cure, hoping maybe anything could help a little. Now and then he'd get so all-fired jinxed by old man trouble that he'd hop into his house, and stand there before Badra, looking like he couldn't make up his mind, his eyes popping this way and that—like they'd given him a prayer book where 'The Lord is My Shepherd' was all mixed up with 'The Song of Moses'.

'Well, now, ole woman!' says he, and his voice is low. 'What am ya feelin' now?'

'De Lawd'll help, ole man.' Badra, she drawls and she sighs.

'Dat ain't no answer!' He's boiling over and laces into her with a shout. 'Ah'se a-askin' ya: What am y'feelin'? Is we got anythin' yet?'

'Ah still cain't tell . . .'

'Goddam yo' pappy, an' yo' chile-bearin', an' dis here Jewish Agency an' Draf' Board t'gedder! Dey sh'd all bu'n in hell a t'ousand times! What a Goddam mess dey's made o' mah life! . . .'

Then he'd jump on Badra, mad as a hornet and plumb out of his mind, and he'd grab her and throw her down on the bed.

'De door . . . shet de door . . .' she'd cluck, all crumpled up beneath him, like a hen. 'Shame . . .'

'Shet yo' mout', ya Goddam no-good an' yo' no-good pappy!' he'd huff and he'd puff. 'Ah'se agoin' t'kill ya!'

II.

Day by day, this gripe that was eating Sa'adya's heart got stronger, and all this time he couldn't speak with her a word of peace. The least little thing would set him off, and he'd boil over and spill his words out on her in a fit of temper. It didn't help Badra nohow that she'd listen to his scoldings and keep quiet. Contrariwise, her being so soft and humble made him hate and fume at her even more. And he'd already thought some about giving her a divorce, but he was going to wait until they straightened out his case in the Appeals Board, seeing as how he'd sent up an appeal and was pinning all his hopes on it.

This was what he told her once when he was boiling:

'Now looky here, y'bitch, if dem dogs on d'Appeals Bo'd don't let me go, ah pity ya. Ah'se agoin' t'have t'give ya a dee-vorce, an' den y'kin go straight t'hell a t'ousand times. Ah ain't agoin' t'put mah life in no danger 'cause o' you. Hit am all, all yo' fault! If'n y'da on'y give me a little boy o' gal befo', ah wouldn't be havin' none o' dese here troubles. But ah ain't expec'in' no hope f'om you. Look't all de toil an' trouble ah done had fo' ya, an' hit ain't done no damn good. Ah'se good as dead a'ready! Ah'se weak as a baby, an' mah knees is shakin'! Damn yo' pappy, y's gotten t'be like a good-fo'-nuthin' mule. Y'pour water in a leaky dam, she keeps on runnin'! Damn yo' soul, ah'se been asweatin' an' adyin' fo' a barrel o' nuthin's!'

Badra, she didn't answer him none. She just shook her bosom, real scared and her eyes apopping, and she whispered:

'Oh Lawd! De Lawd protec' me!...'

But though he gave her the miseries and treated her so all-fired bad, and was fixing in his thoughts to do her dirt, still he never stopped from loving her. That was just his trouble, that his heart was like split in two, and his hating and his loving were getting all mixed up and fighting one another, and he couldn't tell what would be the end, and he didn't know what he would do. When he'd go home and see her face, he couldn't stand her and he'd fret and fume and want to tear her up like a fish, to smash, to kill and destroy. But when he'd go out into the street, right away he'd blame hisself and go crazy as a loon with knowing he'd done wrong, and with wanting her and feeling sorry for her.

'Dere ain't never been no trouble like mine!' He'd shrug his shoulders and get to feeling awful sorry for himself and awondering. ' 'Tain't bad 'nuf dat ah hates her, but ah'se gotta see her side too an' be alovin' her...'

Once he came back home from the street with his heart full and thinking to make things up with her. He found her sitting on the ground and chanting a tune, kind of sad and mournful, over and over, like the childless women in Yemen used to chant at the spring of Rabbi Salim Shabazi, and her eyes were running tears and her thin face was lit up with a brightness a little like a beautiful sunset:

> Fader o' Peace, strengt'en mah heart,
> an' give what ah'se a'askin'.
> Ai, help, holy fount'n
> an' give me a son.

He stood there an looked at her out of the corner of his eye, and it was like a storm passed over in front of him, and he changed from loving her to hating her, and his body shook and he shouted at her:

'Git outa dis here house, y'ugly bitch! Git outa mah sight! Ah'se sick an' ti'ed o' seein' ya, damn yo' soul!'

'What ah done?' She was scared and tried to make up with him. 'Ain'tcha mah honeybunch, mah lover boy, de light o' mah eyes, an' ain't ah in yo' hands like a no-good she-donkey . . .'

'Ah'se atellin' ya: 'nuf o' dat!' Sa'adya boiled over and yelled. 'Y'd better git on outa here quick, so ah don't see yo' face again! So ah don't feel yo' smell in here no mo'! Ah'se sick o' ya, y'bitch!'

As if that wasn't bad enough, things got even worse. Once Sa'adya even raised his hand against her and hit her. This was something new and something to wonder at, seeing as how he'd never been like this and never played that game before. Right away, when she saw what he was at, she bent herself low and turned her face and her arms up to him, and her voice was abegging him in a whisper, like she was asking him to keep one of the Commandments:

'Beat me, ole man, so's ah kin make up f'all mah sins. Mebbe de good Lawd'll have mercy on me, an' mebbe he'll give me a son 'cause o' yo' beatin's. Beat me, beat me, much's ya like. Ah'se all yourn, mah back's yourn, an' dese here arms is yourn . . .'

Then he controlled himself and stopped hitting her. He left her and went off to a corner and sat down and put his head between his knees.

Badra stole after him, quiet-like, and sat down, and she kept her eyes on him and shook her head and just mumbled with her lips and kept still. But after a few minutes she began speaking:

'Y'see, ole man, dat y'didn't beat me, after all! You'se a good man, you is, and y'ain't no trouble maker, and y'd be 'shamed t'beat yo' wife . . . Me, hit don't matter t'me nohow, ah'se ready fo' yo' beatin's. Why, ah'd sho' 'nuf like it if'n y'd beat me, yo' beatin's feel sweet t'me, but hit's better y'don't do hit. Y'don't want, God fo'bid, de Lawd Protec' us, t'git inta no trouble over me an' do no sinnin' 'fore de Lawd. Better disaway, better. Never min' dat ah keeps quiet an' ah'se ready t'take hit all f'om ya, even so hit's better disaway, better fo' you. May de Lawd be good t'ya fo' mah sake, so y'don't do somethin' y'll be 'shamed of, an' give d'ole man Debbil chance t'git atcha. Ah'se contented, ah'se contented...'

From then on he took this to heart and didn't raise his hand to her, but only kept lacing into her with his tongue. When the evil spirit got into him he'd take his two fists and beat on his own face and heart, or he'd hit his head against the wall. Except for three or four times when he beat her and she was willing and they both knew it. But those beatings had no sorrow or shame in them, they was a kind of medicine-beatings—seeing as how there was some jokers done give him a tip that he ought to beat her on her middle after he'd atussled her, the way some hits the cow after the bull, to make sure of her seed. So he did the same, and he hit her with all his might, and after every blow he gave her he'd say, over and over again:

'May de good Lawd give us dat we'll sta't bein' f'uitful an' amul-tip-lyin'! May de good Lawd give us dat we'll sta't bein' f'uitful an' amul-tip-lyin' !'

Badra, she'd take these beatings from him with love and keep urging him on:

'Mo', mo'! Beat me mo', ole man, mebbe dat ain't 'nuf fo' me...'

III.

The days went and the days came, days of anger and wrath, days of weeping and brawling and troubles. Day by day the little sum of money left from the old days kept shrinking, till Sa'adya, he was kept busy working at how to keep their few pennies together, and they was eating less and less.

This was pretty hard on Sa'adya, and he started getting afraid of the hunger-sickness.

'Name o' God, what'll 'come o' me?' He put the fear of the Lord into hisself and trembled with terror. 'Pretty soon ah won't have nuthin' lef', an' den we gonna die, t'die! Who kin help us, who'll listen? Nobody knows our trouble, or gives a damn fo' us!'

Badra, she made up her mind to help him and get her some maid-work with the Ashkenazis. But she just didn't know how to tell him about it so he wouldn't get into a fit and spoil her whole plan. She could tell without asking that he wouldn't like the idea of her working for others. He done told her more than once, before and after they was married:

'No, suh! Ah ain't goin' nohow t'have ya gettin' ti'ed aworkin' fo' no strangers. All ah wants is dat y'set at home like a queen, dat y'be dere awaitin' fo' me when ah gets home, an' ah kin be lookin' at you, an' y'kin be lookin' at me . . .'

So one day she fed him up with black-eyed peas and cornbread, since there was nothing set on his stomach easier and pleased him more than cornbread, and soon as he was asitting there all heavy-like and his hands was hanging loose and his soft side showing, she came over to sit with him.

She took ahold of herself and chose her words carefully and began talking to him real loving-like, and her tongue ran with milk and honey:

'Looky here, ole man, ah wants y't'take hit real easy-like, eatin' an' drinkin' an' strollin', an' ah'll go do some maid-work like ah useta, an' whatever ah make'll be 'nuf fo' us two, wid de Lawd's help. What y'grievin' 'bout? Why does y'let dem dere no-good Ashkenazis make y'life mis'able an' hunt after ya fo' dis here draf'? How much dey goin' t'pay ya? Six o' seven pounds. Mebbe,

mebbe—nine pounds! We don't wan' none o' dat! Y'take yo'sel' out an' stroll, till de time'll pass an' de war'll be t'rough.'

Sa'adya, he shook hisself a bit and threw a look at her and inspected her over and sat there awondering. And after some two or three minutes he hopped up on his legs, real spry and chipper, as if she hadn't filled up his belly at all with lots of black-eyed peas and cornbread, and he yelled at her:

'Who's de man in dis here house, me o' you? Mebbe y'd like t'be awearin' de pants here an' let me wear yo' dress, y'ole bitch? Y'wants me t'be awaitin' on de money y'll be agivin' me? . . .'

For a long while he kept on fretting and fuming at her, and the longer he kept at it the hotter he got. Till he himself felt that he couldn't keep his hands from doing something.

So he picks himself up and starts to leave the house.

'Ah'se agoin' t'de draf'!' He turns to her as he's going out the door. 'Ah'se agoin' t'd'Ashkenazis! Be a soldier man! No damn use! 'Nuf o' dat! 'Nuf o' dat, damn yo' soul!'

Boiling with anger, he can't find no rest, so he keeps on the move, shuffling along from street to street and from alley to alley.

'Ah hates her! Ah hates her!' He kept on saying this to himself, practicing the words in anger and in sorrow, repeating them to make them stick. 'Ah hates her guts! . . . Ah'se just gotta give her a dee-vorce, an' get rid o' dis here trouble, ah'se gotta, ah'se gotta! . . .'

It seemed like the Lord had fixed that day to be one of bitterness and foolishness for Sa'adya, a day when old man Devil was dancing inside him. Dark, without no light. That day he got himself mixed up in a street-fight with Yichye Hamuda ('Loudmouth'), and then a big crowd gathered round and bothered him, and there was anguish and terrors.

This is the way it was. After he'd grown tired out from all his fuming and his troubles and his shuffling, and he wanted to rest—he runs plumb into the business of Yichye Hamuda. This 'Loudmouth' meets him in the middle of the street and stands there ajoking at him like he usually does, he being lightheaded by nature, a funny man and a shrewd customer; but nobody pays no attention to his talk, really, though he's always strutting about with all his business, and saying he can tell fortunes and cast out spells, like the witch-doctors.

So that Hamuda, he stops him and says:

'Hi, Sa'adya, how's d'ole woman? She still dry?'

'De Lawd have mercy,' says Sa'adya and sighs. 'De Lawd have mercy.'

'Mebbe she really *dry,*' Hamuda winks at him, with a laugh and a fooling in his voice. 'Mebbe you'se gotta take her t'de *mikve*-bath an' leave her dere t'ree o' fo' days—mebbe she'll get a little wet dataway . . .'

'Lemme 'lone!' says Sa'adya without any patience. 'We a'ready done hit all.'

'Could be, Sa'adya ole boy, dat de good Lawd, He done made *you* dry wid her, an' she ain't de one dat's dry?'

'De Lawd knows. It's all de Lawd's doin'.'

'But dere's a cure fo' dis here,' says Hamuda, casual like.

'What cure?' says Sa'adya, getting fearful.

'Ah knows dis cure. Ah kin do hit.'

'What cure? What cure? Ah swear, y'se gotta tell me. Ah'se awillin' t'give mah eyetoot'.'

'Ah kin do de trick real quick.' Hamuda takes his time. 'Ah'se studied all 'bout dat dere stuff!'

'Ah swear t'God, if ya kin do dis fo' me an' save me—y'll jes 'bout save me f'om death! Ah'se awillin' t'give ya mah soul, not jes money!'

'Ah ain't a-askin' fo' yo' soul or fo' nuthin'. But ah kin promise ya, word o' honor, dat ah'se a real expert in dis here cure line. Wid de help o' de Lawd, y'll fin' ev't'in' fine an' dandy in a jiffy.'

'Ah don't gitcha,' says Sa'adya, in a wonderment. 'Kin y'give me dis here cure right now?'

'What's de hurry!' Hamuda smooths down his beard, and his eyes is aglistening like two wet olives. 'Dis here is agoin' t'take a little time, ole pal. Like de good Book says: T'eve'y t'in' dere am a sea-son, an' a time t'eve'y pu'pose . . . a time t'em-brace an' a time t'ree-f'ain from em-bra-cin'. Watch yo'sel'! . . .'

'Well, when?'

'Whenever y'wants hit.'

'Ah wants hit dis here day,' says Sa'adya in a hurry. 'Dis here day.'

'O.K., smaht boy.' Hamuda, he swallows a smile into his moustache. 'Y'send yo' ole woman t'me, an' res' easy dat when she leaves me she'll be abelchin' a'ready.'

'Abelchin'?' Sa'adya can't follow. 'What kin' o' cure is dis y'll be givin' her?'

'F'om de stron' an' f'om de sweet an' f'om de goat . . .'

'Am dis here cure a sure-as-hell-fire one?'

'Oho! Dis cure is de one an' on'y! Ah'll open her eyes, an' she'll see de mid-night stars. She won't come out from under mah han's widout she's satisfied, so satisfied she'll be abelchin'. Ah ain't like you, pal, dead lazy, a good-fo'-nuthin' stiff . . .'

When he'd spoke that far, Sa'adya started in ashaking, and he got so angry he wanted to kill him.

'Damn ya, and damn yo' soul, y' rat!' he yelled out loud. 'Basta'd! Whoremaster! Dirty mout'!'

'Shame, shame.' Hamuda stretched his hands out to him and preached at him a bit. 'Y' really is one ungrateful cuss. Here ah was athinkin' o' yo' good, so dey wouldn't be atakin' ya t'de war, an' 'stead o' thankin' me y'starts acussin'.

'Basta'd! Pimp!' Sa'adya grabbed a stone and jumped on him. 'Y'is an ole goat, damn yo' soul!'

Hamuda, he slipped out of his hands and shook a hot leg, and was ahopping and ajumping and arunning like a deer. Sa'adya, he ran after him, yelling as loud as he could:

'Rascal! Scoundrel! Y'is a son-of-a-bitch! Y'is a hell-cat! . . .'

Right away, all the children in the street was running after them, ahelling and ayelling, and after them came the grown-ups from the street and the grown-ups from the yards, and they took hold, and they all got into two gangs, one gang around Hamuda, and another around Sa'adya.

'What's agoin' on?' they all shouted. 'What's happened 'atween ya?'

'Kee-razy! He's jes plumb loony!' Hamuda honked like a goose, wiping the sweat from his forehead with his hand, and complained. 'What do he want f'om me? Why do he keep on achasin' a'ter me? Ask him, what he want f'om me, dis here crazy loon?'

'Y'is a no-good son-of-a-bitch! Scoun------drel! . . .' Sa'adya, he choked and he fluttered, his face got pale and his eyes popped and his lips trembled. 'De t'ings he says t'me, d'ole goat! He's fit fo' de hell-fire! Fo' t'git a fu'nace an' t'row'm in de flames! . . . It's dogs like 'im brin' wars in de worl', an' den dere's mu'ders an' troubles an' dead sons, all 'cause o' dem dere rascals, damn dar souls! If y'on'y knew de t'ings he done said t'me, y'all'd bu'n'm yo'sel's, y'd mu'der'm! . . .'

IV.

Now Sa'adya he was tired from all the trouble he done had with his wife, and he felt like a man that has stuffed himself like a pig till he is so fed up he has no strength, and now he's alooking to just set, doing nothing and resting up a little.

'It's like de good Book says: Ah'se afindin' de woman more bitter dan death . . .' he mumbles to himself, feeling all-fired weary and fed up with Badra, and with a laziness in all his bones.

Even so, when he came to do his usual with her, and she excused herself from it and with good reason, he blew his top at her and wanted to tear her to pieces till she was dead.

But when the time came that she was clean again, he'd be atussling her and rejoicing in her like the day they was married.

Those days he was athinking that this time his work'd not be for nothing in the eyes of the Lord. To make double sure he began being one of the first in the synagogue, every morning and every evening, and he put his mind and heart to it, and he'd say special prayers and 'Our Dear Lords' and Hallelujahs, in a loud and weepy voice, and the whole congregation would come to him and bless him: 'May de good Lawd hear yo' shouts, an' may He open t'ya de gates o' His mercy'—so that he was pretty sure that his salvation would be coming soon. It was clear as day, plain as the nose on your face, and no ifs or maybes, God forbid and may the Lord protect us.

From then on he didn't think no more of giving Badra a divorce, but he loved her more and more, and he'd be atussling with her from night to night and from day to day.

'Give her a dee-vorce?' he'd be athinking to hisself. 'Nohow! Woe is me if d'angels o' Hebben done prayed a'ready dat ah'se gotta do dat ter'ble t'ing. How'll hit be a'ter ah done give her a dee-vorce? How'll ah be acomin' home t'an empty house, widout no Badra in hit? Where'll be her face when she's gone, an' her body all shiny an' bright? Where'll be de fun in her heart an' her talk, an' de way she keep busy all de time 'roun' de house an' fix t'ings jes right? Mah God! Mah God! Ah'se gettin' tetched in de head! Here ah'se jes athinkin' 'bout it-all, 'bout leavin' her, an'ah'se afeelin' loony a'ready! De whole i-dee am plumb crazy. If ah'se agettin' tetched right now, how'll hit be when de Sabbaths'll roll 'roun' an' de holy days an' synagogue time. Ah'se athinkin' dat no woman ah aim t'take'd be worth de shoes on her feets. Ah'se been 'roun', an' ah'se got eyes in mah head t'see d'udder women-folks—ain't none like mah woman! No, sirree! whatever come, ah ain't gonna let d'ole man Debbil git aholt o' me, nohow. Dey say, hoss-sense is better'n cash. We'se gotta t'ank de Lawd dat He done give us some o' dat dere hoss-sense. What's dat? What kin' o' tomfoolery ah been thinkin' t'do? If'n ah be gone from her jes one night—ah kick d'ole bucket! Ah bus' a gut! No sirree! Ah be a crazy loon. Ah be a basta'd if'n ah chase her 'way. Fo' dem dere sons-o'-bitches Ashkenazis wid dar wars, is ah gonna lose mah wife? Betcha life! Dat ain't never gonna happen!'

It wasn't always he was thinking thisaway, but now this and now that: now she's beautiful and now she's ugly, and between times he's sick of them both. Them days, Badra, she keeps ahoping and amoping, and Sa'adya, he keeps asinking into debt to keep body and soul together, just atoiling and amoiling and not knowing what to do.

Then one day he got an invite-card from the Appeals Board asking him to come and lay his case before them. So he went and stood before the three members of the Board, with his heart beating and his lips aquiver.

They began talking thisaway:

'Well, what's your story?'

He took ahold of hisself, and shifted from one leg to the other, stuck his eyes in the ground and then raised them to the Board members, and his lips they got twisted up in a miserable sort of smile:

'Gen'l'men . . .' and he coughed two or three times like the whiskers of the corn done got stuck in his throat. 'Gent'l'men, or feller cit-zens, whichever y'like . . . Whats done got int'y'all? Ain't-cha got nobody else but jes me t'be adraf'in'? Ain't dere t'ousands o' men fit fo' de draf', but ya gotta be apickin' on poor little me? Jes take a look't me an' see how po'ly ah'se lookin', jes skin-an'-bones. Why, a little ole rifle, she heavier dan ah is. An' it's on'y jes me y'is awantin' t'make a soldier man? Ain'tcha got no better help in dis here war but jes me? . . .'

From minute to minute his talk got better, and he felt hisself getting stronger.

'Ain'tcha'all afear'd o'de Lawd Almighty?' he complained, and his face was straight and his head high. 'Is it me y'all am chasin' a'ter t'get inta dis here draf'? Y'gonna come t'sinnin' 'fore de Lawd 'cause o' me! Ain't hit writ in de good Book: "What man am dere dat am fearful an' faint-hearted? let'm go an' ree-turn t' his house." Ah'se a man what am fearful, ah is. When ah sees two cats afeudin', ah'se afear'd o' dem. What'll ah do if y'all sends me t'dis here front o' de war where t'ousands o' de little guns an' de big guns is ashootin' all 'roun'? When ah hears dat, ah be dyin'! 'Nudder t'ing, ah ain't got no chillun t'come after me, an' how y'all athinkin' t'wipe mah name off de face o' d'earf when ah ain't yet kep' de comman'men' t'be f'uitful an' mul-tip-ly? Mebbe y'all is thinkin' t'dee-stroy de Cre-a-shun, God fo'bid an' de Lawd protec' us? What'll y'gonna have t'say on de Day o' Judgment? . . . Y'all oughta go t'dem as has t'ree or fo' chillun, dem as has a'ready kep' de comman'men' t'be f'uitful an' mul-tip-ly, an' dis here law was made fo' dem an' not fo' me, seein' as how ah ain't got no chillun. No suh, gen'l'men. Y'all gotta help me t'bring mo' souls inta Israel, so's ah kin work 'gainst de B'itish Gov'men' what ain't lettin' in no im'grants. Sho' 'nuf! Y'all am good Zionist believers, an' y'se gotta help, an' 'specially a man like me what am atryin' wid all mah might. Why, if'n ah co'd even b'ing in twins eve'y year, ah wouldn't beg off, nohow . . .'

He spoke fine, real fine, that time and that place, good sense and from the heart, and he got louder and louder and more excited till it was like trumpets blowing.

Now the members of the Board, they had a real good time alistening to his speech, and they was winking at each other and laughing. But their hearts was hard, and they didn't see things hisaway.

'That's why,' they said. 'You've got to be drafted because you have no children. That's the law.'

'Whatch'all mean, no chillun?' says he, standing there in a

wonderment and looking them in their eyes. 'Dey'll be acomin', dey'll be acomin', dey'se a'ready on de way. It's de Lawd's doin'.'

'If you'll bring a certificate from a doctor saying that your wife is pregnant we'll give you an exemption.'

'Why, ah been a-askin' her an' a-askin' her,' says Sa'adya ahumoring them by a tone and a tune and a manner of speaking. 'An' she he'sel' still don't know is she on de nest, is she ain't. T' go t'de doc—she ain't willin', fo' shame. But she boun' t'git in de way o'de wimmen, she willin' o' not, nex' day o' nex' week. Soon, ve'y soon . . . Ah'se a'ready doin' all ah kin. Ah ain't agoin' t'let her 'lone, not fo' a single hour, be sure o' dat. Y'all is good folks, an' y'll do de right t'ing, ah knows dat. An' me too, ah'll do de right t'ing by y'all an', seein' as how ah'se a ca'penter, ah'll make y'all a little chess set like we makes here in Israel, wid all de trimmin's, so'se y'all kin spen' some o' yo' time aplayin' dat dere game, an' den y'll fo'get 'bout me, an' y'all won't be rememberin' me all de time, an' y'all won't be thinkin' o' me fo' dis here draf' . . .'

But Sa'adya was talking to a stone wall, and they didn't listen and didn't pay him no mind. Finally he left them, all bent and broken, and his eyes was dark, and his knees was aknocking together.

V.

When he came home he let hisself down to the ground and sat like a mourning man with his dead one laying before him.

'What's t'do, ole woman?' says he in a squashed and trembling voice. 'Ah'se still in de same ole trouble. Dey's apushin' me plumb inta dis here draf'. Look't how ah'se agettin' bald, here and here. Dey sticks to dar guns, an' you sticks t'yourn, like'n empty stove—no chillun, an' still no chillun. What'll become o' me? De Lawd pity me, Mammy, dat y'ever done bo'n me, t' dis here draf' an' t'dis here great trouble dat ah'se agotten inta. Where'll ah go an' what'll ah do? Dere ain't no mo' hope, no mo' hope in dis life . . .'

'De Lawd'll have mercy,' says Badra like always, sighing and standing there, fine and skinny, and her eyes are low and her face is small and sharp, but all lit up like a cloud at twilight.

'What's dis here "Lawd have mercy' talk o' yourn!" he complains. 'We'se adyin', we'se los', ole woman!'

'De Lawd'll have mercy,' says Badra again, and she thinks her own thoughts all to herself. 'Ah'se even ready now—t'swaller leeches. Ah'se ready.'

'What leeches?' says Sa'adya, raising his eyes to her in a wonderment.

'Whatever happen, ah don't care. If'n ah live—ah live, an if'n ah die— ah die. Who care? . . .' says she, bending her head with a sad smile. 'On'y jes dat y'll be wid me, ole man . . .'

'What's dat? What's dat stuff?' Sa'adya gets excited. 'How y'talkin'?'

'One o' de Ay-rab womenfolks, ole man,' an' she bends her head still further, 'she gimme de word dat ah sh'd swaller leeches in d'even'in' o' de night ah goes t' de *mikve* bath fo' mah monthlies. But dis here trea'men's a matter o' life or death. Mebbe de leech, she grab aholt o' mah heart an' choke me, but if she go down deep den ah'se a gonna git us a chile. Who care? Ole man, you hunt up one o' dem leeches an' ah'll swaller her. De Lawd'll have mercy, de Lawd'll have mercy . . .'

Then a kind of cloud came down and covered up Sa'adya's face, and his eyebrows kissed one another, and it seemed like that very minute he was going to jump on her in his anger. But he didn't jump on her, nohow, and he didn't say a word, but he sat and squeezed his head between his knees, and his back was moving, and his shoulders was shaking.

THE JUDGMENT OF SOLOMON

by Yehuda Yaari

I.

EXCUSE ME for bothering you. I know, you are busy, but I simply must speak . . . No! No! Please don't put me off for some other time. I have to talk about it now, otherwise my very heart will break . . . What? No! I wouldn't like to talk about it to a woman. If a woman were to hear me, all kinds of instincts would stir inside her; and where instincts are in charge there can be no fair judgment, and all the boundaries between truth and falsehood simply fade away. Can you understand me? Yes, only a man can listen to me without being biased or prejudiced . . . Oh no! I'm not asking you to pass judgment. I know that even King Solomon, the wisest of all men, would find this case a hard one. The important thing is that you should listen to me with understanding. Well then, I shall begin at the beginning. I shall try to tell it all without any unfairness. I shan't hide anything and I shan't add anything; just as though it were another woman I were talking about.

It began three years ago, in Germany, at the time of the November riots. There was terror and murder everywhere, and the flames from the burning synagogues seemed to be taking hold of each of us. We were a small family—my husband, I myself, and the boy of five. This is his photo. This is what he looked like then, when he was five years old. A lovely boy, isn't he? . . . Anyway, by that time it was clear to us that we had to get away. It was impossible for us to stay any longer in that accursed country. Yes, you may well stare at me in astonishment. What queer people! you must be thinking to yourself. Had it been such a Paradise in Germany before that? Hadn't they realised earlier that they would have to run for it? . . . Yes, I know. But I must tell you: We were doctors, my husband and I, and when the Nazis came to power we decided we must stay on in Germany as long as possible. We felt it was our duty. Most of the Jewish physicians simply fled all over the world, and the Aryans were forbidden to treat Jewish patients. Now you know as well as I do that the entire Jewish community couldn't get away. What was to happen to them? Who was to look after them and attend to them when they were ill? We couldn't leave our suffering and tormented folk without any medical help.

Yes, it was our Jewish conscience more than anything else that told us we must stay. Of course, we didn't find it a Garden of Eden. We went through really terrible times, and if I were to tell you the whole story I would never be done. But we thought we were doing our duty, and we bore our fate courageously and proudly. Until November, 1938.

When that dreadful time came we suddenly saw how weak and helpless we were, and we forgot all our brave resolutions. The burning, the murdered, the tortured, the fear—no, it was impossible to put up any longer with it all. We had to get away! To get out of that inferno as quickly as possible! But where could we go? Of course we wanted to go to Eretz Israel—my husband and I had always been Zionists—but we couldn't go there. We were simply idiotic, we never bothered about getting a certificate while we had a chance. Now it was too late. Other countries also slammed the door in our face. We cabled to relations in America and to acquaintances in Eretz Israel, and every day that passed without a reply seemed like a year. We dashed about as if we were mad, helpless and hopeless, without the slightest idea what we should do. And the boy, the boy! We worried about him most of all. If only we could save the child! If only we could get him away while he was still innocent and undefiled.

And then, just when it seemed to us that there was no more hope, people came to us with a proposal about him. A family we knew had been lucky, and received a permit to enter Eretz Israel. They came and suggested to us that they should take our child with them. They had received a permit for three children, but were taking only two. The third had left meanwhile to train in Holland with a youth group, before going to Eretz Israel. They could add our boy's name to their passport, they said. The matter could be arranged. They were good folk, old friends, and they wanted to help us.

And so, you might say, it was a miracle right out of Heaven! But I didn't feel like that. It's interesting. As long as I never saw a ray of hope, I thought that I would send my son over to any pack of thieves or robbers, as long as I could get him out of that pestilential atmosphere. But now I had an opportunity to save him, I didn't want to. I knew I could safely and confidently entrust the child to these people, and they would look after him as though he were one of their own. But in spite of it I did not have the heart to take this step and part from him at such a time. I simply couldn't... Yes, it was strange. I know it. But that's what a woman's heart is like... What can I tell you? I wrestled bitterly with myself. I thought I would go crazy. You understand, there was shame and horror all around; and here were people who wanted to deliver my only child from all this; yet I couldn't find the strength to agree.

My husband entreated me day after day. Sometimes gently and sometimes sternly. 'Look,' said he. 'They will soon be leaving, and I know that afterwards you'll very much regret your stupid, completely inexplicable obstinacy.' Yet at heart I still prayed that the time of their departure would pass and I would be done with all this mental and spiritual suffering.

One day, though, my husband came home as pale as a ghost, trembling all over. 'Listen,' said he as he came in, his voice trembling. 'If you don't want him to go now he'll finish by going as an orphan. Remember my words.'

When I heard this I gave in at once. He stood looking at me with such frightened eyes I was sure he must have heard news outside about some approaching danger. Maybe he had heard that they were about to arrest him and send him to a concentration camp, or something like that. After all, that kind of thing was taking place every hour. So how could I keep on refusing? 'Alright,' I said, 'I agree.' Before my eyes I could see all those children whose fathers had died in concentration camps, and who were then going to Eretz Israel in groups. Those of us who were sending them off used to call them 'the Kaddish Aliya', because all of them had to say the Memorial Prayer for the dead. So I told myself: Yes, better have my son torn from me now, rather than have him going with sad hopeless eyes, like those Kaddish reciters whom I have seen leaving . . .

Next day my husband took the child and led him to the home of our friends, to stay with them until they left. I asked him to do it so that I could be able to part from him little by little, and not all of a sudden at a single blow. A few days still had to pass before their departure so I went to visit him every day. The first day I spent a few hours with him; the second day, only one hour; and less on the third day. And so I parted from him little by little, gradually. I don't need to tell you that when they left I didn't go to see him off at the station. How would I have been able to? How could I have stood watching the train moving off and taking my only child away from me? Particularly as I was certain I would never see him again . . . My husband went alone, while I stayed at home weeping and grieving.

In short, the child went; and as far as I know our friends kept their promise. They looked after him properly, and treated him with as much affection and devotion as though he was their own child; maybe even more. The first letter they wrote to us was filled with happiness and wonder. The sea-trip, they wrote, had been wonderful. The whole country was bathed in pleasant sunshine, and the whole atmosphere was one of freedom. Here a man could breathe deep, here he could feel at home. Above all, the children were healthy and happy. You can imagine how glad we were, my husband and I, when we read that letter. The miracle had happened, and the child had been saved.

II.

But the letters which followed were written in a mood of depression and bitterness. The good sun, the air of liberty, and the sense of being at home were not even mentioned. Instead came rain that pierced to the very bones, the feeling that they were strangers, and worries about tomorrow. They had already been so long in the country, yet they had not been able to buy a proper home or find a source of income. They were full of complaints and dissatisfaction. You know, just the kind of letters usually written by greenhorns of that type who have not yet settled down in the country, or grown used to its conditions. In spite of that, they wrote, there was nothing to worry about. They would make every effort possible to provide for the children at least, to provide for their board and enable them to get their schooling. And naturally whatever they did for their children they would do for ours. So there was nothing to worry about.

Time passed. We got another letter from them in which they joyfully told us that at last they had succeeded in making arrangements for the children. Now they were on their own—halutzim, and as befitted pioneers they were going off that week to look for a place where they could live and work, in one of the villages of Sharon or Galilee. And what arrangements had they made for the children? They had sent the children to an educational institution in the Emek for children from Germany. But our boy they had entrusted to a certain very-well-thought-of woman in Jerusalem. This was a Mrs. G.—please excuse me, if I don't tell you her name—who was well known for her generosity and high-mindedness. She also was from Germany, but she had gone to Eretz Israel many years before and had a fine house in one of the lovely quarters of Jerusalem. A well-to-do widow without children, she had gladly responded to the request of the committee which handled such matters when they asked her to take a refugee child from Germany into her home. It was our duty to praise and thank God at this piece of good fortune for the child. It would be impossible to find a better house or a kinder-hearted woman in the whole of the country. They were sure that she would look after him lovingly, and bring him up and educate him with the devotion of a real mother . . .

What can I tell you? I read that letter and then went back and read it again and again. I wept all over it. That my gentle child should have to be kept by others, that my only son should need the charity of the kind-hearted . . . But still, at heart I thanked God that he was not with us but was far far away, in a place full of sunshine, in a safe home, in a place where the air was not full of venomous hatred. For I don't need to tell you that our situation in Germany was growing worse from day to day.

Before long we got a letter from the worthy woman as well. It was a long letter that was really touching in its simplicity, deep understanding, and delicate spirit. She told us about Jerusalem, and all that she had gone through in that city ever since she arrived there. She described her house in detail and her style of life, so that we might know the environment in which our son would grow up. Finally she wrote about the boy, the state in which he entered her home, and about his qualities and character in general. During the few days he had been with her, she had already grown used to him and had learned to love him, so much so that she could not even imagine that there had ever been a time when he had not been there. She was sure he would lack for nothing there, and that she and the child would understand one another well . . . At the end of the letter my boy added a few words in his own hand. She must have helped him, because he had not yet learned to write at the time. He was very happy, he wrote, to be with Auntie G., because he loved her very very much . . .

Why should I deny it? When I read those innocent words my heart fell. I began to feel jealous. Yes, lunacy, don't you think so? But I can't hide it. For the first time in my life I felt this emotion of jealousy, a painful, forbidden emotion. They want to take my son from me, I thought. I did not feel any fear or apprehension for his fate, I really want that to be quite clear to you. I knew that he was in perfectly safe and reliable hands. And yet that knowledge made my jealousy worse. I would have felt better if I had known he was in hands that were not quite so safe or reliable. Can you understand it? It went as far as that! I felt ashamed of myself. Yes, I tried to hide it from my husband, and to bury my feeling deep inside me; but it came floating up again, even stronger than before, like a kind of horrible recurrent disease, with every fresh letter we received. For from this time on we used to receive a letter from her almost every week regularly. Each letter added something to the others. In one the boy began to go to school, in another he began to learn music. Yet each one resembled the other in its fine style and fine feeling. Sometimes that innocent line or two added by the child would be there, sometimes it wouldn't. In either case I tormented myself. If the line was there, I became all the more jealous; and if it wasn't, I would think that he had already forgotten me and didn't even send his love . . .

III.

Almost a whole year passed like that. Meanwhile the war began. All this while my husband had managed to evade the murderers, but now the Gestapo caught him at last and took him off to a concentration camp. What was the reason? Who knows? I never saw him again, nor heard from him. They murdered him there, those degraded criminals; then some time later they told me to come and receive his ashes. I was left all alone in the world, a forlorn widow. I no longer received letters from Eretz Israel. Naturally they stopped at the outbreak of the war. Oh, I would have given my very soul to receive just another such letter, with or without a line or two by the child, as long as I might see that I still had something to hold on to in life, that I had not been forgotten, that I was not left alone in this lion's den. But no letters came. I took the old letters out of their hiding-place. (When the war began I hid them, because it was dangerous to keep such things.) At night I read them in bed again and again, scores of times, from beginning to end. Now they no longer made me feel jealous. No! No! Believe me, you know I was just like somebody in some Godforsaken spot, who suddenly meets a person there from his native city. Back in his native city he had disliked the man, yet here, in this place of exile, he is as happy to meet him as though they had always been the best friends . . . No, the comparison doesn't really fit. Can I say I ever hated those letters? If I had hated them, I would never have kept them so carefully, really risking my life to do so. Do you understand? But let that be, for the time being.

The days that followed after my husband's death were chaotic and hopeless. The whole world seemed to turn black, and those letters were not bright enough any longer to do more than emit faint, dead sparks. I was in a state of absolute despair, simply consumed by my terrible longing for my son. It was like the yearning of a mother on her deathbed, longing to see her beloved child for the last time before she died. And then, then I had the idea, the crazy idea: I decided I must really do something! I made up my mind to get away from Germany at once, and to try and reach Eretz Israel any way I could.

Once this idea entered my head, I decided to act on it. I would get away to my boy, to my boy! No power, no consideration whatever could have made me change my mind. Danger? Was there any danger that could frighten me any longer? In any case I no longer had any kind of life worth living. So what did I have to lose?

I'm not going to tell you all that happened to me before I got here. To tell you the truth, I myself cannot realise yet how I managed it. How I managed to steal out of Germany in the middle of the war, without an exit permit; how I succeeded in slipping through Yugoslavia after the Occupation; and all kinds of things like that. On my journey, I was in a kind of daze, physically and mentally. That seems to be what a human being is like: when he does something which is absolutely foolish and should not be done by all the laws of logic, when he has to tread a dangerous path, then he seems to fortify himself, as you might say, with a kind of armor of dazed senses and consciousness. Otherwise he would be unable to perform the action and would not take even a single step along that road. If I were to tell you some of the things that happened to me on the way which I remember clearly (I have already forgotten a great deal), you would certainly not believe me. It is hard for me myself to believe that these things really happened; it seems as though I merely dreamed them. Anyway, you see I succeeded in doing it, for here I am, sitting with you.

And now I come to the real story.

IV.

One summer day I reached Jerusalem. What I felt you can imagine for yourself. As soon as I left the bus I went into a nearby drugstore, to phone Mrs. G. Trembling I took the instrument in my hand. In just another moment, I would hear my child's voice. It was hard for me to keep my feet. The moment that passed between the first ringing in the instrument and the reply seemed to last forever. At last I heard a voice. It was the maid speaking. Mrs. G. was not at home just then. I told the woman my name, and that I had just reached Jerusalem. 'And what do you want?' she asked. I asked her whether she could tell me where I could stay. Naturally I had hoped that Mrs. G. would invite me to stay with her, but it seems this woman had never heard my name, and had no idea who I was. All it meant to her was that a new arrival in the country had just reached Jerusalem, and wanted to know where to stay; and that did not surprise her at all. She was quite used to it. Her mistress had a name in town and elsewhere for being an active social worker, so dozens of newcomers probably came to her with similar requests. Her answer sounded as though it was a regular standby. If I went to such and such a street, said she, I would find the special hostel for newcomers, and I would be able to stay there.

I thanked her politely and put the telephone back on its hook. And why, you may ask me, did I do that? If I felt that the woman had never heard my name and did not have the slightest idea who I was, why didn't I tell her? Why didn't I tell her that I was the mother of the child in their house, and spare myself an hour of unhappiness? But I shall tell you. Ever since I saw how people bring suffering on one another of set purpose and just in order to hurt, I prefer the suffering that people cause accidentally and by mistake so to speak. I know that sooner or later they will realise their mistake and regret the pain they caused me. And knowing this gives me what I can only describe as satisfaction. Actually, it was with a sense of deep satisfaction that I collected my belongings (they were not so many) and went to that hostel.

Before I had had time to wash and take off my dusty clothes, Mrs. G. appeared. She came alone, without the child. When I saw her, my breath simply stopped. She was so beautiful, I was enchanted. I could see she was a bit excited, but this excitement improved her looks. I am sure that you must know her. And who doesn't know her in Jerusalem? She is so nobly tall, with her healthy young face set in its gray hair, and her soft wise eyes, and her expression, motherly and strong at the same time. Yes, she is remarkably beautiful. Even now, after all that has happened, I sometimes stand enchanted at her looks.

She pressed my hand for a long moment and looked at me with eyes full of kindness. The maid had told her I had phoned and she had come at once. She was exceedingly upset at what had happened. It was true that the had received my letter from Turkey, but she had never imagined that I would be able to get here so fast. Naturally she was not going to permit me to stay here, God forbid. Not in any circumstances! She had already arranged a room for me in a pleasant hotel not far from her home. It was all right, I did not need to worry about expense. She would arrange everything. 'So take your things,' said she, 'and come with me at once.' We have to hurry in order to get home before Michael goes to sleep. He always rests and sleeps for an hour in the afternoon.'

After a few polite words I took my hat and went with her. I did not want to take my belongings, in spite of her insistence. I told her I would fetch them afterwards. But at that moment my thoughts were far from hotels, my heart and soul being set on the child I was about to see in just another few minutes. There was a taxi waiting for us at the gate, but I asked Mrs. G. to send it away. I wanted to walk to her house, in order to have time to prepare myself for the meeting with the child.

It was noon. The sun was blazing cruelly. We walked slowly and silently, or more correctly: I was silent while she talked. What did she say? I don't know, I paid no attention. I was all confused. My head was full of all kinds of questions I could not answer. What should I do if the child asked me this? And if he said that, what could I answer? And suppose he asked me about his father, what could I tell him?

After about half an hour, we reached the house. As soon as Mrs. G. opened the door, she called out in a loud and excited voice, which sounded very strange: 'Michael, Michael! Please come here. I have a great surprise for you!' You understand? A surprise... She had not told the child at all that I was about to come. A surprise... The child came running from the other room, and Mrs. G. pointed her finger. 'Here is your surprise,' said she quietly. 'Do you recognise her?'

The child turned quite pale. To this day I can't explain to myself why I stood as though I were paralysed, why I did not fall on his neck and embrace him and hug him and kiss him as I had intended to do, and as any other mother would have done in my place. Why not? Was I so astounded at the change which had taken place in him during these years? When he left me he had been a delicate little boy with milk teeth that gleamed at a distance, and now I saw before me a growing lad, big for his age, with two teeth missing in his mouth. Was I frightened by the resemblance I suddenly saw between him and his father? Or was it because of the strange surroundings and the presence of that woman? Or maybe I already felt at that moment that there was a kind of hidden barrier between us? Anyway, I stood as though turned to stone, unable to move, as though it were a strange child before me instead of my own son whom I had not seen for three years. And he, the boy, stood for a long moment, staring at me with open mouth but not saying a word. Then he dropped his eyes and whispered as though there were no breath left in him: 'My mother... from over there... from Germany...' And after a brief pause he went on in a more assured voice: 'Yes, Mother. I recognise her.' Maybe he said something else, maybe he asked about his father. I did not hear any more. I managed to see the face of Mrs. G. as she stood to one side twisting her fingers nervously. Her lips trembled, but in her eyes I saw a look of victory. And I fainted.

V.

When I came to, she took me not to the hostel nor to the good hotel nearby, but to a hospital out of town. All the weariness of my wandering, all the mishaps and misery which I had undergone during those years, now set their mark on me all at once. I reeled and simply collapsed. The doctors were afraid my heart was affected, that my lungs were out of order. They put me in the hospital for about a month. During the first fortnight, I lay in bed, lonely and suffering, aching from head to foot as though I were all wounds and bruises, my soul weary almost to death. Mrs. G. came to visit me from time to time and brought me all kinds of good things. She never mentioned what had taken place in the house—just as though it had never happened at all. But the child did not come to see me even once. He had been forbidden to come, lest I grow too excited and it slow down my cure. The truth was, I did not regret it. I didn't want him to see me ill, so that he shouldn't feel sorry for me. I didn't want any pity from him. I didn't think of him in the way a mother thinks of a cherished child, but as a woman thinks of her lover and of how to win his heart. Do you understand?

Well, two weeks passed in bed and I was not getting better. I saw that unless I bestirred myself, unless I overcame the twilight mood into which I was sinking, I might gradually just go out like a candle. So I gathered the rest of my strength and got up. The doctors did not know why I got up, just as they did not know why I had collapsed. In spite of this they kept me in the hospital another fortnight for observation and study. It is just as well they did. It was a good thing they gave me a chance to walk about the hospital corridors. In that way they enabled me to get to know them, and so I even managed to find myself a job. One of the physicians, a specialist in eye diseases, asked me to be his assistant, for that used to be my field of specialization abroad.

I left the hospital next morning, that is the morning after I had spoken to the eye specialist and he had asked me to be his assistant. It was a pleasant day at the end of summer. Lonely clouds were floating up above, like guests strolling about the sky. They shed something melancholy on the earth. But that shadow never penetrated my heart at all. That morning I felt newly illuminated, a great sense of ease; it was as though all that heavy load of weariness and depression which had been weighing on me so much during those last years had vanished. I felt renewed—prepared to begin again, to open a new leaf in the book of my life. With a light and trusting heart I went to town, and the same day I took a little apartment near the dispensary of my chief, arranged it as best I could, and began working a few days later. I was anxious to begin working at once, for I knew that nothing but work would enable me to preserve the tranquillity which had come to me in so mysterious a fashion.

In brief—I worked and found my place. Now there was nothing to prevent me from taking my son to my home, and I decided to do it as soon as possible. My salary is not particularly high, it is true, but it is enough for both of us. So what did I do? First I decided to break down the wall of estrangement between us, to get close to him and bring him back to me. Every evening after finishing my work at the dispensary I visited him and spent an hour or two talking, playing, and reading. Mrs. G. did not intervene at all, and never interfered. The boy and I sat in his room while she sat in the next one, in a large armchair, reading or knitting. Sometimes we got excited while playing and made a lot of noise. But she did not protest or show any sign of dissatisfaction. Sometimes we were so interested in what we were reading that we did not notice how the time was passing, but she never came to interrupt us or to remind us by word or sign that it was already late and time for him to go to bed. Yes, Mrs. G. behaved very well indeed toward me. Whenever I came to her home, she always welcomed me with a friendly smile and a hearty 'How do you do'; and when I left she would accompany me to the door and take leave of me with a pleasant smile and a warm handclasp.

She did not say much and asked no questions. Only once, when the boy wept during my visit, did she ask me as I left why he had cried. When I told her that he had cried because I had told him of his father's death, she asked, 'And how did he receive the news?' 'Very bravely,' I answered. To this the woman responded with a strange kind of praise: 'Yes, I always knew this lad was a brave one.'

But in general, it can't be denied—she treated me very well indeed. Yet I must say that this kind behavior was just what annoyed me so much. She did not behave as though she were doing me any favor, but as though I were doing her a favor; as though she were very grateful to me for coming every evening to look after the child and play with him. You understand? It was as though she would never find a better person, or a more devoted governess in the whole of the country to look after her child . . .

Yes, those were good times for me, before winter came. All day long I was doing interesting work and extending my knowledge, and in the evening there were the hours with the child to put heart into me and strengthen me. Every evening our meetings became more free and natural. I felt that the invisible barrier between us was gradually being destroyed, day after day, and that he was coming closer and closer to me.

VI.

One Sabbath day, I came in the early afternoon, not at all as usual, and suggested that we take a walk together for a few hours. Mrs. G. willingly agreed, and the boy came along very happily. It was a wonderful day. The streets were thronged with children and parents, who had come out to enjoy their Sabbath in the open air. For a long time we walked about together. We jumped about, we played at hide and seek among the rocks, we picked flowers in the fields. Then I took him to see my little dwelling, for he had never been there before. I cannot say that he felt like a stranger, but it seemed to me that he was rather nervous. He moved from one room to another quite freely, taking everything in his hands and wanting to know what it was for. But when I told him to sit down for a while and drink tea and eat some of the cakes, he refused because it was getting late. It was getting dark outside and he had to go home. He left me a few of the flowers he had picked, in a vase, and I gave him one piece of pastry to eat in the street, and we went out.

That evening I spent more time with him than usual. I washed him, I brought him his supper, I put him to bed, and then I went in to Mrs. G's room to talk to her. I had made up my mind to approach her that evening, to thank her for all the kindness and more than kindness she had shown, and to tell her that now I wanted to take the boy; for if not now, when then? As soon as she saw me she rose, intending to see me to the door as usual. I told her I wanted to talk to her. Naturally she understood at once what I wanted to talk about, and I saw that she was afraid of the conversation. She began playing nervously with the white necklace she wore, and without a word went back and sat down again. I sat on the couch facing her and at once came to the point.

'I shan't waste words trying to describe my gratitude,' said I to her. 'Are there any words which could tell you how thankful and grateful I am for all you have done for me and my son? . . . If I were to say that you have been just a mother to him, I would not be saying too much . . . But now, I am here, I am working steadily, I have a dwelling of my own, and I see no reason why the boy should continue to stay with you, or why he shouldn't come to live with his mother . . .'

Oh, how hard it was for me to say it! I don't know why. She sat there facing me like a statue, and her face was as white as chalk.

I tried to read from it what must be going on inside her, but I couldn't. Her face was smooth and expressionless, like a kind of white mask. To rouse her from her stony silence I added:

'Surely you understand me, don't you?'

To this she answered quietly, with a kind of smile:

'Yes, of course, I understand you quite well. You want to take Michael away from me. Please do. Why not? But don't you think it might be better to ask the boy first? Maybe he doesn't want to go to you...'

Those words absolutely stupefied me, just as if she had hit me over the head with a hammer. To go and ask the boy first... At that moment I knew for certain I would never dare to ask him. No! No! For what would I do if he refused? Why, it would simply kill me. And then I also understood why I had been so careful not to tell the boy of my intention while he had been at the apartment with me. After all, I had really taken him there just for that, in order to show him his new home. But I had been afraid. Yes, I had simply been afraid that he might say: I don't want to come. That was the reason I let him go without even hinting what I intended to do. Mrs. G. must have sensed it, I suppose, and that was why she came out with what she said. She knew that those words had simply disarmed me. I waited for her to say something more, but she did not add a word. She sat twisting the white necklace between her fingers very nervously. I was afraid that the string would snap any moment and the beads would scatter all over the floor. I couldn't stand it. I stood up and went away.

VII.

What can I tell you? That night I hardly closed my eyes. I tossed from side to side all night long on my bed, mad with jealousy and rage and pity. Yes, pity as well. I was jealous of the woman and of her confidence. 'Go and ask the boy...' She was not in the least apprehensive about asking him. She was sure that if he were asked he would want to stay. Why? Or maybe she was not at all so certain, but she knew my weakness and exploited it against me. And that was not at all kind. That was what made me angry. You understand: to suggest to a forlorn mother that her only child would not want to go with her! That was an act of cruelty. Yes. I almost hated her for it.

Yet on the other hand, when I pictured the fate of the woman to myself, I felt very sorry for her. For really she was just as forlorn as I was, and maybe even more so than I. Oh yes, it is quite true: she is well off and goodlooking and quite famous for her deeds of charity, yet what does she get out of it all? She is alone and childless. No child's eyes have ever brightened the gloom of her widowhood, she has never known what it is to be a real mother. Now she is growing old and a child has come her way, a really lovely child. She did not kidnap him or try to attract him by any trickery. Good, decent people brought him to her home so that she should bring him up and educate him, since he was as good as an orphan and his father and his mother were far far away. So she treated him just as any woman with a heart would have done—she was a mother to him. Is there any sin in that? She loved the child, and he loved her and called her 'Mother'. A short and affectionate word, Mother, which she had never heard in all her life until this child came to her home. Wasn't that worth as much as all her money and looks and good name? Of course she loves him! How could she do anything else? Is there any crime in it? And now, after they have been living together for a long time as mother and son, comes his real mother whom they had thought dead for a long time; and she wants to take him away from her. Why, if she takes him from her now, her home will be far more desolate than before, and she will be truly bereft. Is that a reward for her good deed? . . . Yes, I pitied her, in all truth. The more I thought about her the more I pitied her. I decided I must ask her pardon for going away without taking leave, and be exceedingly nice to her thereafter. For, when all is said and done, she's a really unfortunate woman.

But when I came to visit my boy next evening I did not find her at home. Nor did I find her on the evening after or on the one following. The boy told me she had gone to Tel-Aviv. On the fourth evening I found her, but she received me very coldly. She didn't open the door, she didn't stand up to meet me and didn't ask how I was. She merely said a languid good day from her armchair, as much as to say: Are you here again? And who told you to come? . . . She did this for several evenings. I suffered dreadfully from it. I simply didn't know any longer where I was in the world. So I decided to put a stop to it. No matter what happened I had to do something. It was impossible to go on any longer like that!

VIII.

Well, this very morning, when the boy was at school, I took some time off from my work and went to her house to talk to her. To clear the matter up at last, and try to find a way out together with her. That was what I thought when I went there, to find a way out together with her . . . But I no longer think so. Now, after the talk we had this morning, I know that there's no solution. I can't tell you exactly what we said. I was excited and she was excited. She sat all the time, twisting her white necklace. If it didn't snap today, then the string must be made of iron. And things were said between us that I would be ashamed to repeat. Neither of us put a bridle over her mouth. But I'll tell you in brief.

After I confusedly stammered about pardon and understanding and so on, I told her there was no reason for strained relations between us, and I wanted to take the child without any delay. She had to understand. To this she answered impatiently, almost roughly: 'Yes, yes, I know. I have already heard it all, once before.' Here my patience began to give way. I reminded her I was the child's mother, and it seemed as though she were forgetting the fact.

To this she answered: 'I have never denied it. I know you are his physical mother. But in a sense I am also his mother. It seems to me you don't want to recognise that fact.'

Then I grew angry. I shouted, I wept and I entreated: 'Give me the boy! Give my child back to me!'

But as for her, the more excited I grew, the calmer she became. 'I didn't take him from you,' said she with quiet assurance, 'and I don't have to give him back to you. If you want to take him away from me, you have a choice between two courses: either you ask him—but it seems that you don't dare to do that, you are not so certain he'll want to go with you—or else you have another alternative: you can take him by force, by going to law.'

I was stunned. 'A new Judgment of Solomon?' said I bitterly. 'Yes, a new Judgment of Solomon,' she answered firmly.

I stared into her eyes and in them I again saw that look of triumph. Oh, how I hated her then! I know it is wicked, I know one mustn't hate like that. But what can I do? I can't get rid of the feeling of animosity that awoke in me then. You understand: I felt she thought that if we were both standing in front of Solomon's throne, *she* would be the one to say: 'Give her the living child,' while I would say: 'Cut him in two.' It's a dreadful thought. Why did she think that of me? Good, I understand she thinks she's the child's mother also, but why does she think I am his mother no longer? Why? Why? . . .

So now my position is this—a mother whose child is alive, but who is bereft. He, the child that is, has two mothers, but I no longer have a child. He is lost to me, and who knows whether I shall find him again . . . What? He is in safe hands? . . . You also say that? Have you ever seen a person who has lost something precious and then consoles himself because what he lost is in good hands?

And please don't remind me of all the children who were left back in Europe. If only I could forget them. They stand before me all the time, every moment, they and their suffering mothers. Oh those dark faces, those wizened, shrunken bodies, those staring eyes—will it ever be possible to forget them? But, believe me, I find no consolation in that thought either.

THE SEVEN

by Nathan Shaham

I.

IT COST us a great effort to scale the hill. The traffic road meandered overmuch, so fancying a short cut we climbed up an unpaved route through dark-reddish dolomite rocks, a thorny jujube shrub, and several mint herb bushes. We pulled up our car where a cluster of trees stood sentinel, to relax a bit in the shade of an oak or flowering carob. Not that I am particularly fond of carob blossoms, but we were very tired. The fact is, I personally might have held out and kept going, had I not glanced at the face of Abbi, my travelling companion.

His health, it is true, had improved a lot, but his face at the moment was very pale. His lips assumed a bluish tint, and his eyes, sunken in their sockets, reflected a dull, weary depression. I had never seen him like this. When I asked him, 'What's the matter, Abbi?' he let out a short 'Ha-a,' which might have been meant for either a groan or a laugh, and explained that his bones were aging a bit. I waited for the color to return to his cheeks and then bucked him up to mount by foot to the summit of the range.

The vegetation, which had been spread out in the valley, grew thick and a little entangled on the hill crest. But there was a clearing on top where two rows of houses stood—six long, white, one-storied structures, looking like railway carriages, which had been an army camp in the Mandatory days. The roofs had peeled off long since, and the walls too were pierced with gaps, partly the rounded work of shells and partly the gnawings of time—a general state of crumbling disrepair. Rusty tin cans; old tools destroyed by rot; broken-down trenches; a sooty, cracked field lamp; and a battery of sand-bags, pressed down into a single mass, and pierced by blades of green grass—all these bore witness to the war that had stormed through here before last winter.

Our view swept over the whole valley and its approaches: a distinct ribbon of road stretching ahead and dipping down into the green groves which petered out onto the sand dunes, a deserted half-ruined Arab village, a group of huts and tents in the vicinity, and a blurred prospect of a distant city congregated around a tall tower. I was tired and felt like sitting, so I found a wooden camp-bed stuck among the boulders and dropped down on it. Long out of walking practice, I found my breath short. But Abbi, much to my astonishment, was in no hurry to take a rest and started nosing around in criss-cross directions on the ridge, as if he had lost something. I felt humorously inclined.

'What are you looking for: last year?' I asked smiling, and he smiled back at me, a little shamefaced. We have been thrown into one another's company for many years, and I had in fact made the same joke once before, but I realised that this time the jest had struck home. Here, on this ridge Abbi had spent a bleak and heroic period of his life. I understood that he was lost in recollections. It seemed to me he appreciated my style: I had apparently sounded the note he was after. He had hesitated to weary me with a load of reminiscences and war stories, but with this hint I had given him an opening. In an instant, he dropped the look of disappointment that had been clouding his face.

He sat down beside me on the camp-bed. I sensed that this way he would be at ease in speaking, as he was spared the need to look me in the face. There was plenty to keep his eyes busy: a light wind had risen and gone, and white clouds floated and flitted in the blue heights. I begged him to speak up, as his voice didn't carry in the wind. He repeated his question:

'Do you know why they call this place "The Ridge of the Seven?"'

I was ashamed to confess I didn't know, but imagined it must have been in commemoration of seven fallen comrades. When the battle had stormed here, I had been fighting in a remote zone, where the only information to reach us had been rumored reports. No newspapers had been available. Completely cut off from the outside world, we had been under the illusion we were the only ones at whom the war was nibbling. Six months later we rejoined the others and soon learned that a single front extended through the whole land.

'Generally', said Abbi, 'I have a particular affection for tracing back my own footsteps. My memory develops the most trifling details once photographed, and I can relive in imagination the powerfully expressive episodes in my life history. A second round. But now that I have come back to this spot, though my worst days in the war were spent here, something snaps in my consciousness, my fancy begins to conjure up a phantom variety of iniquitous folly, and I can't for the life of me put any memories of those days in order. Something balks all my efforts at recall. I come close to fainting and so actually satisfy an urgent, pressing physical need, something which then, in battle, I couldn't do without suffering.'

I was familiar with this style of talk. He always had had a weakness for psychology, and I understood that it was now up to me to declare in the professional manner: 'You must tell this to somebody, and while formulating it you will draw out also by degrees what lies hidden in the subconscious.' But this time my encouragement was not needed.

'The War of Independence was then in full swing and we were all depressed by the enemy superiority in men and materials. I wonder how many were reduced to apathy and despair. Exalted heroism and excessive irregularities had become everyday events. Life was stepped up to a stormy pace, that phase of war when all outside considerations drop out and victory comes to those who throw in everything for a single purpose. The strain and the dread of defeat had so shattered our nerves that battle—you, no doubt, will believe this—battle was our salvation.

'The storming of this ridge—"Camp 617", as it was called—was carried out by our whole company, whose total effectives were barely two platoons of infantry and an auxiliary munitions section. Our platoon went over the top. We lost twenty-nine men, including the C.O. But there was no turning back. Every one of us knew the importance of taking that ridge. You know the old-timers, of course, how every man's son of them took in the tactical, strategical, political and public-opinion aspects of each and every battle line. If anyone had then had the slightest doubt about the importance of the battle, we'd have failed. But a spirit of enthusiasm, something akin to religious fervor, made the capture of this ridge the "idée-fixe" of the platoon. The men had become obsessed, and so the fall of our commanding officer in the assault on the ridge had a sort of symbolic meaning for us: it seemed as if we had finished our job. We were swept at first by a wave of enthusiasm which very soon subsided and froze into apathy. When feelings of this kind overcome an individual, they bear the stamp of shirking and are condemned by society. But once an entire group is seized with the notion that its duties are done with, no reasoning and persuasion in the world can move it.

'I am not sure whether you are capable of grasping what our commander meant to us. I know your C.O., he is no criterion. Ours was an amalgam of the Yogi and the untamed brute. Asceticism and hankering all in one. Short, sharp-featured, with green, penetrating eyes. He was bristle-haired, irrepressible, and always untidy as far as his own person went; but for all that: keen-eyed and with his foot down always on the least signs of negligence. He grafted the men to their jobs by the force of his ardor and application. He seemed to be the focus of the platoon's reactions, subjecting their minds and actions to his whim by some power within. I was seized with envy whenever I watched his knack of assigning everything in its proper precedence; first things first and without fuss or bother, as if some sort of herd instinct had crystallized in this one man. I was in charge of a section in his platoon, and never once did I try to act up to my own ideas without becoming ridiculous. At times I thoroughly detested him—you could never be an independent organism in his orbit, you were immediately screwed down to your proper place. But, personally, he was a sworn individualist, and the standards he had set up for himself merely served all the more forcibly to give his personality prominence, so that with all his eccentricities—he was a vegetarian and carried his ardor for archaeology to absurd lengths—he was not anti-social. In his dealings with the men he was so severely above-board that he was held in awe; he never resorted to intrigues, not even in the most trivial affairs. You could never, for instance, invite him to a closed party unless he was reassured the others knew about it. It was strange, though, that he was notoriously fond of scandal; but it was always in good fun and clear of sordid motives, so that the victims of his clowning regarded themselves as flattered.

'I have merely recounted his merits. To have the makings of a fascinating book you have only to jot down the events of his life in chronological order. But the purest of imaginations would have difficulty in keeping up with the events of that chronicle. How he surpassed himself, how young he was at the time, and the trials through which he successfully led himself and his men! Even those fellows who had known him at his worst respected his abilities, as if he embodied a kind of objective judgment. You won't wonder, then, that when he was gone, we stopped being a unit. There were forty-four of us left, isolated on the crest of this ridge, exposed to the enemy's counter-attacks, wrecked in spirit, browned off by the war, and haunted by a cursed obsession that whatever we kept on doing was just a muffled echo of a bygone epoch. In that state we were called upon to confront the horrors of a fierce, protracted nightmare . . .'

II.

Abbi rocked uncomfortably on the seat, his sleeve getting caught on a branch in the process and torn out of his pocket. The wind ruffled the empty sleeve gently, and it rested on his knee, trembling a little as if it had the shivers. Abbi took up the sleeve with his right hand and thrust it into the pocket, trying meanwhile to give it a round shape, such as might fool an observer. He didn't speak as he did this, and during the pause I was lost in thought. That captain had been the object of my sister's affections, and I knew only too well how hard she was bearing the loss. Abbi too had had his heart set on my sister, or so I imagined, since there was something in his face then that made me think she was in his thoughts. If I am not mistaken, he was secretly and passionately in love with her, and that may be why he sought my company. She left here this week, and I think he is quite put out about it.

A car glided up on the road below and suddenly stopped near ours. Two soldiers got out and examined it, and I became anxious; but finding our car locked the soldiers drove off. I observed that Abbi completely disregarded the incident. I didn't suspect him of manufacturing an interlude in order to make an impression. Recently, he has been apt to forget himself abruptly in the middle of a conversation. I got up and amused myself by throwing stones at the rustling carob leaves, but when I remembered that Abbi was crippled I gave it up. Perhaps making too much of a sympathetic fuss would be just the thing to offend him, but still I am incapable of exercising my limbs unnecessarily in the presence of cripples. Abbi pulled himself together and went on with his story:

'After taking the ridge, we were posted into the positions deserted by the enemy, in readiness for an all-out defensive. We buried the enemy dead in a pit which had been dug, apparently, for garbage. The enemy soon after opened a barrage which lasted till evening. One of our dead lay a short distance from the spot assigned as Headquarters. I crawled up to him and was surprised to see that his leg was mauled up to the knee. A shell doesn't do a piece of work like that. I commented to the lieutenant that this man had been killed by a mine. He then remembered that our men had once planted seven mines on that ridge. The man placing the mines had been killed and the map burned in the shelling. We had no mine detector and . . . we knew there was none at the base. Quite likely, there was none in the whole country at that time. Higher up, this might have been a routine administrative problem, but on the crest of this ridge, where we were, forty-four young men grew old overnight.

'Just imagine: you know very well that the hill is sown with mines and that the moment you get up and set a foot forward a horrible death is waiting for you, and there is no escape. The tension that gripped us when we compared this reality with the leave-and-break-away we all thought we deserved in its stead, shook even the strongest. That first moment, when we broke the news to the men, there was an awful stillness. All at once, like some process suddenly accelerated by a catalyst, the whole company broke up into far-removed, isolated units. Six more men would have to be killed for the dread of the mines to pass off. Each one of us prayed in his heart for the other's annihilation. In the battlefront too you are fearful of your own death or that of your own comrade, but then there is at least reciprocity, and the death of your fellow in line doesn't award you a certificate of exemption; but here the other's death was your direct salvation, with no intervening niceties, with a terrible plainness.

'This feeling sharpened to the point of absurdity. Men not generally too well-liked knew perfectly well that the others were hoping they'd be the victims on that hill of horror. The bitterness they felt as a result led to their refusal to cooperate or turn out for duty, for fear they were being sent to their death. Life became something disgustingly foul. Outwardly we may have seemed to be bickering over trifles, but each and every quarrel was stepping on a mine. There were times when I thought the men capable of murdering one another. Men known for their unpopular political convictions believed that their death would be more gratifying than that of the conformists. It was impossible to go on living here together this way even one day longer. War may sometimes forge men into an exalted comradeship of brothers in arms, but this inevitable slaughter, seizing hold of men with an offensive arbitrariness, not out of their courage or fervor, but out of some need for a stupid sacrifice to the gods of war—this shattered us to such an extent that we were no longer able really to continue functioning as a fighting unit. The pettiest grudge, arising spontaneously from some social irritation, flared up into a barbarous, primeval hatred . . .

'For two days we kept to our rooms, ate what was left, and thought about what might have happened to us had we not known of the mines. We flung our excrement out of the window until the hill was covered with an unbearable stench. Our nerves were shattered to distraction, but we had to get out. Hunger was gnawing us and we had to find a road to transport food under the cover of night.

'In the afternoon, the lieutenant and I decided to patrol the grounds and order the men out of the billets. If anybody got blown up, he would just be unlucky. Fate would decide. That might sound far-fetched, but put yourself in our position. In battle, too, men are ordered to run up against hellish fire, but there the tune is: run, storm, get drugged or drunk, plunge into the whirlpool, and the point of contact is a brief moment. But here . . .

'We went out before sunset. At first I stepped out carefully and wondered at the self-assurance of our lieutenant, since the sole of my foot trembled each time before I ventured to bring it down to earth. I felt exhausted and wanted to sit down, though I had no more than six metres to make. But all at once I pulled myself together and began to tread the crust of earth with excessive firmness. I knew I was pale, and I pictured to myself the look on my face. We went from house to house and ordered the men out. Nobody obeyed. Ah, if you had only seen how lustfully they followed our footsteps, how all their eyes were stealthily glued to the fateful point of contact between the foot and the ground, how their ears prayed for the sound of an explosion, how in their hearts they sought our death, how eager they all were for it, like an excited baby clamoring for something not far beyond his reach. Nothing happened, but nobody came out. When I came back to my room, I flung myself on my sleeping sack and wept in despair all night. So these were your brothers-in-arms! That was the caliber you were giving your life for . . . As I lay there I felt a strange numbing of the limbs. Filled with fear I got up and stood on my legs till dawn, shivering from cold . . .

'That night three men escaped. We opened fire but hit no one. One stepped on a mine and was killed. Five mines, forty-one men. We dug a hole where the mine had been and marked the spot with a stake. You could sketch in your mind some pattern or other for the field of mines and try to guess where you might walk safely. We were heavily shelled that day, and there were two serious casualties. The wound-dresser was afraid to go out to help them until the lieutenant had walked that way before him. When this was over, the lieutenant slapped the dresser across his face, and then he asked me to assume command in the event of an infantry counter-attack. I consented, and he went to his bunk and slept for twelve hours. I inspected the positions and indicated by shouts which group was responsible for each of the posts and how much ammunition was assigned to each section.

'The next morning one of the younger men went out of his mind, a lad from a well-known, respected family. He ran amok in the grounds, screaming like mad. Two of his buddies went out, grabbed him, and tied him down. I knew that our food supply, brought up right after we had taken the ridge, was running low, and guessed that those who had braved the open would pave the way for the others. I waited patiently. That young fellow lay where he had been tied, and tittered. Then he suddenly switched over into clear sane speech: "Bunk", he said. "You really believe I went off the rocks? I just wanted to get the gang to go out." We let him loose. During the night, he gave us the slip. Then we agreed not to sleep so we could watch the men, and we telegraphed headquarters describing the situation. A message came back promising reinforcements.

'The next day the men began to come out into the grounds. They walked around with an accusing look in our direction. But they had no alternative. There was no sense in any further precaution. We waited impatiently to see who would fall. Three days passed and nothing happened.

'That same day we were out on a patrol and took a prisoner. A cruel thought struck our minds. He was a young villager, about thirty, with a defiant, energetic cast of features that incited general antagonism. We took him to the grounds and ordered him to run. He ran out and back once, and nothing happened. We again ordered him to run, and he obeyed again. Nothing happened. The third time we insisted he run around in circles, but he refused. Running around like that to no purpose seemed like abuse to him, so he defied us and refused. At first we were astonished at his insolence, but then we beat him up until he spat blood. He was handsome, and his face depicted amazement and scorn. Suddenly he slipped away and began running down the hill slope. His strides were powerful, and none of us could catch up with him, but he was hit by our gunfire and collapsed and was lost sight of among the bushes. We thought we heard groaning, but we ignored it. To put an end to his miseries, we despatched another round to the spot where he had fallen. We didn't want his death, and since he hadn't been killed by a mine, I felt sorry for him. It was peculiar: when it came to our men who stepped on those mines, I was sorry for each one to the extent that I had or hadn't liked him in his lifetime, but not out of any vague sentiment for the ruin of glorious manhood. As for that stranger, who may or may not have been one of the enemy, I was sorry that he was not killed by those same mines whose explosion would have spelt relief to us; it seemed like a wasteful dying, senseless . . . Have you guessed by now into what a strange morass of notions we had sunk? . . .'

(I nodded. I was wondering why they hadn't got out of this mined zone and taken up other positions, but after considering the tactical importance of this ridge, I decided not to raise the question.)

'The next day we captured another prisoner. This time, an old, good-natured wag, who spun fantastic yarns about the enemy forces. It was I who had to "deal" with him. I didn't beat him or order him to run, but loosened his shackles and treated him as I would my friend. The old man was overwhelmed, and it was all I could do to check his repeated efforts to kiss my hands. The degradation of those who surrender meekly is infinitely repulsive. He did whatever I told him, bringing water, marking tracks, doing odd jobs here and there all the while, under a guard which was quite unnecessary. He always came back to me like a dog to his kennel, and I welcomed him with a friendly smile, thanking him for the services rendered. I had never seen such affection before light up in a human face, such boundless affection and devotion. No one had ever been so fond of me. The outcome was that he kept on going and shuffling along the surface of the ridge until his feet found the mine. We showed true charity by contributing a bullet for his merciful release, and then we cremated his body.'

(Though Abbi went on talking, his words still echoed faintly in my heart: 'No one had ever been so fond of me.' He had uttered them with a strange sort of trembling mingled with a spice of involuntarily suppressed cynicism. Later he said: 'I didn't like it *at all,*' and I sensed something more than mere dislike. This, it seems, was the real Abbi, and this is how he will linger in my memory . . . My aunt would sigh and say, 'Ugh, war, war!' but I wouldn't put that all down to the war. I again recalled my sister, how murderous she could be with her sweet qualities and the charm of her mischief! I had no wish to make comparisons, but I remembered an impression kept by me from childhood. After my first experience with injustice wrapped in a smile, I pleaded with all my strength, young and foolish as I was, for the rules of the game, that the perpetrators of injustice should be properly fitted out with a dire aspect, with ravenous maws and terrifying eyes . . . Ah, the delightful deceptions of nature, the thorns in the rosebush and the worm in the apple, how stupid and happy we might have been without you! . . .)

III.

'Reinforcements were due the next day. We had to decide on a question of principle. We talked it over in the evening and adopted a resolution to keep the newcomers in the dark about the mines unless they had been forewarned at Headquarters. Believe me, there was no alternative. There was no escaping those mines, and ignorance would at least spare their nerves. If they would have had to go through what we had, it is doubtful whether they would have been fit for battle. And we had intelligence that the enemy was preparing a big attack. What we did was ruthless of course, but there can be no doubt we were right; you can't outwit fate, and those destined to survive had better be able to carry out their duties. Don't say that we held life cheap, there was nothing for us to save. But what worried me most was the need to enter into conspiracy with those forty men. We had to join forces on a subject which, from the point of view of command, called for a cold logical estimate, but, from the standpoint of this group of men, meant in effect the vile self-interest of an execrably naked struggle-for-existence. Any two men in an intrigue are thrown into mutual dependence; now just imagine an intrigue that takes in forty men! A conspiracy of brutal silence. Each one of the forty might have an intimate friend in the new platoon, and he might be tempted to try to save him from disaster by passing on the information; picture to yourself what suspicion, what endless hate beset us. It was clear, whoever loosened his tongue would be a traitor. How would the men of that other platoon have judged us, if they had learned what it was that we were conspiring to hold back from them . . . They would never have forgiven us. I recall with what depressing clarity our lieutenant formulated his arguments for the deadly silence, and how quickly the men, no less endowed than you and I with the characteristics of enlightenment, fraternised and united on the darkest of all survival instincts . . . Our shared secret brought us together with loathing. There would seem to be only a certain quota of intimacy permissible in social relations also, to overstep which is—a crime . . .

'The next day, at dawn, the reinforcements broke through. The battle followed swiftly. I went out of my way to be in charge myself of picking up and burying the dead. Two were mine casualties. I watched our men passing near them and saw what a terrible look they threw at the spot where the explosion had taken place. Have you ever heard of the image of man?'

(Abbi's profile which had been somewhat dislocated at the jaw by a shrapnel, was suddenly contorted with abhorrence. I knew that this hate could not be directed against any of the survivors without having some envy in it. Generally, one affected this way by fate naturally blames something or somebody, who figures in his imagination as the prime cause of all that is odious on earth. But if he looks deeper he will readily discover the cause in this factor or the other, in himself and his close friends, and it is only right that he should not reproach the war-weary, but should keep a stiff upper lip and continue to hunt for whatever he may find. Since Abbi has seen cruelty of the murkiest kind springing up in the best of his friends, and in himself too, it is not improbable that he now has something to struggle against, directly; something he can overcome by his own efforts. It is not improbable that he has some definite aim. I have no idea what he intends to fight about, nor where his senses may lead him in the field of battle; but of one thing I am sure, he will be a fighter all his life, never giving in to weariness, and the passage of time will still find him a loyal protagonist, one who will have earned the laurel of happiness when it falls to his lot. I again thought of my sister and wondered whether she would understand Abbi, who was now forged of the same mettle that had defeated his friends, and who had learned to see life from a vantage-point below the earth's surface. My sister is also by character receptive to the lessons of experience and incorporates into her own stock of wisdom the trials and errors of others. Abbi fell in love with my sister because she was young and attractive, but after the initial infatuation, he could not help but continue to love her.)

IV.

'There was a further lull for a few days. We almost ceased to believe in the existence of any more mines. Paths were trodden down in the grounds which we took good care to keep to, and we managed to pass on to the men of the new platoon a word of caution, not too precise or deliberate. We began preparations for a systematic attack on the neighbouring villages. The room which had previously passed muster as Headquarters now had some new faces, among them a petite, serious girl operator; though a lone maid among many men, she held her own quite well. To cultivate the intimacy of a woman in her position, even without giving offence, seemed wrong. Not to be dependent on any one of the men was part of her social function, and a special instinct told her that it would not do for her to be drawn after her whims and fancies. She had no trace of conceit, not even enough to lead her, so mischievously and lightheadedly, to tease those sissies who were subjected to the cheap, musty, and concealed levity of the "manly" ones in our group.

'I remember her first appearance among us that morning, a slip of a girl, unkempt, all agog with excitement, and somewhat bashful on that account; and what a fund of childish curiosity and deference she brought to her work in Headquarters. She flitted around with a rebuked air, overawed by the sternness of our job, though we were quite friendly to her, even somewhat paternal. I don't think she was blessed with too much intelligence, but she was infinitely pleasant. She seemed to have dropped down on this earth to evoke your pity for something. Since she was constantly on the move, I became very anxious. No doubt she thought me a stupid youngster, since whenever I was with her I gave the impression of holding back something I had to say to her. You will surely guess what it was that I wanted to communicate. But I maintained silence, painfully aware of the extent to which any favoritism or digression from the secrecy to which we were all committed would have undermined the profound moral basis of our resolution. This is the position: if you secretly disclose the existence of the mines to one person, you are passing sentence of death on another. One doesn't disturb the nice calculations of Fate. One night I decided that if ever I got out of there, my lips would be forever sealed, but I haven't lived up to that resolution.

'The *hamsinim* afflicted us at this season, drying up every drop of sap in our being. We sank into apathy and fatigue, browned off to suffocation. The sky was bleak and misty as in a sand-storm, and a hot wind passed through our lungs, scorching our breath. We lay stretched on our bunks all day, and even the guards slept at their posts. Suddenly the wind changed and a light rain began to patter on the tin roof. Soon the operator bounced out of the room and started prancing about in the open, her mouth wide open and tilted upwards as she drank in the rain water with an insatiable joy. She then began to dance to the accompaniment of ridiculous gestures until she was seized with stage fright; then she ran to those yonder (he pointed to two trees) as if to find shelter beneath them; and then she again broke into a dance which threw me into a fit of worried consternation. We had never once gone over to that spot, for fear that the unexploded mines might be lurking there.

'I stared at this foppish dance and was beset by appalling phantoms. The dance of death, I thought. My eyes, transfixed with horror, followed the soles of her feet which, tripping here and there, seemed to be tapping the ground and testing it for mines. I saw the men watching her as if from an ambush. They had no compunction. I too was silent. I felt myself caught in a tense, fatiguing state of expectation of the inevitable. I stared mournfully at her slim, childish legs. Suddenly, I restrained my feelings and called her to the room, in tones that implied something urgent was required of her. Nobody could have convinced me it wasn't.

'She ran towards me, coming, not to the door, but to the window.' He again indicated the spot and looked intently in that direction. He then passed the three remaining fingers of his right hand across his brow, apparently trying to collect his thoughts, and added: 'She hung onto the window sill and sang out: "What is it?" I just managed to catch a glimpse of her small hands gripping the window—she was a short one, and her rain-washed hair; and a dewy droplet on her forehead was on the point of slipping into her eye-socket . . . The explosion filled the room with smoke and heavy dust; and beneath the window, where no one had suspected, lay a very small corpse, scorched and footless, exposing forlorn naked parts in vain expectation of what would never be . . .

'A week later we took Halissah (he pointed to the nearby Arab village) and were allowed to leave the place. Now do you understand why it was named "The Ridge of the Seven?" '

He was silent—and I felt it would be much better if we left the place. It was getting late too, and I had undertaken to return the car by nightfall. We began to descend the hill path. I thought about what I had heard, and one point puzzled me:

'Something's wrong,' I told him, 'you said there were seven mines, but you only told about six of them.'

'The seventh hasn't exploded yet,' Abbi said in an undertone.

I was swiftly overtaken by a curious fright and slight shivers, which I checked by a mental effort. The surprise had stunned me, but more than by this, I was frightened to see a strange glint lurking in his eyes.

Why had he taken me there? Had he wished me to sense a bit of that dread they had been fated to bear, or had he in a spasm of despair determined to commit suicide in the presence of the brother of the girl he loved?

But that same moment I was struck by another notion: possibly it was my imagination that had led me astray. I remembered that from the side of his right profile, at which I had been looking, I was being stared at by a glass eye.

THE PARTY

by Aharon Meged

I.

CLICK, CLACK, click, clack, Naftali's crutches rapped on the stone tiles of the room as though drawing sparks from their sheen. *Quite a number of people have come. I don't see Geula.*

'Hello! How good that you've come'—Mrs. Meirowitz welcomed them with open arms. 'We thought something had happened to you!' she added, laughing.

'We were delayed a bit, couldn't help it,' his mother answered bleakly with a thin smile of apology. *The antique chandelier hanging as always from the ceiling. Dazzling light. Brandy on the table. I don't like the brand.*

'Hello, Naftali,' said Mrs. Meirowitz, sincere sympathy in her voice as though condoling with the bereaved, and then to all of them: 'You all know Naftali, I hope, and this is his mother, Mrs. Abrahami.'

Naftali smiled acknowledgement, his mother responded with a movement of the head. *Now they'll all get up for you and make room. To hell. Click, clack—forward march. Raffy hasn't come. Here is Shochet. Pity I came. There, they've all got up from their seats.*

Shochet hurried with long steps. *The thin moustache. How he smiles.*

He stretched out a hand with a masculine movement almost soldierly.

'Hello, there, Naftali! How long is it since we met, boy?'

'A long time,' he answered weakly, resting his weight on the left-hand crutch. 'How're you?'

'I'm always well, you know'—he spoke loudly like one-of-the-boys—'so . . .'—he stammered a moment—'you've come at last, and that's that.'

Trying to cheer me up. I can see it. Phoney. Just like his father in everything, probably gone into the business. I haven't forgotten how he was at high school.

'Yes, at last . . .'

'Fine,' Shochet took hold of his elbow to help him to the table. *Don't touch me!* Naftali wanted to scream. *Where's mother? Whispering with Mrs. Meirowitz. Moaning again. I hate her. 'He suffers terribly, what can I do?' and then the tears. If not for her—everything would come right. I would enjoy myself with all of them.*

The chair. Here, next to Mrs. Jacoby of all people. 'Hello, good, good, thanks.' *Smile. Mrs. Jacoby, if I'm not mistaken. Her son in the Seventh Battalion. You don't have to move, you—don't—have—to—move. There. The crutches against the back of the chair. Crack. The crutch has fallen. Now they're all looking. Stopped talking. Already mother is rushing to pick it up. There's no need, there's no need, I told you. She'll never remember, however much I scold her at home. I hate her. I don't envy her when we get home. Good that Geula is not here.*

He picked up the crutch. *The whole evening spoiled. Slippery tiles, the rubber there must have worn. No matter, no matter.*

'Doesn't matter,' said Shochet and edged his chair a little.

'Now then, folks, why aren't you eating anything?' called out Mrs. Meirowitz. *To distract attention. Can't fool me.*

He felt himself reddening to the roots of his hair. Felt pain in his scalp. The glare of the light bothered his eyes . . . *and the crystal wine glasses, and the glitter of the bottles and the vases and the dishes, and of the faces of the women and the men as though newly scrubbed, and the white table-cloth, and the chatter round about, like a buzzing mist, and the glass-case at the wall and mother talking—to whom this time? And warm air. The crutch fell and was picked up. Shochet. Get a grip on yourself. Who is here, actually?*

Opposite him were Shragai and his wife, cracking peanuts incessantly. *Yes, what do I care about the whole thing after all. Tomorrow this evening will be forgotten too. As though it had never been, and again—the little room with mother. An interesting book, the one about the atom bomb. How long can this go on at mother's expense? Another seven pounds. Yes, and there on their left is Elazari.* Their eyes met.

Elazari half smiled as in greeting.

'I think I haven't seen you since high school'—said Naftali stiffly, dutifully. Elazari sat imprisoned in his starched collar. *He was very small then, the shortest boy in the class. I never thought he'd grow . . .*

'Yes, I was in England,' Elazari replied in a monotonous, formal kind of voice. As though answering questions by the Math teacher.

'Studying?' asked Naftali and drew his right leg in under the chair.

'I was sent to study public relations. I work in the Public Relations Department,' answered Elazari.

Save your joke for some other time. You'll need it.

'Is that so?' said Naftali encouragingly. Elazari smiled gratefully. Behind his shoulder he heard Mrs. Jacoby's whisper in Mrs. Meirowitz's ear: 'It happened near Faluja?' 'Yes, he was almost killed.' He wanted to correct her and say 'near Julis.' *I told mother that we shouldn't go to the party. 'It doesn't matter, you'll enjoy yourself a little,' she said. I'm happy as I am.*

His mother came up to the back of his chair and whispered in his ear: 'Naftali, have some of these biscuits, you like them.'

'Let me alone, will you?' he snapped at her, almost shouted. *This itch in the backside from the friction of the hard chair. Like ants creeping up and down, up and down. Should I move? The chair will creak. No, but it's pricking, burning. Shift a little. You'll still have to sit here for two hours, maybe more.*

Shochet is babbling to his neighbour—who is it?—'You can buy a jeep today for 600 pounds and make a first class car out of it. What are you talking about? It's better than a new one. Don't tell me. I know jeeps. 80 kilometres an hour. Where did you see a car that'd do 80 kilometres an hour? And it's a very small investment. I can fix it with Ginzburg's Garage to have the body changed for you in a few days. I have pull with him, ha, ha, ha, don't ask . . .'

Shragai crushed a peanut between his teeth and grunted under his yellow moustache. 'And where does the money come from?' His wife nodded agreement.

'What's money these days?' Shochet attacked from a new angle. 'Money is losing value from day to day. There's nothing safer than investing in machines or . . .'

His red shoes at school. We used to laugh at him because of them. He went and blabbed on me to the principal. Where was he during the war? Shochet and Shochet, his father's textiles. Shochet & Co. Football on Saturday nights, the stadium. Why don't they have games with cripples on crutches, of hobbling, running. A big crowd. Quite entertaining. A forward line on crutches, ha, ha, ha. On your mark—get set—go! Forward, forward, clap—clap, clap—clap, faster! Amos would probably fall. Shochet in the grand-stand—Go it Naftali, go it!—The door. Who is it? Geula?

II.

The door there in the passage opened. 'Hello, Yair,' came the brassy voice of Mrs. Meirowitz. 'We're all waiting for you.' Yair bent down and kissed his mother. 'Forgive me,' he addressed them all. 'I was busy, on duty.'

Immaculate, and the leaves on his shoulder. Now they all got up from their seats to greet him. 'We were already thinking of drinking without you, ha, ha, ha!' came Shochet's guffaw. Naftali was left alone at the table. *The bottles of brandy, the liqueur. Take a sweet meantime. Imported. What a distance between the table and the group at the door to the passage. Invalids' Department. They should have parties for cripples with amputated left legs. Union of Left-Leg Amputees. He'll come up to you in a moment. Be indifferent.*

From the misty distance the voices rippled.

Mr. Shragai: 'Congratulations on your promotion.'

His wife: 'Yes, Yair. We congratulate you . . .'

Mother: 'I was very glad when I heard that our Yair . . .'

Shochet (breaking in): 'Our! Ha, ha, ha, what do you mean yours—ours! Didn't we share a desk at school and throw paper airplanes once in Mr. Gamzu's lesson? Isn't that so, Yair?'

Mrs. Meirowitz: 'You, Shochet, you spoiled him . . .'

Elazari. That laugh. Yair with the fig leaves. Quartermaster. He used to copy from me in exams. I'm going up to his office tomorrow. Click, clack—on the stairs. Hello, Yair—or Hello, Naftali. I'm glad you came to me, friends always remain friends. I'll go straight to the point: Listen, I've come to ask you for something. You know what happened to me . . . No, not that way. Rather: You know I'm a cripple. No. You know I was wounded at Julis . . .

If I'd only jumped to the left as Binia did. Oh, the leg, the left trouser. Always the same thoughts.

Well—you know it's not easy to get yourself fixed up when you're this way. You're telling me! Listen, don't say anything more, I know exactly what you mean . . .

Papers. Signing papers. Physical condition—amputee. If I'd only jumped to the left . . .

Mrs. Meirowitz came up and whispered in Naftali's ear:

'Yair told me that he won't have a party unless Naftali comes. I didn't know you were such good friends, ha, ha . . . I'm really glad.'

'Yes, a long time.' Too hoarse. 'Yes, a long time.'

'Well, yes, to be sure!'

They're coming back to the table. Yair . . . The glitter. All your life. If Raffy were here, everything would be just right. Yair stepped straight towards Naftali's chair. Left, right, left, arm stretched out stiffly. Formal, happy.

'Hello, Naftali! Thanks a lot for honoring me by coming to my party . . .'

No. You can't get up. Don't try. And maybe after all, he's not as arrogant as I thought.

'. . . I know it was hard for you . . .'

Stop it! Stop it! You can't run away now.

'Yes, I came on one foot, as they say,' said Naftali with a smile.

Mrs. Shragai whispered something to her husband. Her husband replied. 'What can one do? There are many, many like him today'. . . He crushed a nut between his palms. Mother lowered her head.

Yair tapped Naftali on the shoulder.

'Come and see me tomorrow,' he proclaimed. 'Say between eleven and twelve. You know where my office is . . .'

'Yes, my memory hasn't been affected in the least . . .'

Yair did not smile. A weak joke. What have I to do with him? I don't want to see him . . .

'Now—have some of this cognac. You like it, if I'm not mistaken.'

He wanted to sneer: 'Thank you,' or to kick him. It was too late. Yair had gone to his seat, at the head of the table.

'He's a "hundred per cent"!' Shochet exclaimed to Elazari.

Elazari helped himself to a chocolate wrapped in silver paper.

'I see that you've adopted the typical army expressions,' he said to Shochet, sucking on the candy.

'Of course!' said Shochet, 'that's from our front-line lexicon, eh, Abrahami?' He turned to to Naftali.

Abrahami, he calls me! I'd like to let this son-of-a-shopkeeper have it with the end of my patched-up thigh. That would shake him. 'Yes . . .' he muttered.

'Abrahami is in a bad mood today,' said Shochet laughing to Elazari. 'Probably been let down by some . . .'

Mrs. Meirowitz threw a reproving look at Shochet, and he broke off.

'It's not easy to let me down these days,' said Naftali with a bitter smile, as though he had not noticed Mrs. Meirowitz's look. Mrs. Shragai grimaced at her husband. Mr. Shragai shrugged his shoulder and went on chewing. 'Your cake is delicious,' said Naftali's mother to Mrs. Meirowitz.

'Mother, where's father?' asked Yair. 'Our guests are impatient.'

'He'll probably come soon,' she said. 'He's been very busy in the Union lately, you know.'

But at that moment the door opened and Mr. Meirowitz came in, took off his hat and said ceremoniously:

'Good evening all. I hope you've already drunk a toast to my son!' He went up to Yair and patted him on the shoulder. Then he shook hands with all the guests, Naftali too.

If I could run, I would run in and out, in and out. With mincing steps, light and gay. How'd you do, Yair? I would say simply and lightly. You've been promoted in Finance, hey? Slap him on the shoulder. Not a bad career, hey? Congratulations, boy! Touch glasses, a toast to all the soldiers! Go out with him to the Garden Café—joking about the exhibition of Bela's paintings that I saw yesterday. How are things with you? He would ask me. I get around. And Raffy would come in too. Why hasn't Raffy come?

Somewhere in the mist the glittering gilded wine-glasses clinked and Meirowitz's quivering belly, poor dad's old friend, and Shragai's nicotine-stained moustache, and the forced smile in his wife's eyes. Elazari, who knows his place, and the cymbals-and-drum guffaw of Shochet pouring all over the table, and Yair—the tallest of them all. Tall and erect in his uniform, not a crease. A toast, a toast, gentlemen! Have some of the cake, I baked it specially, why don't you take some, mother? I'll manage! And the old crystal chandelier. Drink to all our boys who fought so well, and to the victories of our State. The whole of the Negev, as far as Auja, and Julis too, Julis too, don't forget. To Israel's victory! The jeeps at 600 pounds. Friends, I forgot I had something more for you—Hurrah! It's a long time since we enjoyed ourselves so much—a toast to the State.

I'm on the way to Geula now. Crick—crack, crick—crack, in the dark and quiet street in the north of Tel-Aviv. The pavements echo dully: crick—crack. Tamarisks on both sides and jasmin bushes, the smell of jasmin. Crick—crack. A woman opens her shutters—what's that in the street? Ah, a cripple, I was so frightened. Shuts it quickly. Ha, ha, hey, ghosts in the streets, nocturnal ghosts, frightening people. A prickly shiver. Come, all of you! A victory march and I'm at the head. A light in Geula's window. Should I whistle 'You and I'? No, I'll steal in quietly. The stone tiles in the front garden and the oleander bush near the wall. The steps. Thirteen steps. Get a good grip at the crutches so that they don't scrape. Quiet. One, two, three—thirteen. Knock at the door. No answer. She out? Knock. Who's that?—Geula. Her steps in the passage, coming nearer, nearer, stop your heart-beats. Door opens. Geula. Hello—say it in an indifferent tone. Oh, Naftali! I didn't recognize you! Come in!—Just so. Come in. Thanks. Very polite. As one ought to be to cripples. She in front, and I limp behind her. The plush cloth on the big table, as it used to be. And Grandpa's picture. And the big mirror above the sideboard. Confused, she thinks I don't know anything about Yechiel.—Come, let's go into my room.—Thanks. Very polite.—Do you mind putting these crutches in the corner?—Ha, ha, ha, she shudders.—Tell me, Naftali, how are you?—Just so. Friendly, solicitous. Afraid Yechiel might walk in suddenly. I might hit him with my crutches? No, my dear. I won't do that. I'm not jealous. I'm beyond that.—How am I? As you see, I have an extra leg. I used to have two, now—three . . .—Naftali, really, stop it! I know all you've been through . . .—It's not so terrible. One trouser-leg less. Pity you aren't the wife of a cripple—you'd have less to launder for him—Ha, ha. She does not know what to say. Confused, blushes. Continue.—Well, why don't you say anything? How are you? How have you settled down? That's more important.—Nothing special, as usual.—As usual . . . I hate that expression. Hate her.—Carrying on, right?—Silence. Those eyes, warm and brown, again looking straight in your eyes, as though the old link . . . She's beautiful. Very beautiful. And her body—a mystery again. A closed secret. Finished.—Why are you looking at me, Geula? Don't you know me!—Naftali, forgive me.—There's nothing to forgive. I understand you. If I were you I'd be just the same.—Oh, Naftali, don't speak like that. You hurt me.—Sorry, I didn't mean to. I don't think I'm in a position to hurt others.—If only I could help you.—Thanks very much. There's no need.—On the wall, the Van-Dyck painting I gave her for her twenty-second birthday: 'To the Flower of Spring'.—Why don't you change it for something else, it's boring to see the same painting for years on end . . . Tears in her eyes.—You think I've forgotten everything?—Why this damned sentimentalism? Do you want to force tears out of my eyes too?—Why didn't you write to me anyhow, Geula? One can remain friends . . . I didn't know where you were, and besides . . .—Oh, how I hate hypocrisy!—You were afraid of hurting me, eh?—Maybe. What could I do?—Nothing: I'm not complaining, don't mistake me. I know it's not pleasant to sleep with a fellow with one leg.—Stop it! Stop it! You know that's not true! You know that's not the reason! You know! You know!—Ha, ha, ha, why are you getting excited, I don't understand. What's there to get excited about? You have my best wishes. I suggest you go to Yair! He's just been promoted, he's distinguished himself and been promoted!—You're filthy, you're filthy! Yes, yes, I know, I know . . . I know . . .

'Naftali, is that true? You ought to know!'—called Shragai from across the table.

'Of course, he was there after all,' added his wife.

'Let him alone, he doesn't know. What d'you want of him?' Naftali's mother pleaded.

'I wasn't listening. What were you talking about?' asked Naftali.

'Mr. Shragai says,' explained Mrs. Meirowitz, 'that our own officers were responsible for the catastrophe near Iraq-Soueidan. Is that true?'

'Oh, nonsense!' squeaked Shochet.

'Is it true, Naftali?' Mrs. Meirowitz repeated her question and a silence fell. On the big cake there, the chocolate letters 'To our Yair—Good Luck' seemed to creep like worms, and rays of light glanced off the discarded strips of silver paper . . .

'No, it's not true,' replied Naftali, with an effort. *It had been at Maaleh Akrabim. We were terribly thirsty. We climbed with all our kit. Upward, upward. And there was no shade, not even a hand's breadth, and the sun was beating down. There was no end to it, there was no end, and you couldn't sit down, or rest, or stop for a while. And those rocks. Every step as though you were going up an absolutely vertical staircase. My throat was parched. I wanted to scream. Stop for a moment, Ezra, stop for a moment, the boys are almost fainting there! But it was impossible to stop. And to hell with this country, what did we come here for; to hell with this heat, like no other heat in the world; and to hell with these people, what are they giving their lives up for; and what is it all for, what's it all for, for whom, this waterless drought? And Raffy had come up quietly from behind—a little further, boy, another two hundred steps . . .*

Nine o'clock in the morning. Bus Number Four. First in the queue. Please. Please sit down. To Geula. She opens the door. Naftali! Naftali, Naftali . . . crying.—How I waited, I waited all the time. I couldn't write for pain. Together again. Geula, and doesn't this matter to you . . . No, no, no, how can you think such a thing, I love you more than ever, more than ever . . .

'As the enemy's superiority in numbers and arms was known—it was a blunder to launch the attack to start with,' expounded Yair.

'I heard that the bodies were found completely mutilated,' said Elazari between his teeth.

'Well, yes,' said Yair, 'they were in the hands of the Arabs until the place was finally captured.'

III.

'Why d'you have to talk about such things at this party!' exclaimed Mrs. Meirowitz.

'Really. Enjoy yourselves! Enjoy yourselves! Where are you young people? We're old already, but after all, you youngsters are full of life!' said Mr. Meirowitz to Shochet.

Shochet drummed on the table, burst into song: 'What a Night It Was!'

'We're tired of that,' Elazari whispered to him. 'Sing something else . . .'

The door again. Ugh, Gamzu and his wife, dressed in mourning. Everybody gets up. Now I'd like to get up, to walk up to them. Shake their hands, allies. To say to him, forgive me, forgive me, Mr. Gamzu, forgive me for throwing paper airplanes once in your class. I would go up to him. Would whisper—I was with Mussy when he was wounded. We were pals. I would kiss the mother's hand, say to her—I know, you're Mussy's mother. Where are the crutches, where? They've gone and put them by the wall. I can hop on one leg.

'Naftali, sit down, I beg you,' his mother whispered.

'I'm sitting, I'm sitting.' Now Gamzu and his wife came up to him. Shook hands. 'Hello, Naftali,' murmured Mr. Gamzu. 'Hello, Naftali,' murmured his wife. They sat down next to him. Naftali moved his chair. A glass fell on the table cloth. Wine spilt, on his knees, on the folded trouser-leg, on the dead knee, laid there like a broken beam. He leaned back and smiled—*Ha, ha, what a good-for-nothing.* His mother rushed from her chair and restored the glass. She asked Mrs. Meirowitz for a cloth. 'No, my dear, it's nothing. I have to wash it anyhow,' said Mrs. Meirowitz. Elazari looked fixedly at the folded trouser-leg. Shochet called out: 'Saw your teacher and got confused, eh?' Shragai said to Meirowitz: 'Lucky it wasn't the good cognac, ha, ha, ha!' and rocked with laughter. Yair lifted his glass and announced: 'Now we'll drink to our teacher, Mr. Gamzu, right?' A clinking of glasses. That was over.

'Are you in town now?' Gamzu asked him.

'Yes, I'm living with mother.'

'And what are you doing?'

'Meantime, nothing.'

'Have you tried to find work?'

'Trying all the time, it's not easy.'

'Yes, they're forgetting the war quickly here,' said Gamzu dryly.

'Rightly,' smiled Naftali. He wanted to say to him: I was with Mussy when he was wounded.

Mr. Gamzu let his eyes rest caressingly on the amputated leg. Naftali lowered his gaze to the same spot, embarrassed. Gamzu's fingers drummed on the table and he said: 'Yes, yes.'

'Still, I don't suppose they're neglecting you, not helping you,' said Mrs. Gamzu.

'Oh, no!'—Naftali woke up.

'Oh, how green I was'—the voices around them were raised in song. 'Oh, how green . . .'

'Do they intend making you an artificial leg?' asked Mr. Gamzu, sitting close up to him. He wanted to thank him. 'They've promised . . . I don't know yet.'

'Oh, how green . . .'

'That will be a great help to you,' said Gamzu's wife. Now he saw how much Mussy had resembled her. *The same look of child-like innocence. Don't tell my mother—he had said then. Now I understand why. Now, she knows. He fell. Rolled down from the rock until he was stopped by a thorn bush. Got entangled. Leave me! he shouted. Leave me!*

'Oh, how green . . .'

'Yes! Definitely.' Naftali replied. *Maybe it would be of some comfort to her. An only son. The best loved—are the ones that die. If only I could help her . . .* 'But I've got used to it anyhow,' he added.

'Yes, yes'—Gamzu twiddled his fingers nervously.

'Stop it, Jacob,' his wife whispered to him.

'I didn't say anything!' Gamzu reproached her. *Strange how I never thought that this teacher is also a person!*

'Oh, how green you are . . .'

Gamzu and his wife and Naftali were silent. *Say something to them. You must.* They were silent. *Speak, speak. Tell them you saw Mussy. Tell them he was popular. Say that everybody liked to hear him sing, that he had a fine voice.* Silence and again silence and again, unbearable. 'You are green . . .' *Say that you sympathize with them and understand them, shake their hand. Let them sing, let them sing together with the others. They really must forget. It's their duty to the living and the dead. Tell them that it's bad for you too. Let them go away. Let them go and congratulate Yair, if only to get away from here. Tell them there's no sense in mourning, you just have to get used to things. Say something!* 'You are green . . .' He moved his chair slightly and it creaked. *This brotherly get-together round the table and this happy friendly sing-song.* Over there was the fruit-dish. *That leg, that leg again.* He leaned over the table to get hold of the dish and offered it to Gamzu and his wife.

'No, thanks,' said Gamzu. His wife shook her head.

It was silly of him. 'Oh how green . . .'

'Don't let me down. Eat something,' said Mrs. Meirowitz. *At last.*

The singing dissolved. 'Huh, I haven't sung so much for a long time,' proclaimed Mrs. Shragai.

'Yes, it was good,' assented Elazari.

'Are you tired?' Naftali's mother asked him.

'No, mother,' he answered respectfully.

'I just thought . . .' she apologized.

'How about another song, folks?' asked Elazari without moving a muscle.

Naftali shot a glance at Elazari's wooden face. *He hates me because I'm a cripple. I irritate him. Don't you say anything to him, good or bad. What smugness! What smugness! He's not worth even one look of contempt. See how he empties the chocolate dish. Shameless! If one could smash that face up. Yet—he's so sure of himself. And all because of having one leg more? Oh, stop it.*

An argument was going on about rationed food prices and Mrs. Shragai had the better of it. There was almost a quarrel between her and Mr. Meirowitz, who stood up for the law. Elazari spoke guardedly and let his words filter, one by one, through a crack that opened between his lips. *The hypocrite!* And Yair gave forth judicial decisions. *How does he come to be so bold, or rather—so impudent? How unquestioningly his words are received. He looks so triumphant after every stupid sentence! Look at him, look at him! And they all nod their heads in agreement. Gospel truth. And they fall silent when he speaks. Even Shochet devours his words. And his mother is enjoying herself. See how pleased she is with her son. Throw something in his face, tell him he's lying. You don't believe, smooth words hiding naked emptiness. Smooth words, like slush in which you slip and break your leg, ha, ha—*

Nostalgia suddenly gripped him, for the hospital. *To go back there. If only on a visit. The all-pervading smell of the iodine and disinfectant. And white, everything so white, the bandages, the sheets, the walls, the nurses. Their light-heartedness when you pestered them, and everybody equal. Almost bathed in pus. The dull pain as pleasant as an itch, the sulpha pills—and Dr. Herz. Dr. Herz, have you got any injections for making legs grow? Good morning, Herr Doktor, thank God I have no temperature. Aviva, who was not averse to petting. I never got anywhere with her. The frankfurters for lunch. Frankfurters. What do you think, why do they give us frankfurters every day? That was the old man's joke. The shave in the morning in your pajamas. And how you hated people visiting you, especially relatives. Leave us in peace. Yoel, whose long face made him the butt of everybody's wit. Probably contemplated suicide. Not a bad idea. Go to America, you'll see the world!—Amos used to jeer at him. Ah, yes, he has a rich aunt there! Everybody equal, everybody equal. What would have happened if the whole world had consisted of people like us and no others. Then? It would be like this. Interesting relationships. Society would have developed differently, human nature would have been different. The mail. Letters from mother, and the terrible memory of Geula which became a consuming pain. The beating of your heart when the mail arrived. No. She won't write! Why bother to ask—there's no letter from her, you know that well enough. Don't go. Not today either. Tuesday she has a piano lesson, that means no letter tomorrow. The counting, the counting of the days it takes a letter to get from Tel-Aviv to the hospital. The silly calculations. You wanted to send her a telegram. Good you didn't do it, she wouldn't have answered. And the nightmare vision: she didn't write because she was out with Yechiel. Where? At the seashore, there on the bench, the same bench we used to sit on. What cynicism! She doesn't mind, she has no conscience. No. This evening she's gone to the cinema. Yes, we saw in the paper there's a film with Humphrey Bogart. She loves Humphrey Bogart. She allows Yechiel to remain in her room. In the dark. In the sum-*

mer warmth, with the fragrance of the oleander floating in from outside and the hum of mosquitoes through the window. She helps him undo his buttons... He's grown up since then, she doesn't give a damn... How you wanted to see her name on the list of air-raid casualties—I wonder if there are any people left in the hospital?

'What are you dreaming about, Abrahami?'—Shochet's rasping voice woke him up.

I could kill him for calling me Abrahami.

'About you,' the words slipped out uninvited. A laugh ran round the table. Naftali reddened. *Trapped, and there was no escape. They are mocking. Don't deceive yourself. To-hell-with-this-whole-party, may it be blown to smithereens.*

He did not know where to turn his eyes. Opposite, Elazari smiled shrewdly, penetratingly. *He understands my complexes, does he? Mrs. Shragai laughed as though enjoying a kid's wit. Her husband—pityingly. Mrs. Meirowitz—unpleasantly—annoyed at my coming. I know that, and Yair...*

'Naftali was always the serious one in our crowd,' Yair made a public declaration of affection. *Everybody duly admired that. The swines, all of them.*

'Sure! I remember how...' Shochet was starting, but then the door opened.

IV.

Raffy! At last!

'Hello!' he took them all in in one glance. His dark face glowed from sunburn.

'I can only stay for a few minutes!' he announced as he went up to Yair, to his father and his mother.

Hasn't even noticed I'm here, indeed—our friendship is an illusion. Now he's in cahoots with them, on the other side of the fence. Smiling at them pleasantly, laughing loudly. All pals together. Try to catch his eye.

'Oh, Naftos!' Raffy hurried across to Naftali and thrust out his hand. 'I didn't expect to find you here!'

'As you see,' announced Naftali with a cold smile.

'How are things? Listen, I've been trying to look you up for several days,' he said, drawing up a chair and sitting down next to him. 'Where are you living?'

'At the same place,' he replied wryly.

'Listen, I'm coming to see you tomorrow, must speak to you,' he said, tapping him on the stump of his leg.

Naftali felt relieved. The dense mist dissolved and evaporated. Now he noticed that Raffy had shaved off his moustache.

'What about?' he asked, curious. *How silly of me not to have learned typewriting, always putting it off. But anyway—there are too many clerks. Having an artificial leg one can do various manual jobs.*

'There are things,' Raffy answered mysteriously. He bent down and whispered. 'How is it here?'

Naftali shrugged his shoulders and grinned.

'Not like our parties, eh?' said Raffy.

Naftali surveyed the table and the people round it. *Not like our parties. Tel-Charbieh. Where the tables rattled and Rivka sang 'We Won't Get Drunk on Wine' and everybody echoed in chorus: 'We won't get drunk, we won't get drunk.' And the stolen water-melons. Oded didn't want to go with us . . .*

'What do your hear from the crowd?' asked Raffy.

'I?' His mouth twisted. 'Nothing—you know . . .' He looked meaningfully at the stump of his leg.

'Listen, what's going to happen? Are they fixing something up for you at last, or not?' said Raffy angrily.

'Cheap tickets to the theatre,' answered Naftali. *Don't lose your temper, don't lose your temper, keep cool.*

'I'm telling you, I'd . . .' Raffy burst out, but checked himself.

'Why are you quiet, Belkin?' called Shochet to Raffy.

'What do you want me to do?' asked Raffy.

'Sing something!' exclaimed Shochet.

'Yes, sing, Raffy boy,' pleaded Mrs. Meirowitz.

'Raffy, you sing so well, why not give us the pleasure?' called Mr. Meirowitz from the head of the table.

'Raffy you must do it for me, for friendship's sake'—begged Yair.

'I . . . what d'you want from me . . . I can't sing . . .' Raffy shrugged his shoulders and turned: 'Here—Naftali is a singer from the old days.'

Naftali was silent. He forced a smile, not very successfully.

'Why shouldn't you both sing?' called Mrs. Shragai.

'Two are better than one,' added her husband.

'Well, then, should we sing?' Raffy turned to Naftali.

'No, not we, you sing!' declared Naftali with finality.

'Here, Shochet can sing.'

Let them both warble, Raffy and Shochet. A good pair.

Raffy at last submitted and started: 'We Were All Alone on Guard.'

Shochet joined in, and then, one by one, the rest of them.

Geula hasn't come, won't come either. Best not to go to her at all. Maybe I'll meet her by chance. In a bus. She'll blush. Hello, Naftali, sit down. You sit down, it's easier for me to stand. I won't say a word. We shall keep silent all the way. Only her arm maybe will rub against mine. She won't be able to take it and will get off before her stop.—Goodbye, come and see me, Naftali.—Yes, if I have time. Or I may meet her at a concert. Does she still go often to the subscription concerts?—You really must come and see me some time. Let me introduce you, this is Yechiel, this is Naftali.—I wonder if he's taller than I am. A good-looking fellow, I hear. Just so, as though nothing had happened. She was always cruel, like a spoilt child. I once told her so. I never will again. Fate rules all.

Naftali was carried along with the singing. A bass voice. *Like hammered steel and the roar of the sea. From far, far away. From the past. Manly, like a hairy chest. Strong, like a firm body on two legs. Why are you singing? They didn't ask you to. They did ask Raffy. My bass voice, this low, deep bass, soaked in masculine passion, and so powerful, more than any woman, more than Geula, this confident bass, coming up from the depths, from lonely tents on the sands of the Negev, this bass like the growl of a lone dog. This bass voice, like the death of soldiers in battle.*

V.

Loud applause. 'What a fine voice this fellow has!' *Sure, I could sell it for a loaf of bread. A paying profession. Raffy went. What was it he said before going? Yes, 'By the way I'm joining the Hakovshim Kibbutz. See you later.' That's at Tel-Ariss, if I'm not mistaken. Danny is there, too, and Ike Friedman, actually, all the boys. Cactus hedges on the rocks. And water. Plenty of water. Can you drive a tractor with a wooden leg? Yes. I've heard you can. Or book-keeping. They won't accept you. The chicken-coop, the common shower. Interesting how cripples get undressed in the shower. Just a matter of habit.*

'Want to hear something?' asked Yair. 'We had a man in our platoon who wouldn't shave off his beard on any account. I warned him that I'd punish him if he didn't shave. He wouldn't budge . . . Said there was no such regulation . . .'

'You should have sent him to me,' Shochet interrupted.

Naftali fixed his eyes on Elazari.

'Ha, ha, ha, yes, you're right,' continued Yair, 'but listen to the end of the story. "Where d'you come from?" I asked him. "What's the difference?"—he said—"it's a matter of principle." "This isn't the place," I said to him . . .'

Elazari took a candy, popped it into his mouth, whispered something into Mrs. Shragai's ear and they both laughed.

They're laughing, damn them. What's there to laugh at? At whom? What's this smugness, mocking at the whole world?

Suddenly, something exploded. Naftali's voice boomed at Elazari:

'Why are you whispering? Talk loudly, so we can all hear.'

There was silence.

Elazari shrank back, dumbfounded. Yair stopped telling his story. All eyes turned to Naftali.

'I didn't say anything . . .' Elazari stammered in bewilderment.

'He said some silly thing,' laughed Mrs. Shragai.

'Then let him say something silly, aloud. Since he can't do anything better,' snarled Naftali. They were all stunned.

'Don't you talk to me like that!' shouted Elazari. And then to all of them: 'The nerve! I didn't touch him, he just picks on me . . .'

'There, there, what is all this?' Mr. Meirowitz drummed on the table.

'What's happened? What's happened here?' Shochet put on a blank look, asking for enlightenment.

'What children you are!' exclaimed Mrs. Meirowitz.

'I can't stand being laughed at by an empty-headed . . .' screamed Naftali.

'You've no right . . . ' Elazari flared up.

But Mr. Shragai tugged at his sleeve and said, 'Leave him, leave him,' and Mrs. Meirowitz waved her hands to silence him and Yair came up and whispered something in his ear. *I know what he whispered.* Mr. Meirowitz went into a huddle with Mr. Gamzu. *Yes, Gamzu too.* And Gamzu's wife came up to Naftali and put a hand on his shoulder and his mother came up and pleaded:

'Naftali, you're tired, come home.'

'No, I'm not tired and I won't go!' bellowed Naftali.

The whisperings grew to a murmur. Elazari had cooled off, and smiled to himself as he nervously sucked the candy. Shochet was more upset than anybody and racked his brains to find a way of closing the incident. Yair was already on the point of continuing his story and began:

'So I said to him . . .'

But Naftali raised his voice again and called out to Elazari:

'Don't you dare, again, in my presence . . .'

And all the glasses seem to break, spilling the wine, and the clinking of glass against glass, acrobats whirling around me, and Raffy going to Tel-Ariss in Galilee, Geula didn't come and I won't see her tomorrow either, because she's sleeping with Yechiel, and mother, mother, why do I have to live with her? I wonder if there are any free courses in typewriting. What are they whispering about, damn them, where are the crutches, where? Crick, that was the chair moving. On one leg to the wall, let them see how it's done, come mother, come on, home, home, yes, here are the crutches, let them remain here without me, may it do them a hell of a lot of good, and Yair with the fig leaves, good for him, good for him, home, to hell with the hypocrites. Crick—crack, forward march, one, one more, come on mother, one more, don't turn your head, crick, three more to the door . . .

THE ROLL OF CANVAS

by Benjamin Tammuz

I.

WHEN WE were small and learned that Katz Street, on the other side of Tel-Aviv, was named after the father of Pesach Katz who lived in our neighborhood, we were surprised that he didn't live in the street named after his father. We didn't dare ask him about it, because we were just kids, and he was already then a married man. And although he wasn't much taller than we were, he was almost bald and wore spectacles and his face was always sad, and his eyes used to dart about him apprehensively. Sometimes, when he went down the street, we would feel in the mood for a joke and, hiding behind a honeysuckle bush, would chant in chorus: *Mister Katz! Mister Katz!* But he wouldn't even turn his head. Almost as if he were used to this kind of thing from days gone by and knew that he was only being badgered.

It was only many years later that we understood why he chose to live away from the street named after his father, and why any reference in his presence to the fact of his being Katz's son embarrassed him. As we grew up and outgrew him, we somehow realised that he was so short because he was unable to pull himself up and throw off the burden of his father's greatness, a burden that so to speak weighed him down all his life and drove him to seek refuge in our more obscure quarter of town.

We knew that his wife worked as a clerk in one of the concerns in town. What he did, we had not the faintest idea. We would often see him going to the grocery store or standing in line for ice.

He used to speak in a low voice, in a sad sort of way, as if he had just emerged from sitting *Shiva,* and in spirit was still closed up within the walls of some darkened room, the images with which he had communed in the seclusion of his thoughts still before his eyes. The sound of people's voices seemed to aggravate some psychological wound, and he had the pained expression of someone affected by the sudden impact of daylight.

On Saturday mornings, we used to see him and his wife strolling arm in arm to the seashore with short, slow steps. They would return at noon, to be swallowed up once more in their room. The part of the street where they lived was a good place for us to play on a Saturday afternoon. All the other neighbors would scold us for making too much noise and chase us away, but the Katz's window never opened, and they never shouted at us to stop playing.

On one occasion, I remained alone in the street after my playmates had been called home for the Sabbath meal. I crept up to the wall of their house and climbed far enough up the drainpipe to be able to peep through the slats of the shutter. Even before my eyes had grown accustomed to the darkness inside the room, I could hear Pesach Katz's voice rising and falling rhythmically, with surprising assurance; then afterwards I caught sight of him standing in the middle of the floor, wearing nothing but his underwear, reciting a poem from a sheet of paper in his hand. His wife lay on the couch, listening with closed eyes. In my fear of being discovered, my heart pounded away so loudly that I did not catch what he was actually saying. As I hurriedly slid down the drainpipe, overcome with shame and guilt, my sandals made a scraping noise. I dashed for cover to the honeysuckle hedge on the other side of the road, and from there watched their window fearfully. The shutter opened a little way, Pesach Katz's head popped out, and he peered around with the same pained expression on his face that he usually got from the daylight.

II.

Obviously, I would not have bothered to resurrect this distant, blurred memory of Pesach Katz, had not subsequent events made him famous in our neighborhood.

It all began much later than the time to which I have just referred. The story I am about to tell actually opens with the outbreak of the Second World War, when I and my friends, big boys by then, were members of the underground movement that was fighting the British. Where we lived, all the young fellows without exception were what was called 'terrorists' in those days. We used to go out collecting donations from the people in our quarter, and on one such occasion I found myself knocking at Pesach Katz's door. When he opened, I told him that I had to speak to him privately. He showed me into the room into which I had already peeped some five years previously, and invited me to sit down. It was the first time I had met him personally, and his courtesy embarrassed me. I quickly shook off my thoughts and proceeded to discourse at some length on the purpose of my visit. He heard me out gravely, and as he listened his eyes grew sadder and sadder.

'It grieves me,' he said, 'it grieves me deeply to see a Jewish boy spending his days in such activities.'

'That is our duty,' I replied sharply. 'Everyone has to do his bit. And how can you say . . .'

My voice trailed off, as he seemed to be on the verge of tears.

'No, you have not understood me,' Pesach Katz whispered, and added: 'Of course we all have to do something for our nation, but killing is forbidden . . . You are taking human lives, and that is not being true to the nature of our people . . . it is forbidden. We are not like the other nations. We have to conquer with the spirit, not by force . . . Our cry will be heard from out of the silent depths. A still, small voice . . .'

He fixed his eyes on me as if hoping that I might agree with him and repent then and there.

'So you don't want to give?' I asked dryly.

'Give?' he repeated as if unable to grasp what I meant. 'No, no! Of course not. I want to save you, to warn you . . . It is forbidden, we are not allowed to . . .'

I was not used to this kind of talk in our neighborhood. Most of the people used to give readily, and the few who refused would do so in no uncertain terms and kick me out of the house. I was at a loss how to bring this awkward situation to a close, and repeated with rather stupid insistence:

'So you don't want to give?'

He raised his hands in a helpless gesture, and dropped them back in his lap.

'Well then, Shalom!' I said and got up to go.

'Go in peace,' murmured Pesach Katz. 'Don't judge me . . . Think over what I have said. Mend your ways . . . You are a son of Israel.'

I flung another 'Shalom!' in his face and made good my escape.

Round about that time the World War began. One evening, at the local kiosk, I overheard someone remark derisively that Pesach Katz had gone to enlist in the British Army and had been turned down because he was so miserable and scraggy. A few days after that, he disappeared from our quarter. Not having seen him for some time, the grocer asked Pesach's wife what had happened to him, and so we learnt that he had gone to work in a British army camp somewhere in the country, and was employed as a bookkeeper in army stores.

After a while, he began to come home for Saturday leave. During the six years of the war, it was a familiar sight to see Pesach Katz emerge from the last bus on Fridays, make for his house at a sober pace, and be swallowed up in the darkness of his room until Sunday morning, when he would come out again, mount the first bus, and disappear for another week.

Which brings us to the essence of our story.

III.

Pesach Katz's six years in an army camp left their mark on him. His voice became less diffident, and the light of day ceased to distress him. Before the war, he used to hug the walls of the houses as he went down the road; now he walked in the middle of the street like a man. It was these changes that I noticed in him that inclined me to believe the story I heard from Shaya Goldberg; otherwise I would surely have said that Shaya was making it all up.

But let us go back to the beginning.

The desk at which I am writing this story was made for me by Shaya Goldberg, the carpenter. I was out of work at the time, that summer after the World War, and developed the habit of sitting in Shaya Goldberg's workshop and watching him make my table. That was when I heard about the beginning of the Pesach Katz affair.

One day, Shaya told me, Pesach Katz came to his workshop and asked him to go with him to his house. He said he had a business proposition to put to him. The carpenter who, until that day, had barely exchanged two words with Pesach Katz, was more than a little surprised, but—as he was a good-natured fellow and afraid of hurting anyone's feelings (he used to donate to the underground although he was not wholeheartedly with us, as I learnt from him several years later)—he accompanied Pesach home.

'Would you be so kind, sir, as to feel this cloth and tell me what you think of it?' said Katz.

Shaya Goldberg put his hand on a large, bulky roll of cloth that lay in the middle of the room and felt it.

'First-class tent-canvas,' he said. 'How did you get hold of it? You don't see the likes of it on the market these days.'

'Ha! You're surprised,' cried Pesach Katz enthusiastically. 'Prepare yourself for an amazing story, sir. Please be seated. This roll of canvas has a very strange history, almost symbolical . . .' His enthusiasm subsided into a rapid murmur: 'You do not know me, sir. I do not force myself on people . . . I keep to myself, but my conscience is clear.' (Shaya Goldberg stared at him in amazement.) 'I have always acted according to the dictates of my conscience . . .' 'Yes, of course, but . . .'—the carpenter expostulated.

'Please do not interrupt me, Mr. Goldberg,' Pesach Katz entreated. 'I want to tell you this, because I have a partnership proposition to put to you, and I want you to know everything . . .'

'Partnership?'—Goldberg raised his eyebrows.

'Yes, yes. Partnership. But first hear me out . . . I worked in the British army for six years . . . Before that, I tried to enlist, but they rejected me because I was not strong. Well! A man can also fight without a gun in his hand, not so, Mr. Goldberg?'

'Sure! Of course!' Shaya agreed hastily.

'For six years I fought that accursed fiend, may his memory be blotted out, the arch-enemy of our people . . . And when the hour of victory came, my fellow-workers were mostly sad at losing their jobs; I was the only one who really rejoiced, since we had beaten our common foe. Some of the men said: "What do we get of victory? The British will start oppressing us again. They won't give us any Jewish State!" But I answered them and told them they were wrong, that it was not so. We have defeated the enemy, I said, and the hour of our own salvation is at hand. And they made fun of me. But there was a gentile, a British sergeant, who saw my happiness and understood how I felt . . . He always had a high regard for my wholehearted devotion . . . And that gentile took me by the hand, led me to one of the army stores, and pointed to this roll of canvas and said: "It's yours." '

'This?' Shaya pointed to the bundle.

'This. Precisely,' Pesach confirmed delightedly. 'There are metres and metres of it and it's worth its weight in gold.'

'Yes. That stuff costs a lot now. I think maybe ten pounds a metre.'

'That's the point, Mr. Goldberg,' cried Pesach Katz, 'that's it. This is by way of a reward, a tribute to an upright man—as one might say, "the way of the righteous hath prospered." I have been given my just deserts. All my life I have floundered in the depths, but now I shall emerge from the darkness into a great light.'

'How . . . er, that is to say . . .'—Shaya was still quite unable to make head or tail of it all—'What are you driving at?'

'This canvas, sir. From now on I can be a manufacturer.'

'A manufacturer?'—It didn't make sense to Goldberg.—'I don't understand . . .'

'Why? Why don't you understand? You are a carpenter, and I am the owner of this canvas. Why not do something together as partners? We'll manufacture deck-chairs. You will take care of the woodwork and I will provide the canvas . . . Not that I propose to stand by with folded arms . . . Heaven forbid! I shall help you with the sawing, and knocking in nails, and anything that you will tell me to do. Well, Mr. Goldberg?'

'Well, er . . . yes . . . That's to say, I understand.' The carpenter didn't know what to reply. 'But it's hard, I can't just decide on the spot like this, on the spur of the moment . . .'

'Of course!' said Pesach Katz in quick sympathy. 'Who can understand your position better than I? You want to consult your wife . . . By all means, by all means.'

Shaya Goldberg seized upon this heaven-sent opening gladly, and said that of course that was the difficulty, and he would have to discuss it with his wife.

'And then,' Shaya told me, 'I had my work cut out to keep myself from bursting out laughing. And I left the poor chap's house, thinking: "Good that he gave me an idea. I'll go now and come back in the evening and tell him my wife is against it." And that is what I did. I came to him in the evening and told him my wife was against it.'

Katz's face fell. For a few moments he was silent, engrossed in thought.

'Your wife is against it?' he murmured. 'Why? . . . But do be seated, why should you stand? Your wife did not understand the proposal properly. At times, our wives do not know . . . Although I can't say that about my wife. Oh, no! She understood immediately. Do you know what happened that first evening when I brought the canvas home with me from camp? . . . I had a dream . . . But even before that, as soon as I brought my treasure home, my wife straightway grasped the situation and its significance. "Pesach," she said to me, "we're saved." And I said, "I'm a lucky man to have so understanding a wife." And afterwards, when we went to bed, we took the precaution of rolling the canvas under our bed. We were afraid . . . That you can easily understand . . . And when we had pushed the roll under the bed it made a bump in the mattress, and there I lay on top of the bump and couldn't fall asleep. Eventually I dozed off, and in my dream I saw myself on top of a high hill, looking at the sky. Then I remembered the words of the poet who said: "The extent of the heavens at a man's head is according to the measure of the earth at his feet." And to myself I added: ". . . and the canvas in his house." And right away I looked up at the sky, to see how much that was. And I saw that the sky was made of the same canvas as mine, except that it had stars in it; and when I looked closely I saw that the stars were only holes that had been made in my canvas. Then I woke up in alarm. My wife awoke too and listened to my dream, and said it was a good omen. As I was unable to fall asleep again, because of the package that was pushing up at me from below, we lay awake practically all that night talking of our canvas, and then the idea of going into partnership with you, Mr. Goldberg, was born . . . It's a pity it's not working out . . . But you yourself, if your wife had agreed, what is your opinion?'

'I, er . . . of course . . . Yes, we might have done business, except that . . .'—and Shaya Goldberg concluded the sentence with a shrug of the shoulders.

'Just imagine,' Shaya said to me, 'the poor guy began to console *me,* and told me not to have any regrets. He asked me if I was making a living as a carpenter, and when I said that I was, thank God, he felt better and saw me off as far as the street, expressing condolences as if to someone who's just had a bereavement. What do you say to him?!'

'What happened after that?' I asked.

'After that? I've no idea,' said Shaya Goldberg. 'I didn't speak to him again.'

IV.

In addition to changing Pesach Katz's manners, the six years of war transformed him into a man of action. Evidently the bookkeeping was responsible for that. When he got back home, he took an exercise book and firmly ruled the pages into three columns. In the first column, headed "Name," he wrote the names of all the peoples he had approached with his proposition. The second column was marked "Nature of Proposition", and gave details of what he had put up to each man. The third column, "Remarks", gave the results of the negotiations.

It soon became apparent that Pesach Katz had approached every one of the artisans and craftsmen in our quarter, and we were certainly not lacking in those. Within a month, the man and his roll of canvas had became the general topic of conversation.

'Has he been to you already?' the locksmith asked the upholsterer.

'And to you?'

'Sure!'

'And did you turn him down? Did you forego the millions?'

'I advised him to try Rothschild.'

Even the women in the neighborhood got to hear of his roll of canvas, and they shook their heads: 'That poor wife of his,' they would say pityingly. 'She slaves away in some office from morning to night, and that lunatic is giving the world an industry—a canvas industry!'

In the café where the working-men forgathered for a beer or a coffee, they would raise their glasses and drink a toast:

'Here's to the canvas!'

'Here's to heavy industry!'

Only Shaya Goldberg, the carpenter, said nothing in public, but whenever he happened to meet me in the street he used to ask, with a sigh:

'He hasn't come to you yet?'

'No, he hasn't. But one of these days I shall go to him.'

'What for?'

'I don't know. I just feel like it.'

And one bright day I carried out my intention.

V.

I honestly did not go to him with the intention of saying the things I finished up by saying. I myself can't really say why I went to him. It seems to me that it was more than mere curiosity. Perhaps the memory of my transgression, when I peeped through the shutter at him half-naked in his underwear, reciting a poem to his wife, still troubled me. Or perhaps I simply wanted to have another personal chat with this Katz, son of the man after whom a street in the center of town was named. In any event, I went there with quite a different excuse. At that time, after the World War, the fight between us and the British had become intensified. And although our official institutions did everything in their power to please the

British, all they got for their pains was the contemptuous imposition of even more oppressive laws. And since Pesach Katz had once refused to donate to our underground funds, I reckoned the time had now come to show up his ideas for what they were worth. 'We'll see what sort of line he'll hand me this time,' I said to myself.

And so it happened one day, after I had made up my mind to call on him, I caught sight of him in front of me, going home. He had his back to me, and was just about to go inside.

'Mr. Katz!' I called out, remembering, as I did so, how my playmates and I used to call after him from our hiding place behind the honeysuckle on the other side of the street. This time, however, he reacted by turning round. He looked at me closely, not having recognised me.

'You mean me?' he asked.

'Of course, Mr. Katz. I want to talk to you, but you don't recognise me, do you?'

'I don't really remember . . .'—he murmured.

'I was once at your place, some years ago. I wanted a donation from you for the "terrorists",' I said with a smile.

He smiled back and put out his hand as if meeting an old acquaintance:

'Why, of course! How you have changed! Quite a man.' And he promptly added, with a sudden drop in the barometer: 'I am glad to see you alive . . . Many of your friends lost their lives. Ah, youth, youth . . . The mistakes of the heart of the younger generation . . . Please, come inside. Let's have a talk.'

I found myself in that same room once more. It had not changed at all. I think that even the cloth on the table was the same that held the remains of the Sabbath meal that time when Pesach Katz was reciting from the paper in his hand. There was only one addition to the room: a roll of grey tent-canvas lay in the corner.

'Please sit down,' said Pesach Katz.

'I wanted to resume our first conversation,' I began, lowering myself into a chair. 'In those days, you refused to give anything to the underground. You said that not by force, but by the spirit, et cetera . . . You were loyal to your official institutions. And now the war is over. You were very quick to enlist. You believed them. Well, what about it now? What have you to say? Who was right? Did they give you a kick in the pants, or didn't they?'

'Gracious me!' Pesach Katz screwed up his face. 'What language! What sort of talk is that?'

Even I was ashamed, but the blush that spread over my face seemed evidently to cover up my tactlessness. He looked at me for a long time before replying.

'Yes, reality is hard, and one might say that it has proved me wrong . . .'

'So, we've convinced you at last?' I cut in quickly.

'Ah, no! Perish the thought! What is convincing about this? We do not have to take our example from the deeds of the wicked. Do we want to go in their steps?'

'What then do you want?' I broke in a second time. 'To hold another demonstration in the streets? With the Chief Rabbis heading the procession?'

'Don't be angry, my friend, please!' Pesach Katz lifted his arm as if to ward off my words.

'What then? What are you doing? What do you suggest be done?' I pressed him.

'What am I doing?' He passed a hand over his forehead and eyes, and when he went on his voice sounded suddenly tired, and remote. 'What am I doing? It is true that I am not doing anything for my nation, these days . . . only for my home . . . If that is what you meant, then you are right . . . my horizon has shrunk.'

He sighed and lapsed into silence.

'Because you didn't take the right road to start with,' I said. 'I showed you the way, then.'

'No, my friend.' He was whispering, and I had to move closer to hear him. 'That's not it . . . Even now, after you have told me what you told me and reminded me of my duty . . . even now, there is something that I could do . . . Thanks to you, it is possible that I may really do . . . what has to be done.'

Again he fell silent, sitting motionless in his chair, his eyes closed. I waited without saying anything. I looked around the room and my eyes came to rest on his roll of canvas. Involuntarily, I smiled. 'Poor old manufacturer!' I said to myself. 'What can *you* do for your people, you poor fish?'

Pesach Katz came out of his reverie.

'My friend,' he cried, with a sudden access of fervor, the reason for which I failed to understand at the time. 'You have given me the shaking up that I needed . . . I have to thank you. Let me shake your hand.'

He got up and I quickly followed suit, surprised and curious to know what the fellow was going to say. He pumped my arm up and down and said: 'Tomorrow at the same time, I shall have news for you. Please come back here tomorrow.'

VI.

That very evening, after I left and before his wife got back from work, he sat down at the table, took a clean sheet of paper and, casting a long, sad glance at the roll of canvas reposing in the corner of the room, he waved his hand in the air as if to dispel any doubts he might still have, and wrote:

His Excellency the High Commissioner, Jerusalem.

Your Excellency,

I gave six years of my life for victory over our common enemy. I hoped and believed that with victory would come salvation for my people as well, and the gates of the country would be thrown open to our brethren in the Diaspora. And this is what we got: the White Paper, which is a betrayal of my people.

Therefore, grieved and deeply offended, I beg to return the property I received from the British Government on the termination of my services with the army. Kindly inform me where to apply in this matter.

Yours, bitterly disappointed,
PESACH KATZ

He waited for two weeks before a reply eventually arrived from the High Commissioner's office. It read:

Mr. P. Katz, Tel-Aviv.

Dear Sir,

I have been requested by His Excellency to inform you that in matters concerning the return of property, application should be made to the office of the Official Receiver.

It took Pesach Katz two days to find out where the office of the Official Receiver was located. With head held high, and looking him squarely in the eye, Pesach addressed himself to the first official that he came across in the long hall, and explained his business.

The official was, of course, not a Britisher but a Jew in their employ. When he grasped what it was all about, he glanced quickly to right and to left, and then signalled to Pesach Katz to keep quiet and come out into the corridor with him. When they were outside, he pulled him into a dark corner under the staircase, and whispered in his ear:

'What you are suggesting is very dangerous... You could be thrown into jail for just the few words you've said to me... But *I* understand you perfectly, just how angry you are with the British, and I'm prepared to do you a personal favor and take this material from you. But you must not tell anyone, on your word of honor.'

The official spoke in a hurried whisper, wiping his nicotine-yellowed moustache as he did so, his eyes darting about on all sides.

All Pesach Katz asked was:

'But you will tell the British everything I explained to you?'

'Sure, sure!' the man promised hastily. 'Only you just keep completely mum, for your own safety . . . that's the main thing.'

'Very well,' said Pesach Katz. 'I have just one request to make to you. I haven't the strength to carry the canvas. Could you come to my house for it?'

'Of course,' said the official. 'You daren't bring it here. They'd have you arrested . . . Where do you live?'

That evening, the official came, collected the parcel, and made off as fast as he could.

It was twilight outside in our street. His wife was due back from work any moment, but Pesach Katz wanted a breath of fresh air before he broke the news to her of what he had done. He was all worked up: he knew he had done a big thing, but he knew that in so doing he had harmed his wife. He wanted to gather courage and confidence. Had he had a son at home, a little child, maybe he would have stroked its head now, without saying anything, and drawn courage from the sensation of being a father, one who would not have to be ashamed when the day came and his son asked: 'What did you do in those days for your people and your country?'

But as he had no son, he went outside and strode swiftly towards a group of children playing in the street. He wanted to stroke one of their heads in passing. His heart was full to overflowing.

METAMORPHOSIS

by Shmuel Yosef Agnon

I.

SHE WAS wearing a brown dress, and her warm, brown eyes were moist. As she came out of the Rabbi's house with the bill of divorcement in her hand, she found fair-haired Svirsh and Dr. Tenzer waiting for her, two bachelors who had become friendly with her since the first year of her marriage. Through the tears on her lashes, she could see how overjoyed they were: not even in their dreams had they pictured the happy day when Toni Hartmann would be parted from her husband. They both sprang eagerly towards her and clasped her hands. Then Svirsh took the parasol, hung it from her belt, and, taking both her hands in his, swung them affectionately back and forth. Next Tenzer took them in his large, clammy hands and gazed at her with the cold, furtive look of a sensualist who is uncertain of his pleasures. Toni withdrew her tired hands from them both and wiped her eyes.

Svirsh took her arm in his and prepared to accompany her. Tenzer stationed himself on her right and thought: That albino has got in first. But never mind; if it's him today it'll be me tomorrow. And he derived a kind of intellectual satisfaction from the thought that tomorrow he would be walking with Toni, who had been Hartmann's yesterday, and who was Svirsh's today.

As they were about to go, Hartmann emerged from the Rabbi's house. His face was lined and his forehead furrowed. For a moment he stood there looking about him like someone who has just come out of the dark and is wondering which way to go. Catching sight of Toni with the two men, he looked at her with his hard, tired eyes. 'Going with them?' he asked. Toni lifted her veil to her forehead and said: 'Don't you want me to?' Her voice sent a tremor through him. He linked his thumbs one in the other and said: 'Don't go with them.' Toni crumpled her handkerchief in her hand, raised her sad eyes, and stood looking at him helplessly. Her entire appearance seemed to say, 'Do I look as if I could go alone?'

He went up to Toni. Svirsh drew back and let her arm fall. Tenzer, who was taller than Hartmann, drew himself up bravely to his full height. But he soon lowered his head and relaxed his posture. He said to himself, 'After all, it wasn't from me that he took her.' Waving his hat, he walked off—as his friend Svirsh had done—humming as he went a little impromptu tune.

As they went, they looked over their shoulders at the man who had been Toni's husband. Svirsh mumbled petulantly: 'I've never seen anything like it in my life.' Tenzer broke off his tune and wiped his heavy spectacles. 'By the Pope's slipper,' he said, 'it's enough to make Mohammed wag his beard.' Svirsh shrugged his shoulders and pursed his lips, but at Hartmann's anger rather than at Tenzer's levity.

Left alone with Toni, Hartmann made as if to take her arm, but desisted, so that she should not feel his agitation. For a moment or two they stood silently together. The whole business of the divorce had suddenly become very real: they were still standing in front of the Rabbi, and the old man's bleating voice was still ringing in their ears. Toni gripped her handkerchief tightly and checked her tears with an effort. Hartmann removed his hat for relief. Why are we standing here? he asked himself. Once again he heard bleating in his ears, not the Rabbi's voice, but that of the scribe who had read out the bill of divorcement, and he thought there was a mistake in it. Why was the wretched man in such a hurry? Because Toni and I . . . The whole thing was so strange . . . But as Hartmann could not define exactly what it was that was so strange, he became confused. He felt he must do something. He crumpled his hat and waved it about. Then he smoothed out the creases, crumpled it again, put his hat back on his head, and passed his hands over his face, from temples to chin. He could feel the stubble on his face: in his preoccupation with the divorce, he had forgotten to shave. What a disgusting sight I must look to Toni, he thought. *Ausgerechnet heute*—today of all days, he muttered between his teeth. He consoled himself with the thought that, although the greater part of the day was over, his beard was not yet noticeable. At the same time he was dissatisfied with himself for seeking lame excuses for his negligence. 'Let's go,' he said to Toni. 'Let's go,' he repeated, not certain whether he had uttered the words the first time or, if so, whether she had heard them.

The sun betook itself elsewhere. A spirit of gloom brooded over the street and a harsh melancholy groaned among the paving stones. The windows looked from the walls of the houses, strangers to themselves and to the houses. Hartmann fixed his gaze on a window being opened across the way, trying to remember what it was he had wanted to say. He saw a woman peeping out. That's not what I meant, he thought, and he began talking, not about what he'd been thinking, but about something quite different. And after every two or three words he waved his hand despairingly at the things that were coming into his mouth and that he was laying before Toni. Toni fixed her eyes on his mouth and thought: What is he trying to say? His conversation was generally not beyond her understanding; if only he would speak coherently and calmly, she would understand everything. Her gaze followed his hand as she tried to fathom his meaning. Her mouth quivered. The new crease on her upper lip, near the right hand corner, twitched involuntarily. As she smoothed it with her tongue she thought: Dear God, how sad he is. Perhaps he has reminded himself of his daughters.

Hartmann had indeed reminded himself of his daughters: they had not been out of his thoughts all day. Although he had not mentioned them to Toni, not even indirectly, he was constantly thinking of them, now of the two of them together, now of each one separately. Beata, the elder, was nine, and she was old enough to realise that Daddy and Mummy were angry with one another. But Renata, who was only seven, had not yet noticed anything. When the atmosphere at home had become too strained, Toni's cousin had come and taken the children to live with her in the country, and they didn't know that Daddy and Mummy . . . Before Hartmann could pursue his thought to the end, he saw Beata's eyes, the way they had looked when she had seen Daddy and Mummy quarreling for the first time. Her childish curiosity had been mingled with dull surprise at the sight of grownups quarreling. Hartmann had hung his head before his daughter's eyes as they grew dark with sorrow and her mouth assumed an expression of voiceless anguish. Then she had lowered her eyelashes and gone out.

Once again Hartmann felt the need to do something. Not knowing what to do, he removed his hat, mopped his brow, wiped the leather band inside his hat and put it back on his head. Toni grew sad: she felt as if she were responsible for all his troubles. She took the parasol which Svirsh had hung from her belt and toyed with it. Meanwhile Hartmann had begun talking again. He made no reference whatever to the day's events, but they were all reflected in his voice. Toni answered him vaguely. If she were aware of what she was saying, she would have noticed that she, too, was talking to no particular purpose. But Hartmann accepted her replies as if they were to the point.

A little girl approached them and held out a bunch of asters to Hartmann. Perceiving her intention, he took out the purse and threw her a silver coin. The child put the coin in her mouth but did not move. Hartmann looked at Toni inquiringly: What could the child be wanting now? Toni stretched out her hand and took the flowers, inhaled their scent and said: 'Thank you, my dear.' The girl twisted one leg round the other, rocked back and forth, and then went away. Toni looked affectionately at her retreating figure, a sad smile on her lips. 'Ah,' said Hartmann smiling, 'she's an honest little trader. If she gets money, she has to give goods in exchange. Well, this is one transaction I've emerged from safely.'

Toni thought: He says, this is one transaction he's emerged from safely; that means there was another transaction he didn't emerge from safely. She raised her eyes to him, even though she knew that he was not in the habit of talking to her about his business affairs. But this time he opened his heart, and without any prompting began discussing business. He was involved in transactions he had entered into unwillingly, and now he could not extricate himself. These had led to disputes, quarrels and fights with partners and agents, who had bought merchandise with his money and, on seeing they were likely to incur a loss, had debited the amount to him.

Hartmann had started in the middle, like one who is preoccupied and talks of the things that are weighing on his mind. A person unfamiliar with the world of commerce could not have made head or tail of what he was saying, and Toni certainly knew nothing about business. But he ignored this and went on talking. The more he talked, the more confused he made matters sound, until his patience gave way completely, and he began to vent his anger on his agents, on whom he had relied as he relied on himself and who had betrayed his trust, causing him financial loss and involving him in degrading fights and disputes. He still didn't know how to get rid of them. Realising that Toni was listening now, he went back and began from the beginning, carefully explaining each point to her. He now clarified what he had left unexplained in the first telling, and what he did not explain as he went along, he made clear later. Toni began to get the drift of his story, and what she did not grasp with her mind, her heart understood. She looked at him with concern, and wondered how he could bear so many worries without anyone to share them. Hartmann became conscious of her gaze and briefly recounted the entire story from the beginning. Suddenly he realised that he was seeing his affairs in a new light. Although he had not intentionally set out to prove himself in the right, matters now seemed clearer to him, and he saw that the problem was after all not so insoluble as he had thought.

Toni listened attentively to all he said and realised that his angry mood had been due entirely to his business worries. She applied her new knowledge to the other matter, to the divorce. It was as if he had said, 'Now you know why I have been so short-tempered, now you know why we have come to this, to getting divorced I mean.'

Toni was thinking about the divorce and the period leading up to it, but she did not divert her attention from what he was saying. She lifted her brown eyes, which were full of trust and confidence, and said: 'Michael, I'm sure you'll find a suitable way out of it.' She looked at him again, trusting and submissive, as if it were not he but she who was in trouble, and as if it were she who was seeking help from him. He looked at her as he had not looked at her for a long time past, and he beheld her as he had not beheld her for a long time past. She was a head shorter than he. Her shoulders had grown so thin that they stuck out. She was wearing a smooth brown dress, open at the shoulders but fastened with rings of brown silk through which two white spots were visible. With difficulty he kept himself from caressing her.

II.

Hartmann had not been in the habit of talking to his wife much, least of all about business. From the day he had built his house he had tried to keep home and office completely separate. But business has a way of not letting itself be shaken off. Sometimes he would enter the house looking worried. At first, when their love was still strong, he would fob Toni off with a kiss when she asked him to tell her what was worrying him. At a later stage, he would change the subject. Later still, he would scold her: 'Isn't it bad enough that I have worries outside? Do you have to go and drag them into the house? When a man's at home he wants to take his mind off business worries.' But a man cannot control his thoughts, and they would come crowding in on him, turning his home into a branch of his shop. The difference was that when he was in the shop, his business affairs got the better of his thoughts, while at home his thoughts got the better of him. His father had not left him any inheritance, nor had his wife brought him a dowry; whatever he had acquired had been the result of his own exertions. He applied himself to business and kept away from other matters. That is how it had been both before and after his marriage. While still a bachelor he had thought: I'll get married, build a home and find contentment there; but when he did get married and built a home, he found himself stripped of all his expectations. At first he had solaced himself with hope, but now even that was gone. True, his wife did her best to please him, and the daughters she had borne him were growing up. On the face of it, he had no complaints against his home; the trouble was he did not know what to do with himself there. At first he had had numerous friends, but as time went on he had lost interest in them: it seemed to him that they only came on Toni's account. At first he used to look at the books Toni read and tried to keep up with them. But after reading three or four books, he stopped: the love affairs, dresses, plots and sentiment with which they were filled—what need had an intelligent man to know of such matters? Would I care to hob-nob with such characters?

From the books he drew inferences about Toni, and from Toni about the whole house. Since he knew only his shop and was not in the habit of frequenting clubs, he had no recourse after locking up but to return home. And since, once at home, he did not know what to do, he grew disgusted with himself. He began to find solace in smoking. At first he smoked in order to smother his thoughts; and he went on smoking because they were smothered.

He began with cigarettes, and went on to cigars. At first he smoked in moderation, but later took to smoking continuously, until the whole house was filled with the smell of tobacco. He did not consider that he was in any way harming himself; on the contrary, he congratulated himself on the fact that he was sitting quietly by himself and not demanding anything of others. Every man has his form of pleasure: I derive mine from smoking, she derives hers from other sources. And since he didn't trouble to discover what her form of pleasure was, and he failed to find satisfaction in his own, he became troubled at heart and began to be jealous on her account of every man, woman and child, in fact of everything. If he saw her talking to a man or chatting with a woman or playing with a child, he would say: Has she no husband or children of her own that she has to chase about after others?

Michael Hartmann was a merchant, and he sold his goods by weight and by measure: he knew that to waste a measure meant losing it. Eventually he reconciled himself to the situation, not because he condoned her activities, but because she had come to assume less importance in his eyes.

III.

The sun was about to set. In the fields the wheat swayed silently, and the sunflowers gazed one-eyed out of their darkening yellow faces. Hartmann stretched his hand out into the vacant air and caressed Toni's shadow.

All around him the silence was complete. Toni took the parasol and poked at the ground in front of her. Her action seemed devoid of both purpose and grace, and that bothered him. Once again he extended his hand and caressed the air. By now the sun had ended its course and the sky had become dulled. The countryside took on an appearance of desolation, and the trees in the field grew dark. The air began to grow cool and the cucumber beds were fragrant.

High up in the sky was a tiny star, the size of a pinhead. Behind it another star made its way through the clouds and began shining, and other stars followed.

The houses and barns stood in comfortable silence, and the smell of burnt weeds and of cattle rose from the pasture. Michael and Toni walked along silently. A boy and girl sat with their arms twined about each other, talking; then their voices broke off abruptly, and the scent of hidden desire hung in the air. A light breeze sprang up, but no sound was heard. A little boy ran past holding a burning brand. He too had run like that in his childhood once, when his mother had found herself without matches and had sent him over to the neighbor's to fetch a light. He took out a cigarette and was about to light it; but the scent of the fields took away his desire to smoke. He crumbled the cigarette between his fingers and threw it away. He smelt his fingers and wrinkled his nose.

Toni opened her handbag, took out a bottle of scent and sprinkled her hands with it. The scent reached his nostrils and put him in a good mood. So, so, he said to himself, by way of assent or as a question.

After his talk with Toni, in which he had told her all about that business, he began chiding himself for never, in all those years, discussing his affairs with her. If he had not snapped at her every time she wanted to know something about his doings, perhaps her interests would have grown closer to his, and they would not have come to regard themselves as such strangers to one another. This lesson was good for him at the moment, since it enabled him to blame himself and to justify Toni.

Again he folded his thumbs together and said: 'I can't stand that Svirsh.'

Toni hung her head and said nothing.

Hartmann repeated: 'I simply can't stand him.'

'And Dr. Tenzer?' Toni asked softly.

'Dr. Ten-zer?' said Hartmann angrily, stressing each syllable of the name. 'I hate all the Tenzers of this world. They never seem to try and get anything for themselves. All they ever do is lie in wait for things meant for other people. I know what that fellow Svirsh is after. Whenever I see those pink eyes of his and his manicured nails, I know at once what he wants. But with Tenzer you never know where you are. He makes himself out to be in love with the whole world, but in reality he doesn't love anything. He runs after women, but he doesn't love any woman for herself, because she's pretty, or because she's this or that, but because she's another man's wife. The very fact that someone else has an interest in her makes her desirable to Tenzer.'

Toni lifted her face towards Michael. It was night, and he could not see her eyes, but he felt that they were thanking him, as if he had taught her things she could never have learned by herself. Hartmann, who had been angry with himself for mentioning Svirsh and Tenzer, now experienced a feeling of relief, and he looked about him with a sense of freedom and happiness. He saw a light glimmering in the darkness. He stretched out his arm and, beckoning Toni with his finger, said: 'Do you see that light?' Toni looked and said: 'Where?' 'Really, really, I can see the glimmer of a light over there,' he said. 'It's the lamp of an inn.' 'Is that so,' Toni replied, 'I thought it was a firefly.'

A slight shudder ran through Toni, giving her a mysteriously pleasant sensation. Hartmann's saying it was the lamp of an inn and not a firefly suddenly set her musing about the first firefly she had ever seen. She had been on a visit to her aunt's in the country. It was Sabbath, and she was sitting in the garden at dusk. A spark darted through the gloom and settled on her aunt's hat. Not knowing it was a firefly, she thought it was fire and became frightened.— How old had she been at the time? About seven. Now Beata and Renata were at her aunt's, and she, Toni, was here walking with their father.

'We can rest there and have something to eat,' Hartmann said. 'You must be hungry: you had no lunch. We won't get roast duck there, but at least we can have a meal and rest.'

Toni nodded in agreement. She was thinking, When did I recollect the firefly: when Michael pointed to the light, or when I said I thought it was a firefly? But she felt she must have been thinking about the firefly before, as she had been thinking about her daughters in the country. She shivered, as if the incident had taken place only now.

The road twisted and turned, now to the right, now to the left. The inn lamp kept on vanishing and reappearing. A moist smell rose from the earth. Toni shivered a little, though she did not actually feel cold. She gazed silently into the darkness, which was shrouding both her and Michael. Once more the inn lamp came into view, only to disappear a moment later. Toni drew in her shoulders, and a breeze passed across her body.

'Cold?' Hartmann asked solicitously.

'I think I see people coming.'

'There is no one here, but perhaps . . .'

'I've never seen such a tall person before,' said Toni. 'Do look.' A man with a ladder came towards them. Placing the ladder on the ground, he climbed it and lit a lamp. Toni blinked her eyes and drew in her breath. 'Was there something you wanted to say?' Michael asked her. She looked down and said: 'I didn't say anything.'

Hartmann smiled. 'That's strange, I fancied you wanted to say something.'

Toni blushed. 'Did I want to say something?' She looked at her shadow in silence.

Hartmann smiled again: 'So you didn't want to say anything. But I thought you did.'

Toni walked on silently at Michael's side.

Two shadows became visible. The head of one of them was close to Toni's, while the other was close to Hartmann's. Two young people came in sight, a boy and a girl. The whole atmosphere became charged with their unfulfilled desires. Hartmann looked at them, and they at him. Toni lowered her head and looked at her wedding-ring.

IV.

A little later they came to a garden fenced on three sides. The gate was open, and to the right of it shone a lamp. Some smaller lanterns, in the shape of apples and pears, hung from the trees in the garden. Hartmann looked at the sign and said: 'I wasn't mistaken, this is a restaurant. We'll get something to eat here.' Taking Toni by the arm, he walked in with her.

A plump loose-limbed girl was sitting in front of the house, cleaning vegetables and occupying half the width of the bottom step. She greeted them in a loud voice and lowered her skirt. Hartmann thought: She's red-haired and freckled. Although I can't see her in the dark, I've a feeling that's the type she is.—Toni shook her head at him. He gazed at her in astonishment. Could she possibly have sensed what I was thinking? He took her parasol and laid it on a chair, and placed his hat on top of it. 'Let's sit in the garden,' he said, 'or would you prefer to eat indoors?' 'No,' Toni replied, 'let's eat out here.'

A waiter came up, wiped the top of the table, spread a cloth on it, and handed them a menu. Then he fetched a glass of water and put the flowers in it, and stood waiting until they were ready with their order. Hartmann saw that most of the dishes listed in the menu had been struck out. He grumbled: 'Most of the dishes have already been eaten up.' Looking over Hartmann's shoulder, the waiter said: 'I'll bring you some others immediately.' 'You're hiding your wares under a bushel,' said Hartmann. The waiter bent down and said: 'The dishes we have struck out have all been eaten. Others have been cooked instead, but we haven't had time to enter them in the menu.' 'In that case,' observed Hartmann, 'we ought to be glad that we shall be getting fresh dishes.' 'Your pleasure is our happiness,' the waiter replied. 'Will you have brown bread or white?' 'When you eat in the country,' Toni said, 'you must have brown bread.' 'And what wines do you care for, sir?' the waiter asked. 'Wine,' exclaimed Hartmann happily, as if rejoiced to discover that such a thing still existed for people's delectation. He studied the wine list and placed his order.

'We're in luck,' he said to Toni. 'This is far better than we expected.' Toni smoothed the crease on her upper lip with her tongue, either because she was hungry or maybe because she could think of nothing to say in reply. The waiter returned with their order. Michael and Toni drew up their chairs and began eating. Toni was ashamed to eat too heartily, but her bashfulness failed to blunt her appetite.

The potatoes, spinach, eggs, meat, turnips and other things that the waiter brought them were all excellently prepared. Toni ate with relish. The stars winked at them from the sauce, and from the bough of a tree came the song of a bird. Hartmann covered his knees with his napkin and listened to the bird.

The girl they had seen on their arrival passed by. She gave them a glance of recognition. Hartmann looked at her and said, 'Didn't I say she was a red-head with freckles?' though in fact he did not manage to see whether she had freckles or not.

Toni lifted the glass with the flowers, looked at them and then smelt them. She had always been particularly fond of asters, they were so modest and lovely. She had planted some on her mother's grave, and those asters, not particular about growing in the best soil necessarily, would look at her gratefully when she came for a visit.

Again the girl passed by, this time carrying a basket of plums with both hands. The juice of the overripe plums gave off an odor of cloying sweetness.

V.

Taking his wineglass in his hand, Hartmann mused: Since the day I married her I never behaved so decently towards her as when I gave her the divorce. Unconsciously raising his glass higher, he continued: If a man quarrels with a woman, he has no right to live with her. Marriage without love is no marriage at all. Divorce is preferable to a quarrelsome marriage. He put down the glass, moved the cruet-stand, and selected a toothpick. Following the same trend of thought, he reflected: If a man marries a woman and does not love her, he has to give her a divorce. If he doesn't divorce her, he has to love her. And that love has to undergo constant renewal. 'Did you say anything?' Toni stretched out her hand, pointed to the tree, and said: 'A bird.'

Hartmann looked at the tree.

'Is that the one that was singing,' Toni asked, 'or was it another one?'

'Of course it was,' Hartmann replied with great animation, although his certainty rested upon insecure ground.

Toni leaned her head on her left shoulder and thought to herself, 'That little creature sits hidden in a tree, and its voice brings a thrill to one's heart.'

Hartmann clenched his fingers and looked at Toni as she sat with her head resting on her shoulder. Her shoulders seemed to him to be hidden, and two white specks peeped at him through the openings in her dress where her blouse had slipped down, exposing one shoulder. Now, Hartmann thought, we shall see the other one. Unconsciously he rapped on the table. The waiter heard and came up to them. Once he had come, Hartmann took out his purse, paid the bill and tipped him. The waiter thanked him and bowed profusely: either he was drunk, or else the tip was larger than he had anticipated.

The meal had been a good one, and it had cost Hartmann less

than he had expected. He sat with a feeling of contentment and ordered a quarter-bottle of brandy for himself and a sweet liqueur for Toni. He took out a cigar and trimmed it with his knife. Then he offered his cigarette case to Toni. They sat opposite one another, the smoke from the cigar and cigarette mingling. Above them shone the little lantern, and above the lanterns shone the stars. Toni parted the smoke with her fingers and went on smoking tranquilly. Hartmann looked at her and said: 'Listen, Toni.' Toni raised her eyes to him. Hartmann put down his cigar and said: 'I had a dream.'

'A dream?' Toni closed her eyes as if dreaming herself.

'Are you listening?' Hartmann asked. She opened her eyes, looked at him, and closed them again.

'I don't remember whether I had this dream last night or the night before,' he went on. 'But I remember every detail of it, as if I were dreaming it now. Are you listening, Toni?' She nodded her head.

'In this dream I was living in Berlin. Suessenstein came to visit me. You remember Suessenstein? At the time he had just returned from Africa. I'm always glad to see him, for he brings with him an atmosphere of the far-off places I used to dream of in my childhood. But that day I wasn't glad. Perhaps it was because he came in the morning, when I like to sit by myself. Perhaps it was because in dreams we aren't always happy to be with the people we enjoy when we're awake. He had someone else with him, a young man to whom I took a violent dislike the instant he walked in. He acted as if he had knocked about with Suessenstein on all his travels. But for Suessenstein's sake I treated him civilly. Are you listening?' 'I'm listening,' Toni whispered, as if afraid that the sound of her voice would interrupt his story. Hartmann continued:

'Suessenstein looked around at my flat and said: If I found a flat like yours, I'd take it; I want to stay here awhile, and I'm tired of hotels. I replied: I've heard of a very nice flat that's going in Charlottenburg. To which he rejoined: All right, let's go there. Wait, I suggested, let me phone up first. No, he said, we'll go there straight away. I went along with him.'

Toni nodded, and Hartmann went on:

'When we got there, the landlady was nowhere to be seen. I wanted to tell him off for being so impulsive, but I stopped myself, as my temper was very frayed, and I felt I was in danger of going too far. His companion urged the maid to go and call the landlady. The maid looked at him suspiciously, or maybe she just looked at him without any particular expression, but I hated him so much that I thought she looked at him with suspicion. As she went, the landlady came in. She was dark, neither young nor old, on the short side, eyes a trifle filmy, and one leg shorter than the other, though this did not seem like a blemish in her. On the contrary, she seemed to dance along rather than walk. A secret joy twinkled on her lips, a sort of covert, erotic joy, a virginal joy.'

Although Hartmann was aware that Toni was listening with interest, he nevertheless asked: 'Are you listening, Toni?' and went on.

'The rooms she showed us were very nice. But Suessenstein turned away from them and said: I wouldn't advise you to take this flat. Winter is approaching, and there is no stove. I gazed at him in astonishment: Who was it that wanted to rent a flat, I or he? I have a fine one of my own: I'm very pleased with it, and I have no intention of exchanging it for another. Suessenstein repeated: A place without a stove, a place without a stove, if I were you I wouldn't take it. Here the landlady put in: But there is a stove. But Suessenstein interrupted her: Where is the stove? In the bedroom. But the study, Madam, is all of glass. Are you looking for somewhere to live, or for an observatory from which to view the frozen birds? His words depressed me so much that I began to feel cold. I looked around and saw that the study did indeed consist more of windows than walls. I nodded and said: That's so. The landlady looked at me with her filmy but charming eyes, and straightened herself with a caper. I turned away from her and thought, How shall I ever get away from this cold? My skin was already clinging to my bones. I woke up and found that the blanket had slipped off my bed.'

After Hartmann had finished, he had a feeling that perhaps he ought not to have recounted his dream; and yet at the same time he experienced a sense of relief. In order, therefore, to give expression to both emotions, he assumed a tone of banter and said: 'That was a fine story I told you. The whole thing really wasn't worth telling.' Toni licked her lips, and her eyes grew moist. He looked at her involuntarily, and it seemed to him that it was with just such eyes that the landlady had looked at him. Now there was nothing wrong with her, except... except for something whose meaning he did not understand, but he felt that if Toni were to get up, she, too, would turn out to be lame. However, since that would not seem like a blemish—as he knew from the woman in the dream— it followed that even if Toni were lame, she would not seem crippled to him. He got up, took his hat, and said: 'Let's go.'

VI.

Toni stood up, removed her flowers from the glass, shook the moisture off them and wrapped them in paper. She inhaled their scent and paused a moment or two in the hope that Michael might sit down again: she was afraid lest on the way back something should happen to disturb their atmosphere of calm. The waiter came up, handed Toni her parasol, bowed them out, and followed them until they were out of the garden. When they had gone, he extinguished the lanterns.

The garden and its surroundings became dark. A frog jumped in the grass. Toni dropped her flowers in alarm.

The croaking of frogs rose from the banks of the stream. The electric wires were giving off sparks: something had obviously gone wrong with them. After a few paces the wires and poles disappeared from view, and other sparks could be seen: they were the fireflies, which dappled the darkness with their glitter.

Hartmann stood wondering. What has happened here? he asked himself. His mind was tranquil, as if his question had furnished the answer.

Gradually they reached the stream. It lay there in its bed, its waters gently rocking. The stars cast their reflection upon its formless ripples, and the moon floated on the surface. The cry of a bird of prey was heard in the distance, and its echo pierced the air.

Toni crossed her feet and leaned on her parasol. She lowered her eyelids and drowsed. The waves raised themselves up and fell back exhausted. The frogs croaked, and the river plants exuded a tepid smell.

Toni was tired, and her eyes dropped. The river willows whispered, and the waters of the stream undulated languidly. Toni was no longer able to control her eyes, and they began to close of their own accord. But Michael was awake.

Never in his life had he been so wide awake. The tiniest movement set his mind working, and he looked about him searchingly, lest anything of what was happening should escape him. It was good, he felt, that Toni existed for him in this world and at that hour. But what was good for him was not good for her. She was exhausted, and her legs were incapable of supporting her body.

'Tired?' he asked her. 'I'm not tired,' she replied; but her voice belied her words.

Michael laughed, and Toni looked at him in surprise. He laughed again and said: 'One day I was out walking with the girls. I asked them if they were tired, and Renata answered: I'm not tired, but my legs are.'

'The sweet chick,' said Toni with a sigh.

Hartmann was sorry he had mentioned the girls. He looked around to see if he could find a conveyance to take them back to town. But the earth was silent: no sound of a carriage wheel or motor. He looked in all four directions, to see if he could discover a telephone booth. He was filled with pity for this small woman who had not the strength to walk. Once or twice he supported her with his arm. Her dress was damp from the moist air, and she shivered a little. If he did not get her under a roof, she would certainly catch cold.

But the city was far away, and the air was dank. He wanted to take off his jacket and wrap it round Toni. But he was afraid she might refuse; and he did not want to do anything that would evoke her refusal.

Perhaps, Michael thought, there would be a bed for her at the inn where they had eaten. Taking her arm, he said: 'Let's go back to the inn.' Toni dragged after him, bereft of strength.

VII.

They took the same road by which they had come and found their way back to the garden. Hartmann shoved the gate open, and they went up the stone steps. The house was silent. The waiter was not to be seen, neither was the girl. Obviously the household was asleep, and no guests were expected. Every step they took cried out at the intrusion.

Hartmann opened the door to the house and stepped inside. He spoke a greeting into the room, but there was no reply. He found an old man sitting bent over a table, pipe in mouth, an expression of annoyance on his face.

'Is there any room to sleep here?' Hartmann asked. The old man looked at him and at the woman by his side. It was clear from the old man's expression that he was not pleased to see a couple who had turned up after midnight in search of a haven of love. He took his pipe from his mouth, laid it on the table, and, giving them a look of annoyance, said severely: 'We have one room vacant.' Toni blushed. Hartmann crumpled his hat and said nothing. The landlord took his pipe, turned it upside down, knocked it against the table and removed the ash. Putting aside the ash and the burnt shreds, he gathered the remnants of tobacco and put them back in the pipe. Pressing them down with his thumb, he said: 'We'll prepare the room for the lady.' Finally, raising his eyes, he said: 'We'll find a place for the gentleman as well. When we're full we usually make up a bed on the billiard table.'

Toni inclined her head towards the landlord and said: 'Thank you very much indeed.' Said Hartmann: 'Would you show us the room?'

The landlord got up and lit a candle. Opening a door for them, he followed them into a spacious room in which there were three beds, one of them made up. There was a washstand with two basins and two jugs filled with water, and a large decanter half-full of water covered with an inverted tumbler. Above the made-up bed hung a broken horn with a bridal wreath on it and a ram's head and the head of a wild boar with eyes of red glass hung upon the walls. The innkeeper took the tumbler, examined it, stood it upside down, and waited for Hartmann to leave.

Hartmann put out his hand to test the mattress. Seeing him do so the innkeeper said: 'No one has yet complained of not getting a good night's sleep in this house.' Hartmann paled, and his hand remained dangling. The innkeeper placed the candle next to the made-up bed and said: 'Now sir, if you'll come with me, I'll make your bed for you.' And he waited for his guest to accompany him.

Finally Hartmann grasped the innkeeper's intention. Taking Toni's hand, he wished her good-night. Her hand clung to his, and her eyes enfolded his heart.

A few moments later the inkeeper was making up Hartmann's bed on the billiard table and chatting to him as he did so. His annoyance gave way to affability. Now that the guest was without the woman, he considered him respectable. He asked his guest how many pillows he liked to sleep on, and whether he preferred a heavy blanket or a light one, and did he wish to take anything to drink before he retired for the night. Finally he gave him a lighted candle and a box of matches and left the room. A few moments later, Hartmann went out into the garden.

The lanterns had gone out, but a light from heaven illumined the darkness. The grass and the mandrakes gave off a damp, refreshing scent. A chestnut dropped from a tree and burst. Another chestnut fell sharply and burst.

Hartmann stood reviewing the night's events. After a brief pause he went across to the table at which he had dined with Toni. The chairs had been leaned against it, and the dew glistened on the bare table-top. Underneath the table lay a thick cigar. It was the cigar that he had put down on the table when he began telling Toni his dream.

'Now we'll have a smoke,' he said. But before he could take out a cigar he had forgotten what it was he had meant to do.

VIII.

'What was I going to do?' he asked himself. 'To get up on this little mound in front of me.' He had not really intended to do so, but once he had told himself, he went and did it.

The mound was dome-shaped, wide at the base and narrow at the top and not far across, and it was surrounded by bushes. He drew in his breath and considered: I expect each thorn and thistle has a different name. How many names of thorns do I know? More than I thought. I wonder if the gardener doesn't lavish more care on the thorns than on the flowers. Those gardeners destroy the thorns where they normally grow and plant them in the wrong places. Perhaps the names I know are the names of the thorns growing here . . . Suddenly he smiled: That innkeeper doesn't know what Toni and I are to one another. How annoyed he was when we asked for somewhere to sleep. Now let me see what's here.

He looked down on the mound and recalled an incident of his childhood. He had gone for a walk with some friends, and, seeing a mound, he had climbed it, then slipped and slid down to the bottom. He imagined himself back in the same situation, and began to be afraid he would fall; no, it was rather a wonder he had not already slipped and fallen to the bottom. And if he had not already slipped and fallen, he was bound to do so; although there was no real danger of his falling, his fear itself would make him fall; though he was still on his feet, his legs were beginning to give way and to slip, he would roll down, his bones would get broken.

He took heart and climbed down. When he reached the bottom he was amazed. How high was the mound, a foot or eighteen inches? Yet how it had frightened him! He closed his eyes and said, 'I'm tired,' and returned to the inn.

An atmosphere of calm pervaded the entire house. The innkeeper sat by himself in a little room, rubbing his ankles together and drinking a beverage to help him sleep. Hartmann slipped in quietly, undressed, stretched out on the billiard table, covered himself, and looked at the wall.

Strange, he thought, all the while I stood on the mound, I was thinking only about myself, as if I were alone in the world, as if I did not have two daughters; as if I did not have—a wife.

Hartmann loved his daughters the way a father does. But, like any other father, he did not forgo his own interests for the sake of his children. The incident of the mound had opened his heart. He was both ashamed and surprised. And he proceeded once more to occupy his thoughts with himself.

What had happened to him on the mound? Actually, nothing. He had got onto the top of the mound and imagined he was slipping down. And what if he had fallen? He would have lain on the ground and picked himself up again. He stretched out on the bed and thought, smiling: How ridiculous Tenzer looked when I took Toni away from that albino! There are still things left in the world to make one laugh. But let me get back: What happened on the mound? Not the one I was standing on just now, but the one I fell from. One day I went for a walk with my friends. I climbed onto the top of the mound, and suddenly I found myself lying in the ditch . . . He did not remember himself actually falling, only that he was lying in the ditch. Something sweet was trickling into his mouth, his lips were cut, his tongue swollen, and his entire body bruised. But his limbs felt relaxed, like those of a man who stretches himself after throwing off a heavy burden. He had often fallen since then, but he had never experienced such a feeling of calm on any of the other occasions. It seems that one does not have to taste such an experience more than once in a lifetime.

IX.

He extinguished the candle, closed his eyes, and sought to recollect the event. The details of it were confused, as in a dream. From the walls of the house a cricket sounded, then stopped, and the silence became twice as intense. His limbs relaxed, and his mind grew tranquil. Once more the cricket chirped. What I want to know, said Hartmann to himself, is how long he's going to go on chirping. As he framed the question, he began thinking of Toni. He could see her face, and her movements, and also the two white spots where her skin showed through the brown dress . . . There's no doubt about it, she isn't young. Even if her hair hasn't turned grey, she has many more wrinkles. The worst of them all is that crease in her upper lip. Has she a tooth missing?

He still thought of Toni critically, as he always had, but now he felt that all those shortcomings in no way detracted from her. With a sweet feeling of adoration he summoned up her face, that wonderful face; but then it began to fade away from him, against his will. How thin her shoulders were, but her figure was that of a pretty girl. Hartmann embraced the air with his arm and felt himself blushing. As he was talking to himself he heard a sort of cry. Since he was thinking about his wife, it seemed to him that the sound came from her room. He opened his eyes and lifting his head, listened intently. Help me, O Lord, help me. Has anything happened? In reality he could have heard nothing, for there was a thick wall between them. Nor was it a cry of distress he had heard. Nevertheless, he sat upright on his bed in case he should hear anything, in case anything of her vital being should reach his ears. Perhaps he might be able to help her. Once again she appeared before him the way she had looked that day—lifting her veil onto her forehead, raising the asters to her face, digging her parasol into the ground, parting the cigarette smoke with her fingers. Gradually the parasol vanished, the smoke dispersed, and the asters grew more numerous, until they covered the whole mound. Astonished and puzzled, he gazed in front of him. As he did so his eyes closed, his head dropped on the pillow, his soul fell asleep, and his spirit began to hover in the world of dreams where there was nothing to keep them apart.

SHAITANA

by Moshe Smilansky

I.

IBRAHIM THE hunter was young; just eighteen. His family dwelt far away by the Tigris. While yet a boy he had been accustomed to hunt with his father in the plains which lie between the Tigris and the Euphrates, and between one catch and the next his father was wont to tell tales. Old and replete with days was the father. He had passed through the whole length and breadth of the land, had seen many kinds of men and met with many kinds of beasts; many were the vicissitudes which had passed over him. All that he had heard and all that he had seen he related to his son. Ibrahim listened with rapt attention to his stories and could not say which he preferred—the hunting or the tales of his father. Sometimes they would chance on a leopard by the way, but they would not stop their conversation until it was right upon them, and the nearness of the peril set their blood coursing. When they had done skinning the leopard the father would continue to tell; and the son, to hearken.

And of the Huleh swamp did he hear from his father. Sixteen years of age he had been, and when he heard thereof his heart was filled with a quaking and his soul with a mighty yearning. And he said to his father in a trembling voice:

'Father, I would view the Huleh.'

A shadow had crossed the face of the old man, and he was angered and said:

'Thou art still unskilled, my son. Eighteen years of age was I when I forsook my father at this spot and went awandering across the wide world.'

This Ibrahim remembered, and entreated his father no further; for he knew that the old man would not go back on his word. But after the two years, when father and son were returning from the hunt to their tent, Ibrahim said:

'Father, eighteen years am I this day.'

The matter was not good in the eyes of the old man, but he did not go back on his word. He raised his eyes on high, poured forth his prayer to Allah, and said to his son:

'The East and the West, the North and the South, lie open before thee. Go thou forth whither thou wilt, and Allah bless thy way. And when thou dost return to the place where thy forefathers have dwelt, come thou to prostrate thyself on my grave.'

So Ibrahim kissed his father, took his gun and his wallet and went, walking by night and by day. Seven days and seven nights did he go, staying in no place longer than to cook his kill and still his hunger, sleeping no more than two hours after the sunset. And at the end of seven days he came to the foot of Hermon and the Huleh swamp, and lay him down to rest from his arduous journey.

II.

Now this had been the tale of his father:

When Allah created Heaven and Earth and the whole Universe, Satan, who rules the deeps, envied the Creator. And Satan planned maliciously, saying: come let me perform works like to the works of Allah. So Satan stood watching the works of Allah, and strove to do likewise. And upon the face of the deeps Satan created the like of all that which Allah created upon the face of the earth. And he created great whales, creeping things, fish, fowl, beasts and animals after their kind. Likewise did he create man and woman. In the image of the man and the woman upon the face of the earth did he create them. And Allah was told of the works of Satan; and Allah hearkened but did not storm nor grow furious, and did not ordain that Satan's works should be destroyed. For he knew that his works would not be lasting.

And in sooth Satan did not rejoice in his handiwork. When he went forth to traverse the length and breadth of the world he found that his living things were not as the living creatures of Allah. For the living creatures of the deeps were like to stone, without laughter or tears, lacking sorrow or joy. They did not quarrel and did not grow friendly. They did not do battle and did not make peace. And Satan was sad at heart and sought for that which Allah had done to His creatures, and which he himself had not known how to do. And Satan went and enquired, of the creatures he had made, wherefore and after what fashion they differed from the creatures on the face of the earth. What was it that they lacked? And none could answer, not even the man. But the woman whom Satan had created was wiser than all his creatures. And the woman opened her mouth and said:

'Thy creatures know not the secret of love.'

And Satan knew that the woman was right. And he traversed the earth day and night and sought love and the place whence it came. But none could tell him; for the secret of love is hidden with those who sojourn on high, and on high Satan does not come. And he did grieve, for he perceived that his design had not succeeded.

One generation passeth and another generation comes. Of the creatures which Allah had fashioned—upon earth the first were perished; but they had left their children and their children's children. Yet of the creatures which Satan had fashioned—when one grew old and died no other came to take his place. And Satan saw that evil had befallen him, but knowing that the woman he had fashioned was wiser than all his other creatures, he went and questioned her. And the woman said:

'Let thy creatures go forth upon the surface of the earth that they may learn to love. Then they will return to thee and increase and multiply and become many.'

And Satan knew that the woman was right this time as well, but he did not act according to her counsel; for he said to himself: If I let my creatures go forth upon the face of the earth and they see that it is good, they will return to me no more. And Satan strove to fashion new creatures in place of those that had perished, but he did not succeed, for he had forgotten the secret of creation. So he went to view the works of Allah and to do the like. But Allah had ceased creating, for the creatures He had fashioned in the beginning increased and multiplied of themselves. But all the creatures that Satan had fashioned had perished, and none was left of them saving the woman; for at the end of his work of creation had he fashioned her. And he drew near to her and said:

'Love me and let us raise a second generation, so that the memory of the creatures I have fashioned may not be lost.' And the woman answered him:

'Set me upon earth that I may learn to love.' And Satan replied:

'What surety dost thou give me that, after leaving my domains, thou returnest unto me?' And the woman answered:

'Set me in a spot that is half of the deep and half of the earth. There I shall see the creatures of earth and shall learn from their actions, but unto them I shall not come.'

So Satan did so, and set the woman in the Huleh swamp.

When the woman returned to the deeps, Satan came to her and asked:

'Hast learnt?'

'I have learnt.'

'Then let me come to thee.'

'I have conceived.'

'From whom?'

'From a man upon the earth.'

'I set thee in the Huleh swamp; how didst thou go forth to a man?'

'The man came unto me.'

'How could he?'

'But never returned.'

And Satan was wroth against the woman who had deceived him.

'Be not wroth. Thou shalt receive thy portion. At the turn of the year I shall bear twins. The male shall be thine. Satan like thee shall he be. And the female shall be mine, half of her a Shaitana and half human.

'And after I give birth I shall die. For I shall not live after I have been loved by a man.

'But when my daughter grows thou shalt set her in the swamp, and a man will know her: and of him she shall bear twins, a male Satan and a female, half Shaitana and half human. And thus shalt thou do unto the end of all generations, and the creatures of Satan will never cease in the world. And from Man, from the pride of Allah's creatures, shalt thou take them.'

III.

At midnight, seven days after his eighteenth birthday, Ibrahim the hunter woke and hearkened. That night the sign would come. That night he would hear the voice from the Huleh swamp.

It was the last night of the November moon, and after midnight the first sharp early rains would descend. Ibrahim knew this by the east wind which had begun to blow three days earlier at midnight; by the halo round the moon on its last days; and by the sun, which had been red and flaming as fire at sunset that day. Ibrahim knew that at midnight, with the birth of the new moon, the wind would come from the north bringing the early rains. And together with the north wind and the first sharp drops of the rains the voice of the Shaitana would be heard. For his father had told him that with the first rains she would appear in the swamp.

It was a dark night. Ibrahim's eyes could distinguish nothing around him. The darkness rose from the mountains and the valley; it covered him and pressed upon him. He knew that mountains were all around him, before and behind, enclosing the Huleh; but the mountains he could not see, nor even the Huleh; yet hear it he could. It was whispering quietly. The east wind which had blown for three days had ceased at sunset, and everything had become still and seemed dead round about. But the swamp did not cease whispering. The tall reeds did not end their speech.

And Ibrahim gave ear and hearkened.

From the north, far beyond Hermon, he could hear the beating of the wings of the wind. Then he knew that the rain was come. The air of the Huleh trembled, quivered and shook, and seized the heads of the canes and reeds so that they began to rustle and whistle.

'Hooee hoo hoo hooee yoo . . .'

The wind burst from the north, passing over Hermon which stood in its path, and seized the four corners of the Huleh as though it wished to whip up the swamp and toss it to the ends of the earth. The reeds roared and bowed to the ground, and the canes beat and chattered against each other, struggled together and strove to uproot one another. From the clefts among the mountains on every side came streams of wind, to meet in the Huleh and set about each other; then they united into one force that might overturn mountains and smash rocks, and turn the whole world upside down. The wind wept and wailed, bursting out now and again into the thin, high-pitched howling of a child, saddening the whole valley and wearying every living thing in it. Sometimes it would range and roar like a lion, so that the whole world would be terrified and tremble. Then it would suddenly laugh and whistle like a madcap, and the sound and echo would roll on and on and on. And then suddenly all the voices and echoes would become silent and vanish.

Ibrahim covered himself with his *abaya* and raised it over his head and face, leaving only his eyes uncovered as he sat waiting. The wind ceased; some unseen hand had taken hold of it and set a bridle in its mouth. Heavy black clouds crawled laboriously among the spurs and foothills of Hermon and began to conceal the whole of the Huleh. Low, low crawled the clouds, settling round Ibrahim's head; and the air became moist.

'Drip drip drip,' pattered the great drops of water, descending noisily and beating against the earth. The wind, which had stopped a moment, began to rage across the valley with renewed force. The windows of heaven were opened and sweeping rain, a flood of water, began to fall. Ibrahim swathed his face completely in his *abaya* and bent his ears to listen, while his eyes peered into the blackness of the Huleh.

IV.

Suddenly the lad started to his feet. Before him stood the appearance of a woman who had come out of the reeds of the swamp. A dim radiance from the reeds lit up her face. Thick black hair covered her naked body from head to knees. The hair was wet and glistened with water, and clung to her body. Her face was white as snow, clear and pure, and told of charm, sweetness, and modesty. Between her long black curling eyelashes two eyes black as night gazed at Ibrahim, their gaze full of a quiet sadness; and they seemed to beg, to entreat, to pray. Between the thick black locks that covered the body could be seen her white, translucent skin, and her two round and delicate breasts rose high. From the knees downward her legs were bound about with reeds.

'Who art thou?'

'A woman.'

'What is thy desire?'

'Love.'

'Wherefore?'

'For love I was created.'

'Who created thee, Allah or Satan?'

'Is it not all one to thee? My love both burn and my kisses sear. What hast thou to do with my creator?'

'Human women, whom Allah hath created, do not seek for love.'

'They seek but do not tell of it. All the maidens who see thee long for thy love.'

'Wherefore?'

'Because thou art beautiful. Because thou art young. Because thy sinews are iron and thy blood a fire. And woman was created to love man and desire his beauty and strength in her heart.'

'And wherefore do not the daughters of men tell thereof?'

'Because Allah hath created them thus. The secret of love He hath revealed to them, but the strength to seize love He hath not given.'

'Wherefore?'

'Allah was jealous. Only for Himself hath He taken everything. To others He gave but the half. To the one he gave the strength and the power to seize love, and to the second the secret of love.'

Ibrahim's rage began to scorch like fire. Should evil be spoken of Allah and he the believer stand by and remain silent? 'Be silent, daughter of Satan. All that Allah hath made He hath made good and beautiful.'

The words left Ibrahim's mouth and the face of the woman vanished. A blinding streak of lightning split the heavens and the whole earth was lit up. Thunder rolled like a wheel, rolled and crashed down, down, down to the foot of Hermon. The woman was not there.

V.

'Daughter of hell?' Ibrahim asked the heavens from which the heavy clouds had cleared in the morning, and which were light and bright. But the heavens did not reply. They remained silent. Ibrahim could not account for the doubt that had awakened in him. He did not believe that before him had stood the daughter of Hell of whom his father had told his tale. Could a daughter of Hell have had a face so gentle, so pure, so full of modesty? Are not the mouths of the daughters of Hell filled with wanton laughter, and do they not clamor wildly, and are not their eyes filled with impudence?

'But her mouth was full of maledictions.'

So Ibrahim decided that Allah had sent a Bedouin maiden to try him. And he guarded the matter in his heart.

VI.

On the heights of the Mountains of Naphtali sat Ibrahim, looking down at the Huleh. The sun had risen behind the Bashan and lit up the whole swamp. And the sun was vast, round, and full of light and warmth. The many-colored dancing rays of light which it sent to every side declared that the rain had stopped and the wind ceased. All living creatures had come forth at the sun's bidding and spread far and wide over the earth. Man was gone forth to his labor, to plough and sow. The beasts had gone forth to graze in the fields. The wild animals and the creeping things and the diverse kinds of fowl were out ahunting. The whole Huleh teemed with life.

The Huleh is extensive, beginning at the foot of Hermon and spreading westward to the waters of Merom. And it is broad, keeping the mountains of Bashan on the left from the mountains of Naphtali on the right. It spreads so long and broad that the eye sometimes fails to see the whole of it.

And it is split in two by Jordan, which also flows at the foot of Hermon. Jordan flows down southward in the arms of the Huleh, set about by fresh green herbage grown from its waters. And out of the two ranges of mountains standing sentinel on either side of the Huleh there descend streams of water, spring-water and rain-water, and slip between the rocks on the slopes, winding among the undergrowth and reeds till they join the Jordan. On their way they sometimes rest a while and spread out and stop completely, filling the empty places. And the standing waters become pools and swamps and consume the fruitful ground, so that the whole valley is split up into small portions of dry land and portions of swamp.

The portions of dry land are lush and rich with the fruit of the field; and men sow there three times a year. They plough, they harvest, they water; and again they plough, sow, and reap. Wheat they sow in the winter, durra in the summer after they have harvested the wheat, and melons after the durra is gathered in. Between the dry land and the marshes, tender grasses that are a fat grazing grow all the year round. And the fat grasses are eaten by the big cattle and the flocks; and of the water they drink and become fat, so that the eyes of a man grow bright to see them, and he cannot look on them enough. And the fowl of heaven are many, coming to feed on the creeping things which teem in myriads in the swamp. And the birds grow fat and greasy of flesh, and men trap them. And fish swarm in the streams of fresh water and men eat them; and the buffalo grows large as an elephant, thrusting into the swamp up to his belly and lying there cooling himself in the mud on hot days, eating the grasses till he grows like Behemoth; and men drink his milk. All these are the blessings of Allah.

Yet there is likewise death in the swamp. The standing waters are covered with green, and the marsh sends up a stench on hot days, poisoning the air and winging arrows of death at the men on the dry land so that they must flee to the hills. And in the marshes the papyrus and the bulrushes grow lofty and fine. Sometimes their modest appearance deceives a man, and he is drawn to them until the mud grips his legs and he falls and drowns without his place of death being known. So the entire valley belongs half to life and half to death; half to Allah and half to Satan.

From the mountain top Ibrahim gazed down at the Huleh, delighting in it; for the blue mist that covered it made it a thing of beauty indeed. The blue was translucent and bright, concealing nothing that was in the valley. Far away could be seen a swarm of men separating into small groups and spreading like ants to storm and despoil each separate field and stretch of land. Flocks could be seen grazing in the meadows and amid the rushes. Over and around the heads of men and beasts, flights of birds darted about singing happily.

'Life and death in the one place; blessing and curse arm in arm. Wherefore has Allah fashioned His world thus?'

Such were the thoughts of Ibrahim as he sat on his hilltop holding his staff, his gaze wandering afar, his *abaya* spread over his shoulders and then falling in a wing on either side of him. Across the hill passed a camel caravan on its way from Damascus to Acre. Long, long was the caravan, without beginning or end, every camel striding proudly. Each driver paced alongside his beast holding his staff, gazing head erect, bearing blessings from Damascus.

'Daughter of Adam or daughter of Hell?' Ibrahim returned to his former thoughts as he rose, set his rifle on his shoulder, took his staff in hand and proceeded to the Bedouin tents which lay on the slopes above the valley.

VII.

Where the Jordan emerges at the foot of Hermon there is a hill concealed on all sides, on the north by the Hermon, on the south and east by the Bashan tableland. Only to the west is it open, and it closes the entrance to the valley which leaves the Huleh and passes between Hermon and the plateau. On the west passes the Jordan, and between the grasses and mighty trees on its banks can be seen the Huleh; yet part only can be seen from here: its splendor lies to the south.

And the hill does not grieve because Allah has enclosed it about. It rejoices in his lot. All the year round it watches Hermon, viewing his manifold changes—and which of the lofty mountains have the like fate? The hill sees Hermon when, old age leaping upon him overnight, he turns white down to his middle, all his limbs frozen. Then men no longer dare to ascend to his summit; only as far as the border between Winter and Summer do they mount. The hill sees Hermon in his rage, when heavy black clouds attack him and muster all round him as though to take him captive. Then the old father of the mountains is covered entirely with darkness, and in the darkness universes are created and destroyed. Wheels roll and clatter, and thunders peal, and there is a noise as of many waters. The supports of the world fall one after the other, the whole land trembles and heaves, and Hermon does not know what happens behind the cover of his darkness.

But the hill knows everything in advance. Little by little the clouds disperse. A plenitude of water falls from the mountains. All its clefts and crannies run with water, which foams down from the crest of the mountain to its foot; and the whole valley is filled. Jordan overflows its banks and becomes a raging torrent. And this too the hill knows: fury does not endure for ever. On the morrow the sun will shine from beyond Bashan, its crimson rays will fall on the peak of Jebel esh Sheikh, there will be no further sign of clouds, and the old Lord of Mountains will bestir himself, and become radiant.

Then all the folds in his body are shown and the narrow paths are plain to see, twisting and winding up to his summit. The paths crawl like serpents; all the hills which are his body, and the deep deep valleys between those hills, all strain upwards. The valleys array themselves in growing herbage. The springs run down and become streams, now hiding and now reappearing. In the sun they seem like silver veins along the giant body.

On the slope of the mountain is an ancient fort, gazing through its black loopholes at the hill all covered in fresh greenery and conversing with it, telling tales of olden times. It tells of the great dreams which little men dreamed in it, dreams which fashioned it as well. The dreams have passed, the dreamers ceased to be, but the fortress cannot vanish; it must remain evermore, a witness of the dreams. The happy hill, whose face rejoices for the waters of the Jordan and which shelters under the shadow of Hermon, mocks at the old fortress and its mildewed dreams, which were created but to perish. For the hill knows that it will exist for ever.

VIII.

The sun was about to set when Ibrahim the hunter reached the top of the hill that dwells concealed. There he saw three solitary Bedouin tents, and it seemed a wonder in his eyes. Whose were these tents, and to which of the Bedouin tribes did the dwellers in them belong? At the entrance to one tent which had grown black with age, sat a wrinkled woman spinning. Beyond her, at the entrance to a second tent which was new, sat a Bedouin woman whose face and head were covered and whose gaze was fixed on the hillside. When Ibrahim approached, the two women were sitting silent and angry, and it seemed to him that they had been so busily engaged in recriminations that they had not noticed the guest.

'May your day be blest!'

The old woman raised her head and gazed at him in astonishment. The other woman did not turn her head.

'Be blest!' replied the old woman.

'A stranger am I in this place. To whose tent have my feet brought me?'

'Blest be the feet that knew their way. Thou art come to the tent of Sheikh Rashid.'

'Shall I see the effulgent face of the Sheikh?'

'Ere the sun descends behind the mountains the Sheikh will return from his flocks. And until the Sheikh returns let the guest grace us with the brightness of his face, and sit on the mat in the shadow of the figtree.'

So Ibrahim removed his shoes from his feet and sat beneath the figtree opposite the tent. And he wondered to himself about the women spinning. Was she the Sheikh's mother or his wife? And who was the second woman—young or old, daughter or wife of his bosom? And Ibrahim remembered having heard his father tell of one of the Bedouin Sheikhs around the Huleh, the chief and leader of a tribe, a man of vast flocks and herds and servants without number, a man of independent thought whose voice was heard among the great Sheikhs; and his name was Rashid. When the father of Ibrahim had gone hunting around the Hermon he had lodged as a guest in the Sheikh's tent.

Now Ibrahim wondered still more. Why had the Sheikh separated from his tribe? And where were the tents of all the Bedouins who hearkened unto his voice?

'I see that my guest has the seeming of one come from afar. Where is the mare upon which he rode?'

'Thy servant has never ridden in all his life. A footman am I, a hunter.'

The old woman stared at the speaker with great attention, and as though she wished to recollect something. Then she said:

'Seventeen years ago, when first I came to the tent of Sheikh Rashid, a hunter stayed with us as guest, a footman like thee come from afar, from the land between the Euphrates and the Tigris. Abu Ibrahim we called him, after the lad which his wife had borne him at the beginning of that year.'

'I am that Ibrahim, and my father was your guest.'

The old woman's face grew bright.

'Blessed be thy coming under our roof. A blessing will come to this house in thy footsteps. How the Sheikh will rejoice to meet thee! The name of thy father is still on his lips every day. Is all well with thy father?'

'God be thanked. My father knows how to hunt, even as seventeen years ago.'

While he was still speaking, the whinny of a mare came from beyond the hillcrest. The second woman stood up.

'Behold Sheikh Rashid himself, come from the flocks.'

Ibrahim turned round to see an elderly man come riding a fine mare from the trees that concealed the downward tracks. The other woman raised her head and walked toward the Sheikh with her head raised. Ibrahim watched her, and his heart swelled. Never had he seen so upright a woman, so erect a head and legs striding with so much courage, agility and charm. And he felt angered that the woman had not turned her face toward him, so that he had not seen what she looked like.

'See how she hastens to her husband. She wishes to show him her love, as though it were only of him she thinks as she sits here silent as a stone all day long. If thy father knew, if he but heard of it. Could he believe that in his old age the Sheikh would take a wife in addition to the wife he loved, who guarded him all the days of his life? If thy father but knew.'

The old woman approached Ibrahim and whispered in his ear:

'That a Sheikh of the Bedouin should take to wife one of the daughters of the Druze of the mountains! A Druze woman!'

Ibrahim listened without hearing what the old woman told him, for he was watching the Sheikh, and the young woman walking with raised head toward him. When she drew near, the Sheikh descended from his mare and stood by her. And she bowed to the ground and kissed his hand. Ibrahim's heart swelled. How beautiful was her bowing. And the Sheikh's face was bright. And Ibrahim knew that the Sheikh loved his second wife.

IX.

Sheikh Rashid rejoiced greatly to see his guest. And when his heart was eased by drinking strong black coffee, he whispered to him:

'It was the work of Allah. When thy father came to my tent I had but wedded my first wife, being then thirty years old. And until this year I never took another wife. But this year I have wedded Razali, of the daughters of the Druze who dwell in the mountain. And Allah hath sent me thee, the son of thy father. Is it not a good sign?'

'May Allah's blessing rest on thy house all thy days.'

'My friends and companions have departed and my tribe has forsaken me and removed from me, because I took a wife of the daughters of the Druze. The thing is come about from Allah. Allah led me to the mountains to purchase a flock of sheep. I purchased the sheep from one of the sons of the Druze and saw his daughter; and my soul desired her. So I paid him the wedding price of his daughter—as much as the cost of all the sheep. Did not the matter come from Allah? And the prophet—did he set his ban on the Druze women? The Druze are not one with the prophet; but this is only a woman. And what does a woman know? She does as her husband wills. Is it not so, son of Abu Ibrahim?'

Ibrahim agreed with the Sheikh. But his thoughts were far from him and his words. He was seeking for a solution to the question that had been oppressing him since the morning.

'They say that the Druze have intercourse with Satan. But do the womenfolk know anything of their husband's deeds?'

Ibrahim trembled at the last words of the Sheikh. 'Indeed? Do the Druze go hand in hand with Satan?'

'Allah knows the secrets of the heart of man! Who can say? So the elders tell. Maybe they speak truly, and maybe they utter falsehood. But if the men have eaten sour grapes, shall the teeth of the women be set on edge? Is it not so?'

Ibrahim stammered a reply, and the Sheikh looked at him in surprise. But at that moment the old woman come out of the tent and set upon the rug cakes of bread, a skin of milk, cheese, eggs, and a dish of cooked food; and from the new tent the young woman emerged to sit at the entrance. Her face was uncovered and her eyes were raised to the Sheikh. And Ibrahim's heart died within him.

' 'Tis she, 'tis she!' the terrible thought hammered in his head. Aye! The same oval, dark, sad face; the same deep gaze of the eyes, filled with a melancholy piercing to the deeps; and the same charm and grace. The Sheikh saw how white the face of his guest had become, and he laughed in his heart, thinking: 'What man of all who see Razali would not do the like?' He did not feel jealous. He knew that his young wife loved him with all the ardor of her youth. When she nestled against him her love was fire and her kisses honey. Old the Sheikh might be, but his freshness had not vanished and he was no whit behind the youths. And therefore he continued to speak pleasantly to his guest, pressing him to eat of all the dainties which the diligent old housewife had prepared. Ibrahim heard without hearing, ate without eating. His thoughts were busied with the problem which had been picking at his brain from the morning, and which had now received a fresh turn.

'Which of the two is the woman, and which the she-devil?'

X.

A fortnight passed from the day that Ibrahim first came to the tent of Sheikh Rashid. In the morning and the evening ere the Sheikh went to the flocks and after he had returned, they would hold converse together, but he had not yet revealed his perplexity. He had wished to speak to the Sheikh, to ask him of the Huleh and to tell him of the woman who had spoken to him from the reeds; but he had not dared. He feared lest the Sheikh would grow enraged and drive him from his house. Every evening Ibrahim saw Razali, the Sheikh's young wife, when she went to meet her husband returning from the flock, and when she sat at the entrance to the tent, gazing with love at her husband. But during the day he never saw her, for she remained in her tent. At night the Sheikh would also join her there.

All this while Ibrahim wandered in the neighborhood of the Huleh, clambering amid the mountains and the valleys, hunting game and animals and speaking to all men regarding the Huleh and the district. Only of the matter that was oppressing him would he not speak; for he feared that he would become a laughing-stock. At night he would wander. He could hear the Sheikh's wife nestling to him in love. His ear would catch their whispered kissings and it would seem to him that he could feel their warm breath. Sometimes his heart would fill to bursting, and sometimes he would be drawn to the swamp. He would go and sit beside the reeds all night long and return as he had come. To be sure, he had known when he went that his trouble was in vain. The Shaitana would not appear on nights of moon and stars. Only with the north wind, with the rain and the darkness, would she emerge from the deeps to hover about the swamp and distract the sons of men. Yet his heart persisted in thinking: maybe 'tis a daughter of man pretending to be a she-demon. And the more he saw the Sheikh's young wife the greater grew the perplexity within him.

At the end of the fortnight Ibrahim awoke at midnight to hear a moaning beyond the mountain, which was covered with clouds. Rain is coming, he thought to himself, donned his *abaya,* took his rifle and set out. He came in silence to the place where he had been the first night. Then a sound was heard. The whisper of lips. The reeds below him spread out and a sight appeared before him, and he quailed. It was indeed the very young woman whom he had seen before, and she was the young wife of the Sheikh. The same and no other. His heart stopped within him.

'Son of man!'

'What is thy will?'

'Love.'

Ibrahim never answered, staring at the woman. Her face was so sad, and the charm of her pierced him through and through. Her innocent eyes were filled with a silent grief and a dumb prayer, as though she begged for her soul. His spirit surged. A question trembled on his lips, but he could not find the strength to ask it.

'Love me!' came the woman's voice. And it was so enchanting, so sweet, so compelling. Her long black hair fell over both her shoulders, and covered her tender fresh white body, which drew him and called him as though aloud. Her bosom rose and fell as she breathed heavily, and it seemed as though waves beating within were striving to burst forth. To Ibrahim it was as though a flame from her two breasts was scorching him.

'Who art thou? What is thy name? What hath brought thee hither?'

'A woman am I and thirst for love. And my desire hath brought me to this place.'

'Woman does not seek love. 'Tis the man that follows woman.'

'And what shall the woman do who knows no man?'

'Let her sit and wait.'

'And when her soul is wearied of waiting?'

'Let her pray to Allah.'

'For woman Allah hath hardened His heart. He hath given the world to the man.'

'Wherefore?'

'Allah's eye is baleful. When He created woman He saw how lovely and sweet was the work of His hands and He grew jealous of man. And in His jealousy He cursed the woman saying: "For him shalt thou long and he shall rule over thee".'

Ibrahim's wrath flamed like fire that the woman had spoken ill of Allah. He seized his rifle, aimed at her forehead and pressed the trigger. There was a tumult in the swamp; startled noises were heard, voices of dread, and the woman had vanished.

XI.

From the dawn onward Ibrahim wandered round about the hill, but could not pluck up courage to approach the tents. How would he be able to look the Sheikh in the face? And how would he find Razali? And would he find her? And if he saw her, what would he find in her? Although Ibrahim knew that in a little while the Sheikh would go forth to the flock, he did not approach the tents. Only before evening did he return and seat himself under the figtree. When the old woman asked him where he had been all the morning, he replied that he had found the spoor of a deer on the mountain and had followed it. And he did not raise his head when he spoke. For a long time he sat with his head bowed, fearing to look up and see the young woman. But she did not appear until the neighing of the mare was heard beyond the trees. Only then did the curtain at the entrance to the tent part and the young woman come out with her head raised even more upright and proudly than before.

When the Sheikh sat beneath the figtree and asked after his health and the reason for his absence that morning, he was exceedingly troubled and could not answer clearly. He knew that at that moment Razali was sitting at the threshold of the tent, with her face uncovered and her eyes directed straight at the Sheikh—and he did not look at her.

'Razali, what is the black mark on thy forehead?' the voice of the Sheikh reached his ear, and he heard him as in dream. He raised his eyes to her and saw that in the middle of her forehead, at the very spot at which he had aimed the night before on the brow of the woman in the swamp, there was a black spot like a scorch.

'It is nothing, my Sheikh!'

Her voice was sad, sweet, and quiet as always. Her face was suffused with charm, modesty and innocence, just as ever. Her black eyes gazed straight at the Sheikh, telling of love.

When the Sheikh had ended the evening prayers he blessed his young friend ere his sleep and turned to the tent of his young wife. Then Ibrahim called to him:

'Master Sheikh!' His voice trembled and his face was very pale. The Sheikh turned toward him in surprise and asked:

'Wherefore do you tremble?'

Ibrahim prostrated himself his full length on the ground before him, clasped his feet, and said in entreaty:

'Have mercy upon me, O Sheikh. Hear that which I tell thee. And if I sin with my lips slay me as one of the worthless.'

'Speak, my son, for I hearken.'

Ibrahim led the Sheikh behind the figtree and told him in a quivering whisper of that which he had seen and heard in the swamp. The lad spoke and the Sheikh listened with great attention, his face white and his eyes flickering like fire. And the more the lad told the whiter became the face of the Sheikh, and the more his eyes flickered and glittered. Ibrahim ended his tale and sighed silently; the old man faced him, dumb as any stone. Finally he said:

'Tomorrow, ere the sun rises, I shall take her from the tent and slay her.'

The lad shook as a leaf in the wind.

'God forbid, my master, that thou shouldst raise thy hand against her. Mayhap she is innocent and I have but seen a foolish vision.'

The Sheikh thought a moment, then said gravely:

'Thou art right, my son. I shall test her and see what is fated for her.'

And that night the Sheikh did not go to the tent of his young wife, but stayed in the old tent. And Ibrahim's spirit gave way within him, and he knew no rest all the night.

XII.

In the morning Ibrahim awoke and looked at Razali's tent. It was empty, and the hangings were raised. At the entrance of the old tent sat the old woman, busy embroidering, with satisfied face. The Sheikh's place under the figtree was empty. 'Why has the Sheikh gone to the flocks so early today?' thought Ibrahim. And as though the old woman read his thoughts she told him:

'Today the Sheikh went early to the flocks. Nor will he return until three days are past.'

'What has the Sheikh done to his young wife?' thought Ibrahim to himself. And as though in answer the old woman said:

'The evil designs of the Druze woman have at last been revealed. Tonight the Sheikh returned to me.'

'And she—where is she now?' Ibrahim asked aloud, stammering as he spoke.

'For her the Sheikh has chosen a cool spot and a soft couch. She is at the foot of the hill amid the trees. There she will rest for three days. And if she does not reveal her evil designs, she shall be food for the dogs of the field and the fowl of heaven.'

Then Ibrahim knew that evil had been done to Razali, and it irked him sorely, for he had brought it upon her; and maybe he had incited her husband against her without cause. He descended the hillside and stood among the trees. Looking around him his eyes fixed themselves on the sycamore; under its branches he saw the head of Razali—in the ground. He approached the tree in alarm and his hair rose on his head. A pit had been dug in the ground and Razali thrust into it; then it had been filled with sand till only her head was visible. And Razali's face was calm, quiet and innocent; but the sadness in her eyes was greater than before. It seemed to him that she was looking at him with dissatisfaction and reproach. He drew his sword, ran it into the pit and began to dig.

'Do nothing, great or small. Until the Sheikh has mercy upon me I shall not go forth from here.'

Her voice was low, quiet, and boundlessly gentle. Ibrahim ceased his labors and turned to the mountain. Three days and three nights did he wander on the mountain, neither eating, drinking nor permitting himself to sleep. And he poured forth his prayer that Allah should have mercy upon him and reveal the secret of the Huleh, the secret of the woman who had spoken to him from the reeds and of Razali, the wife of Sheikh Rashid. But Allah never hearkened to him. And at night, when the wind came from beyond the hill, his ears heard a thin wailing.

On the evening of the fourth day Ibrahim returned to the tents. From afar he recognized the Sheikh sitting in his usual place under the figtree. At the entrance to the old tent sat the old woman, spinning with downcast face. On the threshold of the new tent sat the young woman. Her face was uncovered and beautiful, and her eyes, full of love, gazed at the Sheikh. On her brow could be seen the black mark.

'Thy evening be blest, my master Sheikh!'

'Blest indeed, blest!' replied the Sheikh with even greater cordiality than usual, his face bright and joyful. 'Blest be thy return to my roof. Sit thou beside me and refresh thy heart.'

The Sheikh made room for his guest and sat opposite him. And when they had finished eating the Sheikh rose, led his guest aside and said:

'The matter came from Allah to prove her. Nothing but a vanity and a vision didst thou perceive. Her soul is pure; she is free from iniquity.'

XIII.

Ibrahim did not know what to do. He had intended to return to his father and his hunting, but could not. How could he return ere he knew for certain who the woman was that had spoken to him from the swamp in the storm? And how could he go ere he understood the soul of Razali? This and something else. Remorse powerful as death consumed him for the suffering he had caused Razali, and he took counsel within himself as to the way he might atone to her. Whenever he saw her his thoughts became confused and there was no peace in his soul. For whenever he saw the ardent eyes she turned on the Sheikh, his spirit would seethe. He would remember the gaze of the woman in the swamp: had not the same gaze rested upon him? From the time he returned to the tents the nights proved very long. All night long the ardent kisses of Razali could be heard. His soul flamed and his nights were wearisome.

XIV.

It was morning when Ibrahim left the tents of the Sheikh and went to walk beside the Huleh. The Huleh had awakened from the brief slumber of winter and was celebrating the festival of its spring. All the portions of land which men had turned over and made black were covered with a fine carpet of green, fresh, fat, happy green that gaily rose on high. The reeds and papyrus were green afresh, and the slopes of the mountains on both sides lay hidden under masses of flowers. The men, who had completed their ploughing and sowing, lay outstretched in their tents on the slopes among the swarms of flowers, slumbering among the intoxicating scents, resting until the season for new work came. Only the children were scattered, tending the horses, the cattle and flocks which trod the narrow strips between the dry land and the swamp, feeding on the fine green grass. The children watched them to make sure that they did not destroy the seed on the one side, and did not sink into the swamp on the other; the buffalo waded into the swamp up to its neck, and when it ascended from the mud with the green slime on its shaggy hide, it seemed like a creature of the infernal regions. When the beasts had eaten their fill they were full of gladness and began to skip and dance; so that the entire Huleh was filled with a lowing, bleating, whinnying, and neighing. A tall, black, lean, light-footed stallion, speedy as a leopard, tossed its head aloft, raised its eyes, shook its tail, and raced, like an arrow from a bow, towards the reeds. By the reeds stood a mare with her head hidden among the stems; she sensed the one who came to her, brought her head right out, sniffed the air, and stretched her neck its full length.

And the mare was beautiful. She was white as the snow on Mount Hermon, and her flesh gleamed like oil; her tail was long and woolly, and fell to the ground. Her mane was thick and tangled, and her hair fell in curls. Her head was small, her ears tiny, and her chest broad and out-thrust. The stallion did not come up to her but stood still, opened its mouth, and neighed so that the air trembled and was filled with the sound. Her silence was an answer, and he approached her. He shook his tail even more, and his nostrils swelled. He set his head beside hers and smelt her scent. Then she too whinnied tremulously and also twitched her tail. Again the air was filled with his neighing. All the horses near and far answered him, raised their heads and shook their tails, and each began to dash its own way.

The heavens were lofty, broad, and pure and holy. Deep were they as the abyss, and their giant arms embraced the full width of the Huleh; the ends of heaven reached the ends of earth and poured themselves forth in a kiss.

Ibrahim returned to the tents of Sheikh Rashid after sunset. Reaching the tents, he stood still and stared about him in wonder. Everything was still as death. Neither the barking of the Sheikh's dog nor the whinnying of his mare was to be heard. He came to the figtree but found no signs of a meal under it. What was wrong? Had not the Sheikh returned from the flocks? Such was not his wont; why should this day differ from others? His eyes fell on Razali's tent and he was suddenly consumed by a vast desire to know whether the Sheikh had returned from the flocks to the tent of his wife. He approached the tent, though he knew well how evil a thing he did. Among the Arabs one does not look into the tent of a wedded woman.

But he could not control himself. He was in the toils of an inexplicable spell which was too strong for him. As he approached he noticed that the curtains of the old woman's tent were tightly closed. 'She sleeps,' thought he, and the thought diminished his oppression of spirit. The curtain at the entrance to Razali's tent was not pulled tight, but swayed slowly in the air. Ibrahim approached and raised one corner.

The faint light of the moon glimmered through the covers and curtains into the centre of the tent. The couch in the corner was empty. Neither the Sheikh nor his young wife was there. Had his wife gone to him amid the flocks? Would she do this? And Ibrahim felt much aggrieved that Razali had followed her old husband to the flocks.

Deep in thought, he slipped unwittingly through the half-open curtain into the tent. He heard a movement behind him; something warm caressed his neck, and something smooth as a serpent embraced his whole body. A head crowned with black hair rose as though from under the ground, and through the hair flamed two eyes like two torches. A searing kiss scorched his lips. Ibrahim was in the arms of Razali, naked as at her birth.

'Thou hast come to me—dost love me? I have waited for thee—I love thee.'

Ere Ibrahim could speak the clatter of horses' hooves were heard outside the tent. The Sheikh and the shepherds of the flock were come. In another moment the Sheikh's mare stood at the entrance and his happy affectionate voice called: 'Razali!'

XV.

For three days and three nights Ibrahim was held prisoner in Razali's tent. That same night the shepherds of the Sheikh seized Razali by the scruff of her neck, dragged her out of the tent and beat her murderously with their ropes. Ibrahim leapt like a lion from a thicket and brought three of them to the ground under him; but their companions caught him, bound him with cords and cast him down beside the couch of Razali. He lay in the tent three days and three nights, seeing the armed shepherds who stood on continual guard over him, and hearing Bedouins and Druzes arriving and departing. And he heard the voice of the Sheikh instructing and giving orders. On the third day he heard Razali. She moaned as one who suffers grievous torment. When he heard her he shook all over and shouted bitterly:

'Bring Sheikh Rashid hither!'

The Sheikh came and stood beyond the tent. His face Ibrahim did not see, but could hear his voice addressing him:

'Let the son of Abu Ibrahim say that which is in his mouth, for I do hearken.'

'Let not the Sheikh shed innocent blood. Mine alone is the transgression. I alone have sinned. She is innocent. Her hand was not in this. Take me beyond the camp and slay me but do not raise thy hand against her!'

The Sheikh did not answer. Ibrahim only heard the sound of his feet as he withdrew from the tent. Razali's moans did not cease. Her torments still continued.

On the fourth day in the morning three guards came to Ibrahim in the tent, armed from head to foot, and loosed his bonds.

'Go hence and return where thou art come.'

Ibrahim leapt to his feet.

'What has been done to Razali?'

'Come get thee hence!'

Ibrahim turned his face eastward, and went walking toward the Huleh without looking backwards.

Suddenly he stopped on the hill slope. A soft moaning had reached his ears, the sound of mortal suffering. He turned his head toward the voice. Razali sat on the ground beneath the sycamore, her head bowed, her hair falling over her shoulders. Her hair shook slowly and through it could be seen her sad face. Out of her face two bleeding hollows turned towards him.

'Razali!' he cried and sprang toward her. Suddenly he stood stock-still, like a nail driven halfway home. Beyond the sycamore he saw the face of the Sheikh. Old age had leapt upon him. He was pale as death and his eyes spoke terrors. Great was the suffering on his face and sevenfold greater the grief in his eyes. Ibrahim glanced; then turned and went.

XVI.

The north wind came from beyond Hermon and shook the Huleh. The heavens became thick with black clouds heavy as lead. Rain flooded down to earth. Ibrahim did not go eastward to the mountains, but strode back to the swamp. And when darkness cloaked the face of earth and the rain became a flood, Ibrahim stood in the Huleh at the spot where he had already stood twice. And at midnight, as the reeds swayed, the head of a woman rose between the papyrus till she faced Ibrahim. The face was sorrowful, the hair was black, and in place of eyes there were two hollows filled with blood.

'Razali!' cried Ibrahim and leapt down into the swamp.

REB SHMELKE OF SAFED

by Yaakov Churgin

I.

DON'T BE alarmed if you happen to see Rivka Leah standing at the kitchen window while her husband is at work in the neighboring street, and from time to time shaking her hand with its five outstretched fingers, moving her lips in an unheard whisper, and spitting three times on the floor every few moments. Don't be alarmed. Rivka Leah has not gone out of her mind, God forbid. That is just her way of protecting her husband from the perils of the Evil Eye.

Nor is the protection at all unnecessary. But for her, there is no saying what he would be like, Reb Shmelke, her husband. Why, the fellow has no sense at all. Suppose the Creator has left him a little strength in his old age! Does he have to go swanking with it in front of everybody, just like a boy?

Reb Shmelke stands in the narrow street, hairy and broad-boned, his greasy waistcoat shining like a mirror, while under it hang down the tail ends of his *Tzitzit* and the bottom of his shirt, and all the while he loads boxes and trunks onto the roof of a lorry. Every time he heaves up a heavy box with his short powerful arms, Rivka Leah's head spins as though she were looking down into a deep abyss. She peers tremulously in all directions, her gentle eyes viewing the eyes of any passer-by with a furious hatred, prepared to scratch them out if they should but rest on her husband.

But more and more people gather in the narrow street, travellers and plain idlers alike. Scores of eyes observe Reb Shmelke, all full of nasty envy and evil at heart. Rivka Leah sees all this and her heart pounds within her for fear; yet he, the cruel thing, the murderer that he is, isn't at all sick or prepared to feel anything. He heaves up and loads, heaves up and loads on. And Rivka Leah feels like fainting at the sight of the way he is strengthening the unseen foe, and her power of combat weakens. Out of the window she thrusts her head in its colored kerchief embroidered with black and blue little glass beads, and in her plaintive voice you can hear both apprehension and an entreaty for mercy run together:

'That's enough! Even a machine has to take a rest!'

But, as remarked, Reb Shmelke has no sense at all! What does he care for his wife's fears! Why, he wouldn't twitch an eyebrow even if she were to drop down dead at his feet! So Rivka Leah complains to herself weeping in her distress. Her eyes fill with tears. Each and every eye out in the street bears thousands of plagues and troubles with it, all of them just waiting to befall her husband—but he, cruel murderer that he is!—has to heave up and load, heave up and hand the goods to the boy standing on the roof without a moment's rest or interruption, until the boy himself begs him in his exhaustion:

'Just a moment, Reb Shmelke! Let me catch my breath.'

'Catch hold, you molly-coddle! Why, I'm about seventy!'

'Teh-teh-teh,' Rivka Leah interrupts him with renewed fear and dread, 'he's counting out his years already... Better let the boy rest a bit! Have some pity...'

'And maybe you'll spare your tongue as well?' Reb Shmelke feels aggrieved at her concern for the lad.

'I'm taking pity on you as well!' Rivka Leah sees that he is annoyed and laughs in order to calm him down.

'And who'll work instead of me? Maybe father's servants?'

'Take yourself another help!' the woman responds hesitantly.

'And where shall I pay from, faithful wife?' Reb Shmelke continues the conversation without a moment's respite. 'From your father's dowry, maybe?'

And once it reaches that point—just stand where you are and lend your ears! Reb Shmelke will tell you for the umpteenth thousandth time, as he has already done for the past fifteen years, the dread and fearful tale of the dowry he never received. In the midst of his most pressing task he will stand up and wipe his moist eyes, and his running nose, and the sweat off his brow with one stroke of his sleeve—a really expert piece of work. Then he raises his voice so that it can be heard from one end of the Quarter to another:—His father-in-law had promised to give him one whole thousand Turkish piastres as dowry, and had given him only two hundred! The old fellow had passed away twenty years earlier, but Reb Shmelke is not going to forget the loss and shame, and he visits the sin of his father-in-law on his spouse whenever occasion offers.

'Well-well-well, he's beginning already . . .' Rivka Leah takes umbrage, and her head vanishes into the gloomy kitchen. But she does not leave her post. She keeps an eye fixed on him, through a crack in the wall, and continues to whisper her charms and spells so as to weaken the power of the Evil Eye.

Finally work is over. Only then does Rivka Leah feel free of her fear and struggle and returns to her housework, wearily, with moist eyes, as though she has been engaged in prolonged and very tiring toil. Reb Shmelke cleans his hands in his usual fashion, without using any water: he spits on his palms a couple of times and dries them on his knees, which have become so greasy with wiping that they shine as though they have been polished with lacquer. Then he sticks his head into the low kitchen window and growls:

'Prepare the Messianic Repast, Rivka Leah, I'm hungry!'

'Teh-teh-teh . . . Messianic Repast, of all things . . .' the woman echoes after him with stressed and artificial contempt, in order to reduce the effect of his display on anybody who may be listening outside. 'Eats like a bird and demands the Messianic Repast with its Wild Ox and Leviathan . . .'

'Certainly!' Reb Shmelke feels offended at the disrespect shown to his virility, and promptly draws his tried and tested weapon against her. 'And how'm I going to get that wild ox? With the dowry I received from you, maybe?'

'Well, well,' her voice softens to mollify him. 'He's beginning again already! Come in and wash your hands.'

But that's just the proposal which he doesn't approve of. He is prepared to try any job in the world in order to earn a penny: he loads up luggage and burdens, he's a guide to those who come to prostrate themselves at the holy graves, he purifies corpses and digs graves when necessary. There are only two jobs about which he is weak and lazy: they are hand-washing and the grace after food. Reb Shmelke is prepared to trick his stomach and his Maker in all kinds of ways, in order to evade these two duties. And when he succeeds in filling his stomach with all kinds of trifles and can do his duty by the Lord with the mere ordinary blessing—he feels as happy about it as though he had earned a fortune; and for hours and hours his face shines and he feels in the best of moods.

So Reb Shmelke does not take his wife's advice. Instead, he stretches out a hand, uncovers a seething pot, and sticks his hairy head into the cloud of steam to inspect it. The next moment, a large steaming potato appears in his hand. He tosses it from hand to hand to cool it off and puffs a real stormwind at it with his mouth, meanwhile biting bits off, grimacing at the heat and jumping and dancing heavily. But at length the potato vanishes, and for long moments afterwards his mouth steams as on a cold wintry day.

II.

If you see Reb Shmelke at twilight, sitting on the smooth stone in the gateway to his courtyard, keep your distance and don't disturb him. Reb Shmelke is casting up his day's accounts.

And there you are. Reb Shmelke has never been much of a one for figures. Numbers weigh on his head more than a heavy load. The hills looking at him all round, some with their bald tops and others with their heads wildly overgrown with trees, wink furtively at him and smile at one another with a cunning mutual understanding. If they had a mouth they would tell you all about Reb Shmelke's 'gentile' brain when he was little and still a pupil at the Heder, the Hebrew class. But let's not pay any attention to idle tattle . . .

The reckoning seems simple, but the figures mock him. They enter his brain in orderly and respectable fashion, all of them clear and nothing lacking. But when the time comes to add them together, they fall apart and scatter like a smashed string of beads . . . Sometimes they swell up into a real treasure, a great find, while sometimes they dwindle away to nothing . . . For a moment it seems to him that he has earned a vast sum. He's ready to jump from his place with joy and astonish his wife with a present of cheap sweets, as is his habit after a festival: sharing them out to her on Sabbath after dinner with a trembling and economical hand as though he were counting out money. That is the time when both of them sit on the porch of their house, feeding their eyes on passers-by and noisily sucking the sweets in their mouths, enjoying them like children . . . Then all of a sudden Reb Shmelke leans back against the wall in despair: he has suddenly found that the profit is very small. After the imaginary profit which he had just calculated—there is a very considerable loss here. Reb Shmelke feels the loss, and regrets it as much as though the money has actually just fallen out of his hands.

Once again Reb Shmelke needs his wife's aid. In his eyes this refractory reckoning is a deep enigma, and all his calm of spirit depends on solving it. Not that Rivka Leah can reckon better than he does. That is something which Reb Shmelke will never admit. It's impossible for any woman to be better than him at anything. It's simply that his head refuses to work now, while her head, after all, has nothing to worry about.

'Hey, you Rivka Leah! Come and let's see!' he calls towards the house hesitantly.

Rivka Leah knows quite well what her husband is inviting her out for. She appears wiping her hands on her filthy apron, all bashful, her apple cheeks doubly pink, just like a shy girl; as though she were being called to do something which is not quite proper. The knowledge that her big, strong husband requires her aid in reckoning worries her more than it does him. It is not nice for her to be better than he is at anything. He gives her the details of receipts and expenditures which he remembers very well, and lo and behold the account arranges itself quite smoothly and clearly with her aid.

'That's what I also thought,' smiles Reb Shmelke rather confusedly. 'My head simply isn't working today.'

'What with so much hard work and tiring yourself,' Rivka Leah explains the situation to encourage him, feeling even more confused than he does. She forgets that she is called on to aid him every day, and on each occasion his head simply isn't 'working.'

For just a moment Reb Shmelke wonders to himself at his wife's quickness, and steals a sidewise glance of astonishment at her, as though he had seen her for the first time. But he immediately feels a sense of shame which makes him seek some compensation to restore his honor. Rivka Leah turns round to re-enter the house, but he delays her. He stands up, shoving his old hat onto the back of his head with his fist until you can see the broad bulging forehead and the greasy embroidered edge of a skullcap. He waits a little while until there are quite a number of passers-by, then gives his wife his hairy thick hand with an expression of cunning gravity.

'Give me your hand!'

Rivka Leah knows what he is about. She blushes, straightens the kerchief on her head and looks all round, afraid and shy, like a young girl.

'Don't be a child, husband! Come into the house!'

'Give me your hand!' Reb Shmelke sternly repeats his order.

Her plump hand, round as a rolling pin, hesitantly, reluctantly, and with fearful submission creeps into the large male paw which closes upon it suddenly. Rivka Leah screws up her face with pain and cries out, but not too loud.

'Look, just look!' Reb Shmelke pretends to be surprised though the cunning pride of victory shines in his face. 'What are you shouting for?! What have I done to you?'

'Leave me alone! You're killing me!' Rivka Leah quivers with pain mingled with pleasure and pride at her husband's strength. Her eyes gaze at his in wonder and esteem through a thin haze of tears. But she suddenly notices the crowd of curious busybodies who have surrounded them and the scores of eyes watching her husband. With a tremendous inner effort she overcomes the pain, stops twisting, looks mockingly and says, shaking her head contemptuously:

'You can press from today till tomorrow. It doesn't hurt at all...'

'It doesn't hurt at all?!' The astonished Reb Shmelke presses more strongly, with all his strength. 'And now? How is it now?'

'Not now either...' declares Rivka Leah with difficulty, out of her heroic self-restraint, while her smile changes from time to time into a grimace of suppressed pain. Suddenly she gives way, utters a choked scream and begins to twist and quiver and entreat weepingly:

'Enough! Have pity on me! Let go!'

'Ha-ha-ha!' laughs Reb Shmelke at the top of his voice in satisfied victory. Now he lets her go and turns to the onlookers with childlike bravado:

'Have you ever seen such a heroine? I just touch her—and she begins to howl!'

'Teh-teh-teh!' Rivka Leah promptly forgets her pain and also turns to the onlookers. 'Do you suppose that he's such a hero? For whole nights on end he twists and turns with his aches, and he moans and groans . . .'

'Me?!' Reb Shmelke is insulted and all prepared for battle.

'Of course . . .' she answers weakly this time, hesitating to give way and thus leave an opening for the envious Evil Eye.

'Of course . . .' Reb Shmelke repeats after her, feeling it necessary to avenge his affronted honor on the spot. 'Where should I find strength? What should I eat from? Maybe from your father's dowry?'

And the ears of the assembly once again hear the tale of the dowry that was never paid. The tried and tested weapon has its effect at once. Rivka Leah retreats from the battlefield in shame and confusion.

III.

While we chat about the old couple, the sounds of argument and shouting and noise come from Reb Shmelke's courtyard. And be it known and understood: any dispute and quarrel is a greatly desired thing at this place. Men who take pleasure at the sight, and beefy women all glowing with excitement, come running and hurrying. So do the hills and mountains round about, crowding together at the end of the steep street, at the entry just opposite, and watching with grave and solemn satisfaction as though observing a scene on a stage. And here—make way, make way!—here comes burly Mount Atzmon as well, thrusting his broad shoulders between the scamps of hills which start back on either side, bearing proudly his cleft head with the grey turban of clouds, and watching the while . . .

Let us hurry across as well. What has happened? Everybody is opening his mouth, talking in confusion, trying to let us have all the details at the same time. Everybody, men and women and children and the measly old carob tree in the courtyard and the pair of underpants spread wide apart on one of its branches. But here you mustn't depend on rumor. The fine climate of the spot gives rise to magnificent fruit, rounds the cheeks of girls, and brings up a hundred and twenty measures for every single seed of rumor. At the open window are scores of heads. Rivka Leah stands in the corner, abashed and wiping away her tears. Reb Shmelke, flaring and flaming fit to terrify, stands at the window, orating to the assembly about that dowry. It turns out that Reb Shmelke's poor capacity for reckoning is what has caused this sudden quarrel. And this is the story:

In the middle of the night Reb Shmelke woke up to a sound like the clinking of metal coins as they fall into a tub. By the light of the little lamp, kept burning all night for fear of nocturnal possibilities, he saw before him the figure of a woman in a long nightdress with flashing eyes standing motionless with his trousers in her hands. A demon, Reb Shmelke decided, and immediately shouted out 'Hear, O Israel!', pulled his blankets right over his head, turned his back on the demon, and began yelling all kinds of queer and choked howls in a voice that was not his own. These howls roused the frozen female form and she began to calm him and to talk to him in precisely the voice of his wife. Yet not even Ashmedai, King of the demons his own honorific self, was going to fool Reb Shmelke. As a member of the Hevra Kadisha, the Burial Society, he was well versed in the demons and spirits and knew all their signs and distinguishing marks. He poked a furtive eye out of his blanket and, twisting round cautiously, inspected the feet of the thing. And lo and behold! he found no chicken shanks but the worn slippers of his spouse, which had been sewn out of a bald old piece of fur. Then his fears fled and he was prepared to fall upon his wife's neck and kiss her for saving him from the attack of a demon—but he immediately noticed his trousers in her hand, and sat up in the bed full of surprise and suspicion.

'What were you doing with my trousers, Rivka Leah?'

'With your trousers!' She was taken aback. Only now did she notice that in her fright she had forgotten to drop the trousers. 'Nothing at all . . .' she stammered, letting the garment fall onto the chair as though it were some kind of poisonous insect. 'I wanted to mend them . . .'

'At night!' Reb Shmelke grew even more suspicious. 'Thievingly?'

She could not think up any excuse but stood before him like a child caught at some mischief, and trembled all over. Reb Shmelke began to rage at her silence, jumped up and beat his fist on the nearby table:

'If you don't confess, it means a divorce!'

Rivka Leah was trembling all over, but simply couldn't talk. There was another blow on the table and another shout of divorce—and Rivka Leah burst out weeping . . . Then Reb Shmelke thought it over and changed his tactics: he promised to forgive her if she told him the truth.

Rivka Leah took heart at his promise and confessed, with fresh tears, that she had tried to take a few coins out of his pocket in order to get his shoes repaired. He had been walking round with holes in his shoes for weeks now, but he wouldn't give her a penny.

Reb Shmelke did not hear the explanation. All that stuck in his brain was the attempt at a theft. He promptly decided that this could not be the first time she had been going through his pockets! She must have been behaving like this ever since their wedding, that means fifty years on end, night after night. The idea was terrible, and even worse was his attempt to reckon up how much had been stolen from him during this long time: fifty years, three hundred and sixty-five nights each year, and a couple of coins each night! He simply could not reach any definite sum and for this very reason the indefinite figure rose frighteningly, menacingly, agitating his mind to madness. So it was not by chance that he had remained poor and needy to this very day! He had been toiling and laboring and working, all for a pocket with a hole in it. To begin with, of course, she must have stolen and given to her father in order to deprive him even of the miserable part of the dowry that he had received. Now she was doubtless sharing it out to her brothers. All of them were fattening up and having a good time on his account.

Once again he jumped over to the table and beat it with both his fists:

'I've had enough! It's a divorce tomorrow!'

Rivka Leah trembled and wept. She tried to beg for mercy. It was the first time she had ever tried such a trick and after all what she had done she had done only for his sake! But in vain. That indefinite figure swelled from moment to moment in Reb Shmelke's brain and received the very concrete form of piles and heaps of coins, of hundreds of pounds. In his imagination he began searching among the pillows in the homes of his brothers-in-law and discovering piles of money—all his, the quintessence of his heart and blood. They had murdered him, slaughtered him, drunk up all his blood—and all by the advice of his father-in-law, may he roast in Gehenna and never rise at the Resurrection, when the dead come back to life! No... and another terrible bang: 'We're getting divorced tomorrow!'

He promptly began to regret his concession. How could he simply let her go and leave all his money with her brothers? He demanded that she should return all she had stolen, to the very last farthing. Her oaths and protestations did not convince him. Nobody was going to fool Reb Shmelke. That was why his young brother-in-law had been looking so fine and bright lately. Now he understood where his older brother-in-law had found himself the money to buy a goat. All that wealth had been sweated out of his own flesh and blood, they had gone and slaughtered him, murderers that they were!

'We'll get divorced tomorrow!'

And to prove the point he went out into the corridor. Henceforward she was forbidden to him like a strange woman. He was not to have anything to do with her. And Rivka Leah remained standing where she was, weeping.

IV.

Next morning they went out to go to the judges. Reb Shmelke was in advance, heavy, fuming, without a coat after his fashion. Behind him trailed Rivka Leah, her hands covering her face as she wept without a sound. A large retinue quickly gathered behind them: onlookers, busybodies, single trees, houses, the miserable carob with a host of buzzing hornets and the outspread underwear on one of its branches, a shrieking quarrelsome wind, and behind them, like a rearguard to the host, all the mountains and hills of the neighborhood. It isn't every day that such a fine show as that is to be seen. Some of the women armed themselves for the journey with roasted sunflower seeds, to increase their pleasure and ensure their patient endurance.

Acquaintances and kinfolk tried to persuade Reb Shmelke to change his mind. It was of no avail. For a moment, to be sure, he thought of his children and the shame of it. His ears caught the weeping of his wife, and it struck a chord of pity in him. But that vague and uncertain amount promptly jumped to the fore again and bore down twice as heavily on his heart. He only had one answer, without pausing as he went:

'There's going to be a divorce!'

By the time they went down the sloping alley paved with slippery stone steps, almost all the town was behind them. This time all the rows of houses on the slope joined the procession, with a cow from one of the courtyards that stank of fresh manure, two roofs where grits were spread out to dry, a roof covered with dry grass on which was a bearded billygoat with a bell on his neck, and yet another roof on which a cottonwool maker was at work preparing quilt stuffings, with his queer machinery which looked like a giant harp. The closer they came to the Court the more did Reb Shmelke begin to feel the influence of a sort of sudden fear. Now he began to pray silently for somebody to intervene and reconcile him with his wife. Not for pity's sake—he would never admit such a thing to himself. But merely in order to save part at least of the stolen amount. Yet nobody tried, and Rivka Leah too made no attempt on her own part. She just walked along weeping . . .

But near the gloomy entry Reb Shmelke suddenly turned about, beckoned one of the crowd over, and told him, turning his face away from his wife as he did so:

'Simon, tell that woman there that if she returns me half the sum, I'll forgive her.'

In spite of the fact that he was speaking at the top of his voice and Rivka Leah was standing next to him, the messenger passed on the information. Poor Rivka Leah weepingly swore that she had nothing.

'Then in that case,' Reb Shmelke categorically declared, 'there's going to be a divorce today!'

And once again he turned on her his broad, rather bowed back, from which two large old patches peeped. But his fear kept growing from moment to moment. How would he sleep alone at night? He, the hefty one, was as frightened as a child when it came to sleeping without anybody there and without a light in the room. And what would he say to his son? He had a grudge against him, to be sure, for marrying a woman without a dowry. He had long been thinking of doing something to him which would stick in his memory for good and all. But still he felt nervous at heart because of the lecture he'd be read. Once again he turned round, his face to one side.

'Simon, tell that woman there that if she returns me a quarter of the sum, I'll forgive her.'

Once again came the same answer: tears and oaths that she had not taken anything.

'If so—it's a divorce today!'

Yet at the very gateway of the courtyard, where the Rabbinical Court was, Reb Shmelke suddenly felt darkness coming before his eyes. He, who was strong enough to work a whole day long without resting, suddenly found himself panting and his knees giving way. That terrible vague amount became more easy, and no longer oppressed his heart. Reb Shmelke remembered that his brother-in-law had not yet bought the goat, but had only discussed the purchase with him. And he also remembered that his other brother-in-law had been looking miserable lately, and had even come to ask him for a loan.

'Reb Simon,' Reb Shmelke tried once again, 'tell that woman there that if she tells me at least how many times she's taken money out of my pockets—I'll forgive her.'

And Rivka Leah wept and swore by all the oaths: only one time.

'If so, there'll be a divorce at once.'

This time he raised his voice in order to convince himself and his wife of his irrevocable decision. But when he stood at the door to the court-house and the beadle asked him what he wanted, he started back a bit and didn't answer. Suddenly he felt sorry for Rivka Leah and himself. Once again he turned and said:

'Simon, ask her whether she promises not to sin again.'

'I promise,' came the weeping reply as hope reawakened.

'Ask her if she promises to be a faithful wife!'

'I promise,' she replied like a penitent child.

'Tell her to swear to it!'

And out of her mouth poured a gush of oaths, full of emotion, with a flaming will to promise and prove without end.

'Well then,' he turned his eyes to her and added in a businesslike tone, 'go home, Rivka Leah, and prepare something to restore the heart!'

'Shmelke!' She burst out weeping afresh, 'Shmelke . . .' But she suddenly felt abashed in front of all those people and also went on in a businesslike tone, all her body trembling with choked tears, 'I'm going at once, husband . . . Don't forget to have your shoes patched . . .'

'And you,' only now did Reb Shmelke notice the huge crowd and thunder at them, 'what are you doing here? A wedding maybe? Home with you, you rogues, you scamps!'

V.

The crowd dispersed in fright and sorrow. What a pity that the fine show had stopped in the middle! Men and women dispersed. The burly mountains fled away, together with the mischievous hillocks. The measly carob went striding backwards, limping dot-and-go-one on its crooked trunk, the host of hornets buzzing busily after . . . and the pair of underpants chasing along too, one leg flapping in the wind, swelling like a sail in the effort to flee for its life. The only one who did not run away was the roof with the belled billygoat. It went on eating the withered grass while the bell rang softly and lazily.

Reb Shmelke went back to work. The houses on either side looked after him in annoyance for spoiling their fun . . . He had to hurry to cover the theft. With one swipe of his sleeve he wiped his nose and brow and eyes, which were moister than usual. Doubtless Reb Shmelke would have said that they were wet with sweat. But nasty tongues whisper: No, they were wet with furtive tears . . . Still, we're not the ones who need to listen to any such scandalmongering . . .

COUNTRY TOWN

by Yitzhak Shenhar

I.

HOW OLD is this township? Originally its site was occupied by a tiny, sleepy village, dismal and cut off from the world: windowless clay houses and rusty tin shanties. Dejected *fellaheen* used to sit in their shade gasping with exhaustion; skinny she-goats would walk about swinging their udders encased in leather bags; and children with festering eyes would climb onto the dung-heaps that had accumulated in the course of years.

Now the place is occupied by solitary houses set about haphazardly. There are large, unfinished houses, still imprisoned in their scaffolding and boards. There are small houses with temporary roofs bending their shoulders to take the weight of another story when the time comes for it to be added.

For months the air was filled with the beating of hammers, the grinding of concrete-mixers, the pounding of brick-making and the protesting groan of pumps. Then the bustle stopped abruptly, and everything became silent. Only here and there is a solitary worker to be seen, his body bent as he digs a pit or mixes lime in a wooden form. His naked back glistens with sweat, and his backbone quivers and stretches like a bamboo cane, and the skeleton building stares at him through the gaping hollows of its windows.

Now the sun beats down out of the blue sky, and the world's nakedness lies stretched out before it. Man and earth lie exposed to the glare, with no tree to rest its shade upon them. The new settlement has not been able to muster the strength to draw its houses together; and so they stand about, creating a mere suggestion of streets, from which paths branch off into the untilled countryside and reach as far as the foot of the distant mountains. Bars of heat-haze pass across the large expanse of naked earth, silently quivering like the waters of a lake when the wind blows off-shore . . .

II.

The Shalva Restaurant had its door wide open, and the green awning spread its wings at an angle over the little tables set outside. Reb Zalman Liebman, the owner of the restaurant, had for the third time traversed its length and breadth, sprinkling water on its concrete floor. He stood plunged in gloomy thought, eyeing his solitary customer with unreasoning disfavour. A customer! He and his like will never provide you with a living! That fellow—Zimran is his name, an official in the Government Department of Forests—has been sitting there a whole hour, silent and preoccupied, without moving a limb. His shirt-sleeves are rolled up, and his tie flows crimson down to his middle. A pipe protrudes from between his teeth. Was it from his English bosses that he learned the art of silence? It is a wretched art, for it has the capacity to make a man neither cheerful nor successful, and it never produces words that ease the mind or solace the ear.

Perhaps he is merely listening with a rapt expression to the murmur of his unseen forests? For he has already planted countless trees in hill and valley: conifers among which the wind whistles flute-like; eucalyptuses which beat their knife-shaped leaves together; stubborn stone-pines which rattle the bells of their cones; and stately cypresses towering in sacred majesty. True, our eyes may grow dim with age before they behold even a trace of their shade. However, it is a clean, respectable occupation, and it furnishes spiritual and aesthetic satisfaction; all the more so as it is connected with a secure post in the public service.

Each day the young man passes by in his open and dilapidated Government car. On the seat next to him, sitting bolt upright with all the impudence of a beggar, is his grey dog, pointed ears erect and tongue lolling out. Zimran gets down in front of the Shalva Restaurant, lays his pipe-clayed tropical helmet on his knees, pushes the dog under the chair with his feet, and slowly sips his bubbling lemonade. The heavy silence of forenoon rests upon everything. The washing on the line shrivels in the sunshine, and its white glare dazzles the eye. Zimran is well aware that over there, on the slopes of the high hills, on the patches of ground amidst the barren rocks, the *fellah* laborers are now cursing him roundly as they help themselves to an hour's idleness and carelessly expose the tender nurslings to the burning heat. He is well aware that, when he gets to the office, he will find Mr. Johnson sitting in his customary posture with his feet on the desk, his hollow eyes exuding boredom and disgust.

'Hallo,' Mr. Johnson will say in answer to his polite greeting. He will not turn his head an inch, but will go on staring in front of him through the open window, watching the revolving sprinkler as it scatters its bead-like drops around the nursery.

Somewhere in a city overseas his brother, young Zimran—no, young Singer, for he has *not* changed his name into Hebrew—is leading his life of dissipation. He is a gambler and a drunkard; his temples are sunken, and a greenish pallor lies in the hollows of his cheeks. When he smiles, he displays rotting, yellow teeth. Like a nightbird which flees the sunlight, he prowls about in dark alleys. He expends all his energy among dissolute women, and he would at any moment be liable to arrest, deportation, and all manner of trouble, were it not that his elder brother sends him enough money to live on.

It is all done quietly, without complaints or bitterness and without demanding accounts: on the first of each month, half his salary is set aside and cast into the jaws of that distant city, where it sinks like a stone in the mighty waters. The younger man does not even send letters. Why should he? He is burning up the remainder of his youth there and casting its ashes to the winds: can that be compressed into the lines of a letter? Should he write back to express his gratitude in whining tones when he is striking at the very roots of his being and making game of the whole world—when he even scoffs at his elder brother who is so anxious for him and is still hesitant to abandon him to his fate? Zimran goes on carrying his burden and living frugally. Could he bring his brother over to this country? Even if he were to agree to come, what would a worn-out roué like him do here? How could he adapt himself to the vast silence? How could he hang his rotting smile upon this wilderness of generations?

It is an open secret to all the local inhabitants. The old women are sorry for him. The men consider it 'quite natural'. The young girls have an intuitive feeling that there is something more to Zimran's personality—that he, the 'King of the Forests' who is restoring the country's ancient glory by replanting it with trees, also carries concealed within him a germ of the kind that has manifested itself in his younger brother: something stormy, fiery, and consuming. But Reb Zalman Liebman is of the opinion that Zimran has made a poor deal, and that he would be well advised to have nothing further to do with his brother. But absolutely nothing! What have you in common with him? In times like these it's each man for himself, eh? If you find a stranger's hand resting on your shoulder, you have to brush it off; and if he climbs onto your shoulder and rides on it, you're most definitely obliged to throw him down. It's a question of the individual, and there isn't the time to spend on anyone else. Every Jew has to take stock of himself and see whether he has any strength in his loins. If you have, get up and save yourself, by whatever means and in whatever circumstances. Don't turn left or right, and don't stop to indulge in introspection, about yourself or people in general. For instance, over there, at the *kevutza* of Ramot, they have already missed the boat. It's perfectly simple: they live, so to say, outside of time—everybody climbing onto everybody else's back, and they won't let go. It's as if a boatload of shipwrecked people were floundering in the water, with the weaker ones holding onto the stronger ones, so that in the end they all sink together . . .

But Zimran does not mix with people a great deal, and he is not a ready talker, and the freckled forehead that tops his short body displays no sign of wrinkles. Is he thinking, when he's silent like that? A small lizard darts out from nowhere and scurries along the ruts of a path. It distends its neck voluptuously in the sunlight, and its pink belly rises and falls. Zimran watches it and guides it across the road with his eyes. Now it's climbing the wall of Reb Ozer Mohr's house. A curious structure: a shop with a verandah fronting it! The verandah is green and narrow, and three stone steps lead up to it. The shop doors are opened flush with the walls and are loaded with a display of wares: funnels, brooms, paper bags, handkerchiefs, and colored posters advertising chocolate—a tasteless jumble of articles put together by a male lacking in imagination and love. But in one window a pyramid of canned goods rises up against a background of green corrugated paper with the appearance of celery. The moment you look at it you perceive that it betrays the refined taste of a woman—of the woman who is now coming through the shop door, making a sudden entry, as if pushed onto a stage set specially for her.

III.

The lizard tears itself away from its perch and jumps to the ground. Zimran removes the pipe from his mouth and bows from his seat. Chava Mohr stands on the green verandah in front of her father's shop and smiles. There is nothing arrogant in her smile, but it does suggest that she is in possession of a fragment of knowledge which is withheld from others. If you observe closely, you will notice that both her hair-style and her smile are contrived: one ear is uncovered and displays a drooping earring, while the mass of her hair falls across the other ear, covering it and part of her cheek. This is by no means a sign of vanity or coquetry, but merely a device to hide a small scar, as red as a beefsteak, near the ear.

'Will you be coming to "The Nurses" this evening?' Zimran asks from across the road.

Chava twirls the colored parasol which she holds open across her shoulder and nods an assent. She will certainly be there this evening. She will turn in at the hospital huts and go into the spacious room where the two nurses live. Clearly nothing has changed there since the last party took place. There will be the same 'Oriental Corner' contrived of empty tins, mats, and potted palms; and there will be the same old tunes on the gramophone. Once again there will be tea in glasses, and peanuts, almonds, and nuts on a burnished copper tray; and, over it all—the piercing laughter of the girls. All the same she'll go this evening: there's nothing else to do.

Zimran climbs into the car followed by his dog. Before it starts, the overheated car splutters and quivers for a few moments. At the sound, Chava's father emerges from the shop, skull-cap on head. A column of bluish smoke is carried along the smooth road, which lies stretched out like a shining black ribbon. Reb Zalman Liebman takes a step toward his neighbor and waits for him to open his mouth. A long summer's day draws itself out in scorching boredom. The sky is gradually melting and dripping into the troughs of the west.

'Hot,' says Reb Ozer.

'Well, well, some place this!' Reb Zalman gleefully sails into the attack. 'It's neither town, country, nor desert. Is it surprising that things are the way they are? After all, our American brethren are mixed up in it. As we know, a Jew plain and simple is a man with imagination, and an American plain and simple is a bluffer. Now just imagine what a combination of American and Jew must be like!'

Reb Ozer flaps his hand to drive away the flies: the heat makes them sluggish, and too lazy to change their perch. Reb Zalman examines his grey handkerchief intently, to see if he can find a dry corner with which to wipe his large pate. Chava smiles. Abroad, where she lived before, her father would never have deigned to consort with a type like Liebman: a bow-legged creature who goes about all day without a coat, his braces engraving lines of sweat upon his shirt. When he goes to serve a customer, he leans both hands on the table, fixes a pair of demanding eyes on him, and breathes over him the compounded fragrance of tobacco, beer, and onions. As he likes to spare his body any unnecessary exertion, he does not take the trouble to go up to the kitchen hatch to place his orders, but turns his head and shouts from where he happens to be standing: 'Hey there! One plate of hamburger and potatoes!'

His wretched wife, who is never seen beyond the threshold of her home, becomes flurried and makes a clatter of crockery in her hidden recess amidst the snake-like hissing of the primus stoves. No, in their old city her father would not have started a conversation with a man like that. But here, in this country, everything has become blurred. Can you tell here what a man is really like? Who and what his people were? What his occupation was before he came here? People just have no past at all. There's been a complete shake-up, and the old social distinctions have been thrown to the winds. It's like a sort of mill, only it grinds human beings instead of ears of wheat. That is why in this country her father makes his way along slowly, like a snail in its shell, blinking suspiciously at everyone who draws near.

Her father bears himself a grudge: he, the experienced businessman whose intuition had never failed him before, had been taken in by the schemes propounded to him by proud and eloquent emissaries from the Land of Israel. They had visited his town; they had unfolded illustrated maps before him; and they had quoted him figures. They demonstrated conclusively that here—in this precise spot!—a large town was destined to arise. It would spring into existence all at once, American style. Every Jew capable of looking ahead and seeing what lay before him was absolutely bound to have a hand in the venture, and whoever was lucky enough to be one of the first—and so on, *ad lib.* And he, Reb Ozer, had been gullible enough to believe all he heard. He went and sold all his property, receiving in exchange a sum in zlotys ending in several noughts. He quickly changed the zlotys into dollars, and the noughts were cut down in a twinkling. The dollars he exchanged for pounds with Hebrew lettering at the bottom, and the noughts were still further reduced, to a heartbreakingly low number. When he suddenly found himself denuded of everything, the firm confidence he had felt in himself was undermined, and for the first time in his life he was seized with terror. When his fellow-townsmen came to take leave of him, the tears welled up in his eyes in jealousy of the little people who were staying in their warm nests, their lives laid out for them, for the time being, according to a fixed pattern. Throughout the journey, by sea and overland, he was pursued and frightened by his thoughts, and his eyes would wander and his spectacles become clouded. As if out of a spirit of perverseness, he avoided the three main cities and hurriedly settled in this forlorn spot—as though afraid of missing his opportunity and finding that someone had forestalled him.

IV.

Reb Ozer has a feeling of guilt towards his daughter. Indeed, he doubts whether she ever really wanted to live in the Land of Israel. At times it seems to him that he forced her to come against her will. It is not his habit to discuss matters with her and speak of the things that weigh on his mind. But it is clear to Chava that he has not yet reconciled himself to his environment: to the little shop which does not even remotely resemble the business house he used to own in the old days; to giving up his established position in the community; to the ugly feeling that he has come down in the world and now counts for little in this new and heterogeneous society.

He has been overtaken by the fate of every man, Chava thinks to herself. A man may be walking along with a feeling of assurance, and then suddenly, without rhyme or reason, he turns aside. Isn't it that which gives life its main charm? What a pity not everyone is able to smile when it happens! One's face darkens over, there is a burning sense of regret, life is drained of its sap, and the thought of tomorrow holds out no cheering prospect. Yet, as Chava is well aware, if a dusty car should draw up and disgorge an unknown tourist or one of those fleeting travellers who buy everything they see, the two of them—Liebman and her father—would immediately converge on him and shake him cheerfully by the hand:

'This place? Oho, you simply can't imagine what a future it has! Would you like to see where the shopping centre is to be built? Now this is where the park is to be laid out; and over there is the site of a large theatre and the Government buildings. It's a splendid project, as everyone knows. The plans have been elaborated down to the last detail!'

This is the kind of talk with which they inundate the tourist as he relaxes comfortably and quickly makes a note of figures and jots down abbreviated items of information. The anger is forgotten, the rancor momentarily disappears, and things look brighter in the eagerness of the unfortunate to cover up the mistakes of their lives. Chava is usually not standing about when travellers' cars pull up. They have a way of staring at her with a mixture of curiosity and pity. That is how she herself used to stare out of the train window when she passed little village girls as they stood at the edge of the fields, heads upraised, gazing with stupid jealousy at the train flying by. But generally cars do not make a long halt here. They pass by, with their passengers and loads, sounding their horns as if to flaunt their disregard for the open spaces of the new township. They and their clatter give off an odor of strange countries, and their off-handed contempt causes a feeling of resentment. For a moment the place endears itself to you: the large, empty, desolate market-place, the white skeletons of the houses, and the bald, fenced-in enclosures named after somebody-or-other. The tarred road running through the center of the township sets off the vast surrounding half-built area all the more sharply. Not one house is built actually adjoining another. Indeed, it would seem as if life does not form a pool between them, but drains away and disappears, slipping off like the cars with their loads of tourists.

But when day draws to a close, the shadows stretch out, bridging the gaps between the houses and filling all the empty spaces. The paths seem to be returning from distant gutters to which they had gone. Evening comes, bringing with it a cool breeze which straightens the stems of the plants, which raises up something solemn that was crushed by the tread of day. Solitary trees draw near and huddle together, and somewhere the last train whistles. At this hour you could imagine that a city was really situated here, mysterious but invisible. And as the local inhabitants go out for a stroll, they straighten up and walk towards solitude as if that were their goal. Some look casually behind them to see whether anything has happened, whether by chance the formlessness has been redeemed, whether perhaps it has meanwhile taken on material shape.

Reb Ozer goes back behind his shop counter and pays no attention to his daughter. Chava is distressed to see her father's world enclosed within such narrow confines. A man like him should have stayed in his birthplace, to lead a placid existence and live out his life to the end, until the great storm came to uproot him altogether. People like him should gaze with open eyes at the ruin that is finally destined to overtake them and not hurry to seek out a haven of refuge. It was a mistake on his part to try and anticipate the catastrophe. He came to the Land of Israel to salvage the remainder of his life and property. And here he hopes to carry on and pick up the severed thread. That is his second mistake.

After coming here he has suddenly begun to have thoughts about his daughter, hidden thoughts which have not found articulate expression, either because of family pride, or because he feels abashed before his grown-up child who has deferred so submissively to his will.

Poor father! If only he would open up and talk things over with her, she would explain to him, calmly, that this is the kind of thing that happens to people: all of a sudden and with full knowledge, you turn from your path, and that is known as Fate. Just as happened to her with that mean-souled man who thrust his way into her life, turned it upside down for her, gathered his harvest, and went off before she had time to realise that it was not he whom she had wanted. It was a mistake; and as a result here she is, alone, at the age of twenty-eight. If her father were to ask her what she thought, she would whisper gently into his ear that on no account should he distress himself for her sake. On the contrary, ever since that episode she had been secretly yearning to go to some other country, and it might just as well be the Land of Israel. It was as if someone were drawing her to distant places and saying: Here a person can turn over a new leaf. Here your life will be renewed, here you will find the way back to your youth. If your hopes have been dashed, Father, it is neither your fault nor mine, nor even that of this strange country. For such is the way of far-off lands, and such is the way of dreams. If only Mother were alive! But Mother quitted this world nine years ago, before anyone imagined that her family would pull up its roots and go wandering. That was before any of the young settlements around here had come into existence, before the Mohr house with its green verandah had been built. This house has never known the expression on Mother's face, has never heard the sound of her footsteps. A dusky Yemenite woman pads softly about the place in her bare feet. She cooks, cleans, and makes the beds. And Father sits in his shop, alone and slovenly, and for lack of anything better to do he transfers bundles of goods from one shelf to another.

Chava is absolved of all domestic duties and does nothing. But people here have a habit of asking you what your occupation is the moment they set eyes on you.

That is the way people here get to know one another, as if one's hands were a clue to one's entire personality. Her hands are elegant and white, and her fingers long and tapering. On being asked her occupation, Chava usually replies: 'Oh!'—making that single syllable sound richly pregnant with meaning. But to Golani, a member of Kevutza Ramot, she once confided that her chief occupation was to stand on the river-bank of life and watch it streaming past. Golani looked at her in surprise. Without meaning to, he turned his head and surveyed the landscape, as if in search of something he had not seen there before: ranges of hills covered with purple gauze, their rounded peaks supporting the vault of heaven. A story-book camel seemed to be walking across them, stepping lightly and hovering, swaying his humps as he moved. Light clouds floated high overhead, drawing their train of shadows over the hill slopes; and the shadows glided slowly downwards, spreading out like transparent carpets of muslin, transforming the earth. The vestiges of a pristine world still lay concealed there: some element of the earth must surely have been poured then into his sky, and something sky-like must have been mingled with his earth, and between the two passed a succession of many generations bearing mortal crowns and divine legends.

V.

If Chava raises her eyes as she stands on the verandah, she can descry in the distance the water-tower of Kevutza Ramot. The buildings themselves are hidden behind a wood of cypresses and casuarinas. Only their roofs peep out of the deep well of piled-up greenery. Chava can picture to herself the entire village yard, square in shape and strewn with stones, and puddles dragging across it from the drinking troughs at the foot of the water-tower. When she went to visit the village during the first few weeks after their arrival in the country, Golani used to join her and show her round the farm. He would walk in front, his body turned sideways to her, eagerly explaining everything in full. Chava, on those occasions, seemed to herself to be a tourist, to whom detachment is an advantage, and she had no other purpose than to gather beautiful reflections at every prospect she beheld. She listened to Golani with a smile. As she did so, she derived enjoyment from her blue dress, with its accordion-like pleats, from the body encased in them like an unplayed melody, and from the attractive poise of her high-heeled shoes on the broken board placed across the damp manure.

'This is our Holstein steer,' said Comrade Golani as he stood at the entrance to the cattle-shed. 'He's a young fellow, two and a half years old.'

A pungent smell assailed her out of the gloom. Drawing in her head, Chava could make out no more than two white spots moving upon a black and terrifying mass. She heard snorting nostrils, a rattling chain and the stamp of a mighty hoof. At that moment one of the young women of the *kevutza* passed by dressed in shorts, one hand carrying a pail of water, the other stretched out into the air. She had fat thighs which swayed as she walked, but her face had a housewifely expression. As she passed, she darted a hostile glance at Chava and pointedly broke into loud song:

Once there was a lad who drove
To the road . . .

Chava flinched, as if the girl had stopped and splashed her with cold water from the pail. Everything around her seemed to turn darker. The houses of the village looked very faded and somber to her, the trees were yellow and covered with dust, and Comrade Golani seemed to be taking longer than necessary in the cowshed. Could it be that he was ashamed to be seen in her company by the young woman of the *kevutza?* And why did he want so much to introduce the bull to her? Strange man!

Golani came from the same home-town as herself. At the time she lived at home she had thought of him very rarely, as she would of a strange-looking figure at the roadside. The first time she saw him she was still a high-school pupil in all the freshness of her youth. In those days she could still dream with delightful naïveté of queening it in a tiny kingdom set amidst fields and forests, yet only a few hours' distance from the provincial capital.

Golani was at that time a member of the Hashahar Society. He used to immerse himself in books and pamphlets, and was busily engaged in attending meetings and taking part in discussions. Chava never found herself in his company. She had by chance heard that his family were very religious but not very well off, and that they lived in a little house on the outskirts of the town. To this day she does not know whether his parents are still alive. She has an idea that his father must be dead, and that his aged mother has found herself a refuge in her married daughter's home. Golani did not help his parents, as he did not earn anything. All his time was dedicated to the Hashahar Zionist Society, whose members would foregather in the evenings and speak Hebrew amongst themselves. Chava at that time was not interested in political trends or parties. All her attention was directed to the whisperings of her girl-friends about young men: the set of this one's head had something 'piquant' about it; that one had a *je ne sais quoi* about the way he spoke; and that one had a Byronic expression.

Only one meeting remained engraved upon her memory. It took place one morning in the Great Synagogue. She had come there by chance with two of her girlfriends All three had their hair plaited like wreath about their heads, and they all wore aprons closely fitting round their hips. They came in with linked arms, spluttering into their handkerchiefs with inexplicable mirth, darting sidelong glances and screwing up their faces, as if conferring a favor upon 'those Jews' by attending their gathering. The meeting was held in an atmosphere of impending elections, but she has no recollection of what all the excitement was about. A large crowd pressed into the synagogue. All the parties had mustered for the fray, ready to do battle. Veteran orators mounted the platform and harangued the assembly, each with his characteristic way of speaking and gesticulating. Some of the more hotheaded members of the audience would throw in interjections, like rubber balls, and the agile speaker would immediately toss them back, to the plaudits of his adherents and sympathisers. It grew warmer; voices began to wilt and throats to become constricted. Then a stir passed through the crowded audience. Chava, too, rose on tiptoe and saw that a lane was being cleared for a thin youth with a heavy forelock who was calmly passing between the rows of people, adjusting the edges of his black shirt as he walked. It was Golani. He spoke in Hebrew, and the entire audience seemed to be listening to him intently. Even the confirmed hecklers desisted of their own accord and kept silent. Chava did not take in anything of what he said, but she heard her neighbors whispering:

'Doesn't he speak beautifully!'

'One would think it was his mother-tongue!'

'A charming fellow!'

It was only then that she began to take note of him. She does not remember what the outcome of the contest was, only that he was the hero of the day. Each time she met him in the street after that she would fasten her smiling eyes upon him and enjoy the sight of the confusion that spread over his face. Then she would mischievously pout her lips and dismiss him from her mind. Gradually she forgot him altogether. Some students came to spend their vacation in the town, and there began a series of gay strolls to the pine wood, intoxicating conversations filled with innuendoes, and the excitement of love on moonlit nights. Chava learned, quite casually, that Golani had left town to join a group of young people who were going to settle in the Land of Israel. The news evoked no echo within her: what was it to her if one of the young men living on the outskirts of the town chose to go out into the wilds of the desert? She herself was walking along springtime paths whose sad fragrance cause one's heart to flutter and one's eyes to grow moist. Golani went off and was forgotten, and the years followed their course and brought changes in their wake. It was only when Reb Ozer began trying to overcome his fears on the eve of their departure that he casually mentioned Golani's name, apropos of nothing in particular. Except that as he mentioned it he averted his eyes from Chava. Oh, poor Father! How sweet he is when he tries to practise some deception, as if she were still a little girl of seven!

When she met Golani in the Land of Israel for the first time, she said: 'Ten years ago, you wouldn't have believed you'd see me here.'

He replied smiling: 'On the contrary, I was sure you'd get here some day.'

Something inside her trembled as she heard his words. Or was this just a polite formula for all new settlers?

'You see, we've chosen to settle in the town near your village. Wouldn't you say it was the hand of fate?'

'I'm very glad of it, really, extremely glad, because . . . because there are so few people from our home-town.'

Yes, Chava laughed inwardly, according to the accepted conventions, the answer you gave me should have been something like this: What a pity it is only the hand of fate, and not of your own seeking . . . She covertly examined his face and noticed that it was deeply lined, and that parts of his heavy forelock had turned silver. Why are the men in the *kevutza* so wrinkled? After all, some of them are quite young. And why is it the girls show signs of fading, quite unlike farming folk? Perhaps it does not show outwardly at first, but it lodges like a disease in a corner of the heart. It is as if an unseen crevice had opened up in the life of this country, draining off strength, youthfulness, and heart's joy.

VI.

When Golani took her to see the *kevutza* dining-hall for the first time, Chava felt it was she, and not the others, who was on view. The large room was filled with a confused hum as closely woven as a spider's web, although the people seated there were not talking. This was the resort of solitude in the midst of comradeship. Some of them were sitting with legs outstretched, leaning their backs against a table and smoking. Others were leaning forward, heads cupped in hands, reading newspapers. Chava put on a bright expression and conferred her dazzling smile on each of the people in the room. But they returned a concentrated, chilling stare, like that of people who have suddenly gone deaf. It was as if she had addressed them in a language they did not understand. Someone got up and made room for her to sit down, but she did not accept the offer. Golani, who was standing next to her, mumbled something. A blush suffused his sunburnt face, and he clasped his hands as he used to do in his youthful days when for a moment he found himself face to face with her in the street. Out of the window, the familiar scenery was visible: distant ranges of hills bathed in silent light with cloaks of indistinct purple spread across their folds. The scenery had its continuation in that white room and in the life within it. Where was the truth of that life? Chava looked around. A modest bookcase stood in the corner, its glass panes glistening. Near it was a black notice board embellished with tattered pieces of paper. Above the bookcase hung a grey picture: an old man, his forehead hairless, his shoulders seeming to wait for the pigeons to come down and perch on them, and a dreamy, understanding look in his eyes.

'Why did you take the skull-cap off that Jew's head?' asked Chava, elevating her chin in the direction of the picture. 'It doesn't suit him to be bareheaded.'

One of the members of the *kevutza* coughed into his hand. The others looked down at the floor.

She rocked to and fro on her heels with an air of independence. No, she thought, these people do not live here seriously. Each one of them suppresses his awareness of it and tries to cover it up. I am almost inclined to think that they have agreed among themselves to put on a front. They are sitting and waiting for the train to carry them back home, to that wonderful place which is always there for you at the end of your road. You will find no reward there for your tribulations; but there may be a kindly, forgiving grandfather who will pat you on the shoulder and show you that all your exertions were for nothing. And that too is good.

If one could take the life stories of all these individuals and weave them into a single fabric! Take that squat young man over there with the patched white shirt that is too wide for him. And that other fellow with the slight stoop and the parchment-like bald patch surrounded by the remnants of what had once been a headful of chestnut curls. And all those young women looking like roses which have been disappointed in their thorns until finally all their barbs were worn away!

'It's amazing,' she said to Golani as they were leaving the dining-hall. 'You've been through so many years of hardship and toil, yet you haven't become a sceptic.'

Yes, that was the word she used to him: sceptic! She didn't remember what he said in reply. What did it matter, anyway? The main thing is that he should catch the inflection of her voice, that he should ponder the question embedded in her matter-of-fact words: Have you still the strength to walk in springtime paths, to close your eyes in the awareness of what you are doing and allow yourself to be swept away by the storm?

Golani's greying forelock looked attractive, and every breeze would ruffle it and fill it with dimples as with a caressing hand. At such moments his head looked like an unruly tree-top, and there was a stubbornness about his neck and about his shoulders, which drooped slightly. What winds had raged around that tree? It has now become quiet and calm, it seems, and encased in so thick a shell that he is oblivious even of the 'Chinese' eyes that are resting a stolen glance upon him—the eyes of Rachel Winter.

Rachel had at one time been a member of Ramot, and she had been generally regarded as 'Golani's girl.' But now she is the wife of Dr. Walter Gideon Winter, physician. For two years she had worked at his side and accompanied him on his rounds of the hospital hut. Finally she had married him and gone to live with him in the nearby township.

'Such is the country and such are its ways,' Reb Zalman Liebman says with reference to that affair, pointing into the distance and rolling his eyes. 'These customs were unknown to our fathers and grandfathers. It is completely unnatural. Wantonness and lawlessness.'

VII.

Chava Mohr does not lie in wait to intercept Rachel's glances. She noticed them by chance one day when they happened to be together in Zimran's car. It was a holiday, and they had taken a trip to see the newly planted eucalyptus grove. Golani had also been invited. He sat in the front, next to Zimran, and 'the ladies' had the back seat to themselves. Zimran placed his hairy arms on the steering-wheel and drove fast. While the car was in motion, no one uttered a word. Chava covered her face with her light-blue kerchief, the ends of which fluttered behind her like wisps of steam that refuse to evaporate. Through this mask, she suddenly detected

Rachel's eyes exploring the back of Golani's neck. What were those eyes asking? What did they want?

If someone doesn't say something, Chava thought, I shan't be able to restrain myself from touching Golani on the shoulder and asking him to turn round.

Once or twice more the wind buffeted against their faces, and the car came to a halt.

'Here we are.' Zimran's words filtered through above his pipe, and he pointed with his hand. Across the broad plain stood row upon row of reddish saplings. A short way off a five-year-old grove of trees made a gentle, primeval rustling and spread their scant shade upon the ground like fine strands of hair. The saplings stood wondering and intent, anxious to know what was happening in the hollows beneath them and looking anguished, as if the fibres of their roots were paining them greatly.

'When can we come here and pick mushrooms?' Chava asked, clapping her hands.

Zimran stood there, hands in pockets, one eye closed on account of the smoke from his pipe. The other was surveying the woodland.

'A forest of willows for *hoshanoth*,' he shot out the words as if mocking at himself. Rachel lowered herself gently and sat among the saplings, bending forward and gently caressing their wasted leaves. 'It seems ages ago,' said Golani shading his eyes with his hand and gazing towards the white settlement which seemed to spring up in the distance. 'Six months before the Arabs left the village, I went to buy some tobacco plants from them. At that time no one thought the village would simply disappear from the map and that this new settlement would arise in its place. Remember, Rachel?'

'I remember,' Rachel answered softly, raising her eyes to him and putting her hands to her bosom. Golani gave a restrained but penetrating laugh which had in it an element of elation, of confidence in his own powers, and something of a triumphant victor's cruelty.

Chava Mohr suddenly felt her spirits gutter. Here, then, was the consolation of living in this strange country. And what had she brought here ? Where would she cast away all the surplus baggage she had dragged with her out of her past—that delightful, intoxicating past which brought a tear to the eye? Suddenly she became angry at her sharp heels, which were sinking into the loose earth at every step. She seemed to feel the breath of those hills, which lay there like a herd of drowsing buffalo. Golani seemed to be standing over them, legs apart, like a trusty shepherd: in another moment he would call them, and they would rise and go towards new times.

VIII.

Where then are the new times? This country seems to grow twin-like days, drought-ridden and turning in the circle of a single fate, and every soul is called upon to undergo penance and seek an interpretation in them. Chava is standing on the verandah of her father's shop, looking at the road which leads to Ramot. She is aware that no one is going to come from there at midday. Most of the members of the *kevutza* are at work in the fields on the other side of the settlement. Perhaps Golani is at this moment eating his dry crust, or maybe he is sitting in the shade of the slope rolling a cigarette. Or maybe he is jolting up and down on the tractor as it crawls along, obliterating the shape of the earth in its path. The sky is dripping with heat and silence; the hours are lazily crawling by; and that same phantom camel is flying in the hills, springing from peak to peak, but never coming nearer. Towards evening one can go down to the road, turn into one of the narrow paths and abandon one's face to the light westerly breeze. One can walk, leisurely and aimless, breathing in the scent of the hot earth. Marked out for the buildings of the future city, it is now simply uncultivated land. There are still green plants at its verge, and its reddish color seems to be mingled with clotted flames. The hem of the sunset is sinking into the corners of the horizon, and you have a feeling that your haste was in vain, that there is time, and that many gates are still beckoning to you. Go and knock, and you will be answered.

Chava sometimes looks back, and her past life takes on the aspect of a house of several stories studded with rows of windows. Some of them are dark and opaque, like eyes that have clouded over; others are brilliantly illuminated. At such moments she feels a void in her heart, a void that only Warsaw, Nice, or Paris is capable of filling. What has she in common with this tiny country and its inhabitants, who bear their dedicated lives with so much diffidence? The country is a patchwork of East and West; of poverty, lofty ideals, and the cruelty of everyday existence; of high-sounding phrases about life and of an illusory national revival. Its people go about their business, humming to themselves, as if they had succeeded in winning a comfortable and familiar security. But they secretly follow each other with jealous eyes, as if asking: Have you already crossed the hidden bridge and fallen among those silent ones who have reconciled themselves and made all the concessions demanded of them?

Sometimes she gives rein to her fantasy as she lies on her bed at night, when a bewildered mosquito gets entangled in her mosquito-net and sets up its unceasing whine. The moonlight streams in through the slats in the shutters, and the night pours in from the wide-open spaces of the streets. She sees in imagination the Bedouin encampments which are sometimes pitched amidst the stubble, and their dwellers seem to her like enchanted princes of the desert. By day they sit about idly, cross-legged and huddled in their garments, while near them stand mangy, evil-smelling camels drooling at the mouth. But the moment night touches them with its magic wand, they change, and the camels become transformed into fleet-footed dromedaries laden with mysterious merchandise. In a trice they cross the empty spaces and bring the entire desert to her window-sill. Chava is seized with terror: How did she get here? Should she get up, part the curtains of her mosquito-net and go, barefooted and white-fleshed, into her father's room (he isn't asleep, she knows that), and say: Father, let us flee from here for my strength is failing. I forgive you for the mistake you made, but I can't carry on any longer. I simply cannot, Father.

There is no need to flood him with words. He is aware of what is taking place in her heart, and her silence must surely cause him severe pangs. Were she to speak up plainly at this compassionate hour of midnight, he would certainly return with her to their birthplace, taking upon himself the burden of disgrace it would entail, as well as the risk of utter impoverishment. Or else he would sail with her to a new but inhabited land, to a great city with multitudes of people crowding between its fortified walls.

Clearly, her father would follow her like a penitent child. While still a high-school pupil she used to chat with her girl-friends about men and their manners and ways. It was the age of yearning glances, of stolen kisses, of verses written in albums. All the girls agreed then that men were nothing but great babies. The same kind of feeling comes over Chava now, sometimes, when she converses with Golani. She laughs inwardly: He thinks he can deceive her! He has undergone all the vicissitudes this taciturn country can impose upon a man it wishes to conspire against, yet he is still a baby!

IX.

'At one time during my youth,' he told her shamefacedly, 'I was about to become religious and observe all the commandments in the most rigorous manner. I experienced starvation at that time, that is to say, spiritual starvation. But since I have been here I have been feeling very contented, and I no longer yearn for God.'

He was walking by her side as he spoke, his hands clasped behind his back and his sun-browned face bowed towards the earth.

'And you no longer feel any hunger at all?' Chava asked with a smile.

His hands tightened their grip behind his back. 'This country, this country . . .' he mumbled.

For some moments they walked silent and solitary in the broad plain. Golani turned his thoughts in a different direction, and after a few moments he laid a crumb of them before her:

'The Jews have to return to the East. They have finished their task in the West. When they leave it they must close the door with such a bang that the whole place will shake.'

'Really? And perhaps you'll set up harems as well? You know, Golani, you'd be wonderful as the master of a large harem!'

He did not pay heed to her levity: a long, unseen trail extended behind them, and it disturbed him.

Chava immediately changed her tone and said seriously: 'Doesn't a person have to be a citizen of the world at large if he wants to take root in this country too? If so, what is one to do if the main part of one's life has been spent in a medium-sized town, and if all one has ever aspired to is a fistful of *petit bourgeois* contentment?'

He looked at her in astonishment. Every utterance of hers harks back to one single thought at the centre of her mind. The mincing high-school girl has indeed grown up. She no longer celebrates the events of her life as if they were set next to one another like the beads on a necklace. She is like a ripe fruit hanging from a bough, which never sees the blue of heaven, but is forever gazing down at the earth, at the earth.

A slight contortion swept across Golani's face, and he licked his dry lip with the end of his tongue. He would like to be revenged on Chava, just a little, for all the contemptuous looks with which she used to lash him in their home-town; for the scented arrogance with which she inspired dread in his young heart; and for all the inchoate emotions which, as a result, were doomed to strangulation at birth.

'The Jews are like flies crawling over a map of the world. They hop with ease from the green to the red. and from the red to the yellow; but not a trace of those colors clings to their feet.'

Chava nods: All right, my dear, I'm listening, I can take it. Go on, sting away, hit as hard as you like. Will it make you feel any easier?

The joy of vengeance takes hold of Golani. He begins to hurt Chava, using subtle and delicate methods. He gives a new twist to the conversation and talks quietly of the return to nature, of the greatness of the Jewish 'revolution,' which is altering the course of development of world society. He takes out of his verbal armory all the outworn stereotypes that have grown rusty with disuse. He would not venture to talk that way in the dining-hall of Ramot: his comrades there would surely look at him with undisguised derision.

She walked by his side, striking her folded parasol against the heads of the salvia and wild mustard that sprang up all around. She felt like interrupting his flow of words and asking him: 'You, who are the friend of all the young women who walk about in shorts and tire themselves out with hard work—why do you become so agitated at the touch of a woman with delicate hands and a lightly made-up face?' But her tongue was stricken dumb in her mouth as if laden with weariness. Gone were the days when she would lie asleep dreaming that she was dancing on her toes on the spires of the church steeple, her hair disordered and the bells ringing out in the night breeze.

What a pity her father is not walking between them and taking part in the conversation. I wonder whether Golani would have spoken like that in his presence. But her father never goes beyond his own front door. Only once, at midday one Sabbath, did he bestir himself to go and see the *kevutza* of Ramot.

'It's lovely there,' he told Chava on his return. 'A real country estate. They have cows and poultry and cereals. All kinds of good things.' The wrinkles on his broad forehead smoothed out, and his face lit up. He seemed to be standing in a posture of supplication, as if to say: You see yourself what great deeds have been performed here. Does it not atone, at least in some measure, for the fateful mistake I made? 'And Golani is one of the leading people there. Our Golani; you remember, don't you?' But Chava pretended not to be listening. Since that day he has not been to visit the *kevutza* again. And on the occasions when Golani came to visit him at home, he behaved differently with him. He would slap him on the shoulder and grunt: 'Well, how's business? How much has our deficit grown, eh?' As he spoke he would wink in the direction of his daughter and smile.

'When I see you,' Chava said to Golani once as they took a walk together, 'I begin to believe again in the strength of man, in his power to adapt himself, to suffer, to carry a burden on his back.'

Golani looked at her sideways, and his eyes narrowed: 'And why did you ever stop believing in the strength of man?'

Well, well, it must be hurting you a great deal, Chava thought; and out loud: 'Everyone carries his past with him, doesn't he? And everyone draws his own conclusions from it.'

'Maybe,' said Golani, staring into the distance.

Are you still thinking of Rachel? Chava wondered. Unconsciously she had moved a step away from Golani, and her face took on a sullen expression. 'Every country is endowed with a characteristic feature by which you can easily identify it. Russia has its steppes, Italy has its gondolas. But what is the distinctive feature of this country? Perhaps there is nothing really authentic about you or the life you lead; perhaps it is an unreal life based on an arbitrary rule?'

'Our life is founded upon a rule to the extent that art is founded upon a legend, no more,' he answered without conviction, as if under a compulsion to say it.

Chava hung on his words for a moment and then said ironically: 'The old orator in you seems to have woken up. I don't altogether follow your meaning. But that isn't what I wanted to say. What's going to happen to the individual? He has always been waiting for a little bone to fall to his portion, and he has been conditioned to go and hide himself away with it in his den and gnaw away at it . . .'

'Well, speaking for myself, I'm already past these questions,' Golani smiled.

'Are you sure?'

'It's hard to explain to a bystander.'

A great bitterness welled up in Chava's heart. 'A bystander? What do you mean? You all walk around here as if you were keeping some closely guarded secret; as if you belonged to a different race with its own mysterious language and a mode of behavior on a superior plane. Even those who have left your secret band and have gone their own roads—even they go on guarding the mystery, as if by disclosing it they were to render themselves liable to some severe penalty.'

'What, what?' Golani stammered incoherently, and brought himself up with a jerk. The wind filled his shirt like a white sail. He bent down, plucked a dry stalk of grass and straightened up, his composure regained. He smiled and repeated what Chava had said before, giving emphasis to the words: 'Everyone carries his past with him and draws his own conclusions from it.'

What do I want from this man at my side? Chava admonished herself. Does he really attract me?

When she took leave of him, she put her long fingers into his broad hand, and his calluses touched her fair skin. She looked into his eyes, and he smiled at her in confusion. Meanwhile dusk had descended, that strange, scented hour, when day and night are cast into the plain, opposite one another, like sections of a fruit that has split in two. The blue deepened, and the outlines of the distant hills grew fainter and put veils of light mist on their heads.

X.

Chava is walking towards the railway track, heading for the station. A gloomy stone building erected by the Turks, it stands in an odd position, as if a wagon had chanced to pass by there in the noonday heat, and a box had dropped from it without the driver's noticing. The loading platform is always damp, and two or three trucks stand lined up before it, woebegone, discolored and featureless. The miserable place evokes nothing of the excitement a person feels in a railway station in the great world outside. It does not serve as a gateway to vast expanses; it does not make you want to put on the mask of strangeness to yourself and to others, to envelope each commonplace traveller in a cloak of marvels, and to hear in every whistle of the locomotive the clarion call of miracles and mighty deeds. This station is altogether prosaic: it is the personification of lethargy and helplessness. The stationmaster is a Christian Arab, his uniform cap looking a little shabby, his face shining with fat and exertion. On seeing Chava he blinks his eyes and calls out, resorting to French for the occasion: *Bonjour mademoiselle!*— as much as to say: What have we two in common with all the things for which people here struggle and risk their lives? Our eyes are turned to Europe. *Comment ça va, mademoiselle?* Chava smiles and nods to him, involuntarily feeling her hair to see if it covers up the little red scar behind her ear.

At that hour of the day, Dr. Winter is likely to pass by on his roan, his knees working their way up to its neck. Absentminded and always in a hurry, he forgets to adjust the stirrups to the length of his lanky legs. In this manner he goes from one *kevutza* to another in the area, rain or shine, fearlessly picking his way along hillside tracks and paths through the fields. His instrument bag bumps against his thigh, and his eyes are red from lack of sleep: each case of malaria fills him with a new flurry of anxiety.

'Shalom to you, Chava Mohr,' calls Dr. Winter, bobbing up and down in the saddle. He twists his long, thin neck, which rises up from the opening in his shirt. It is a pale neck, which never gets sunburned, and it cries out for a high stiff collar to hide in. 'Chava Mohr, we're soon going to start building the new wing of the hospital. I have been given a definite assurance about it.'

'Really?' Chava replies, waving her parasol at him. 'That'll be fine. We'll have a splendid hospital. I'm so glad. Please give my regards to Rachel, Dr. Winter.'

'Certainly,' he replies. A ray of light crosses his tired face, and he urges on his horse by digging his ridiculous heels into its belly.

Dr. Winter is riding home. His wife Rachel will no doubt come out to meet him: she will be standing at the top of the steps while he is extricating his feet from the short stirrups. Chava is sorry she has never been there on one of those occasions. That Rachel with her 'Chinese' eyes, her broad forehead and the furrow of bitterness running down to the corner of her mouth! She is not her bosom friend, but she likes to call on her of an evening and sit with her in the room with its ever-present smell of laundry and disinfectant. Whenever she goes there she is sure to find an overnight visitor, some member of one of the collective villages in the district who has come to the town on business affairs. They are young men, and they wear cloth caps and khaki puttees round their legs, but through that exterior one can discern vestiges of the gentility of a respected family in a distant East European township, one which by now may have altogether ceased to exist. On such occasions Chava muffles up her personality, hides herself on the settee, which stands in the shade, and watches Rachel with a frozen smile on her face. Rachel sits erect in the circle of light cast by the shaded lamp and converses with the guest. She asks about the farm at his *kevutza,* about the field of clover and the Beirut cow. She asks about so-and-so, who has moved to a smallholders' settlement, and about so-and-so, who has gone abroad. Rachel wears a most serious expression, her eyes overflow with the intimacy of friendship, and now and then her voice casts a note of hardness in the direction of Chava Mohr, the stranger and outsider.

The guest sits with his back slightly bent and his hands between his knees. He talks freely, disregarding the barrier that has sprung up between himself and Rachel, a barrier whose visible indications are the tall lamp poised on one leg, the soft settee with its colored cushions, and the glassware gleaming on the wide sideboard. He pretends not to notice that Rachel is listening with only half an ear, while the main body of her attention is in the dark upper room where her only child, little one-year-old Uri, is sleeping.

Without realising it, Rachel is yielding step by step. She still wears print frocks cut in the *kevutza* style, but she no longer goes about with a kerchief on her head. On festive occasions she still joins in the round dance of the *hora,* with its stamping feet and necks thrust back. But at times she murmurs, almost unconsciously, something about a trip to Europe in the summer.

Her friends notice it, Chava Mohr sees it; only Dr. Winter is completely oblivious. He gazes at Rachel with eyes as eloquent with love and admiration as in the early days, when she used to walk about softly in the darkened hospital hut at Ramot, rustling behind him in her snow-white coat and listening to his instructions with charming seriousness. He, Dr. Winter, is content with his open-necked shirt, his crumpled trousers and his large, dusty boots. And if Rachel decided to put an elegant walnut desk in his room to work at, no doubt it is all very right, proper, and altogether unexceptionable.

So, Chava silently asks as she gazes at Rachel, what was the point of all those years you spent in the *kevutza,* and what did you get out of them? Perhaps it was just a momentary deviation, after which your feet are returning with disgraceful ease to their accustomed path—except that you, my dear Rachel, are slowing down their pace from a stupid sense of shame? How do you rationalise this change to yourself—for it is quite clear how it is going to end. I dare say little Uri occupies a by no means incidental place in your rationalising, eh? It would be interesting to know whether the transition is at all painful, or whether it is simply like a spring that has been stretched for a little while and is now reverting to its original state with a joyful sensation of relief? And if it does hurt, my dear Rachel, can it be more painful than the feeling you experienced when you left the comfort of your parents' home to work in the laundry or cowshed of the *kevutza?* After all, you can't go on forever hiding behind the back of that great baby of a husband of yours! If anyone were to come and tell him that you were suffering at all from heartache, he would open his innocent eyes wide: What, his little Rachel suffering? In all likelihood he would take the blame for it upon himself, he might even go down on his knees to you at night and weep his heart out. Poor man! For you are the pure one, the lovely one, the honest one, the one who is all perfection, goodness and idealism! Everyone knows you used to be Golani's girl. The only one who doesn't know is your husband: he simply has no place for such knowledge in his mind and heart.

XI.

Every time Chava returns from a walk with Golani, she encounters Rachel Winter. Is it purely a coincidence, or has she been standing in the window, peeping through the muslin curtains? Rachel joins her and accompanies her a short distance.

'Beautiful weather,' Rachel exclaims.

'Yes.' Chava straightens the folds of her dress and sways her hips slightly.

'Zimran visited us today,' says Rachel suddenly.

'Indeed?' Chava drawls languidly, adding: 'I expect he sat there without uttering a word.'

'He's an interesting fellow,' Rachel observes in a serious tone.

'I dare say.'

'He'll shortly be getting a raise.'

'Is that so?'

'And his brother is going to go to America. After all, it is time that matter was finally settled.'

Aha, you're a persistent one, my sweet, thinks Chava; you're doing everything in your power to push me into Zimran's arms. You seem to be forever saying: Hands off Golani, keep away from him! Zimran's the man for you, he and none other.

'You know, Rachel dear,' says Chava sweetly, giving her a sidelong glance, 'I saw little Uri today. You simply must get him a new suit, knitted blue silk with tassles, to go with his blue eyes and fair curls.'

Rachel nods smiling, and the pucker of resentment fades from the corner of her mouth. 'I've already thought about it. But I'm rather worried: he's been eating very little lately. I'm thinking of consulting Dr. Winter'—that's how she refers to her own husband!—'about it. Maybe we should have a change of air for his sake.'

'What, another change of air?'

'What do you mean by "another"?'

Chava laughs. 'Oh, nothing; nothing at all. For some reason I just remembered that you once belonged to a *kevutza.* Tell me, Rachel, don't you sometimes feel a longing for life in the *kevutza?* Silly, eh?'

'Me? I've never broken my ties with that life,' Rachel answers coldly. Her eyes narrow, and she shows signs of haste. 'Well, I must be getting back to little Uri, he hasn't yet fallen asleep properly. Will you be coming to "The Nurses" tonight?'

Yes, of course she'll be there. That is the absurd highlight of her day: 'The Nurses' room'!

XII.

If she were back in the days of her youth, her heart would probably beat faster at the prospect of the party: a fresh glow would mantle her cheeks, and her hands would tremble with impatience. But now?

She will go home, spread a tablecloth on part of the table and quietly have supper with her father. She will sit with him a while, talking desultorily of this and that. Then she will go to her room and stand before her wardrobe mirror. She will slowly put on her tight-fitting black dress. First she will insert her head and shoulders, pausing a moment in the rustling darkness, and feel a hollow listlessness well up in her.

Who is that staring out of the mirror, all dressed up and with touches of red upon her cheeks? O where art thou going tonight, most beauteous of women? For thou art come to most excellent ornaments, and splendor rests upon thine brow, tra-la-la, tra-la-la...

Suppose Golani were to come to her now and say: Chava, I am ready to leave the *kevutza* for your sake. I'm ready to throw up everything. I'll go to the big city and find a good job, and then I'll bring you to me. Would she burst out laughing and say: Are you he, the prince of my dreams, who reigns over a hundred and seven and twenty legends? Will you bring with you the key to the riddle of my heart? Have you weighed matters in your mind and found that my hour is past, and that I am no longer worthy of anything but the fate that you have appointed for me with your own hands?

Or would she wrap herself in a simple shawl, take a small bundle in her hand and follow him, chastened, subdued and with a ready heart?

'Going out?' asks Reb Ozer, lifting his eyes from his newspaper and looking at his daughter over the top of his spectacles.

'If I'm back late, don't worry,' Chava replies, unable to muster the courage to give him a piece of her smile.

The house is desolate, the furniture is in mourning, and the place is full of shadows. A mixture of smells seeps in from the shop, which is shrouded in darkness. Above the electric lamp a tiny bird is wheeling and fluttering, trying to get at the light. But in vain: its wings do not get singed.

XIII.

Chava goes outside. The night already extends from horizon to horizon. The world has doffed the rugged mantle of day and put on the silken raiment of darkness. A handful of lights peep out modestly opposite myriads of stars. The black road crawls on its belly, straining forward in the darkness to reach its white brother, the Milky Way. In the bushes, crickets are sounding their note of yearning. The solitary trees are whispering, and the shadows of severed heads are set in the curtained windows. A group of young men are seated at the small tables in front of the Shalva Restaurant, engaged in noisy discussion. Their upper arms stick out of their rolled-up sleeves like pieces of burned wood. Their words vibrate in the intense darkness. Terror lies at every door and envelops every yard. One is afraid to set one's foot down upon this earth, lest it give way underneath, and one will be left with one's leg dangling and swinging like an empty pail above a well.

'God in Heaven,' Chava mutters to herself.

A good thing there is a God in those heavens!

Chava, dressed in black, is completely swallowed up in the dark. Her high heels stumble against the uneven surface of the hidden paths. She skirts isolated backyards and enclosed spaces overgrown with thorns. She crosses avenues-to-be and squares-of-the-future named after various personalities, passing between all those masses of life that have been heaped up there, like so many embryos or messy after-births. Sharp scents of night suddenly assail her nostrils, and something painful stirs in her heart: O land, O land . . . Chava feels herself dwindling into insignificance; the pure vault of heaven above her grows higher and higher; and the night rises up like a wall on either side of her and causes her to shudder. As she walks into 'The Nurses' room', her lips are moving slightly and her face is pale; but her pallor becomes her . . .

From afar she can hear the expressive voice of wide-hipped, goodhearted Nurse Dinah; and the nervous fragments of laughter of Nurse Ruchamah, with her slender back and flat chest, and the long curve of her arm giving a pleasurable feeling of comfort to all who behold her. In a corner sits Zimran, his feet beneath his chair and his extinguished pipe drooping over his lip. Rachel Winter is bunched up on a little stool, her hands to her bosom and her head on one side. In addition, there are two young men in a state of convalescence. Their illness has left a trace of yellow in their faces, and weakness fetters their limbs.

The awkwardness of the first hour still hangs over the room. One of the convalescents hesitantly starts telling a musty joke, his eyes darting among the guests as if in search of a worthy listener. Only Ruchamah responds nobly and gives a long laugh. Zimran shifts in his chair and passes his hand over his reddish hair, which glistens with moisture. Dinah goes about with a tray full of sandwiches and bends over each of her guests with a movement of the shoulder acquired from the hospital.

The gramophone hidden among the potted palms sets its needle racing and opens with a tune played on Hawaiian guitars—those guitars which sob and quaver at the end of every cadence, pouring out their hearts and bewailing the vanished paradise.

'More girls than boys again,' says Ruchamah, pretending to be overcome. She picks at the edges of her blue blouse, looking about anxiously to see how the couples will form. When the jokester comes up to her and asks her to dance, she quickly places her long arm on his shoulder and closes her eyes.

Zimran dances with Chava. He is somewhat shorter than she, and he looks up at her with a mixture of awe and devotion. He is not a tempestuous dancer, and he does not bump into other couples. He keeps to a small section of the floor and leads his partner carefully, as if apologising for every additional movement he troubles her to make.

A pleasant coolness is wafted through the open window, and tiny stars twinkle above. The impressions of the night are still floating like wisps of cloud in Chava's heart.

'I could go on dancing with you for hours on end,' says Zimran in a hoarse voice.

'Really?' Chava drawls distractedly, giving him a clipped smile. Rachel Winter is sitting on her stool, nodding her head in time to the music and looking at them contentedly.

'And where is your dog, Mr. Zimran?' Chava asks loudly, to make sure Rachel hears her poking fun at him.

'He's outside. No need to worry about him,' Zimran replies, compressing his lips.

With the second dance comes Chava's turn to sit it out. In a leisurely manner she cracks almonds, not looking in the direction of the dancers. But the pairs of legs pass within her field of vision, without expression or grace: they kick, turn, step, hurry forward and pause regretfully. The guitars of distant Hawaii go on whining, lamenting the passing of the beautiful life, and so liberally drenching their song with tears that even the pale palm-trees in the corner seem to be straining with a sigh to release themselves from the bondage of their pots.

Dr. Winter suddenly appears in the doorway, waving his hand and displaying his large teeth.

'Shalom, Doctor! Come and dance,' Dinah calls out in her chesty voice, releasing her partner.

'I? Oh dear no. I've only come for a moment, just for a word with Rachel,' the Doctor mumbles as he drags after Dinah, who is pulling him by the sleeve.

'Is the child asleep?' Rachel asks, turning her head as she dances.

'Yes, he's asleep,' her husband nods, picking up his long legs and tiptoeing across the room until he is standing at Chava's side. 'Isn't it a lovely night?' He bends down towards her, his face bright and proclaiming love of his fellow-creatures and a guileless soul.

'Come on, come on, Doctor, dance!' Dinah says reproachfully. 'Don't stand about doing nothing!'

'Steady there, my young bucks,' the Doctor calls out cheerfully to the two convalescents. 'Don't get too warmed up, or I'll have to pop the thermometers back into your mouths.'

Zimran dances with Chava again, obstinately moving in a small circle around her. Ruchamah throws her head back and casts fragments of laughter to the wind as she urges her sluggish partner to move faster.

'There was something I wanted to ask you,' Zimran begins again in a hoarse voice.

'Better not ask,' Chava interrupts him, hardening her face. 'I have no answers to questions.'

The flush on Zimran's face deepens, and the freckles stand out as if about to drop off. His cheeks clear suddenly, and his eyes grow deeper.

I expect he looks like his younger brother now, Chava speculates calmly. I'm sure that rake knows how to get his way with women. Not like his elder brother.

'Chava Mohr, take that wicked expression off your face!' Dr. Winter blithely calls out to her, as he steps assiduously in his large boots, embracing Dinah's waist with both hands.

'Very well then,' Chava smiles penitently. She moves a little and openly studies Zimran's form. Maybe they're right? Perhaps it is she who has been blind, and the man now holding her in his arm is the one destined to build a protective wall around her? Without intending to, she brings her rouged cheek nearer to his, and the touch is very soft and careful. His hand resting on her back trembles, and his legs are thrown off the beat.

From the end of the room Rachel sends them a glance of her

slanting eyes, and with her eyelashes extinguishes the spark that flared up in them for a moment. She silently detaches herself from her partner and turns round and round on her own, slowly, singing in tune to the music with suppressed joy.

As dance follows dance, and one word succeeds another, the night grows older. These feet are still sad, and so is this gaiety. In vain do the guitars moan and proclaim their anguish, here in the centre of the far-off township, about to switch off its lights and sink into slumber . . .

XIV.

The head of the mounted watchman suddenly appeared in the open window, his white teeth gleaming beneath his black moustache. 'Hey, you merrymakers! There's a fire!' The couples whirled round suddenly and stopped. The encircling arms fell limply apart.

'What's happened?'

'A fire?'

'Where?'

'Some Arabs set fire to the grove.'

'Why?' asked Ruchamah innocently, blinking her large eyes. Her arm was still clinging to her partner's shoulder, unwilling to let go.

The watchman disappeared into the darkness once more, and they all crowded outside. In the distance, beyond the roofs of Ramot, there was a red glow on the horizon, and a light cloud of smoke could be seen rising above it. The flames burst forth at the corner of the sky, and the moon rode delicately above them, as if afraid to singe the hem of her robe.

They stood in a group, silent and indecisive. The night was in a contrary mood and was beginning to recede. Voices broke out from the adjoining streets and the more distant houses. From the window the remnant of the Hawaiian guitars' plaintive wail was still issuing forth.

'My little Uri!' Rachel burst out with a strangled cry. She tore herself from the spot and rushed towards the house, as if the flames had taken hold of the rafters in the upper room where the infant lay asleep. Dr. Winter disappeared wordlessly, without anyone noticing. The 'Nurses' stood in the doorway of their room, trembling and pressing one another close.

'Whose car is this?' The voice was that of an unfamiliar figure which suddenly sprang into their midst from nowhere.

Zimran got into his car, his lower lip hanging down loosely. After him climbed the two convalescents. The car made a grinding sound but refused to start. Zimran threshed about in his seat, all his limbs jerking, and let fly a hail of Arabic invective. Opposite, the dog was running up and down and barking, demanding his rightful seat, which had been usurped by a stranger.

In a few moments Chava Mohr found herself standing alone. Her arms, with nothing to occupy them, pressed close to her ribs. She moved and began walking towards her house. She would change into her soft dressing-gown, pour herself a glass of tea, and settle down on the verandah to sip it as she watched the distant fire. Young tree trunks are now standing there like great lamps, making a protesting sound as they yield up their souls. The fresh sap is pouring down, bubbling and giving off its aroma. Green leaves, rudely awakened from their sleep, are folding up like charred wings and slowly dropping to the ground.

Chava takes a few steps and then stands still. She purses her lips: Zimran's trees are also on fire yonder. There is no wall, no door fastened with bolt and padlock, nothing at all. Over there is his young brother in the bustling city, and here—Arabs on the hill slopes.

Chava gazed at the bright flames, and her eyes quickly filled with scorching tears, as if the fire had come close and set light to their pupils. All around her was silence: no one was to be seen, nothing stirred. There was no light in the world save the fearful brilliance that rested above Ramot. The members of the *kevutza* must now be slithering down the hillside in their hurry to reach the burning wood. Some people are sitting on their verandahs gazing at the spectacle of the fire; others are rushing to put it out. Chava imagines she can see Golani running, his hair unkempt, his shirt bellying out on his back. Perhaps he is crying out as he runs; pehaps he is stumbling and falling. To whom will Golani cry out when the fear of the fire is upon him? As Chava crosses the desolate darkness of the level plain, something lights up inside her: Golani! The word beats in her heart like the clapper of an invisible bell. He is the person, the only one, the one specially for her: it is he who has all the while lain hidden in the secret recesses of her life; and she never knew. There is but one road open to her, the one that leads to him. All the other roads she has traversed have been merely sidetracks, merely the resentment of defeat. Now she will arise and go to him, bringing with her all the lofty words she has thought of, sometimes seriously, sometimes in fun, since the days of her youth. Now she will gather them together, one by one, like the grains of her heart, and lay them at his feet as a tribute to the victor.

The shadows of horsemen loomed in the darkness. Hoofbeats rang out upon the road and died away. Out of one of the yards came a cart hitched to two mules, a broad-shouldered young man urging them on with his whip. Chava Mohr lowered her head and ran towards the creaking cart. She lurched after it a few paces in her high-heeled shoes and flung herself into it. The cart was lined with wet sacks which gave off a foul smell. She fell on her face amongst them, and her black satin dress immediately became wet and soiled.

'Where to?' the young man asked angrily.

'Only as far as the *kevutza,*' said Chava ingratiatingly, and she held on to the sides of the cart with both hands.

There was a moist sheen on the smooth surface of the road, and on the stars above. The mountains turned their heads towards the crackling flames; the whole of the tiny country seemed to be converging towards that point. I must see him now, come what may, Chava thought. All I will say to him is: I've come, I've come!

The cart turned off the road and began jolting over the broken ground at the sides of paths, swerving and rattling, the hoops threatening to part company from its wheels. I've come, I've come!

Chava sat hunched up, her hair disarranged, facing the back of the cart. The damp chill of the sacks sent a shiver up her spine. The sound of the guitars was still ringing in her ears, and a tearful melody throbbed in her heart: Suppose he doesn't understand what I tell him? I shall tell him that I'm asking nothing of him, I'm just bringing him an offering. I've come to return him his life's loss, that's all.

Near the cypress grove she jumped down. The cart topped the crest of the hill and raced down the other slope with a clatter. A heavy silence brooded over the *kevutza* yard. They had nearly all hurried off to the blazing wood and were working there with feverish haste. With their wet sacks they were fighting the flames and tenderly enveloping the scorched trees. Chava leaned against a slender cypress, and all the shadows gathered together round her. The watchman would not notice her as he passed by humming and yawning, rifle on shoulder. She would wait for Golani here: he would turn to this spot when he came back from the fire, and would find her. Maybe she would say nothing to him when he came: she would take him by the arm and pull him silently after her onto the wide, desolate stretch of uncultivated ground as it lay aching in its stones and still giving out the heat of the day. A heavy dew would descend upon the two of them, blanketing the earth, and the grass would grow damp and turn, as it were, into wet rags provided by God to wrap around His creatures in the midst of a conflagration.

She suddenly had a vision of her father standing alone and forlorn on the steps of the little verandah, awaiting her return and feeling twinges of remorse. Reb Zalman Liebman goes out to him, holding his trousers up with his hand, his braces trailing behind him. 'Well, Reb Ozer,' he says, 'a fine country this, eh?'

The pathetic figure soon became blurred and faded away. Chava was tired. She picked up her heavy feet and made her way to a corner between the fence and the shed where the Holstein bull was kept. She sank down on the ground, leaning against the wall. The bull roused himself and stirred in the darkness of the shed. He put his head up to the narrow grating above and stamped and snorted angrily, as if seeking to tear his nostrils from the ring which held them. Chava sat motionless, outstretched and secluded. The hours passed, and the stars above her head grew dim.

Never mind, she would wait. It would soon be dawn.

POLKA

by Yigal Mossinsohn

I.

THE MOUTH-ORGAN jerking to the movement of his tapping body, Yoshka stood among the dancers, who brushed occasionally against his outstreched elbows and touched the rolled-up sleeves of his glistening white Sabbath shirt. His eyes, squinting in the flecked light flickering from the rows of cracked lamps in the dining-room, followed the movements of the dancers rushing wildly from one end of the hall to the other in whirling circles, sweat dripping from the swinging couples. The mouth-organ's hoarse metallic tone pierced through confused voices of people huddling together against the walls and gazing at the great circles whirling in dizzy rings, a whirlpool of dance: the high-pitched notes accompanied their steps, their quick short breath, breaking into the stamping feet, the din, the raucous cries and noisy laughter.

Baruch Talman, a wizened bent farmer with a thin neck like a tortoise, wearing felt socks and an embroidered shirt flapping above gabardine trousers laced round his calves, stamps his foot with the force of a hammer blow upon the concrete floor. His brown hands, the hands of an old peasant, clasp and squeeze the ample bosom of his partner, Rina Taborit, whose massive, slightly bandy legs revolve slowly as he turns her heavy feminine body round in a circle. His hot breath flutters her golden hair, and her perspiring odorous body intoxicates him so that he lets out a hoarse roar to the ceiling of the hall and to the madly-playing Yoshka, tapping with his toes to the rhythm of the tune: 'Hey! Ho! Ho! Hop!'

'Hey! Ho!' Yoshka answers him, full lips parting in a wide beaming smile.

Hans, who looks after the vineyard, dances with Ma Friedman, the cook in the old folks' kitchen. In the slow grace with which they move it seems that not the polka accompanies them, but the strains of a Strauss waltz in a scented spring garden under the light of bright-colored lanterns, which circle slowly before Ma Friedman's half-closed eyes. They move slowly, languorously, Hans' hands caressing this body which had borne so many children, a body made up of trembling shaking circles, enveloped in a black silk dress and giving off an odour of naphtalene and old desires grown cold. Yoshka drums on the floor with the tip of his shoe: 'Hey, Ma! Pick up the load, Hans!'

Hans dances on with her, painstakingly leading her in peaceful, slow steps.

Around him, girls leapt like kids, hands on the shoulders of their partners, spinning them with arms around their waists and warm sideways glances of longing. Yoshka's drumming never stops, and his hand works the mouth-organ ceaselessly: They are still sitting in the corner, side by side on the same bench, and talking, heads close together. Maybe they will get up and leave the room together while I'm still playing! The devil take that guest! Why did he have to take up with my Ruth, damn him? He must clear out of here—go away and leave us alone! My world has become black since he came here four months ago—even though I'm smiling now for the dancers! Hey! Ho! Ho! Hop!

The hour is three after midnight. The dairymen leave the circle, abandoning their partners, hurrying through the kitchen shrouded in darkness, past pools of liquid manure to the cattle-shed. Black clouds cover the forest on the hill, flowing like a viscous stream to the valleys, blotting out the moon's cold light and scattering showers over the sowed fields, on the plots of barley and wheat and on the tin roof of the dining-room.

Now they are getting up, Yoshka is thinking.

The visitor, the theatrical producer Yitzchak Urbin, leans against the notice board, deep in thought, and Ruth pushes through the tight-packed crowd to a dim corner, wrapped in darkness, where she sits down on a table piled high with benches. The three exchange no direct glances, but eye one another's movements secretly. From behind a hand held casually to his forehead, Yitzchak Urbin inspects the broad-shouldered man, with his pug nose and small eyes, standing in the middle of the bustling crowd and sending out discordant music—like a fiddler in the market-place, he thinks. And Ruth rests her body, grown suddenly so heavy, on her arms and looks silently at the depressed stance of the producer, standing alone, aloof from the gay crowd, his great height surmounting a sorrowful face, his hand rumpling his hair in troubled thought. Yoshka seems to see nothing except the sweating bodies revolving round him in the movements of the polka and stamping on the down-beat with all their strength—those people whose world has been muddied by bad seas of rain, but who now seem suddenly to have revived in the festival atmosphere.

II.

Ruth supports her chin on her palm. She leans against the white wall, one leg folded over the other. So this was the end to months of drunken senses—Yitzchak was going tomorrow and would not return. No more would his long sensitive face stoop to her hands with a sigh of passion, the wide thin lips caress hers, sending shivers of desire down her yielding body. And there stands Yoshka, simple and deceived, deceived.

Ruth shivers. Is it the chill wind creeping on her from an open window—or Yoshka's smile falling on her over the heads of the dancers?

Yitzchak Urbin will go back to the little café, Ruth thinks, where his friends gather to talk of this and that, the artists and actors sipping cup after cup of sweet black coffee and sending spirals of grey-blue smoke up to the ceiling until midnight, until long after midnight. He will lean his lithe body against one of the town women, passing his fingers over her neck, her ears, the vermilion-smeared lips of the café woman reminding him of her kisses: 'There was a woman. In the kibbutz. She loved me. Don't even remember her name. After the rehearsals she would slip into my room. We would snatch a few hours together—until she had to go out into the night, to her husband Yoshka the tractorist. And I would lie on my back on the white bed, smoking under the quiet of the lamp. They invited me to produce a play for their tenth anniversary celebrations. It was rather an amusing experience.'

Ruth looks at the pale face and blond locks across the wide space of the dining-room. Yitzchak Urbin lights a cigarette, his fingers moving delicately as if aware of their beauty. He stands a little away from the moving wall of people, quiet, indifferent, observing the strange faces lit with a wild unfamiliar gaiety.

That woman sitting in the corner now—whom I talked with only a few minutes ago—what is she thinking? That placid mask was stripped off when we were together in the little room. Perhaps you never know a woman until she is stripped of all clothing and stands naked before you, undisguised—aflame with lust. And this clumsy Yoshka has never seen the whole of the woman in her, made for a man's love. Ruth for him is only a seed-bed, ploughed first and then sowed. Yes, with those heavy hands, blue from dragging chains through mud and dirty with grease. Maybe that's why she was drawn to me—because of my white skin and my hands, which have never worked with earth and ploughs. Tomorrow I'm going with the kibbutz lorry, leaving behind this woman and the whole affair. If I miss her—I'll drink a few more glasses of cognac in the café. But why must it always be the same ending:

settling the affair leaves a bitter heart. She just told me: 'I'm having a child.' Imagine, a little Yitzchak Urbin walking about the cattle-sheds and tractors! No, it's not certain at all, not at all. And if I've already reconciled myself and wished them luck, she and Yoshka both, why does she watch me with bewildered eyes, half crying, and get up and rid herself of me so suddenly?

Yitzchak Urbin drops his hands feebly, and moves the weight of his body from one leg to the other.

Why does every woman I meet want to bind me to her with cords of flesh forever? Maybe it would be good to clip my wings—my aimless life of never-ending holidays. But am I expected to become a swaddler of babies in napkins, standing beside the laundry tubs and cleaning infants' backsides?

It was hard to tell whether Yitzchak Urbin was curling his lips with disdain or smiling with regret.

Yes, Yoshka is probably better off, living here with his friends, leading their dance on holidays, not afraid to be imprisoned between four walls with a woman. While I go barren all my days, free of soul and barren—without a woman and without sons! Maybe it's better for Yoshka, near the clods and sowed fields, and in the din of dancers, sweat dripping from them but not stopping even when dawn approaches, and I among them—a stranger, a foreigner.

Yitzchak Urbin walks over to the window and looks out on the muddy yard. Next to the door of the cattle-shed, under a single electric light, stands a cart loaded with green fodder. Dairymen clean milk cans and carry them inside.

What sort of a life is this, of waking in the dead of night to manure heaps and to cows dripping with mire? While I walk along the city pavements on my way to bed, they get up to work. Perhaps this effort of theirs is a sign of strength, or perhaps they haven't strength to fight their monotonous fate of fatigue and toil, day after day, year after year.

Pondering the lives of those who worked and slaved for their bread under heavy burdens, Urbin stands with his back to the uproar, chin pressed against the glass for a long while.

III.

'Hey! Ho! Ho! Hop!' Yoshka turns round on weary legs, beating time with tired movements. 'Heeeeeey! Hoooooop!' he cries to the sweat-stained faces—to Baruch Talman, whirling dizzily and trying to keep up with the rapid movements of Rina Taborit, whose shirt clings wetly to her skin, exposing her fleshy breasts—to Ma Friedman, dancing with half-closed eyes—to Ruth, withdrawn into herself in the dark corner—to the narrow back of Yitzchak Urbin—to the wild hair and dim-lit faces of the dancers.

'Hey! Ho!' Tomorrow Yitzchak Urbin will go, and Ruth will return to her own quiet self and stop this nightmare sleepwalking of the last few months. It's good I said nothing to her. She thinks I don't know anything about it. She thinks . . . 'Hey! Hop!' And Yoshka clutches his mouth-organ with renewed strength and starts a new tune.

The heavy rains had flooded the fields, washed away fertile soil and interfered with the planting. In the intervals between downpours Yoshka goes out to plant the sodden fields. The tractor chain presses down the heavy earth, dragging behind it heaps of sticky loam mixed with seeds.

Yes, that's how it is, Yoshka thought. All winter the cattle fodder wasn't cut in the flooded fields. The dairymen had no food for their animals. The lucerne was stricken by rust. Good lands were spoiled, the work of many years ruined. The best soil was lost, the fertile upper layer. And my field also has been ruined, Ruth spoilt by this city weed. Damn Urbin! And the child—is it mine?

'Hey! Ho!' Yoshka shouts suddenly. 'Come on, Baruch! Faster, you old plough horse! Lift your legs!'

Ruth looks at him, at his eyes shining with unaccustomed fire. His voice is hoarse. Yes, it is Yitzchak Urbin's child, Yoshka. When a person wakes after drunkenness he still has tortures ahead of him. Maybe all those months of intoxication, of nights without sleep, were nothing but a mocking dream—and the touch of Urbin's hands never made my body shiver with passion. Perhaps I never went in a trance to his room and surrendered myself to his arms. Perhaps those endless days of mud and rain, of screaming children in the nursery and midnight rehearsals, have blinded me, have hidden Yoshka from me. The fragrant cigarettes, the starched shirts and white neck, the long hands and exciting, tender caresses—were all a dream. And the new life in me, flowering in my flesh? He said to me: 'Congratulations, good luck to you and Yoshka!' Doesn't he know this is his son? Yes, Yitzchak Urbin, do you think you will find the answer out there in the darkness by the cattle-shed? My world is destroyed. When I came home from rehearsals tired, saturated, trembling from the touch of Urbin's naked body, Yoshka never reproached me. He always made a place for me in the wide bed. 'Tired, Ruth? Come,' he would say, and fall asleep holding me against his hairy breast. A deceitful and miserable fraud. Two people whose world had collapsed, pretending to sleep peacefully in one another's arms! It is good that he was so patient with me—a man like that can forget, can let the memory of the bad times pass away. If I'll go into the circle and dance until all my strength is gone—perhaps I'll rid myself of this last link to Yitzchak Urbin.

Ruth rests her burning face against the cool wood of the table.

Maybe I'll go into the circle and dance a mad polka until it becomes a dance of blood for me! To be rid of everything, free again! Yoshka will dance with me, and all our comrades will see me dancing, will see my answer to the desire flaming in me for Urbin! And Yoshka is sure this is his son! Yoshka, it's not true, it's a fraud, a perverse and wicked lie! And when Yoshka met me going towards our room, early one morning, when he returned from night ploughing because the tractor had broken down, what did he say? 'Good morning, Ruth! Where are you going to so early?' and was off without waiting for an answer. 'Something to do at the garage,' he said. Yes, something broke down. Nothing is as it used to be. The barrier will always be between us, this man who made me crazy for a while. Yoshka, tapping with his foot—how little people know of what torture he has gone through, how wise and understanding he is! He didn't destroy our lives because of a foolish interlude, thank God!

Ruth slides down from the table and makes her way through the crowd, towards Yoshka.

I must be careful, she thinks. Nobody must guess what I want to do.

She prepares herself for the plunge into the whirlpool. Yoshka's silent strength chills her heart for a moment, freezing the warm blood in her veins. She pays no attention to the significant glances cast at her by people she elbows aside, glances of curiosity and surprise: she's walking queerly, with fixed eyes, this woman who has been sitting moodily in a corner and now suddenly can't wait but must push forward hastily to the heart of the circle—and to her husband.

Yitzchak Urbin turns on his heel and searches for Ruth in the crowd.

A real night-bird, that's what you are, thinks Yitzchak Urbin to himself. A night-bird. While the sun is out you prefer to doze in a room guarded with shutters so that no light can enter, a china ash tray choked with cigarette ends on the carpet next to the bed. Year after year goes past, and the wonderful plans for the future are forgotten. And no one knows—and I least of all—what purpose there can be in this life of haunting city streets at midnight, of walking always alone, making a living from imagination and visions, supported by a father growing old behind the counter of a small pharmacy at the street-corner. Here at least these people have done something concrete—even if their nails have become ingrained with black—and after sowing they reap sacks of grain and make flour. No, these are not amateurs like me, these people who go out to plough at night, these dancers who find the strength after a week of fatigue to form merry circles and forget the early risings in the bitter cold and darkness, the rain soaking through to the bones in the open field, and the long hard hours of labor until the body rebels from weariness. And I am—an amateur producer! What emptiness, what a waste of a life!

He turns to look for Ruth, lighting another cigarette and crushing the old stub under his heel. 'There she is—next to her husband!' Urbin thinks, looking at the couple.

IV.

'Yoshka. let's dance,' says Ruth.

Yoshka lowered his head towards her. He had not heard, or had not understood, what she had said—or had not wanted to understand.

'Let's dance, Yoshka?'

He looked in bewilderment at her outstretched hands, her moist eyes and trembling chin.

'What's wrong, Ruth?' he asked.

'Nothing—come on, let's dance!'

Yoshka stopped playing. He pressed the mouth-organ against his chest. The dancers came to a standstill and separated slowly, walking away and leaving Ruth and Yoshka alone in the middle of the hall, the focus of curious eyes.

'What's wrong, Ruth?' he repeated anxiously, his mind working slowly with almost visible effort.

'I want to dance, Yoshka, to go ma-a-d! Perhaps it'll be a dance of blood . . .'

'This isn't a play rehearsal, Ruth. You can't dance in your condition.'

He was referring to the growth pressing inside her.

'Yoshka, I want to forget everything about the play and—and that man, Yoshka.'

They stood close to one another, forgetting the crowded hall.

Yoshka patted her neck gently. 'You can't do it, Ruth. It's crazy.'

Yitzchak Urbin came towards them, face wax-white and eyes burning into the couple standing silent and tense. Without speaking, he took the mouth-organ from Yoshka and squeezed a few cracked chords out of it.

'Want to dance?' Urbin asked them, his eyes looking past them, hearing clearly again the cry of a tipsy dancer in the café: 'I'm bored to death!' A wry look of derision hovered over his thin mouth, and he passed his tongue nervously over his twisted upper lip.

'What shall it be? Tango—foxtrot—or some pi-on-eering tune?'

'Well—play!' growled Yoshka.

Ruth caught the hate for Urbin in these words that Yoshka flung at him. This was not the same understanding, gentle, easy-going man she knew. This was Yoshka standing at the entrance to his cave, and prepared to defend his woman with brute strength if necessary. His broad, hairy chest rose and fell heavily, and he glared aggressively at the pale face opposite him.

'Play, Urbin! Play a polka!' Yoshka placed his hands on Ruth's waist, swung her in a half-circle and shouted: 'None of your teasing town tangoes! A polka! Hey! Ho! Ho! Hop!'

At first the rhythm kept slow. They moved evenly, gracefully, past a solid wall of onlookers. And after they had moved a few times up and down the length of the dining-room—one solitary couple dancing in all that space—the pace began to quicken. Their faces lighted up, their breath came shorter, their legs began to dance by themselves dizzily.

As they danced, Yoshka bent down and whispered to Ruth: 'What's going on? They're all watching us!'

'Never mind, Yoshka. Don't worry about them.'

Yitzchak Urbin played on, his eyes never leaving the couple. All the time she had given herself up to his caresses, he saw with a sudden knife-thrust of bitterness, her face had never been as radiant as it was now. Her eyelashes trembled on half-closed lids, the mouth twisting itself into an expression of mingled pain and lust. Each step, each turn, thought Urbin, each movement in those clumsy farmer's arms wipes away those nights we spent together, as dawn erases the darkness: with the dance melted away the fierce, silent hours in the little room—melted the image of that Ruth who stripped herself of her clothes, throwing them over a chair and giving herself up to Urbin's long arms.

She danced on, eyes shut, a mist of thoughts before her, oblivious of anything outside the rhythm of the music. Her legs moved like separate beings, not needing instructions from her brain or heart, not needing Ruth herself. Yoshka breaths heavily: his shabby khaki trousers flap in the dance, his broad back and his knees bending in the dance.

It was Baruch Talman who had whispered to him that night in the field: 'Urbin doesn't only come here as our guest, but he must make himself at home with another man's wife.' Baruch Talman whispered this to him down by the camp-fire in the field where they ploughed the land for the summer crops.

The ground was damp, and the tractors, crawling through the darkness behind lamps which intensified the gloom surrounding them, dragged behind them rows of sharp plough blades. They spun on their chains, sliding from the uneven road to the furrow, making the earth leap and spring under the shock which heaped it with black waves behind the plough; they felt their way behind the swirling lights into the heart of the night, startling the sodden fields with noise, the smell of grease, flying clods of earth.

It was a chilly night, and Baruch Talman sat hunched up on a straw mattress, peeling potatoes by the light of a damp wood fire and watching the tractors' lights groping in the dark.

Around him lay scattered barrels of paraffin, grease tins, boxes. And Baruch Talman let the peels fall to the ground between his knees and thought of Yoshka's Ruth, the wife of the man coming towards him on the noisy tractor.

His rifle was hidden inside his jacket, the leather strap for the bullets lying at the edge of the mattress. A field lamp stood on a tin inside a box of cutlery, blackening its glass with the murky flame. Frogs croaked in the nearby swamp. Baruch Talman dropped the potatoes into a bucket of water, poured oil into a four-legged frying pan placed over the fire and cut the potatoes into pieces, letting them fall into the pan, where they sizzled with little explosions of frying fat. Baruch Talman lifted his head and stared into the darkness, watching Yoshka's tractor come closer to the fire. Baruch was part peasant and part one who watched over these people ploughing in the night and attended to their needs. When they were eating, he said to Yoshka: 'Urbin doesn't only come here as our guest, but he must make himself at home with another man's wife. . . .'

Yoshka said nothing, didn't answer a word. He chewed the coarse bread, the potatoes, the bitterness that rose up in him, hearing Baruch's words. He remained silent until just before he started the tractor to go back to the fields. Then, only then, he turned to Baruch Talman standing beside a petrol drum: 'Don't stick your nose into other people's business, Burka!'

And Baruch pushed his thin bloodless neck towards him excitedly, bursting into speech: 'Haven't you eyes to see, Yoshka? Everybody's talking about it. After the rehearsals she goes to Urbin's room, Yoshka.'

In the roar of motors Baruch heard Yoshka's shout and saw two massive clumsy hands coming towards him and gripping his coat lapels, and a grime-streaked face shone menacingly above him, eyes glittering in the light of the fire: 'Burka, listen, Burka—it's my business, and no one has the right to interfere! It's my life that's being ruined, you understand, my life! I've kept quiet because you can't change emotions by force. You can't force emotions. That swine Urbin has nearly wrecked us, our world together—but she must come back to herself before she comes back to me. And she mustn't think I stole any happiness from her. She'll come back, Burka. She'll come back with a whole heart if I won't press and force her now, taking away from her her feeling of freedom, the air she breathes. Married life isn't a prison, Burka. If I'll keep the keys of a jail in my pocket I'll lose her, she'll run away—and I want her so much, in spite of this Urbin who has blackened my world. Do you hear, Burka?! If you interfere again—I'll give you a beating you won't forget in a hurry!'

Having finished this rush of words with a grunt, Yoshka did not let Burka go at once, but held him for a moment, then pushed his wizened body away with a force which threw him against the empty barrel: 'Go to hell, all of you!'

He climbed on the tractor, and began travelling towards the black furrows. Over the ravine were fields of wheat, planted before the first rains, and beside them vetch for hay. The rows were regular, evenly-spaced. Afterwards they would plant summer crops here—sorghum, sunflowers, corn. Yes, the world included also summer—and Yitzchak Urbin wouldn't be there. Better not think about it. Yes, there are seasons of winter crops and summer crops, the legumes enrich the earth with nitrogen taken from the air, and return to the soil its richness removed by the grains—and a man who had been tortured by life—what would reward him? Better not think about it . . .

Yoshka dances. Sweat drips from his body in heavy drops, running over his flesh. Ruth turns between his arms, feels a mist rise and cover her eyes, a thick fog blotting out her vision. The people against the walls seem pale, blurred, caricatures of themselves. The clock on the wall dances with her. Its hands spin ceaselessly at a tremendous speed. The arms holding her waist are steel pincers, holding her fast, pressing her. Who is this dancing with her? Yoshka? Urbin? Maybe a sweating body was dancing, and those hairy arms were apes, leaping from tree to tree with wild cries. Grey flowers drop their petals over her forehead. Grey flowers hang on the hands of the clock: behind them lies Urbin on his back in the bed.

V.

'What's wrong!?' Yoshka asks.

Ruth falls to the ground. People run towards her, bare feet shuffling over the concrete floor. An abyss opens, people falling inside it. Ruth stretches out a hand: 'Urbin, don't do that . . . please don't . . .' Ruth groans and gulps: 'Uhnnnnnn.' Her eyes are glass. Yoshka bends down and picks her up in his arms. He carries her, half fainting, into their room, near the dining-hall, feeling with relief the warm blood pulsing through her body.

'Nothing! Everything's all right!' he calls over his shoulder to the people following him. 'She's feeling a bit faint . . .' He hears Yitzchak Urbin coming up behind him on the gravel path. Those steps that Yoshka hated, light, as if floating on air.

'What is it, Ruth? What is it?' Yoshka groans desperately to the limp figure in his arms. Ruth sighs, opens her eyes for a moment and closes them again. Pain forces a long shuddering cry from her: 'Aaaaaah!'

Yoshka goes down the wooden steps, feeling Urbin's steps behind him. My shadow, Yoshka thought. I haven't said anything to him yet— don't let him force me to curse, to pour my anger on his white face—don't let him force me.

Clouds were moving over the roofs, very heavy clouds.

'Well—better, Ruthie?' Yoshka's winking eyelashes and quivering lips spoke louder than the barely uttered words.

Yitzchak Urbin walks beside Yoshka. He wants to say something, but he feels a suffocating feeling in his throat and can't speak. At last he comes out with a rush: 'What happened?'

'Nothing,' Yoshka growls, and it seems as though the word comes from a hollow deep down inside him.

Urbin's great height seemed to shorten, from the slope of the ground or from nervousness. 'But—I saw—she fainted,' he stammered. 'She fell in the excitement of the polka.'

Yoshka reached the door of his room. Urbin hurried to open it before him, switched on the electric light and squeezed himself into a corner of the creeper-covered porch. Yoshka placed Ruth tenderly on the bed, returned with heavy steps to Urbin.

'Listen, Urbin,' he said deliberately, 'I've nothing against you—but get out of here! Take your things and go, before the day breaks! Get going, Urbin!'

Urbin tore some leaves from the creeper and examined them, head downcast. 'I wanted to say something to Ruth before I went,' he murmured, looking at a leaf falling broken from his hand.

'Listen, Urbin! My child's dead!' Yoshka whispered hoarsely.

A note of threat crept into the stillness hovering before the dawn. Yitzchak Urbin slid a sidewards glance at Yoshka, and made off with hurried strides in the direction of the hill.

At the same time the rain began battering on the tin roofs, and in the dining-room they were sweeping the dusty floor.

THE LATEBORN

by Yehoshua Bar-Yosef

I.

HUNEH'S GRANDFATHER was a clever man, who could see far ahead. Seventy years ago he wound up his business abroad and went to live in Jerusalem, the Holy City. Having more money then he knew what to do with, he went and built a large courtyard, which unto this very day is called, after him, 'Reb Moishe Duvid's Courtyard.' This courtyard was consecrated by Reb Moishe Duvid as a foundation for fifty scholars, who were to live there free of charge with their families: every five years new scholars, chosen by lot. Later, his son Reb Nuhemtche demanded three napoleons a year from the lodgers. And when Reb Nuhemtche died and left a widow and a son, they asked five pounds a year. So nowadays the courtyard is neither a foundation nor real estate. Not a foundation, because the lodgers pay five pounds per year; and not real estate, because one cannot call five pounds rent. The upshot is—today the tenants live almost free of rent, and the widow and her son Huneh make a decent living out of it.

A man amongst men was Reb Moishe Duvid, even on the brink of the grave. When he was nearly eighty, he married a young girl of twenty and gave her a darling baby boy who was the praise of all Jerusalem. When the boy had reached the age of thirteen, his young mother had already been laid to rest on the Mount of Olives; but Reb Moishe Duvid partook of a rich pie in honor of his son's bar mitzva. Only after he had heard read the engagement contract between Reb Nuhemtche and his first wife, and he was satisfied that his son had been delivered into faithful hands, did the old man make up his mind and decide that the honorable place in Paradise, which was his by due, was to be preferred to a simple house in Jerusalem. And so did Reb Moishe Duvid take his leave from the pleasures of this sorry world.

His son, Reb Nuhemtche was also a man of good sense; but as he was born in Jerusalem, worse luck, he was neither as strong nor as rich as his father. Not as strong, for he had not eaten fattened geese abroad; and not as rich, for the courtyard which was his patrimony was a foundation and did not bring him more than a hundred and fifty napoleons a year. Nevertheless, he was one of the few people of importance in Jerusalem. His hair was as soft as silk, his skin like velvet, and his looks like the pure oil in the silver Hanukka lamp. His speech was like plucking a fiddle's thinnest string, and his prayer like a wounded bird which had fallen to the ground. The miracle-workers of Jerusalem expected great and mysterious wonders of him. Reb Nuhemtche took two wives and divorced them both, the first after ten, the second after twenty years. Neither was blessed with children from his weak loins. But then there came the third, a healthy old spinster, and she brought Huneh into the world. Fifty years old was Reb Nuhemtche when his son, the last effort of his manhood, was born, and thus made him as happy as a young man of twenty. Never had Jerusalem seen a circumcision feast like that of Huneh. Twenty strong porters were busy all day carting the drunk home; for a true son of Jerusalem, as soon as his feet lose contact with the holy earth, immediately cleaves to it with his whole body, so that there is need for two strong porters to detach him. Thus Jerusalem welcomed Huneh, and thus they rejoiced in his father's joy. Had they foreseen his end, they surely would not have been so glad at his birth.

It would seem that the heavenly Powers had mercy on Reb Nuhemtche and required his presence above before he could have much 'pleasure' from his son. Huneh was the son of an old father, but his flesh and bones were like those of a young bull. Fire burned in his body and flames in his sinews. When he was three years old, no child's face remained unscratched in the courtyard; by the time he was five, all its windows were broken and all its earthen water-jars in shards. Nothing, large or small, was safe from his hands. And because he was the only son of the young widow who owned the courtyard, nobody dared lay a finger on the boy. The mother, a good and simple woman whose only chance to have her own way was due to the little heir, spoilt her strong son as if he were a tender little bird. All the unspent energy of her widowhood was expended in kisses and caresses and embraces on the unwilling little boy, who would object by crying and striking her with hands and feet. To the young widow, his kicks were as sweet as her own kisses and caresses. But if she felt relieved by them, Huneh reacted differently. After every such outburst he was angry with himself and with the whole world. If his face had been beaten and his body whipped, he would not have been as upset as he was by his mother's kisses.

As long as he was still a baby, people sometimes gave him a smile or a friendly look. They forgave him his naughty pranks and put the blame for them on his unusual situation. But when he began to grow up, people would get angry with him. Mothers kept their children away from him, children of his own age were afraid to meet him face to face. Even the adults regarded him as a strange sort of creature. 'Something is not quite in order with Huneh Late-born . . .' they all said. And he was really different from other children. The ordinary games did not attract him; every toy, anything made to last, annoyed and frightened him, and he was not satisfied until he saw it smashed to bits. He liked to see children's faces screwed up with weeping, and those of grownups—confused and ridiculous. Then he would laugh his loud and hearty laughter. And even though he could not see his own face when he laughed, he noticed the spark of fright in the eyes of those who looked upon his laughter. 'There is something unsimple, impure, in the boy's eyes,' a woman once whispered. His teacher at the *heder* also said something similar. From the Bible and the prayerbook Huneh ran away as from the plague. He stayed in the *heder* only as long as this gave him a chance to make some other child burst into tears, and to find occasions for his own loud laughter.

Before many days had passed, his name was in every mouth. Even Rabbi Michale the Judge felt that it was his duty, in his mild manner, to sermonize the unruly boy. And though Huneh could take a hard push in the ribs which someone might give him in secret, he was unable to forgive Rabbi Michale the Judge for his bland admonitions. So, for the first time in his life, Huneh thought a long while of some way to revenge himself.

One day he waited for several hours for a mouse to come out of its hole. When it came out—he caught it and put it in a box, which he then closed. That whole day long the box stayed in his pocket, whispering like a glowing coal; and no less heatedly did Huneh's imagination whisper about the gentle wrinkled face of Rabbi Michale the Judge. Rabbi Michale was a fine man, spick and span, dressed all in white on Sabbath and weekdays alike. There was no spot on his coat, no grain of dust under his fingernails. Also, he had a snuffbox, curiously wrought in silver with all manner of delicate cusps and curlicues; the box was kept in a silken cover in the pocket of his gabardine, and was Rabbi Michale's joy and pride.

That day in the Beth Midrash, Rabbi Michale did not see how the burning, whispering eyes of Huneh followed him as he went to a certain place. As soon as the gabardine was hanging on a clean nail near the entrance, Huneh went up to it and did whatever he did . . . Rabbi Michale returned with measured step to the Beth Midrash, dipped his white fingers in the water, wiped them on the towel and, leisurely and composed, joined a group of people who had come to pray, and began to discourse of heavenly matters with the learned men beside him. In due course, after this and that, it was time to enjoy a pinch of snuff. Rabbi Michale turned his eyes upwards, relieved his delicate features with a few suitable grimaces, raised his hands as one might lift a precious Torah scroll, inserted his long fingers in the pocket of the hanging gabardine, carefully pulled out the silken cover, put his thumb and forefinger into the opening of the cover and winked modestly, as if to say: 'Such a snuffbox! In all Jerusalem you will not find another one like it!'—and lo! his fingers held, not the snuffbox, but a frightened mouse! Instead of jumping on the floor, as Rabbi Michale might have wished, the sharp-nailed mouse climbed with quick jumps up into the sleeve of his white shirt... and shouts of laughter filled the prayerhouse. Running and noise and confusion! Only one, a boy of ten, stood on the side and looked quiet-faced at the whole spectacle, his eyes agleam with lust and enjoyment.

II.

When he was thirteen, Huneh discovered that something had been wrong with his brain even before he was born, something that was at the root of the whole trouble. That, at least, was what people thought; and though Huneh himself did not think that such things were as important as all that, something within him was shocked when he heard what was said about him. He began to hate people and to be afraid of them. When he stayed alone, he was somehow afraid of himself, at times his mind showed signs of an inexplicable melancholy. His mother, who became frightened at all these rumors and whisperings, decided to cure her only son with the aid of holy caves, incantations, and sorcery. When these were of no avail, she took her life into her hands and went to those new sorcerers, the European doctors of all kinds—but that was no use either. At night and when no one paid attention, the boy of thirteen would sit and tremble with fear like a three-year-old. One of the doctors told his mother that the cause of his fear lay in his blood; that is to say,

Reb Nuhemtche had been born when Reb Moishe Duvid was old and afraid of death; and Huneh was also born in his father's old age.

Huneh's fear, though, was no fear of death, but rather fear for its own sake. Only when he laughed his wild laughter or when he was getting ready for it, was Huneh free from his fear. Like a starving man who performs his work for the sake of his daily bread, so Huneh exerted himself to invent new tricks every day, so as to be able to laugh. All those wise observations which relatives made to him sagely and carefully—such as that a person should not run about aimlessly in God's good world, or that it was a bitter and evil thing to skip one's prayers and to grow up without learning—fell on deaf ears. While they were talking to him solemnly, he would gravely consider the chances of pulling away their chairs from behind them, of sticking a pin into a certain spot in their trousers, of pasting on them a donkey cut out of paper—and similar tricks designed to cause huge enjoyment to their perpetrator, and confusion to their targets. Even when he did not carry out these plans in reality, for fear of his mother's kisses and the caresses which would follow her bitter weeping, his imagination would perform them in every detail—and there would sound his laughter again, a sudden laughter which left people with their mouths gaping and made them shake their heads, as if to say: 'There is no hope for the poor devil . . .'

So Huneh grew up, lonely and forsaken in the large courtyard. When he walked in the street, people would point their fingers at him and shake their heads: 'Have you seen Reb Moishe Duvid's grandson? Why should such a pious man have deserved all this?' And when Huneh heard such pitying words, he felt as if pins were stuck into his heart. But instead of paying attention and considering the right and the wrong of his way of life, he would make all kinds of faces, stick out his tongue, mew like a cat or bray like an ass, and finish up with some salty curse.

In those days, Huneh came to realize that a man's mind is more sensitive than his body and began to annoy people through matters of the mind. He ceased to use *tefillin* and boasted openly of it. On the first of May, he assembled the children of Meah Shearim and marched them about in the streets with a red flag waving above their heads. During prayers, he would stand at the window of the synagogue and sing or whistle the tunes of the 'halutzim.' All these produced familiar and foreseeable movements of people's bodies, which filled him with waves of laughter and relieved to some extent the incessant feeling of fear.

His most daring exploit was that of the cigarettes on Sabbath. He would climb to the roof of the house, wait patiently until the people came out of the synagogues, and as they walked home through the pleasant, narrow, clean lanes, he would call out to them in his merry voice: 'A good Sabbath to you, good Jews, a good and blessed Sabbath!'—and straightaway a match would be struck and he would be puffing at a lighted cigarette. Down in the street scores and hundreds of people would come running, shouting, waving their hands, throwing stones and cursing roundly. But he would carry on. Only when a long ladder would be brought and portly, perspiring Jews had climbed its rickety steps with angry, vengeful gestures, would Huneh's legs withdraw and jump from roof to roof, until his body disappeared in one of the passages.

Those were full, stormy days. And at night he would dream: confused dreams and clear dreams of the day's events; he dreamed, and wondered about the meaning and interpretation of his dreams. He was outlawed and ostracized by his neighbors. Even his mother began to look at him with sorrowful reproaching glances, glances which sometimes hurt him more than all the curses and insults of other people. Nevertheless, no one touched him; perhaps because they respected the memories of his father and grandfather, and perhaps because they were afraid of his mother's retaliation.

When he was eighteen, Huneh began to notice the soft hairs which sprouted on his cheeks and chin. First he played with them like a cat with its whiskers, but afterwards he started to shave, out of a secret desire to annoy the people of the courtyard and of the neighborhood, who all let their beards and earlocks grow. In those days, he had for the first time a good long look at himself in the mirror on the wall. The face which he saw there was a frightening discovery: he felt like one who sees an abyss suddenly gaping at his feet. And indeed, there was reason enough for fright: a pointed, bald head—for most of his hair had fallen out during his childhood; a pale, yellow-tinted face; a long, crooked nose; a wide mouth, distorted with mockery; a sloping, narrow forehead; eyes in which a fire of fear and madness flickered; and a long, thin neck, bent forward like that of a camel. And this face rose up out of a body powerful with wide shoulders and hard-muscled flesh. A strange feeling of shame overcame him. Thereafter, he felt as if all eyes were staring at his ugly face. In his dreams his body would rise before him, member after member, and each would instill a different creeping fear in him. Even when awake he would recall the movements of these dreams, and from time to time he would run to the mirror to find out how much truth there was in his frenzied imaginings.

If hitherto Huneh had only known fear in general, he now felt all the special kinds of fear which our sages mention. There is a fear which turns only the tips of your members into stone: a sort of chill possesses your fingers and toes and the tips of your ears, while in the chest something keeps boiling and trembling. Another kind of fear is the exact opposite: hands and knees tremble—and the heart turns to stone. Sometimes you want to hide yourself and to creep away to some far corner, where you hope to find cover; then again you feel like running away from yourself, in any direction. At times melancholy and a desire for sleep combine within you; then again a stormy desire for battle and the lust of revenge arise in the heart. The kinds of fear are different and manifold, like the tints that can be discerned in a ray of sunlight. But worst of all is when the source of all fears is within yourself, when you fear the memory of your own face.

All these fears passed through Huneh's mind and left their imprint upon it. Sometimes he felt as if his ugly face had left his head and entered into his very self and turned it to dust and ashes. On those days, he would sit gazing at his countenance in the mirror. He would no longer go down into the lanes of the neighborhood to play his tricks, but would sit in his mother's house, weary and trembling because of his thoughts. Sometimes he would go out, pale and silent, onto the large balcony which overlooked the courtyard, and would stare without interest at the commotion of the noisy life below. People did not recognize him. In less than a month's time he had changed completely. His wide mouth had become pinched as if by tongs, and he would look back at people with quiet, fearful eyes, so that an uneasy feeling would force them to leave him alone.

III.

One day Huneh noticed Zipporah. The girl came out of the house door to return a pot to the kitchen. The sunlight fell on her face; the girl lifted her hand to shade her eyes, and her white chin was lifted a little and uncovered her throat. Now Zipporah had not fallen from the sky. She had first seen daylight in that selfsame courtyard. Hundreds of times had Huneh seen her play with the children, but he had never noticed her. Now he suddenly trembled all over. Her soft, hesitant posture stuck, as it were, in his throat. All at once he noticed the black line containing her eyes and brows—this line dominated her face as if it had been stuck on by an unskilled hand—and the living pulsating pallor round her mouth and chin. She was sixteen years old and fully grown; her figure was average, neither fat nor thin. Her hair was black and full, and the two long tresses which hung down on her feminine shoulders were poorly plaited; above her ears, whorled like a delicate shell, locks of disobedient hair escaped. When Huneh saw the girl that day, something broke within him. That whole night he kept seeing her image before him, as a drowning man sees death before his eyes.

Thereafter, his old fear left him and something new took its place. Only one question occupied him: how to approach the girl? How to get permission to stand near her or to feed his eyes on her, even from afar? For she was sure to be afraid of him, to regard him as half crazy; in the days of his wild pranks, he had harried her parents often enough. The more he thought of it, the more he felt a weakness and a strange shame. He remembered the ugliness of his face, his bad reputation and the enmity by which he had become surrounded, and said to himself: 'Ai, Huneh, Huneh, you are the most miserable man in the world. Everyone thinks you are crazy. You have not studied Torah. You have not gained wisdom. What good are the merits of your ancestors to you and how can the inherited income of the courtyard help you, if you yourself are an abominable branch?' Thus he spoke to himself day and night, and thus he wandered about, full of shame and despair. He was in mortal fear of approaching Zipporah. From afar, from a safe hiding place, he would look at her, at the movements of her playful head, at her walk which constricted his heart, at her slender erect figure, and each single one of her limbs assumed a painfully pleasant meaning. More he did not dare. He kept this all within his heart, as a precious secret to be shared with no one. He enjoyed his secret, turning it over and over, awake and in his dreams, and he was happy—if one may call such a feeling happiness.

It is difficult to say what connection there was between his new secret and the strange desire which overcame him, to make closer contact with people again. His dreaming body was attracted by the continuous tumult of the Beth Midrash, with its festive and lively activities. And though he himself used no *tefillin* and prayed neither alone nor with the community, the very fact that he came to the Beth Midrash was a submission. At first, people were suspicious of the way he would be quietly standing there, feeling sure that he was preparing some new prank. But when they looked at his face, which was sorrowful like the face of one who repents, they would whisper amongst themselves: 'Surely the merits of his sainted ancestors in the other world have come to his aid, and thoughts of repentance have entered his heart.' And indeed, in those days Huneh loved to hear the sad melody of prayer. He felt a slow tremor filling his wide shoulders, and a strange desire to lean his forehead on the table and to cry as he had never cried before. But for all his trying, the choked tears could not come up out of his throat. That was a great defect of Huneh's—he could not cry. Crush him in a mortar—not a tear would come out. He had never cried. Perhaps that also was the fault of his fearful blood. So he sat miserable and sad, but tearless, amongst the same people who only yesterday had feared him like death.

It's an odd thing about people: either you lord it over them or they lord it over you—they are incapable of leaving a man alone in the privacy of his dreams. That was what happened with Huneh. As long as he plagued them with his pranks, everything was fine and dandy; but as soon as he stopped meddling with their affairs, they began to pester him. It was as if they felt that all his strength had faded away. One snapped his fingers against his nose, another turned his hat around, yet another pinched his cheek as one does to a child of four; one laughed provokingly in his face, and someone else told rude stories about him—and all this while Huneh sat and smiled, humbled and abused, musing about himself and his surroundings. He was like a dreamer overwhelmed by a great trouble in his dream: though he may think he knows how to avert it, he cannot lift a finger.

One of the members of the community was Zipporah's father, a

Jew from Poland with a heavy beard, pious and innocent in the Beth Midrash, but cunning and sharp in his trade. He had a poultry shop, which supported him in luxury, for he was a rare expert in the art of stuffing fowls with all manner of fodder to increase their weight before selling them, and he could blow up a meager chicken till it looked like a fat hen, fit for a king's table. One bright day this man's black eyes shone with a greasy smile—he looked at Huneh as if he were a strange toy, and waited patiently for the end of the prayer. They all, including Rabbi Michale the Judge, had already gone home, and he and Huneh were left alone—he with his meaningful smile, and Huneh with his endless musings. Huneh was sitting, as was his wont, with his head on his hand and dreaming of forgotten yesterdays, when suddenly he felt a soft hand on his shoulder. Huneh looked up into the hairy face of the other, and it seemed to him like the face of an angel, soft and friendly—like Zipporah's face.

'Ai Huneh, Huneh,' sighed the hairy face. 'You have strayed from the straight path, you have forgotten whose son you are. You do not use *tefillin,* you do not keep the Sabbath, you have not studied the Law, you are outlawed and despised by God and man. Who will want to take you as a husband for his daughter? Who will even look at you in a year or two, when you are an old bachelor? And that is only in this world—what will be your fate in the next? Have you ever thought what it means to hang and fry thousands and ten thousands of years in the fires of hell? Look, here is a little match. Just light it and hold your little finger in the flame for a moment, while I count till ten . . . You should really try it, really . . .'

And he pushed a box of matches into Huneh's hand. Huneh looked at him, frightened and speechless. He had never thought of hell. That terrible punishment he had always put off until later, much later. And here came this man and offered it to him in a box of matches . . . They looked at each other, and out of the whole speech only the words 'Who will want to take you for a husband for his daughter?' rang in his ears. By pure chance the other had touched Huneh's weak spot. Huneh's gaze was fixed on the ground; the words seemed to force themselves out of his throat:

'And if I repent, will anyone let me marry into his family?'

'He-he-he!' laughed the other over the whole width of his beard. 'Even I myself would give you my daughter . . . it all depends on you, only on you . . .'

'What!' interrupted Huneh. 'What, you also would give me your daughter, Zipporah?'

'He-he-he!' laughed the beard again. 'And what am I, not a Jew like other Jews? The main thing, Huneh,' he continued in a solemn voice, 'is that from today on you must try to better your ways. You are not a woman that your face should be smooth like a baby's, but a man in Israel. Let your beard and earlocks grow till you look like God's likeness. Take a teacher and study Talmud and books of morals like all decent Jews . . .'

His words penetrated Huneh's heart like red-hot steel. He remained sitting submissively in the same place and smiled, as a sheep does when the butcher strokes its head. The next day Huneh started to use *tefillin* and to pray loudly out of the prayerbook, and a needy student instructed him in the Talmud and in the Bible with Rashi's commentary. The sound of his full voice poured into the empty courtyard, his beard grew and his earlocks became longer. The women shook their heads in wonder at the miracle that had happened to that unruly outlaw, and the men smiled at Huneh's awkward attempts to be like them. 'Huneh the Penitent,' they began to call him. And Huneh actually felt like a penitent, like one who, having been dirty, washes his body with boiling water and soap, so as to be able to enter the house of a great prince. And who was the prince? Zipporah's father, of course. But that sly Hasid stood aside and looked on with an air of innocence in his eyes and enjoyed having been able to make Huneh forsake his evil ways, pretending that he did not know why this sinner had suddenly repented. As for Huneh, Zipporah seemed to dance before his dreaming eyes, between the lines of the book and between the folds of the prayer-shawls. He knew now: it all depended on him. If he would become acceptable to people, this man who had befriended him would also receive him into his house as a son-in-law, and if not—all was lost.

IV.

Meanwhile Huneh longed for Zipporah. He looked at her from afar as one looks at a costly gift which in due time will become one's own. He would follow her walks, and his heart rose at the sight of her movements while she attended to her housework, and of the clean tiles in front of her door. On the Sabbath and on fair weekday evenings she would go for a short walk with her girl-friends: Huneh would count the flowers on her printed dress, and his eyes would caress her thin black stockings; his dreamy glance would fondle the abundance of her shining black hair; and he would smell from afar the smell of her pink-white body, that smell which fills a man's head with a kind of vertigo which is part dream and part vision. And though they had never spoken to each other even with their eyes, he know her voice well enough. There are things in which a man sees whatever he wants to see. He may look at the clouds on a half-clear winter day and see anything in them, from the wrinkled face of Rabbi Michale the Judge to the tail of a cow who, by your leave, is relieving herself. He may listen to the sounds of the night and hear anything from the braying of a faraway donkey to the muted tune of a hymn. So it was with Zipporah's voice. It is difficult to give you an idea of the wonderful melody which he heard in it, because it did not leave the circlings of Huneh's blood but ran around in the complex pathways of his veins, like the voice of a tree's growing which is retained in the hesitant motion of the smallest leaf. But his throat burned, as if red-hot needles had been stuck into it; his chest was compressed inwards and felt as small as that of a day-old baby; and his eyes bulged like those of a cow in labor.

Only once did he actually speak to her. It happened on an ordinary, pleasant winter morning. All the residents of the courtyard had received their cans of water from the man in charge of the tap who sold the water ration. Huneh remained standing motionless, as soon as he saw her. There were still traces of sleep on her face, her hair was uncombed, and a few bits of white down clung to it here and there. That moment, somehow, he felt particularly close to her. His feet were rooted to the spot, and his eyes opened wide and devoured her body's movements. The cans were full, and Zipporah bent down to lift them and carry them into the house. Immediately Huneh, with a strength that was not his own, lifted the cans from the ground as if they had been feathers and ran with them to the kitchen of her house. Blushing and disturbed, Zipporah stopped at the door, and Huneh blushed as well.

'Why did you take the cans?' she asked, as if speaking to herself.

'Because . . . because . . .'—more than that his throat could not let pass.

Neighbors stuck their heads out of the window. The large courtyard started to move. Zipporah noticed it and was annoyed and confused.

'I always carry the cans myself. I need no help.' Her lips shut tight and turned white.

Huneh remained standing there with bent head and hanging shoulders, as if his face had been slapped. He did not know what to say. He felt guilty before her and did not know how to free himself of his guilt. She looked at him, as he stood there in his misery, and clear laughter suddenly burst out of her white throat and her slightly trembling breasts: 'He—he, Huneh Lateborn! He—he, Huneh Lateborn!' Huneh did not know whether to be offended or glad because of her sudden joy. A stealthy look at her face revealed to him only goodheartedness and friendliness. She is glad because of what I have done, he thought. Involuntarily he straightened his head, his face cleared, and he looked openly into her eyes. He felt as if her smile entered straight into his throat and penetrated the whole width of his chest, a sensation which was to return whenever he recalled the movement of her smiling face. That day, he seemed to hear his own voice:

'You know, Zipporah, I . . . I am . . . I have repented . . . I pray already . . . study Torah . . . I . . . I . . . will be . . .'

If she had kept silence, perhaps he would have been able by the warmth of his words to make her pity him a little, to make her look at him more favorably—for he actually looked better since he had started to grow a beard; but she burst out in a loud, mocking, and contemptuous laugh which cut off the words he was trying to speak and made his throat feel hoarse. With faltering feet, he escaped in the direction of the Beth Midrash, pursued by her healthy laughter.

Soon enough people started to accept Huneh as one of themselves. They saw his application to study, his face steeped in dreams and devotion to his prayers. They listened to his quiet talk on worldly and heavenly matters, discerned in some chance remark of his the wisdom of one who suffers silently—and all the childish pranks were forgotten. In all respects he was like one of them; in one sense he was even better, for his livelihood was assured for the whole of his life. The marriage brokers began to regard him as a respectable prospect. And Huneh himself was already silently planning how he would send a marriage broker to Zipporah's parents and how he might persuade them to agree to the wedding (in those days his memory concealed her mocking laughter from him). But then a rumor spread in the courtyard: Zipporah had become engaged to a cousin of hers, an excellent young man who had just come from Poland. At first Huneh refused to believe his ears. Was not Zipporah his own? Had she not been promised to him, if he would repent? When he found out that the rumor was true, he fell silent. That whole day he wandered about, quiet and withdrawn, and listened to the insult that burrowed in his mind. That fellow with his heavy beard did not think him even important enough to fear his revenge. Huneh simply did not exist for him. The whole revolution in Huneh's life did not really matter to him at all . . .

Only in the evening, in the Beth Midrash, when Huneh saw the handshakes and congratulations and the fat smile on the man's beard, his whole body seethed and the ice of his astonishment melted. Suddenly he jumped at him, grasped the black beard with his iron fists, and shouted in a mechanical voice: 'Robber! Murderer! Robber! Murderer!' Over and over those words broke out of his mouth, as if someone else were shouting them from inside his breast. The people who had come to pray turned pale with fright. For a long while they looked at each other, until they finally made up their minds to separate Huneh from his victim. The terrified shopkeeper held his plucked, blood-flecked beard and cried: 'What does this madman want of me? What does this madman want of me?' while Huneh struggled against the dozens of hands which held him, threw his arms and legs about, and in a hoarse voice uttered strange, unintelligible noises. Only after Zipporah's father had made his escape from the Beth Midrash did Huneh relax somewhat; with a queer look, he stared at the wisps of black hair that remained in his fist. When the people let his body go, Huneh remained standing on the spot and looked at them speechlessly, with increasing astonishment, as if awaking from a nightmare. A hatred of strange faces arose in him, and his look passed from the one to the other, full of contempt. The people were not surprised by his stare and looked at each other meaningly; one shrewdly remarked, as if to himself: 'When a man has a little screw loose, nothing can be done for him any more . . .'

In the days and nights that followed, Huneh suffered a purgatory of sounds and sights that seemed to grow out of his blood. As he shaved his beard, the old restlessness of his childhood flowed again into his body. It was as if every human face or sound touched him at the very center of his nerves and forced him to do something to annoy people. 'Huneh has turned bad again,' decided the courtyard. Each one made a different guess as to the reason, but no one knew of his secret; the only one who sensed it was Zipporah. After Huneh's fight with her father, she no longer showed herself in the courtyard. She kept herself locked and silent in her room, and was busy sewing dresses and bed-linen for the wedding, the date for which had been set now with special haste. Even the room for the young couple had been rented, secretly, in an out-of-the-way lane.

But Huneh noticed everything. He noticed, and his whole body was in an uproar. He would creep to the window of the little room and look in at the two wide, low beds loaded with a wealth of pillows and cushions; at the large wardrobe, which smelled strongly of mothballs; and at the little straw mat which had been laid between the beds so that the dear young man would not, Heaven forbid, chill his tender feet in passing from one bed to the other. And once, through the chink of the curtain, he saw Zipporah herself sitting, needle and thread in her hand and her eyes fixed on the floor, lest they should look too much upon her healthy thighs trembling in expectation. Everything, Huneh saw; and even more than with his body's eyes, he saw in his mind. All the angels from on high, and all the devils of hell, took on Zipporah's likeness and laughed her soft, mocking laughter. His teeth chattered with fear as he closed his eyes at midnight; and his knees were covered with clammy sweat when he opened them at daybreak. Many thoughts of revenge passed through his mind, but one single movement of Zipporah's remote face was enough to make him shake them off, like some unclean thing that had stuck to his body.

V.

Unlike the old inhabitants of Jerusalem, the Polish Jews hold their weddings on any ordinary weekday; they also have real musicians: fiddles and trumpets, drums and cymbals. It seems that, not having been born near the Wailing Wall, they are not aware of the feeling of mourning for the destruction of Jerusalem, and when they rejoice, they like to do so with their whole body and soul.

As if to annoy Huneh, a sumptuous wedding had been arranged in the large hall of a big hotel. The lighted windows shone in their full glory, and tempestuous tunes burst forth through them. Huneh, walking up and down on the pavement below, could feel how up there they were amusing themselves and dancing, drinking and gorging themselves, while Zipporah, dressed up in her best clothes, washed and bathed and joyful, smiled in all directions. And he—he longed to be near her, and could not. There were moments when he wanted to plunge into the merry crowd and smash everything; but immediately he remembered Zipporah's mocking laughter, and his feet halted and his arms grew weak. For a long while he walked about in the dark street, turned his crazy eyes upwards and felt his nostrils tremble at the smell of the dishes and the wine which filled the empty space, until he feared that his heart would burst from pain if he did not do something. Thus, on feet that seemed not to belong to him, he ran about in the half-dark streets, like a mad dog running away from fear of itself: ran about without noticing whence or whither, until his feet halted before the window of the room which had been rented for the young couple.

Exhausted, he leaned his head against the open, half-barred window, and the smell of ironed linen and mothballs penetrated his breast. Quickly he climbed up to the window and squeezed his body with difficulty through the narrow space between the bars and the window frame. Once within the small room, his head was turned even more strongly. The fresh smells were breathtakingly close. His fingers began to touch the bedding and stroke the furniture, and his body to fondle all the objects in the room, small or large. In his tenseness, he began to speak to himself, to talk and laugh with the furniture and the bedding, and with the smells in the room. This crazy conversation would no doubt have lasted until daylight, if he had not been disturbed by the sound of footsteps and voices. It was the family, who were accompanying the young couple to the marriage room. Suddenly Huneh remembered that he was in a strange room, that in a moment the door would open and he would be discovered. He tried to jump to the window and go out the same way he had entered, but just then the family said good night to the young couple under this very window, accompanying their farewells with loud good wishes. Huneh ran back and forth as if caught in a trap, until finally, as he heard the key turn in the lock, he threw his large body under the nearer of the wide beds.

The bed was long and low, and concealed his trembling body perfectly. When the couple and their parents entered the room, he felt nothing but an expectant fear. Even the entering footsteps were hesitant, as if waiting for something new. Only after they had lit the lamp did they begin to talk.

'Well, Rivka,' said the father to his wife: 'let's not keep the children too long. They are tired from the fast and the wedding . . .' 'True, true,' coughed Rivka. 'May we only see pleasure from them . . . May my sainted forefathers intercede for you . . . May . . .'

'Now then, Rivka, enough.' The father halted her tears, which threatened to break out in a swelling stream. 'It is already past midnight.'

'All right, all right,' she answered, frightened by his aggressive voice, and trailed behind him with the old submissive step of Jewish wives, weak and devoted to their husbands.

The room fell silent, a silence which made audible the nervous breathing of Zipporah and the movements of the body of her husband, who did not know what to do with himself. Soon the key could be heard turning in the lock, and a voice-that-was-no-voice sounded in the room:

'Shall we go to bed, Zipporah?'

There was something in the voice and in the question which annoyed both Zipporah and Huneh. It was like someone saying to his servant: 'Shall we scrub the floor?' Huneh forcibly held himself back, lest he should do something which would betray his hiding place, while Zipporah remained silent, offended and annoyed. Her feet shuffled on the floor, and her fingers with their pink nails touched her eyes, which filled with unwanted tears.

The young man seemed to regret his voice, which had played him false, for now he repeated the same words, only more tenderly, so that Zipporah lifted her eyes slightly, pouted her lips with a movement of slyness and self-indulgence, and said:

'You know, my head hurts a little... Just see whether I'm not a bit feverish.' Now the young man became totally confused. Now the girl was a total stranger to him. He was not prepared for all these uncertainties. Now he didn't know how to carry on with what had been broken off.

'How should I know whether you have a fever?' he asked as if in anger.

'Just feel my forehead, just a little...' Her voice pleaded like a cooing pigeon.

And Huneh saw hesitant shoes go up and down, approaching Zipporah's chair determinedly. A leaden heaviness spread through his heart.

'You have no fever,' said a hoarse voice.

'Hold your hand there a little longer,' she continued to plead. 'It is so good when you stroke my head... just so... more... more...'

And Huneh in his imagination saw her smiling head, surrendering itself between the hands of the man, and his throat was strangled and his eyes bulged with anger and lust and jealousy.

'Come to bed, it is late . . .' and now the voice was the assured, quiet voice of a practical man who knows what to expect.

And again Huneh's eyes had to look at the shoe which slowly dropped from Zipporah's foot, at the pink knee revealed from under the hem of a dress lifted without any fear; and the pincers which choked his throat grew larger and larger, hotter and hotter. And as if on purpose to annoy Huneh, the young man went and stretched out on the bed under which he lay, and Zipporah stood with her bare feet next to his nose. A long time she stood there in her white, wide shirt, dreaming and hesitating, rubbing one foot against the other, her knees trembling.

'Why don't you lie down?' asked the young man.

'Do I know? Just so . . . I am cold, cold . . .'—and her whole body shivered, though it was a June night.

'If you feel cold, surely you shouldn't remain standing like that . . .' said the young man hesitantly.

And she listened to him and came to bed. Then she burst out in a strange sort of laughter which lasted a few moments.

'What is there to laugh about?' The young man was thoroughly frightened.

'Your beard tickles, he-he!' And her laughter was goblets of silver and gold.

'But you haven't even touched my beard?' He could not stop wondering.

'From afar it tickles, from afar . . .' She kept quiet for a little while, and then started asking anew: 'And do you know how to kiss? No? Close your eyes for a moment, open your lips, like this . . . like this . . .' A soft, caressing, licking sound was heard in the darkness, and then more sounds, muted and near.

Huneh's throat burned like an oven. For some reason or other his memory recalled a small white kitten. The other cats stayed away from it as if by secret agreement. It would let its little white, striped head hang low, and sniff with its nostrils and blink its eyes with babyish, pitiful movements; but its comrades looked upon it with open hatred. Then the little kitten bowed its head, closed its eyes with a slow offended movement, and called: 'Miaow!' and exactly this same 'Miaow' suddenly came out of Huneh's throat.

At first the couple were frightened, but immediately the young man mustered his courage and called in an assured voice: 'Psst, psst!'

'Just a kitten ...' Zipporah assured him, and the muted caressing sounds began anew.

But again and again the cat's cry returned, as in a dream.

'The cat is in this room, perhaps under the bed ...'

'What does it matter?' she answered. 'Anyhow there is nothing to eat here ...'

Such equanimity was too much for Huneh. So he could not even hinder them! Memories of his childhood, when he tried to annoy the people and they only laughed at him, came alive: involuntarily he repeated all his noises of those days: dog's bark, donkey's bray, camel's grunt, cock's crow. And each single noise came out of his throat with its right tone and strength. Huneh had always been good at imitating animals and birds ...

At first, when the young couple in bed heard the dog's bark with its heart-rending sad wail, they were frightened and held on to each other as if they sought shelter. Then, when the other sounds came, human in their cry for pity—they were gripped by the age-old Jewish fear of ghosts and devils. The young man called out in despair: 'Hold on to my *tzitzioth,* Zipporah! My *tzitzioth!* Say: Hear, O Israel!'

She obeyed him, with chattering teeth. Her voice trembled:

'There is something wrong, something wrong ... I was afraid something would happen ... That madman, that Huneh, always looked at me with unclean eyes ... he stabbed me with his looks ...'

The word 'madman' struck him like a bolt of lightning. Suddenly her whole attitude towards him became clear. For her he was mad, and that was all. His body rose up in a great anger, and he lifted the bed with the couple and all.

The terrified cries of the struggling couple rent the quiet night and aroused many people from their beds. Neighbors ran to the room, axes split the locked door, while Huneh ran around like crazy, with the bed on his back. When the door broke down, Huneh ran out with the bed into the courtyard full of people. Many ran away in fright when they saw the bed floating in the air, but others, discerning Huneh, closed in upon him and bound his arms and legs, while still others poured water over the couple, who lay fainting in the bed, which had broken when it fell down.

For a long while Huneh heard nothing of all that was happening. A terrible weakness filled his bound body. When he began to open his eyes, he heard someone saying these words, full of mixed fear and enjoyment: 'A fine joke Mad Huneh thought up! A joke that might have sent scores of people to their grave . . .'

VI.

The next day Huneh discovered that what he had done—was regarded as a great deed! Everywhere there was huge laughter. In every shop and at every corner people stood and whispered to each other the heroic story of Huneh. Beards were full of sibilant laughter; toothless old women's mouths twisted to hold back the glee that filled them. All that day Huneh walked about, miserable and dejected in his longing for Zipporah; but people patted him on the shoulder, and accosted him with sly smiles and friendly questions: 'Huneh, where was the couple when you lifted the bed? Huneh, what did the bride say when she heard the cat mew? Huneh, why did you hide under the bed and not between the pillows?' Everywhere he was asked such questions, and as he looked at the greasy gleams in the eyes of people, something whispered within him: 'There is no pity in the world!' His own heart ached because of Zipporah's shame and suffering, but they—had something to laugh about! All those days he walked about as in a daydream and looked with hate and contempt upon those who cackled around him in order to pick up another crumb of ugly laughter. When this feeling began to weigh upon him, he kept to his house and gave himself over to melancholy thoughts about the behavior of people: about that young man from Poland, who had unwittingly robbed him of his Zipporah; about Zipporah herself, who had not wanted him because she had thought him crazy from birth; and about her beauty and charm and his own ugliness. Strangely enough, though: for all those beautiful warm thoughts, he found it difficult to forget that Zipporah was married to someone else, that she never would be his. Thus he began again to plot ways and means to make her husband hate her, so that he should divorce her and he, Huneh, would marry her when she was miserable and forsaken.

And so there began a ridiculous chapter of persistent persecution and interference in little things with the young couple's life. For hours and sometimes days on end, Huneh would keep himself concealed in a hiding place not far from the house of the young couple, waiting for an opportunity to crawl into the kitchen. Whenever he succeeded in entering, he would throw salt and pepper or sugar in the saucepans; strew tacks on the floor of the room or between the sheets; or blow sneezing powder through the open window before they went to bed. All these little things, which cost him great effort, bore their fruit in Huneh's glowing imagination. For hours on end he gave himself over to his imaginings and laughed long and deep as he thought of the husband making faces at the food which Huneh had prepared for him, or of the couple sneezing on their couch throughout the night. It was a laughter which grew out of his body and made his face turn ugly and his eyes bulge strangely. Sometimes he looked into the mirror when he laughed thus—and his face turned pale at the sight which he discovered there, and his breath was choked. Yet he clung to this laughter, like a drowning man clutching a straw.

One day, when he was about to creep into the little kitchen, Zipporah herself suddenly stood before him. She wore an apron printed with blue flowers, and her shaven head was charmingly covered with a tight black kerchief. She stood there before him and looked at him with her large black eyes, her body bent, her hands hanging down, and her prominent mouth, as usual when she spoke to him, half pleading and half angry.

'Huneh, what do you want from me?' she asked in a voice which made him tremble all over.

Without being aware of it, he looked into her eyes. They were filled with large, round tears. For the first time in his life he saw her eyes wet.

'Huneh, what evil have I done to you?' she added in a tearful voice.

Slowly, with much effort, Huneh lowered his head; and in doing so he noticed that her face had become very pale and her belly bulged a little. 'Good Heavens, she's pregnant! . . .' The thought flitted through his head. And now he looked with something like curiosity at the beautiful body which was slowly being broken down by the new body growing within it. Her pitiful weakness seemed to whisper to him: 'Huneh, I need you no longer. Whatever has been done has already been done to me, and I have no more use for you and the likes of you . . .' And he was overtaken by a great compassion at the sight of her pale face and the belly which had begun to bulge under her apron. A warmth flowed through his trembling body, a feeling that in reality not he had been sinned against, but she. It was she who needed pity, not he. He was sound and hale, she pregnant and ill. Now he remembered all he had done to her, all the suffering and sorrow he had caused her, and his knees began to tremble. He wanted to say something, but could not. Tears choked his throat. For the first time in his life, he wept like a little child.

And this first crying changed Huneh in every respect. All his anger against Zipporah and against himself disappeared, as if it had never existed. His weeping, which was not intended to make others pity him but give relief to himself, showed him that his enemy was in truth no enemy; and his hatred, no hatred. Zipporah was dear to him like a good dream which fills the dreamer with warm and pleasant feelings. For whenever he remembered how pitifully she stood there, he was moved to that same quiet weeping which opens the gates of Heaven to man. His blood calmed down, his body felt light, and a desire to sing and rejoice, alone with himself and in secret, never left him. All the beautiful melodies which he had heard in his life he sang to himself in those days. All the pleasant sights which he had seen in childhood and in his dreams, he discovered anew in their pristine freshness. He seemed drunk with the sights of his imagination and the sound of his blood. Slowly he discovered that his ugly body was really not ugly at all, but full of pleasant things he had never known. As if without trying, he discovered the ancient secret, that the Creator fills our flesh and blood with treasures of joy and pleasure which man may discover in moments of grace. Such moments became plentiful in the lonely life of Huneh, who rarely sought the company of people. And he was well aware that all this had come to him thanks to the pallor in Zipporah's face, the wetness in her eyes, and her little belly which bulged under the apron.

VII.

Many years have passed since then, nearly ten years. Zipporah is beset with children and poverty and trouble, like most women in the poor quarters of Jerusalem. Her husband goes about with bent back, worried and troubled about the little shop which must provide his hard breadwinning. All the beauty of Zipporah's maiden days has faded away. Now her body is swollen with unhealthy fat, her face is creased, the light in her eyes has long gone, and her dresses, dirty and worn, make her whole body ugly. Huneh, though, has changed little since then. He still shaves, his body is still strong. But there is a different light in his eyes and a quiet smile on his lips. In the course of time, many marriages have been proposed to him; apparently, people think that he is fit now for human company, particularly since his livelihood is easy and secure, while theirs is hard and uncertain. But Huneh will have nothing whatsoever to do with the marriage brokers. In his imagination he keeps a precious secret, the secret of the looks of Zipporah in those days, Zipporah of the large black eyes shining with a slight wetness, and with the half-smiling, half-pleading lips moving in a frame of the most delicate pallor. He does not dare to take a wife and have children, for fear they may steal that pleasant picture away from the walls of his imagination.

Often he enters Zipporah's poor house, enters as if driven by devils, enters and asks unconnected questions, in a slightly hoarse voice, about how the children are and what they are doing. She receives him with a feeling of inferiority: she is forced to accept the help of his money, which he gives her without saying a word. Her body moves about nervously, as she offers him the best chair in the house, and her swollen cheeks are filled with a false blush. But he feels like a debtor who has paid only a small part of his debt. He knows: with one look, Zipporah gave him more than she has given her husband in all the ten years of their marriage.

ENIGMA

by Yisrael Zarchi

I.

THAT YEAR I was living in a distant quarter of Jerusalem, filled with crooked alleyways, houses huddled together like a collection of bent misshapen old crones, and poverty-stricken inhabitants reduced to beggary in order to exist. There I had rented a small room far from the bustling town, hoping to find in it a haven of rest. But when I would return from the noisy streets of the town to my lonely room, dragging my tired legs behind me and mortally weary in soul, the spirit of loneliness would come out to greet me with outstretched arms, caressing my breast in a stifling embrace; then I would come awake again, and instead of lying down and snatching a brief rest on my narrow bed, I would rush back to the busy town, as if escaping from a vile den.

During those days when restlessness would drive me from the town to my room and when loneliness would banish me back again, I found refuge in a little out-of-the-way café situated in a corner of a street in the upper part of the town. This café was a peculiar one, and did not look like the usual café in the least. Its waiters were not dressed in black waistcoats and white shirt fronts; there was no gay music, and none of the hustle and bustle usually associated with public places. This café of mine was nothing but a small hut stuck together from old boards—an old wooden shack that had remained standing from years gone by. The entrance was through a small door resembling that of an actual shop, and here were sold a modest selection of small cakes and buns. At the back of the shop there was another and smaller door which opened into a tiny garden furnished with a few tables for regular customers. Indeed, it was not even an ordinary garden. It was merely a small courtyard, surrounded by a crude stone fence, like all the other broken-down fences of Jerusalem. In one corner there grew a gnarled and withered old vine, its bark peeling with age, yet somehow still managing to grow fresh branches covered with a profusion of foliage, which, as though bowed in prayer, cast their shade over the whole of the small courtyard, covering it with a mantle of green; and the customer at each table was cut off from his neighbors, as if hidden away in the garden. In season, fruit hung from the branches, clusters of tiny grapes that never ripened, and its tendrils would clasp the stones of the fence and cling to them stubbornly.

This was the very place that my soul craved, when it was attacked by loneliness and longings. Secretly, I would examine the few coppers in my pocket, and if I reckoned that there was enough for a cup of coffee, I would come to the café and sit alone, hidden under the vineleaves.

Not many people came here, but those who did were regarded as members of one family. Actually people did not greet each other, much less speak to their neighbors, yet in spite of this there was a feeling of silent kinship, as if a secret pact had been formed among them. In the small shop, behind the narrow counter, sat the proprietress—a woman in the early twilight of her life, whose hair had begun to whiten before the wrinkles showed in her face. She would welcome her visitors with a show of cordiality expressed by a quiet smile and a slight nod of the head; she spoke no more than was necessary and bothered no one with her questions. Only her eyes would follow her visitor affectionately as he made his way to his accustomed place in the vine-covered garden. A stranger coming to the shop would be welcomed politely but coolly, and served by her dexterous fingers; but she was glad if he would make his purchases and go his way in peace without interfering with her guests in the garden, for all the world as if she were completely disinterested in the matter of profit.

Toward dusk I would always see, seated on my right, a tall thin-faced man, in the prime of life, with an aquiline nose and ears plugged with cotton wool. As he enters he makes his way to the table reserved for him; and if it is occupied by somebody else, he lingers beside it for a moment, looking as lost as a shipwrecked mariner—until the waitress, seeing his confusion, makes the intruder vacate his regular place. Safe in the harbor of his table, he pulls out a cigarette from his breast pocket, splits it into two and compares the two butts to see if they are fairly divided. One half he lays down before him; the other, he lights immediately, and the burnt-out match he replaces carefully within his box of matches. The cigarette butt lit, he then buries himself for a full hour in a welter of newspapers specially placed for him on the table. When he has completed his reading, he extricates himself from the batch of newspapers, lights up the second half of his cigarette, and requests the waitress to give him a cup of coffee. Finishing his cigarette, he drains his coffee to the last drop, rises, unobtrusively pays out his few coins, and leaves the garden with light quick footsteps that seem incongruous with his long legs.

At one table, close to the entrance, there sits a woman who is not very young. She wears spectacles with thick lenses, and, sunk in thought, her face clouded by a great sadness, she seems completely indifferent to her surroundings. Suddenly stirring, as if bringing her gaze back from a distant prospect, she begins hastily devouring the round cake which has lain before her since her arrival; then, with the last crumb still in her mouth, she rises distractedly and leaves, as if she has stayed longer than she intended.

One of the occasional visitors to the garden is a student from Mount Scopus, who always carries an enormous bundle of books under his arm. He retires to a corner in order to study, but soon he pushes his books aside, thrusts his hand into his pocket and pulls out a short letter, a scrap of paper folded over many times. Again and again, his burning eyes travel over this crumpled piece of paper with great intensity, as if some holy gospel is inscribed there.

Sometimes groups of white-uniformed nurses from the nearby hospital enter. The younger ones amongst them snatch honey cakes and sponge cakes and eat them with splendid gusto, bending over to one another and whispering secrets into each other's ears. They burst into laughter, light and restrained like the chatter of rolling nuts. For a little while they introduce an unaccustomed murmur into the still atmosphere. The older ones amongst them sit patiently at their places, gazing fixedly in front of them, as if the sorrows of man, which they have left behind for a while in that white house of suffering, have made their mark for ever on their faces, have banished joy from their hearts, and they will never know happy laughter again.

Soon I became a regular visitor to this spot, accepted by everybody. The other visitors regarded me with a favorable eye, the waitress knew my order in advance, and the proprietress also would welcome me graciously with her quiet and soothing smile. I soon learned, like the other regular visitors before me, that this place was a sanctuary for those who had no home.

II.

One evening I sat there gazing at the electric lights fixed in the branches of the old vine and illuminating the garden so charmingly. Although it was summer time, cool breezes blew from the Jerusalem hills, pleasantly caressing the skin. Suddenly I was aware that the waitress kept coming to my table, putting an ash tray on it, and then removing it. She was hovering around me in an odd fashion, most unusual in this place, where the visitor was not generally addressed until he himself had first given his order.

I looked at the waitress in amazement and sought the reason for this behavior. This waitress was a beauty, with lively dancing eyes; a mature woman, she was long past the age of innocent youth, but at times its afterglow would still betray itself on her face. The atmosphere of the café would induce her to behave with quiet decorum and there her eyes would not dance too much, nor would she swing her hips more than was necessary. But sometimes, sitting concealed in my corner until midnight, and leaving just a little while before her, I would see young men waiting for her at the corner of the dark street; and when she came out they would link their arms in hers, and disappear into the heart of the city. Now, I searched her face in perplexity, not understanding the cause of her agitation. I saw that her eyes were glistening with a strange light, her lips were trembling, and her whole face was as if stricken with excitement. When she saw the surprise on my face, she gave me a significant look, and directed me with her eyes to a small table hidden under the vine, as if to provide me with an answer to my bewilderment.

And, indeed, I saw an unusual sight there. At a small table modestly concealed among the vine branches, sat a young couple; the man was handsome, dressed in grey, and facing him on the opposite side of the table sat a girl younger than he, dressed in a light-blue embroidered blouse, her fair plaits falling loosely and attractively over her shoulders. Both the beauty of a woman and the charm of a child were equally visible in her face and gave it a striking appearance. They sat opposite each other, their hands clasped on the marble-topped table, gazing into each other's eyes. Motionless, they were deeply absorbed in one another, as if lost in some fascinating dream. There was a wonderful purity about their attitude, and the fervent intensity of their expression reminded one of an old legend of enchanted castles.

The waitress gave me a triumphant look, as if to say: From now on you will understand my excitement. But when she saw no sign of comprehension on my face, she bent towards me, her breast brushing my shoulder, and whispered in my ear with bitter scorn:

'What do you say to that? Is such a thing possible in this day and age?'

I remembered her meetings with young men at the corner of the street, and I knew that if she had seen this young man and woman kissing and embracing one another before our eyes, she would not have been astonished; but because they sat silently thus, with their hands firmly entwined, and looked into each other's eyes with serene devotion, she could not bear the sight of their joyous innocence. I pitied her. Perhaps her sharp derision was nothing but unconscious envy and a reminder of the bitter memories of first love and fervid longings for the days of her youth which would never return.

When she realized that I did not share her surprise, and that she could not wring out of me even the slightest sign of agreement with her mood, she stopped hovering around me. With an openly aggrieved air, she removed the ash tray from my table and turned away from me, swinging her hips, with the cool disdainful glance of an insulted princess . . .

I felt contrite at having unwittingly offended her, but did not attempt to make amends. I remained sitting in my place a long while, and tried to conjure up pleasant thoughts that might ease my depressed spirits. But from time to time I would turn my head, involuntarily, furtively watching the pair of lovers who still sat there raptly gazing at each other, oblivious to everything and everybody else.

Suddenly the man got up, removed his jacket quickly and put it round the girl's shoulders, whose thin transparent blouse was inadequate for the cool Jerusalem evening. As the garment touched the girl's body, she quivered a little, and her shoulders shrank for an instant as if touched by fire. But she did not remove her gaze from the young man's face, and her eyes suddenly smiled and lighted up her intelligent, lovely face with the soft radiance of a wondrous love.

At that precise moment, a pang of utter loneliness shot through me. My heart ached with an intolerable yearning. I rose and paid my bill to the proprietress, and, wishing to avoid her eyes, I left hurriedly and fled from the town to my isolated room, as if some great salvation might await me there in my lonely little cell.

III.

Some years passed and that little cake shop, in the upper part of the town, with its vine-covered garden, had almost become a forgotten memory. I no longer lived in a small room in a slum area. Sorrows that had once seemed mountainously heavy, now felt as light as thistledown: the weight of new burdens had softened the severity of the old. But still it happened once that days of idleness came and reminded me a bit of those lonely times. I do not know exactly how, but one day, as if by some mysterious association of feelings, the vision of that little café suddenly rose to my mind, and, without conscious volition, I found myself walking in the upper part of the town towards the old wooden shack.

High-storied buildings had been erected recently and had pushed the cake shop into a corner. But the small hut and the tumble-down stone fence surrounding the vine garden were still there; nothing had changed. The proprietress sat, as always, behind her narrow counter, and greeted me cordially, but with no overt sign of affection, just as if I had quitted her shop only yesterday—but a momentary gleam in her eyes betrayed the feelings of a mother silently greeting her long-lost son. In the vine-shaded courtyard, too, nothing had changed. The withered vine was still shedding its bark, and green clusters of grapes still hung from its boughs, whilst its tendrils were still entwined with everything round about, as green and fresh as ever.

I sat down at my old place, empty at the time, as if it had been reserved for me during my long absence; and at once I saw to the right of me the thin man with the aquiline nose, his face thinner than ever, absorbed in his newspapers with his half-cigarette still lying beside the ash tray. To my left sat three healthy young nurses, chatting with great animation as they munched their cakes.

The waitress came at once, looked at me for a while as if trying to recall my face. Then her eyes, around the corners of which a few tiny wrinkles had been added by the years, twinkled as she exclaimed in a tone of surprise mingled with reproach:

'It's a long time, since last you were here . . .'

I looked shamefacedly at her, and asked for a cup of coffee. Since the days when I used to come to the café, I had taken to other drinks, but now I felt as if all the latter years of my life had been wiped out and I was sitting here again in my corner, as I used to do in the old days, when I would have to examine secretly the few coppers in my pocket. So I ordered my usual cup of coffee.

As I sat and waited, I turned my head here and there, searching the place which had so long served me as a refuge for my reveries. Meanwhile the nurses had finished their cakes, but not their conversation, and they left the garden still chattering vivaciously. Turning my head to a part of the garden concealed by the vine, I saw a lovely young woman sitting beside a table slowly stirring the contents of her cup. My gaze lingered on her and my heart began to beat rapidly. Even though her hair was coiled high on her head, as was now the fashion for town women, I immediately recognized the girl with the long plaits who had sat here with her lover on that memorable evening and who had looked into his eyes with such enchantment. After that evening, I had seen her many times here with the same man, whom she no doubt had married, sitting with him for a while beside the marble-topped table, drinking coffee, speaking a few words, and then leaving. She, too, had seen me here in those days, and she had become, like the others, 'one of the family.'

Still stirring her cup languidly, she raised her eyes and met my glance. She was now grown into a ripe and beautiful woman, her girlish charm having left in its place the beauty of maturity, her eyes dark and filled with understanding. I do not know whether my glance was a bit strange, because of this unexpected meeting, but it seemed to me that she inclined her head slightly as a sign of recognition. I was too startled to return her greeting, and made an attempt to turn my face away in order not to disturb her.

Even as I tried to force myself not to pay attention to her loveliness, I saw her reach for her handbag and take out a cigarette, then fumble vainly for her matches. At a loss, she turned around looking for a light for her cigarette. Since the waitress had not yet returned, and the thin man was oblivious to what went on around him, I unconsciously reached into my pocket, and finding some matches, made haste to give her what she wanted. She took the burning match from my hands with her long slender fingers, thanking me with charming humility and apologizing for disturbing me. Then in a pleasant tone of voice, hesitating slightly, she said:

'I believe I haven't seen you here for some time . . .'

I was overcome with confusion and replied haltingly that that was so, I had not been here for a long time. As I turned to go back to my place, she looked over at my table and, seeing that it was empty of dishes, said softly:

'If you have not yet had something to drink, perhaps you would join me at my table?'

My confusion increased, and, seeing my dismay, she quickly added:

'Perhaps you are waiting for someone? Forgive me. I didn't mean to disturb you . . .'

Then I recovered a little and replied:

'No, no. I'm not waiting for anybody, but—I thought . . . perhaps *you* are waiting for someone. I don't believe I have ever seen you here alone.'

She smiled sadly, pushed the empty chair beside her table, as if inviting me to sit down, and said:

'Yes, yes. You have a good memory. I used always to come here with my husband . . .'

I stood silent, at a loss for words.

'But tonight,' she continued, and blew cigarette smoke through her teeth, 'tonight, I shall sit here alone—that is, if you refuse to sit down with me . . .' she concluded, laughing a little to cover up her embarrassment.

I sat down beside her on the vacant chair and looked at her with an astonishment I could not conceal.

'Let me tell you as simply as I can,' she continued in a quiet but firm voice, as if anxious to open up her heart completely and at once—'I was divorced this week from my husband . . .'

I looked at her, amazed, lacking words to express my grief. Just then the waitress approached the table where I had formerly been sitting, carrying a tray of dishes, and seeing that I was not there, she turned her head from side to side until, in surprise, she noticed my new position. My companion raised her hand and beckoned the waitress to bring the coffee to her table. The waitress paused a moment and then, without a word, did as she was bid, placing the coffee before me and turning her back on me in silent disapproval.

IV.

Again we were left alone. I secretly scanned the face of my young companion and saw that it was flushed. I realized that I had not yet said a word to her.

'But why? Why? . . . I thought you loved one another so much,' I mumbled, not sure that I was saying the right thing.

She forced herself to smile, but I could see that she was very upset.

'Of course, of course we loved one another very much,' she

replied, raising her voice. 'That's what makes it all the more dreadful . . . so much more dreadful! . . . But I must tell you everything right from the start, otherwise you will never understand at all; and maybe even after I tell you everything you may still not understand. I don't know whether I can explain things properly, for I myself can't grasp all that has happened or the reasons. These matters are so intimate, so delicate in feeling, I haven't even told them to my closest friends . . . because it's so difficult, nothing tangible, no particular incident that one can speak about; only feelings, only emotions. How can I possibly tell you? Yet perhaps I should tell you everything without shame or embarrassment. I'll tell you the whole story. The waitress once told me that you are a writer. You write stories, don't you, and writers are like doctors—you don't feel ashamed to stand before them in all your nakedness . . .'

She stopped speaking, stubbed out the rest of her burning cigarette, and nervously gulped down a little coffee. And I sat mute before her, trying to contol my turbulent heart. She recovered a little and began in a quieter tone, like a person reading from an old volume of memoirs.

'I became acquainted with him in Tel-Aviv immediately after I had left school. My graduation was to be celebrated by throwing a big party at my house. All my girl-friends were invited, and it was decided that each one of us should bring just one boy-friend—we thought ourselves grown-up young ladies, and many of us already had boy friends from our schooldays. I, too, had had many boy friends, but I was not in love with any one of them. Still I chose one of my friends and invited him to my home, so that I too might help carry out our group decision. Just as the party was ready to start, one of my friends came, all excited and confused: she was ready to join us at the party, a new dress had been made for her, and her boy friend had already called to take her, when suddenly the door opened and there stood her cousin from Jerusalem who had come down especially to congratulate her on her graduation. She just didn't know what to do. Suppose she were to come to the party with her regular boy friend—then how could she leave her guest at home? But if she were to go to the party with him—she'd have no fun at all without her sweetheart. At that time we were very naïve and thought that the heavens had fallen in and spoilt all our plans. After a long and heated discussion, we finally decided that she should be allowed to bring both boys—that this was something out of the ordinary for which she could not be blamed.'

She kept playing with the leather ornaments on her handbag, twisting it in all directions, winding and unwinding the delicate tassels. Then suddenly she stopped and said, as if wishing to free herself from the many memories crowding in upon her:

'I shan't use many words. This cousin, before his arrival at my party, sent me a bouquet of white roses. And when he entered and I saw him—he captured my heart right from the start. I can't describe to you how he looked. Perhaps he was really very ordinary. Grey-eyed, well-built, cultured and clever, courteous and pleasant—not one of our young friends could compare with him; and all this cast such a spell on me that I walked about as if in a dream. This was the first time in my life that I felt the stirrings of my heart, and when he came towards me and danced with me, my knees went weak. Suddenly all my good sense left me—I had the reputation of being a sensible youngster—but there I was, just a foolish girl who had fallen head over heels in love. He spent a whole week in Tel-Aviv, and that whole week my friends kept talking about us. Perhaps they also ridiculed me or laughed at me—but I didn't care a fig. All those days we went for walks in the nearby villages, went rowing on the Yarkon, and wandered about in the shade of the tall trees growing beside the river—in short my hand never left his all that time. When his vacation was over he returned to Jerusalem and promised to write me long letters.'

Here she paused, laughed to herself, and again took hold of the leather ornament, tugging at it excitedly:

'How can I tell you? Not a day passed after he had returned to Jerusalem without my longing for him. I could find no peace of mind, and my life without him seemed empty, as if he had bewitched me and I was no longer a free agent. I walked the streets moonstruck, and looked at the passing vehicles without really seeing them. Then suddenly I saw a large bus, and the name on it seemed to leap out at me: *Jerusalem.* My heart jumped: this was a sign! Quickly I rushed home, and told my mother that my friend, who lived out of town, had suddenly taken ill and that I had to visit her; that perhaps I would remain there all night and that she should not worry about me if I didn't return home that same evening. Then I left the house and boarded the bus for Jerusalem. I knew his address and found his house easily. It was already dusk when I knocked at the door. I had plucked up enough courage to ask someone where I might find him, but fortunately for me he opened the door himself. Even now I can still see his look of astonishment when he saw me standing there. "You!" he said, as if I were a ghost and not flesh and blood. "Me," I replied. "Are you on a hike? What brings you to Jerusalem?" he asked, his astonishment growing. "Have you relatives here?" I smiled nervously and said, 'No, no, I didn't *happen* to come to Jerusalem, and I have no relatives here. I came here just to visit you, to see you for a while! . . .' 'Me?' he almost shouted. 'For a while! But at this hour it's impossible to get back to Tel-Aviv!' he finished, anxiously. 'What of it?' I said with affected calmness, 'I'll stay here. Maybe you can find a place for me . . .' I can still see his great confusion as he ushered me into his room and gave me a chair. His eyes glowed like fire, and his composure was completely gone.

'He lived alone in one room, a bachelor's existence, and he didn't even have a cup of water. After we had sat a while, silent and embarrassed, he took me out to have supper with him. We went out and walked for a long time until we arrived at a funny little café, and there we sat. That funny little café was this very place where we are now sitting. It was here, in this vine-covered courtyard, at this little table. Here we sat, without speaking. Actually there's nothing I can tell you about that evening, but I will never, never forget it. I have already told you that my life has been without great events, only feelings, emotions . . . All that I remember about our sitting here that evening is a sort of wonderfully clouded, enchanted dream. I believe we sat silently and with clasped hands. What was I thinking about then?—I don't remember, I couldn't tell you a thing. Only one moment comes back to me, brief and unimportant—I don't know why—that moment is engraved on my mind for ever. He was sitting opposite me, in his grey suit, and I was dressed in a blue, transparent blouse. In Tel-Aviv the nights are not as cool as in Jerusalem, and I had not brought any warm clothes with me. Indeed I had brought nothing at all, not even a nightdress. The Jerusalem evenings are cool—but I felt nothing. Then suddenly my friend rose from his place, took off his jacket and draped it over my shoulders, over my long plaits—I had very long, fair plaits. That's the only moment I remember out of that whole evening, how my heart trembled at the touch of his coat, and how then I knew surely that this man was destined for me, only me . . . And that night I stayed with him in his room.'

V.

'Before many days had passed I married him. True, at first, my parents objected to the marriage; they argued that I was still too young and that, because of my abilities, I should continue with studies on Mount Scopus as had been intended. But I took no notice of them. I told them I was sufficiently grown-up, perhaps more than they realized, and that I thought it would be immoral for me not to follow the dictates of my heart. My ideas on morals always seemed peculiar to my parents and relations, and my beliefs seemed nothing but the foolishness of youth; but I—I had never wanted to do the conventional thing, but rather to follow my inner compulsions. Until then I had never encountered anything serious that put me to the test, and this was the first time that I had come to grips with an important problem. I decided to fight. When my parents saw that I wouldn't budge from my decision, they became reconciled, and though at first they had threatened they would never give their consent to the marriage, nonetheless they came to the wedding ceremony and shared in our joy. What shall I tell you? I was not disappointed in him at all. Today I know it was a bold and impulsive action. To live with a man, night and day, in the same room; to eat with him from the same dish; to wash in the same bathroom; to sleep in the same bed—no, all this is not the same as a fleeting encounter at a party. Yet I must say that I was not disappointed in my heart's choice; on the contrary, he was the best man I have ever known. He loved me, and he spent all his free time in my company, sometimes taking me with him on his business trips so that I should not remain at home alone. We had a beautiful home, one of those old houses which are to be found only in Jerusalem; it was in a courtyard surrounded by an ancient wall of moss-covered stones and far removed from the neighboring houses; it was situated amongst some very old olive trees—a small house, with just a couple of high and spacious rooms, like they used to build in Jerusalem. A quiet, peaceful atmosphere reigned there. The distant sounds that reached it from the street were muffled and muted, as though they came through a thick curtain, and their far-off echoes made our solitude even sweeter.

'During the day I would busy myself a little with the work of my small home, read a book or play the piano, and in the evenings we would sometimes go to the theatre or the cinema. On our way back we would drop into this little café, and sit a while at this very table, drink coffee, eat cakes and smile at one another: we didn't have to speak much in those happy days in order to understand one another. I can tell you in four trite little words: we were very happy . . .'

She drained her cup quickly. Her nervousness increased and she stared at me for a while with feverish eyes, as if she was suddenly asking herself: Why am I telling you all my secrets? But I had lowered my eyes, and she continued in an excited voice:

'Then came that night. Yes, that night. But again I must tell you: you mustn't think that anything special occurred then, some terrible incident. No, no, on the contrary, it seemed like an ordinary night, like any other night, and yet . . . how can I describe it . . . that night cut through my life, although nothing really happened, just my heart... I can't open my heart to you, I only remember the outward appearances, but these I remember so well that they have become ingrained into my very soul, so that sometimes I substitute them for the real causes, as if these outward signs brought about what happened later . . . Well, that night I awoke suddenly from my sleep, and, as sometimes happens, I didn't know where I was for a moment. Then my eyes were attracted to the window gleaming in the darkness of the room. It was a still night, and the moon shone on the window with a dull, silvery glow. I told you before that our house was situated amongst ancient olive trees. One of these trees stood just outside the window, almost touching it. That night a faint breeze stirred its branches, and the soft leaves brushed against the window-panes, the upper part reflecting the moonlight whilst the lower was wrapped in shadow. The rustling leaves caressed the window, as if they were trying to call to me dumbly, and the light in the window cast a mysterious, sinister patchwork of shadows onto the opposite wall. Suddenly my mind cleared, and I realized where I was. I looked at my bed and saw my husband sleeping beside me, his breathing quiet and regular as usual. I couldn't distinguish his face, untouched by the moon's pale light. But at once I was filled with misgivings, and a deep inner voice spoke from within and filled me with panic: What am I doing here, beside this man, this stranger . . . Memories of my childhood and youth flooded my mind, and an odd sensation attacked me suddenly . . . Husband? What is a husband? . . . At that moment I could not understand for the life of me why I had tied myself to this man, this man and no other . . . So powerful were the doubts that assailed me that I was filled with terror and my whole body began to shiver. I began to rebuke myself and told myself that I was nothing but a foolish child, that this man was my husband and I loved him, and that we were bound together forever by the ties of the flesh. I pulled the blanket over my head so that I shouldn't be able to see the olive leaves brushing the window-panes, and I kept repeating to myself how foolish I was; but the voices would not be silenced. Instead, their echo grew louder within me until I was completely terrified, and I could do nothing to quiet them. I pressed myself closer to my husband as if seeking protection from my terrible loneliness, but the pounding of my heart did not awaken him. He was sleeping so soundly that he seemed hardly aware of me, except that his hand stroked me for a moment, as a husband's hand will, then relaxed, and again he was sunk in a deep sleep. The terrible voices were still pursuing me. I was in the grip of some cruel power and kept looking at the weird, dimly-lighted window, seeing the rustle of the olive leaves and the gruesome pattern of shadows which struck my heart with horror—until the moonlight faded, and the wind stopped, and the night gave way to dawn. Only then did I fall asleep, and I slept fitfully and uneasily. When I opened my eyes I was alone: my husband had gone to work.'

She suddenly stopped speaking: looking around I saw that the waitress was coming in our direction, carrying an empty tray in order to clear the dishes from our table. Quickly she took the empty cup away from the young woman, without even giving me a passing glance; then, about to remove my cup, she paused a moment and said sarcastically, as if wanting to make a fool of me:

'My, you're very absent-minded today. You've been sitting before that full cup all this time, and you've not yet touched a drop . . .'

I looked at her at first in astonishment, but when I got her point I pulled myself together and mumbled apologetically:

'Yes. Of course. I haven't started to drink . . . I was waiting for it to cool off. I don't like hot coffee . . .'

Raising the cup I drained it at one gulp and returned it to the waitress. She placed it on her tray of empty dishes, loitered a moment to give me a suspicious look, and then shrugged her shoulders slightly as she turned away from us.

VI.

When we were once more alone, my companion said, staring after the waitress as she passed through the small door:

'I don't like that woman.'

I answered with a vague, meaningless smile, and she continued her story:

'At first I tried to rid myself of those strange voices I had heard at night. I tried to forget what I had seen and to control my feelings, but it was no use. That very feeling which had taken hold of me in the dead of night would not leave me and clung to me like some evil spirit. A great change had taken place in my life. But again, as I have told you over and over again, there was no outward change. On the surface everything was the same, but only on the surface . . . I don't know whether you are married: if not, it may be hard for you to grasp my meaning. Our life together had not changed one iota, and yet it was not as it had been at first. We had never spoken very much to each other, but (how shall I describe it to you?) our silences had been charged with meaning and content; the little trivial things that we did each day had been full of interest and joy; if our hands met by chance, when we both reached for the teapot on the table, an invisible tremor would pass from body to body, like an electric current, and our faces would suddenly become radiant . . . But now, after that night, everything was different. The silence was nothing more than a profound emptiness, as if one fine morning we had suddenly woken up to find that we had nothing more to say to each other; the daily happenings of life were nothing more than trite events of little interest, and when our hands met it was merely a dull contact, dead bodies, like wires which had been torn from an electric circuit and caused the electric current to break . . . And from then on the magic circuit of my husband's house was broken. Suddenly my eyes were opened to things that I had never noticed during all the days of my married life. I saw that there was a pulsating, busy life outside the walls of my house. There were many young men—some better-looking, some worse-looking than my husband—and they all caught my eyes and aroused my curiosity. But, please, don't misunderstand me: I never at any time desired to break out of the circle of my life, and if any of those young men had shown any interest in me, I would have turned my back on him with contempt; but still, now I could no longer close my eyes to the world that streamed beyond the wall of my house. Whether I cared or didn't, it existed; and so I lost my joy in life, and my desire for my husband died.

'Before many days had gone by, he sensed the change that had taken place in me, and began to probe me for the reason. I hinted to him that I doubted our mutual love, that things were not going well. He looked at me in wonder, unable to believe his ears, and then began to laugh as if I were joking with him. But in the course of time he realized how serious the situation was, and he did his very best to cheer me up and to seek all possible ways of lightening my depression. But all his efforts were in vain. My inner voice ruled me and made me see things as they really were: I felt him to be my husband no longer but a stranger, and the contact of our bodies—was like an act of obscenity. I wanted to say to him: Perhaps we should separate a while, I'll return to my parents and look into my heart in solitude; but he wouldn't listen. The good man, he still believed that the wound might heal if only I were not to break all the threads that we had woven together from the time of our wedding. He begged me to remain in our peaceful and pleasant house, and he would go away for a long time in connection with his work—until this dark cloud would pass. I did not have the strength to make any objections to his entreaties, and I agreed. He would write me long letters about his travels throughout the country, of the people he met and the things he did; but to that matter, which lay hidden within our hearts, he did not refer. He did not bother me with questions and did not attempt to rouse my pity. Not a thing, not a thing—but every Sabbath eve he would send me flowers, even if he was not in Jerusalem, a bouquet of white roses at all seasons of the year, excatly like the white roses he had sent me before he saw me at the party. He was so good and so fine, until I began to think at times that I had made a mistake: that the whole thing was nothing but a quirk of fate, and that I still loved him as I had at first. But when he would return home for a day and look at me like a beaten dog begging for a kind word, expecting some faint signs of hope—perhaps I had changed my mind and all my feelings of depression had vanished like the morning mist—then the inner voice would suddenly burst forth and cry out to me, that this man is nothing but a stranger, whom I do not love, that it is wrong for me to live together with him. I do not know how to make it clear to you. You probably think this is nothing but the caprice of a woman who hasn't got to worry about the struggle for existence. But please don't think of me in this way. I know for sure that this feeling which wracks me with such force could not be a mere caprice; and that it might attack any woman, whatever her class. Perhaps if a woman were absorbed in the care of children and beset by economic difficulties, she would have to suppress the voice of her heart, but still I'm quite sure that that voice would torment and plague her for the rest of her life. But I've already explained to you—I have my own ideas about morals;

and I wanted to be true to myself then as I had been at first, when I obeyed my impulse and went to the man I loved, not calculating and caring for nothing, neither for my parents nor for public opinion . . . So again now, I made up my mind to leave him, since the invisible cords which had bound us together were broken. I wanted to follow my own instincts faithfully to the end, to defend the wholeness and truth of my emotions, taking notice of no one . . .'

She grew breathless and paused a moment. Her hands caressed the marble-topped table nervously.

'Some months passed. I realized that there was no other course but divorce. Why should I torture this good man, why should I deceive him, knowing very well that the rift could never be healed? But he would not listen to the idea of a final divorce. He still thought that everything could be patched up and that I was merely the victim of some transient mood. Once I decided to put an end to this terrible situation which had been created, and when he returned home, I sat beside him and said in a soft and conciliatory tone: "Look, my dear, we cannot possibly live together any more; why shouldn't we finish with this outer tie, once and for all?" Again I saw spread over his face that terrible sadness, which I could not bear. And he shouted: "Why? why?" But I hardened my heart and said harshly: "Are you blind, that you can't see the reason? Do you think I just sit here like a widow in mourning when you are not at home? Can't you realize that I am a young woman with the best years of my life before me? Are you still so naïve, that you ask me—why?"

'I lied to him! There wasn't a grain of truth in all that I had said. He was my beloved, of my flesh, my first and only love, and I have never been unfaithful to him to this day. Only my heart—my heart had not stood the test . . . When he heard my bitter words, his face fell and he grew deadly pale. He sat before me dumbfounded, without uttering a word, only his eyes reflecting his great despair. From then on he never raised any more objections, and before many days had passed we went together to the Rabbinate to make preparations for the divorce.'

VII.

'Why should I break my heart again with these bitter memories? The wound is still very fresh. I'll tell you the rest of the story very briefly, and not weary you with long speeches . . . Well, we went to the Rabbi together, tortured and broken in spirit, my husband's eyes like those of a lamb being led to the slaughter. We came, said what we had to say, and waited a long time until the divorce papers were completed. I sat in a corner and waited while my husband was negotiating with the attendant. He is the best of men: even at this final hour, he was trying to make things easier for me. Then suddenly the old Rabbi approached me and said: "So woman, perhaps you will change your mind and return home . . . the both of you—there is still time . . ." I looked at him with unconcealed hostility and said: "If we could have changed our minds, we should not have taken the trouble to come before Your Reverence." He looked at me with such sorrowful eyes that a shiver ran down my spine. Then he turned to go, only turning his head a moment to say quietly: "Do you know, young woman, that our sages have said: Every man who divorces his first wife, even an altar of stone shall weep for him . . ." How could I answer him? I suddenly felt an agonizing pain as if my heart had broken. But the cup of bitterness was not yet completely full. We still had to receive the fateful document. My husband stood before me, ashen-faced, holding the divorce papers in his hand; and, when he had to hand me the parchment, he shivered, his fingers trembled and his whole body shook like a thunder-stricken tree. I was so alarmed that I wanted to fall on his neck and kiss his pale face, that I know so well and that I had loved so much, to comfort him with kind words

She now removed her hands from her face and spread them out as if presenting herself to me for judgement. With rising excitement she cried:

'Well, maybe you can tell me: *How* shall I answer him? We, simple people, what do we know? We are like nothing more than the fingers of a clock rushing endlessly through our cycle of hours, on and on, and we don't know why... But you tell me: are we nothing but animals who follow the blind call of their blood, and is the game of love nothing but a beautiful amusement? Tell me, tell me: why did I go after him at first as if I were moonstruck, and why did I suddenly reject him for no reason? And why am I eating my heart out now that I have cut myself away from him? Tell me, tell me: why did all this take place? For what reason?!'

She seized my hand that lay beside hers on the marble top and drew it towards her fiercely. I felt its hot and trembling contact, and prepared myself to reply, like a child that is brought to task by his elders. But when I lifted my eyes and saw her flushed and burning eyes, her quivering eyelashes and uplifted eyebrows—I did not know how to reply. I lowered my head and was silent...

THE WHOLE LOAF

by Shmuel Yosef Agnon

I.

I HAD NOT tasted anything all day long. I had made no preparations on Sabbath eve, so I had nothing to eat on the Sabbath. At that time I was on my own. My wife and childern were abroad, and I had remained all by myself at home, so that the bother of attending to my food fell upon myself. If I did not prepare my meals or go to hotels and restaurants and cafés, I had to put up with hunger inside me. On that particular day, I had intended to eat at a hotel; but the sun had flamed like a furnace, so I decided it was better to go hungry than to walk about in that heat.

In all truth, my dwelling did not keep the heat from me either. The floor was as hot as glowing fire, the roof fevered like piercing fire, the walls simply burned like fire, and all the vessels simply sweated fire, so that it was like fire licking fire, fire of the room licking at the body, and the fire of the body licking against the fire of the room. But when a man is at home, he can soak himself in water if he likes, or take off his clothes when he wants to, so that they do not weigh on him.

Once the greater part of the day had passed, and the sun weakened, I rose and washed myself and dressed, and went off to eat. I was pleased to think that I would be sitting at a well-spread table with a clean tablecloth on it, and waiters and waitresses attending to me while I ate properly prepared food that I had not needed to exhaust myself about. For I was already tired of the poor food I used to prepare for myself at home.

The day was no longer hot, and a gentle breeze was blowing. The streets were filling up. From the Mahneh Yehuda Quarter to the Jaffa Gate or nearby, the old men and women and the lads and girls were stretching their legs all the way. Round fur hats and caps and felt hats and turbans and tarbooshes shook and nodded, on and amid hairy and hairless heads. From time to time fresh faces joined them, coming from Rabbi Kook Street and from the Sukkat Shalom and Even Israel and Nahlat Shiva Quarters, and from the Street of the Prophets which people have the bad habit of calling the Street of the Consuls; as well as from all the other streets to which the authorities had not yet managed to give names. All day long they had been imprisoned in their homes by the heat. Now that day was past and the sun was losing its strength, they came out to glean a little of the atmosphere of Sabbath twilight which Jerusalem borrows from the Garden of Eden. I was borne along with them till I came to my own path.

II.

While I was being carried along, an old man knocked at his window to draw my attention. I turned my head and saw Doctor Yekutiel Ne'eman standing at the window. I hurried over with great pleasure, for he is a very considerable sage, and his words are pleasant. But when I came there, he had vanished. I stood looking into his house until he joined me and greeted me. I greeted him in return, and waited to hear some of those magnificent thoughts we are accustomed to hearing from him.

Doctor Ne'eman asked me how my wife and children were. I sighed and answered, 'You have reminded me of my trouble. They are still abroad and want to come back to Eretz Israel.'

'If they want to come back,' said he, 'why don't they come?'

I sighed and said, 'There's some delay.'

'Verily the delay comes from a crooked way,' said he, rhyming on my word. And he began to scold me. 'There's some laziness about you,' said he, 'so that you have not devoted yourself to bringing them back; and the result for you is that your wife and children are wandering about without father or husband while you are without wife and children.'

I looked down at the ground and said nothing. Then I raised my head and turned my eyes to his mouth, in the hope that he would say something consoling. His lips were slightly open, and a kind of choked rebuke hung from them, while his fine, grayshot beard had creased and grown wavy, like the great sea when it rages. I regretted having brought his wrath down on me, and causing him to bother about such trifles. So I took counsel with myself and began to talk about his book.

III.

This was a book about which opinions were largely divided. There are some scholars who say that whatever is written in it as from the mouth of the Lord(. . . .) was written by Yekutiel Ne'eman, who neither added nor took away anything from His words. And that is what Yekutiel Ne'eman declares. But there are some who say this is certainly not the case, and that Ne'eman wrote it all himself and ascribed his words to a certain Lord whom no man ever saw.

This is not the place to explain the nature of that book. Yet this I must add, that since it first became known the world has grown slightly better, since a few people have improved their behavior and somewhat changed their natures; and there are some who devote themselves body and soul to doing everything in the manner described there.

In order to make Ne'eman feel more pleased, I began proclaiming the virtues of his book and said, 'Everybody admits that it is a great work and there is nothing like it.' Then Yekutiel turned his face from me, let me be, and went his way. I stood eating my heart with grief and remorse for what I had said.

But Doctor Ne'eman did not remain annoyed with me for long. As I was about to go away, he returned with a packet of letters to be taken to the post office and sent by registered mail. I put the letters in my breast pocket and placed my hand on my heart, as a promise that I would perform my mission faithfully.

IV.

On the way I passed the House of Study and entered to recite the evening prayers. The sun had already set entirely, but the beadle had not yet kindled the light. In view of the mourning of Moses, the congregation did not engage in the study of the Torah, but sat discoursing and singing and taking their time.

Stars could already be seen in the open, but complete darkness still held sway within the building. At length the beadle lit a light, and the congregation rose to recite the evening prayers. After the Havdala ceremony, which brings the Sabbath day to a close, I rose to go to the post office.

All the grocery stores and other shops were open, and people crowded round the kiosks on every side. I also wished to cool myself with a glass of soda water, but since I was in a hurry to send off the letters, I kept my desire in check and did without drinking.

Hunger began to oppress me. I considered whether I should go and eat first. After starting, I changed my mind and said, Let me send off the letters and then I shall eat. On the way I thought to myself, If only Ne'eman knew that I am hungry, he would urge me to eat first. I turned myself about and went towards the restaurant.

Before I had taken more than two or three steps, the power of imagination arrived. What it imagined! What did it not imagine! All of a sudden it brought a sickbed before me. There's a sick man somewhere, I told myself, and Doctor Ne'eman has been told about it and has written him down a remedy; and now I have to hurry and take the letter containing it to the post office. So I got set to run to the post office.

In the middle of my running I stopped and thought, Is he the only doctor there is? And even if he is, does he promise that his remedy is going to help? And even if it does help, do I really have to put off my meal, when I haven't eaten anything at all the whole day long? My legs grew as heavy as stone. I did not go to eat because of the force of imagination, while I did not go to the post office because of intellect.

V.

Since I was standing still, I had time to consider my affairs. I began to weigh what I ought to do first and what I ought to do later, and reached the decision to go to a restaurant first, since I was hungry. I turned my face at once to the restaurant and marched off as quickly as I could before some other thought should strike me; for a man's thoughts are liable to delay his actions. And in order that my thoughts should not confuse me I gave myself good counsel, picturing all the kinds of good food for which the restaurant was well known. I could already see myself sitting, eating and drinking and enjoying myself. The force of imagination helped me, producing more than an average man can eat or drink, and making good to my taste each article of food and drink. Undoubtedly the intention was for the best, but what pleasure does a hungry man have when he is shown all kinds of food and drink but is given no chance of enjoying them? Maybe he can find satisfaction from this in dream, but it is doubtful if he will do so when awake.

This being the case, I went back towards the restaurant, thinking over what I should eat and drink. At heart I was already happy to be sitting in a pleasant building at a spread table, among fine folk busy eating and drinking. Then maybe I would find a good acquaintance there, and we would spice our repast with pleasant conversation which satisfies the heart and does not weigh on the soul; for I would have you know that Doctor Ne'eman had weighed somewhat on my heart.

Remembering Doctor Ne'eman, I remembered his letters. I began to feel afraid that I might be so carried away by my talk with my friend that I would not send the letters off. So I changed my mind and said, Let us go to the post office first and be done with the job, so that afterwards we can sit comfortably and the letters will not keep on burdening my mind.

VI.

If only the ground had moved along under me, I would have done my mission at once. But the ground stood still, and the way to the post office is hard on the feet, because the ground is broken and uneven with heaps of earth and stones; while when you do get there the postal clerks are not in the habit of hurrying but keep you hanging about, and by the time they finish whatever it is they are doing, all the food will get cold and you will find no hot dishes so that you are bound to remain hungry. But I gave no thought to this and went to the post office.

It is easy to understand the state of a man who has two courses in front of him: if he takes one, it seems to him that he has to follow the other; and if he takes the other, it seems to him that he ought to go along the first one. But at length to his joy he takes the course that he ought to take. Now that I was going to the post office, I wondered that I could possibly have been doubting it for a while and wishing to give my own trifling affairs precedence over the affairs of Doctor Ne'eman. And within a short while I found myself standing at the post office.

VII.

I was just about to enter when a carriage came along and I saw a man sitting in it. I stood and stared in astonishment: now, when as much as a horseshoe is not to be found in town, a man comes along in a two-horse carriage. And what was still more surprising, he was laughing at the wayfarers, and driving his horses along the pavement.

I raised my eyes and saw that he was Mr. Gressler. This Mr. Gressler had been the head of an agricultural school abroad, but there he used to ride a horse and here he drove a carriage. When he was abroad he used to joke with the peasants' daughters and the simple folk, and here in the Land of Israel he fooled about with anybody and everybody. Yet he was an intelligent and polite person, and although he was a fleshy fellow, his fleshiness was not noticed by reason of his intelligence.

This Mr. Gressler had something about him which attracted all who saw him. So it is not surprising that I was also affected. On this occasion Mr. Gressler sat leaning back in his carriage, the reins loose in his hand and dragging below the horses' legs, as he watched with pleasure while people passed on either side and returned to the place from which they had run, and jumped about in front of the horses, the dust of their feet mingling with the dust of the horses' hooves; all of them alike as cheerful as though Mr. Gressler were only out to please them.

This Mr. Gressler was my acquaintance, one of my special acquaintances. Nor do I exaggerate if I say that from the day I know him we have never ceased to have a liking for one another. Now, although all and sundry like him, I can say that he prefers me to all of them, since he has taken the trouble to show me all kinds of pleasures. When I used to tire of them he would amuse me with words of wisdom. Mr. Gressler is gifted with exceptional wisdom, of the kind which undermines all the wisdom you may have learned elsewhere. Never did he ask for any compensation, but he gives of his bounty and is happy to have people accept it. Ah, there were days when I was a lad and he went out of his way to divert me; until the night my house was burnt down and all my possessions went up in flames.

The night my house burnt, Mr. Gressler sat playing cards with my neighbor. This neighbor, a converted Jew, was a dealer in textiles. He lived below with his wares, while I lived above with my books. From time to time my neighbor told me that there was no great demand for his goods, that all his textiles were like paper since they were made in wartime; now that the war was over, textiles were being made of proper wool and flax again, and nobody wanted to make a suit out of the substitute stuffs which wear through and tear as soon as they are put on, if he could get himself real material. 'Are you insured?' Mr. Gressler asked him. 'Insured I am,' he answered. While they were talking Mr. Gressler lit a cigar and said, 'Drop this match in this rubbish heap and take your insurance money.' He went and set his goods on fire, and the whole house was burnt down. That convert who was insured received the value of his goods, while I, who had not insured my possessions, came out of it in a very bad way. All that I had left after the fire I spent on lawyers, because Mr. Gressler persuaded me to take action against the Municipality for not saving my home and, what was more, making the fire worse. That night the firemen had had a party and grown drunk, filling their vessels with brandy and beer, and when they came to put the fire out, they made it burn even more.

For various reasons I kept my distance from Mr. Gressler after that, and it almost seemed to me that I was done with him for good and all, since I bore him a grudge for being the cause of my house burning down, and was also devoting myself to Ne'eman's book. Those were the days when I was making myself ready to go up to the Land of Israel and neglected all worldly affairs; and since I was neglecting these worldly affairs, Mr. Gressler let me be. But when I set out for Eretz Israel the first person I ran across was—Gressler, since he was travelling by the same ship as I was; save that I travelled on the bottom deck like poor folk do, while he travelled on the top deck like the rich.

I cannot say that I was very happy to see Mr. Gressler. On the contrary, I was very down in the mouth for fear he would remind me of my one-time deeds. So I pretended not to see him. He noticed this and did not bother me. Then it seemed to me that since our paths did not cross on board ship, they would do so even less on the land. But when the ship reached the port, my belongings were detained at the Customs, and Mr. Gressler came and redeemed them. He also made things easier for me in my other affairs until we went up to Jerusalem.

Thenceforward we used to meet one another. Sometimes I visited him and sometimes he visited me, and I don't know who followed the other more. Particularly in those days when my wife was away from the country. I had nothing to do at that time, and he was always available. And when he came he used to spend most of the night with me. His was pleasant company, was Mr. Gressler's, for he knew all that was going on, and had the inside story even before the things happened. Sometimes my heart misgave me, but I disregarded it.

VIII.

Seeing Mr. Gressler in front of the post office, I signalled and called him by name. He stopped his carriage and helped me up.

I forgot all about the letters and the hunger and went along with him. Or maybe I did not disregard the hunger and the letters, but I put them aside for a little while.

Before I had begun talking to him properly, Mr. Hophni came towards us. I asked Mr. Gressler to turn his horses to one side, because this Hophni is a bothersome fellow, and I am afraid to have too much to do with him. Ever since he invented a new mouse-trap, it has been his habit to visit me two or three times a week, to tell me all that is being written about him and his invention. And I am a weak person, I am, who cannot bear to hear the same thing twice. It is true that the mice are a great nuisance, and the mouse-trap is very useful; but when this Hophni goes gnawing at your brains, it's quite likely that you would prefer the mice to the conversation of the trapmaker.

Mr. Gressler did not turn his horses away, but on the contrary ran the carriage up to Hophni and waved to him to get in. Why did Mr. Gressler think of doing this? Either it was in order to teach me that a man has to be patient, or because he wanted to have some fun. Now I was not at all patient at that time, nor was I in the mood for fun. I stood up, took the reins out of his hands, and turned the horses off in a different direction. Since I am not an expert in steering horses, the carriage turned over on me and Mr. Gressler, and we both rolled into the street. I yelled and shouted, 'Take the reins and get me out of this!' But he pretended not to hear and rolled with me, laughing as though it amused him to roll about with me in the muck.

I began to fear that a motorcar might pass and crush our heads. I raised my voice higher, but it could not be heard because of Mr. Gressler's laughter. Woe was me, Mr. Gressler kept on laughing, as though he found pleasure in dusting himself with the dust of the horses' legs and fluttering between life and death. When my distress came to a head, an old carter came along and disentangled us. I rose from the ground and gathered my bones together and tried to stand. My legs were tired and my hands were strained and my bones were broken, and all of my body was full of wounds. With difficulty I pulled myself together and prepared to go off.

Although every part of me was aching, I did not forget my hunger. I entered the first hotel that came my way, and before entering the dining hall I cleaned off all the dirt and wiped my injuries and washed my face and hands.

This hotel has an excellent name throughout the town for its spacious rooms and fine arrangements and polite and quick service and good food and excellent wine and worthy guests. When I entered the dining hall, I found all the tables full, and fine folk sitting, eating and drinking and generally enjoying themselves. The light blinded my eyes and the scent of the good food confused me utterly. I wanted to snatch something from the table in order to stay my heart. Nor is there anything surprising about that, as I had tasted nothing all day long. But when I saw how importantly and gravely everybody was sitting there, I did not have the courage to do it.

I took a chair and sat at a table and waited for the waiter to come. Meanwhile I took the bill of fare and read it once, twice, and a third time. How many good things there are which a hungry man can eat his fill of, and how long it seems to take until they are brought to him! From time to time I looked up and saw waiters and waitresses passing by, all of them dressed like lords and ladies. I began to prepare my heart and soul for them, and started weighing how I should talk to them. Although we are one people, each one of us talks ten languages, and above all in the Land of Israel.

IX.

After an hour, or maybe a little less, a waiter arrived and bowed and asked: 'What would you like, Sir?' What would I like and what wouldn't I like! I showed him the bill of fare and told him to fetch anything he wanted. And in order that he should not think me the kind of boor who eats anything without selecting it, I added to him gravely, 'But I want a whole loaf.' The waiter nodded his head and said, 'I shall fetch it for you at once, I shall fetch it for you at once.'

I sat waiting until he came back with it. He returned carrying a serving dish with all kinds of good things. I jumped from my place and wanted to take something. He went and placed the food in front of somebody else, quietly arranged each thing separately in front of him, and chatted and laughed with him, noting on his list all kinds of drinks which the fellow was ordering for his repast. Meanwhile he turned his face towards me and said, 'You want a whole loaf, don't you, Sir? I'm bringing it at once.'

Before long he came back with an even bigger tray than the first one. I understood that it was meant for me and told myself, That's the meaning of the saying: the longer the wait, the greater the reward. As I prepared to take something, the waiter said to me, 'Excuse me, Sir, I'm bringing you yours at once.' And he arranged the food in front of a different guest most carefully, just as he had done before.

I kept myself under control and did not grab anything from others. And since I did not grab anything from others I told myself, Just as I don't grab from others, so others won't grab my share. Nobody touches what's prepared for somebody else. Let's wait a while and we'll get what's coming to us, just like all the other guests who came before me; for it's first come, first served.

The waiter returned. Or maybe it was another waiter and, because I was so hungry, I only thought it was the same one. I jumped from my chair in order to remind him of my presence. He came and stood and bowed to me as though mine were a new face. I began wondering who this waiter could be, a fresh fellow or the one from whom I had ordered my food; for if he were a fresh waiter, I would have to order afresh, and if it were the same one, all I had to do was to remind him. While I was thinking it over, he went his way. A little later he returned, bringing every kind of food and drink, all for the fellows sitting to the right or the left of me.

Meanwhile fresh guests came and sat down and ordered all kinds of food and drink. The waiters ran and brought their orders to them. I began to wonder why they were being served first when I had been there before them. Maybe because I had asked for a whole loaf and you could not get a whole loaf at present, so they were waiting till they could get one from the baker. I began rebuking myself for asking for a whole loaf, when I would have been satisfied even with a small slice.

X.

What is the use of feeling remorseful after the deed? While I was bothering my heart, I saw a child sitting holding a Sabbath loaf with saffron of the kind that my mother, may she rest in peace, used to bake us for Purim, and which I can still taste now. I would have given the world for just a mouthful from that loaf. My heart was standing still with hunger, and my two eyes were set on that child eating and jumping and scattering crumbs about him.

Once again the waiter brought a full tray. Since I was sure he was bringing it for me, I sat quietly and importantly, like a person who is in no particular hurry about his food. Alas, he did not put the tray in front of me but placed it in front of somebody else.

I began to excuse the waiter with the idea that the baker had not yet brought the whole loaf, and wanted to tell him that I was prepared to do without it. But I could not get a word out of my mouth because of my hunger.

All of a sudden a clock began striking. I took my watch out of my pocket and saw that it was half-past ten. Half-past ten is just a time like any other, but in spite of this I began to shake and tremble. Maybe because I remembered the letters of Doctor Ne'eman which I had not yet sent off. I stood up hastily in order to take the letters to the post office. As I stood up, I butted in to the waiter fetching a tray full of dishes and glasses and flagons and all kinds of food and drink. The waiter staggered and dropped the tray and everything on it fell, food and drink alike; and he also slipped and fell. The guests turned their heads and stared, some of them in alarm and some of them laughing.

The hotel keeper came and calmed me down and led me back to my place, and he asked me to wait a little while until they fetched me a different meal. From his words I understood that the food which had fallen from the waiter's hands had been intended for me, and now they were preparing me another meal.

I possessed my soul in patience and sat waiting. Meanwhile my spirit flew from place to place. Now it flew to the kitchen where they were preparing my meal, and now to the post office from which letters were being sent. By that time the post office doors were already closed, and even if I were to go there it would be no use; but the spirit flew about after its fashion, even to places which the body might not enter.

XI.

They did not fetch me any other meal. Maybe because they had not yet had time to prepare it, or maybe because the waiters were busy making up the accounts of the guests. In any case, some of the diners rose from the table, picking their teeth and yawning on their full stomachs. As they went out, some of them stared at me in astonishment, while others paid me no attention, as though I did not exist. When the last of the guests had left, the attendant came in and turned out the lights, leaving just one light still burning faintly. I sat at a table full of bones and leavings and empty bottles and a dirty tablecloth and waited for my meal, as the hotel keeper himself had asked me to sit down and wait for it.

While I was sitting there I suddenly began to wonder whether I had lost the letters on the way, while I had been rolling on the ground with Gressler. I felt in my pocket and saw that they were not lost; but they had become dirty with the muck and the mire and the wine.

Once again a clock struck. My eyes were weary and the lamp was smoking and black silence filled the room. In the silence came the sound of a key creaking in the lock, like the sound of a nail being hammered into the flesh. I knew that they had locked me into the room and forgotten about me, and I would not get out until they opened next day. I closed my eyes tight and made an effort to fall asleep.

I made an effort to fall asleep and closed my eyes tight. I heard a kind of rustling and saw that a rat had jumped onto the table and was picking at the bones. Now, said I to myself, he's busy with the bones. Then he'll gnaw the tablecloth, then he'll gnaw the chair I'm sitting on, and then he'll gnaw at me. First he'll start on my shoes, then on my socks, then on my foot, then on my calf, then on my thigh, then on all my body. I turned my eyes to the wall and saw the clock. I waited for it to strike again and frighten the rat, so that it would run away before it reached me. A cat came and I said, Here is my salvation. But the rat paid no attention to the cat and the cat paid no attention to the rat; and this one stood gnawing and that one stood chewing.

Meanwhile the lamp went out and the cat's eyes shone with a greenish light that filled all the room. I shook and fell. The cat started and the rat jumped and both of them stared at me in alarm, one from one side and the other from the other. Suddenly the sound of trotting hooves and carriage wheels was heard and I knew that Mr. Gressler was coming back from his drive. I called him, but he did not answer me.

Mr. Gressler did not answer me and I lay there dozing until I fell asleep. By the time day broke, I was awakened by the sound of cleaners, men and women, coming to clean the building. They saw me and stared at me in astonishment with their brooms in their hands. At length they began laughing and asked, 'Who's this fellow lying here?' Then the waiter came and said, 'This is the one who was asking for the whole loaf.'

I took hold of my bones and rose from the floor. My clothes were dirty, my head was heavy on my shoulders, my legs were heavy under me, my lips were cracked and my throat was dry, while my teeth were on edge with a hunger-sweat. I stood up and went out of the hotel into the street, and from the street into another until I reached my house. All the time my mind was set on the letters that Doctor Ne'eman had handed over for me to send off by post. But that day was Sunday, when the post office was closed for things that the clerk did not consider important.

After washing off the dirt I went out to get myself some food. I was all alone at that time. My wife and children were out of the country, and all the bother of my food fell on me alone.

BIOGRAPHICAL AND CRITICAL NOTES

AGNON, SHMUEL YOSEF.

Born in 1888 in Galicia, Agnon has lived in Israel since 1909, with intervals of residence in Germany, Poland, and elsewhere. Eleven volumes of his collected works have been published by Schocken, and his rare style has been a challenge to translators in fifteen languages. *The Bridal Canopy* (1937), *In the Heart of the Seas* (1948), *Days of Awe* (1948), and scattered stories have appeared in English.

Metamorphosis: The giant among the earliest pioneers of modern Hebrew fiction reflecting life in the land of Israel, Agnon also has deep spiritual roots in the world of Europe, especially that of Polish Jewry. This tale of divorce and reconciliation 'somewhere in central Europe' illustrates some of the more universal aspects of his stories with European settings.

A Whole Loaf: In the wide range of Agnon's effects, there is an important area which might be characterized by saying that it has affinities with Kafka's symbolic and mytho-poetic tales. However, though Agnon and Kafka seem at times to be wrestling with similar psychological and existential problems, Agnon does so, almost always, within the terms of traditional Judaism. He is thus at once broader in his canvas and more difficult to translate than Kafka, who, though a Jew with Zionist affiliations, as Max Brod has made clear, rarely made these elements of his psyche explicit in his stories.

'A Whole Loaf' is steeped in the atmosphere of modern Jerusalem during the Mandatory period, on a realistic level; but it can also be interpreted allegorically, in a fashion which makes it an important key to the understanding of all Agnon's works. A note on its probable allegorical significance is printed separately at the conclusion of these Notes.

BAR-YOSEF, YEHOSHUA.

Born in 1912 in Safed, Bar-Yosef may be considered the senior member among the 'younger' writers represented. A fifth-generation Israeli, he received an Orthodox training in Yeshivoth; and he has worked as a newspaperman. He usually writes about the tradition-steeped lives of the old Ashkenazic communities—especially in Jerusalem, where he spent much of his youth; but he has also depicted Sephardic and Bukharian Jews.

'The Lateborn' is the first in a group of three Jerusalem stories. Lusty, and almost Rabelaisian in its moments of satirical humor, it is above all a frank and penetrating character study. There is universal truth in Huneh, lateborn and afraid of life, who seeks relief from his inner conflicts in pranks and violent laughter.

CHURGIN, YAAKOV.

Born in 1899 in Jaffa, long before Tel-Aviv was on the horizon, Churgin is the only one of a middle generation of writers here represented—including Hazaz, Yaari, Shenhar, and Zarchi—who was born in Israel. He has edited a publication for young people and has also written stories about Arabs.

Churgin's fondness for strong, primitive types is well exemplified in this tale of a hearty laborer in the picturesque little town of Safed, in Upper Galilee. The plot of a quarreling couple is a perennially amusing one, and somehow these two seem vaguely familiar; however different the setting, we might have encountered them in one of Sholem-Aleichem's humorous sketches of Jewish life in a South-Russian village.

HAZAZ, HAYIM.

Born in 1897 in the Ukraine, Hazaz lived in Paris during the exciting '20's, and came to Israel in 1931. The senior member of our 'middle generation', he is also its most daring stylist and explorer of new realms of experience. He has ranged from penetrating realism to the 'prose poetry' of *The Bridegroom of Blood* (translated by I. M. Lask for *Yisröel*); and in subject-matter from the Russian Revolution to the lives of the Yemenite Jews, both in Yemen and Israel, about whom he has written two full-length novels.

The picture of the Yemenite in the stories by Shamir and Hazaz, as relatively primitive in his social concepts and incapable of understanding national or international problems, true as far as it goes, is of course incomplete and probably not representative. Hazaz's focus here is on the delicate problem of a loving husband and a sterile wife—with World War II in the background; and his humor is of the profoundest kind, the sort which wavers on the boundary line between laughter and tears, between comedy and tragedy. The Negro dialect has been used in the translation in order to capture some of the qualities of Hazaz's Hebrew and should not mislead the reader into thinking of the Yemenite as Negroes in any racial sense.

MEGED, AHARON.

Born in 1920 in Poland, Meged came to Israel in 1926 and spent his childhood in the village of Ra'anana. After completing his studies in Tel-Aviv, he began in 1938 to follow a double career as writer and worker: in kibbutzim, in quarries and on roads, as a porter on Haifa's docks, and as a fisherman. Most of these experiences are reflected in his stories and, since 1949, his plays; he has also written for the radio.

Since 1950, Meged has been living in Tel-Aviv. One fruit of this latter experience has been his best-selling *Hedva and I* (1954), a satirical treatment of life in Tel-Aviv, which has already run through a number of editions and been dramatized (translation of the play, Youth and Hechalutz, Jerusalem, 1957).

'The Party' was included in Meged's first collection of short stories, *Wind of the Seas* (1949). Though there is much talk here of Israel's War of Independence, the emphasis is rather on the complexities of the post-war present as reflected in the tortured consciousness of one of its crippled veterans.

MOSSINSOHN, YIGAL.

Born in 1920 in Israel's very first moshav (Ain Ganim), near Petach Tikva, Mossinsohn studied agriculture, and from the age of seventeen worked as a guard and shepherd, and on roads and in quarries and orchards; finally, he joined a kibbutz (Na'an), where he lived for twelve years. One of the founders of the Palmach, he has had a stormy and varied career; since leaving the kibbutz, besides doing writing and public relations work, he has maintained a small farm in a moshav.

Mossinsohn has written novels, plays, and stories, as well as a highly popular series of children's books. 'Polka,' which takes us into the intimate life of a kibbutz, was included in his first, highly successful, collection of short stories: *Sack-Grey* (1949).

SHAHAM, NATHAN.

Born in 1925 in Tel-Aviv, Shaham in his adolescent years followed a pattern familiar for many of his generation, of military service in the Palmach ('commando' group organized by the left-wing kibbutzim) and membership in the Beth Alpha kibbutz—where he continues to live, following a double career as agriculturist and writer. His stories and plays have been appearing in a steady stream since 1948.

'The Seven' was first published in a collection of soldiers' writings. This war yarn *par excellence,* later transformed by its author into a highly successful stage-play, has been translated into a number of languages and acted in London and elsewhere in England.

SHAMIR, MOSHE.

Born in 1921 in Tel-Aviv, Shamir's youth was largely devoted to the Hashomer Hatsair (The Young Watchman) youth movement including six years spent as a member of the Mishmar Ha-Emek (Guard of the Valley) kibbutz, in the Valley of Jezreel. There he wrote his first novel, about life in a collective colony; and, since his leaving the kibbutz in 1947, his career can be summarized in terms of a series of plays, novels, and short stories, culminating in the recent best-selling historical novel, *King of Flesh and Blood* (1954), and the historical drama which was its sequel, *The War of the Sons of Light* (1955).

The present story, which treats of a conflict in the life of a German-born doctor and his family brought to a crisis by his son's being called to arms in World War II, is from a collection published in 1952, *Women Waiting Outside.*

SHENHAR, YITZHAK.

Born in 1905 in the Ukraine, Shenhar emigrated to Poland in the early '20's and then to Israel in 1924. He worked as a laborer and farm-hand until he established his reputation as a writer of fiction and as a translator from the Russian, English, German, and French. Later, until his death in the summer of 1957, he was associated with the Schocken Library in Jerusalem. A volume of his stories has appeared in English: *Under the Fig Tree* (1948).

'Country Town' was published in *From Land to Land,* a volume of stories concerned with the wanderings of Jews in our generation and the problems of settlement in the Land of Israel. This is Israel's version of the Western 'boom-town' which fails to really 'boom'—Affulah, in the Valley of Jezreel, during the 1920's—set in juxtaposition with a nearby collective colony. Shenhar's skill in the evocation of environment and atmosphere, and in the probing of character, make him a psychological realist of the first water.

SMILANSKY, MOSHE.

Born in 1874, in the Ukraine, Smilansky was the oldest of the writers here represented. Settling in Israel in 1890, he was one of the founders of Hedera, and for some years served as head of the Farmers' Union. He died in 1953.

Much of Smilansky's writings was in the vein of history and memoirs; some of his biographical sketches, for example, have been translated and published with the title: *Unknown Pioneers* (1946). But he was also one of the first to break literary ground by writing about life in the new colonies; as one who had left Europe behind at a tender age, his very first story (1906) already revealed a rootedness in the new land. Above all, he contributed a rich vein to Hebrew literature in his many stories which reveal a profound understanding of the psychology and folklore of the Arab (*Palestine Caravan,* tr. I. M. Lask, London, 1935).

The Huleh swamp, where the 'Shaitana' ('She-Devil' in Arabic) appears, is on the northernmost boundary of Israel. Now being drained to make the land suitable for agricultural settlement, its waters and mysteries will soon pass into history.

TAMMUZ, BENJAMIN.

Born in 1919 in Russia, Tammuz came to Israel in 1924, and is thus practically a sabra. He studied at the Sorbonne in Paris, and since 1948 has been on the staff of *Ha'arets,* where he writes art criticism and edits a special edition for children. During his first few years on that paper, he achieved great popularity by creating the figure of 'Uzi', prototype of the satirically humorous sabra, whose daily comments on events in Israel, widely quoted and enjoyed, were later collected in a small volume.

In addition, Tammuz has published a volume of stories, dealing with childhood in Israel: *The Golden Sands* (1950). 'A Roll of Canvas' appeared in the *Yearbook of Ha'arets* for 1954-55. It reflects the gap between the generations in Israel, and carries one of

Tammuz's perennially questioning youngsters from thoughtless childhood, through dogmatic adolescence, to a wiser, or at least more knowing, maturity.

Pesach Katz is an ambivalent symbol for the exalted ideals of Judaism and human brotherhood on which the State of Israel was founded, and in the light of which the youth of Israel has been educated. On the one hand, these are seen as unrealistic and ineffectual: Katz is subservient to the ruling British, and unsympathetic to the youthful patriot in his struggle (the other side, of course, as in the Irish rebellion, called him a 'terrorist'). On the other hand, as our narrator grows up, he feels that he has to come to terms with the very human reality of Pesach Katz and with the ideals he preaches. The end of the story leaves this ambivalence still unresolved.

YAARI, YEHUDA.

Born in 1900 in Galicia, Yaari came to Israel in 1920 and was one of the founders of the Beth Alpha kibbutz in the eastern Emek (Valley of Jezreel). During a three-year period, he completed his studies in America.

In 'The Judgment of Solomon,' an intensely dramatic story is presented of a struggle between two women contending for the love and custody of a son, one very humanly tragic result of Hitler's inhuman persecutions. The Jerusalem environment, taken for granted by the narrator, is an appropriate setting for this apparently insoluble conflict between the claims of a real mother and a spiritual parent. How would Solomon himself have been able to end it?

YIZHAR, S.

Born in 1918 in Rehovoth, S. Yizhar (the pen-name of Yizhar Smilansky) is the son of a writer, Ze'ev Smilansky, and a nephew of the late Moshe Smilansky. He has been a teacher and principal (of the Gymnasium in Rehovoth), and a soldier and an officer in

Israel's army. He has been a member of the Knesset since its inception.

'The Dead and the Living' (we have supplied this title) is the only selection in this volume not written as a self-contained unit. It is a climactic chapter from Yizhar's first novel, *The Grove on the Hill* (1947), which depicts the self-defensive stand during a single night of an agricultural settlement; the period is that of the troubled years of 1936-1938 when Arab attacks such as these were especially common. The death of the group's much-beloved leader, the first casualty of an unexpected skirmish—obviously imposed on young men whose deepest desire is not to fight but to work the soil and live at peace with their neighbors—results in a crisis for the group as a whole, and a 'soul-accounting' by some of its members.

In the chapter which follows in Smilansky's book, the British police come and restore 'law and order' by forcing the group to abandon the settlement they have been defending at such bitter cost; and proper care is taken of the wounded Arab.

ZARCHI, YISRAEL.

Born in 1909 in Poland, Zarchi came to Israel in 1929 and worked at first as an agricultural laborer. He later graduated from The Hebrew University in Jerusalem, the Holy City he loved and about which he wrote much; and he always remained especially sensitive to the problems of Israel's youth, her hard-pressed students and artists, and her immigrant population. This moving tale of atmosphere and mood, whose perplexed heroine may be (in some respects) a fairly typical young sabra, is from a collection of Zarchi's Jerusalem stories. It is characteristic of the work of a young writer who continued to mature and grow in stature until his premature death in 1947.

"A WHOLE LOAF"

Like Kafka, Agnon seems to think spontaneously in symbolic modes. Consider, for example, in 'Metamorphosis,' the dream passage, the skillful use of description and atmosphere, and the incident on the mound which Hartmann recalls from his childhood: 'It seems that one does not have more than one such experience in a lifetime.'

However, Agnon's debt to rabbinic legend and commentary often brings him closer to explicit allegory. Thus, 'A Whole Loaf' can be appreciated on an obvious level as a somewhat morbid fantasy of modern life in Jerusalem; but Dr. B. Kurzweil, an important critic of Agnon's works, has revealed deeper levels of meaning in this particular story. We can permit ourselves here only a brief glance at his analysis.

The second sentence introduces the general situation: 'I was a lonely man at that time. My wife and children had gone abroad and I was left alone in my home.' Section III provides the most important key to the allegory: Dr. Yekutiel Ne'eman is a veiled allusion (but obvious enough to the reader steeped in rabbinic lore) to Moses, and the Book he is said to have received or written is, of course, the Bible; 'the Lord (. . .)' is Agnon's way of writing the Sacred Name of God (YHWH).

With this key in mind, the reader himself may unlock some of the further meanings hidden in Agnon's narrative: the letters he must post, then, are religious commandments, or some sort of religious mission; the hunger for food represents the life of the senses and bodily appetites; Mr. Gressler, with his carriage, becomes a sort of Mephistopheles; and the desire for 'a whole loaf' represents . . .

what? I'm not sure: Dr. Kurzweil takes it to signify the unbounded, egotistical desires of the flesh; but I feel in it, also, a somewhat pathetic desire for completeness and 'wholeness' in a drastically imperfect world. The word 'whole' here is profoundly ambiguous. The reference to 'the mourning of Moses' at the beginning of Section IV is an allusion to the tradition that Moses died at the expiration of the Sabbath, in commemoration of which fact the Orthodox act as Agnon describes them: this is both a realistic detail, then, and a development of the Mosaic theme.

And so forth. But, of course, the possibility (or necessity) of this sort of interpretation does not make the heat of Jerusalem here less hot; the people in its streets, less busy; or the narrator's hunger and loneliness, and the polite but inefficient (or malicious?) waiter, and the rat, and the cat—less 'real.'

GLOSSARY

All foreign words are from the Hebrew, unless otherwise indicated. Of the place-names, chiefly those significant for the story are included. The guttural letters (for lack of a commonly accepted transliteration) are variously written as h, ch, and kh.

abaya: a loose, sleeveless outer garment, worn by Arabs (Arabic).
aliya: lit. 'going up', in common use for immigration to Israel.
Ashkenazi: generally refers to the western European Jew.
Ashmedai: a demon (Asmodeus).

Bar Mitzva: lit. 'subject to the commandments of he Law'. A Jewish boy enters upon his religious majority at the age of thirteen, and the occasion is observed by his first public observance of rituals, before the congregation in the synagogue.
batlan: idler.
Beth Midrash: House of Learning, often located in the synagogue.
Bilu: the first modern movement for immigration to Palestine from Russia in the 1880's, whose name was formed from the first letters of Isaiah 2:5: 'O house of Jacob, come ye, and let us walk.'

Chacham: lit. 'a wise man'; used as a title of respect, and by the Sephardic Jews as the equivalent of Rabbi.
Chacham Bashi: the chief wise man (Arabic); the term for Chief Rabbi among some eastern Jews.
Chag Habatsir: The Harvest Festival.
Chalabs: natives of Aleppo, province of Syria.
chala: white bread eaten on the Sabbath and holidays.
chalutz (pl. -im; also *halutz*): the term applied to an Israeli pioneer.
chalutziuth: pioneering.
Chanukah (also *Hanukka*): The Feast of Lights (or: of the Maccabees).

Druze: a people and religious sect dwelling chiefly in the Lebanon mountains, Syria.

El Kuds: 'The Holy,' an Arabic name for Jerusalem.
erets: land, as in Erets Israel, the Land of Israel; often abbreviated to 'The Land' (*Ha'arets*).
Even Israel: Rock of Israel, quarter in Jerusalem.

fellah (pl. -een): farmer or peasant (Arabic).

Galut: the Jewish dispersion, exile, or diaspora.

Gerer Rebbe: the Rabbi from Ger, one of the well-known Hasidic rabbis.

Gut-Yom-Tov: Happy holiday! (Yiddish).

Hakovshim: The Conquerors.

hamsin (pl. -im, also *khamsin*): a hot southwesterly wind, from the desert, said to blow for about fifty days each year (Arabic for 'fifty').

Hashachar: 'The Dawn'.

Hasid (also *Chasid*): lit. 'pious' or 'saintly'; a member of a Jewish sect, first founded in the 3rd century, B.C.E., and later revived in 18th century Poland by Rabbi Israel Baal-Shem (of the Good Name), who stressed joy of living and worship. Also used loosely of a pious Jew more given to 'enthusiasm' than to learning.

Havdala: the prayer at the conclusion of the Sabbath, 'dividing' the sacred from the secular.

Hawaja: Mister (Arabic).

heder: the elementary religious school.

Hevra Kadisha: 'Holy Society'; a charitable society which cares for the sick and buries the dead.

Hoshanoth: from the Hebrew phrase, 'Hosha-na!' meaning 'Save, we pray!' (cf. 'Hosanna'). Used to refer both to certain prayers, and to the willow twigs used in connection with those prayers, on the Feast of Tabernacles (Sukkoth).

Huleh swamp: located in the far north of Israel, among the sources of the Sea of Galilee; now being drained.

Jebel esh-Sheikh: 'The Mountain of the Sheikh' (Arabic).

kasher (kashruth): food fit to eat according to the Jewish ritual.

kevutsa: a kind of kibbutz.

kibbutz: a collective settlement based on the communal ownership of property and of the means of production.

kreplach: a kind of boiled meat pie (Yiddish).

Kurds: natives of Kurdistan, a region in Western Asia, mostly in Turkey, but partly in northern Iraq and Persia.

lange kapotes: long coats, of the sort worn by Orthodox Jews in East Europe (Yiddish).

L'hitraoth!: 'Au revoir!'

Ma'aleh Akrabim: 'The Scorpions' Ascent,' a place in the Negev.

Meah Shearim: 'A Hundred Gates,' Orthodox quarter in Jerusalem.

melamed: teacher, usually poor, in a *heder*.

meshugas: craze, foolish notion (Yiddish, from the Hebrew).

mikve: the ritual bath, prescribed for women after their monthly periods.

Misnaged: an opponent of the Hasidim.

moshav: settlement; used in Israel to refer to a cooperative village, based upon individual farm units and cooperative marketing and purchase, and in which each family lives in its own private house.

Mount Atzmon: near Mount Canaan, both in the neighborhood of Safed.

Mugrabis: 'The Westerners,' an Arabic name for Moroccans.

nahag: driver, as of taxi or bus or truck.

Nahlat Shiva: Portion of Seven, quarter in Jerusalem.

Negev: South; Israel's equivalent of the 'Wild West,' from Beersheba to Eilat.

Palmach: 'commando' unit, organized by left-wing kibbutzim during the British Mandate.

peyoth: the long earlocks worn by certain Orthodox sects (*peyes,* in Yiddish).

sabra: lit. the cactus. Used of the native-born, or locally educated, youth of Israel, with the explanation: He has a rough exterior, and his thorns may prick, but inside he is very sweet.

Seder: lit. 'order.' Used for the Service of Passover.

Sephardi: originally a descendant of Spanish Jewry; but the term is often used loosely in our day for the Oriental or eastern Jew.

shadchan: match-maker.

Shaitana: a feminine form of Satan, the Devil (Arabic).

Shalom! lit. Peace (be with you)! Used for both 'Hello' and 'Goodbye.'

Sharon: the coastal plain of Israel, from Haifa to Tel-Aviv.

Shema Yisroel! Hear, O Israel!

shiva: lit. seven. Used as an abbreviation for 'sitting shiva,' the seven days of mourning.

Shmelke: an affectionate form of Shmuel, or Samuel. 'Reb Shmelke' is a Hebrew equivalent of the Irish 'Mister Paddy.'

shul: synagogue.

Succoth: The Feast of Tabernacles.

Sukkath Shalom: Tabernacle of Peace, quarter in Jerusalem.

tarboosh: red cap, worn by Turks and other eastern nations (Arabic).

tefillin: phylacteries, worn by Orthodox during morning prayer.

Torah: the Law, or Pentateuch.

tzitzith (pl.-ioth): fringes; the twisted tassels worn on the corners of the *tallith,* the prayer shawl.

Urfals: natives of the ancient Edessa, a fortified town in Aleppo.

wadi: the channel or ravine of a river, dry except in the rainy season (Arabic).

ya Allah: Oh, God (Arabic).

yallah: Let's go! Scram! (Arabic).

Yeshiva (pl.-oth): a Jewish academy of religious study.

Yeshiva-bachur: a student in a Yeshiva (Yiddish).

Yishuv: settled community, used for the Jewish community of Israel.